Karin Baine lives in Northern Ireland with her husband, two sons, and her out-of-control notebook collection. Her mother and her grandmother's vast collection of books inspired her love of reading and her dream of becoming a Mills & Boon author. Now she can tell people she has a *proper* job! You can follow Karin on Twitter, @karinbaine1, or visit her website for the latest news—karinbaine.com.

Cursed with a poor sense of direction and a propensity to read, **Annie Claydon** spent much of her childhood lost in books. A degree in English Literature followed by a career in computing didn't lead directly to her perfect job—writing romance for Mills & Boon—but she has no regrets in taking the scenic route. She lives in London: a city where getting lost can be a joy.

MIDWIFE'S ONE-NIGHT BABY SURPRISE

KARIN BAINE

WINNING OVER THE OFF-LIMITS DOCTOR

ANNIE CLAYDON

MILLS & BOON

First published in Great Britain 2024
by Mills & Boon, an imprint of HarperCollins*Publishers* Ltd,
1 London Bridge Street, London, SE1 9GF

www.harpercollins.co.uk

HarperCollins*Publishers* Macken House, 39/40 Mayor Street Upper,
Dublin 1, D01 C9W8, Ireland

Midwife's One-Night Baby Surprise © 2024 Karin Baine

Winning Over the Off-Limits Doctor © 2024 Annie Claydon

ISBN: 978-0-263-32162-3

06/24

This book contains FSC™ certified paper
and other controlled sources to ensure responsible forest management.

For more information visit www.harpercollins.co.uk/green.

Printed and Bound in the UK using 100% Renewable Electricity
at CPI Group (UK) Ltd, Croydon, CR0 4YY

MIDWIFE'S ONE-NIGHT BABY SURPRISE

KARIN BAINE

MILLS & BOON

With thanks to Catherine and Karen for sharing
their midwifery knowledge with me.
I may have used some artistic licence,
and any mistakes are entirely my own!

CHAPTER ONE

'I *AM* ENJOYING MYSELF. Honestly.'

Melissa Moran adjusted her sparkly pink cowboy hat, careful not to smudge the glittery make-up dabbed at her temples, and forced a smile.

Lydia, who was more like family than a friend, wasn't fooled, heaving out a sigh of disappointment. 'Mel…this was all for you.'

Melissa's smile faltered. 'I know, and I appreciate everything you've done. Thank you.'

Lydia folded her arms, straining the leopard print fabric of her jumpsuit across her ample bust. 'Look, I know you've had a rough eighteen months, but this is your thirtieth birthday. Not your hundredth. You're still young. You have a life to live.'

'Unlike Chris,' Melissa mumbled.

'It was an awful, tragic thing, losing him like that when you had all those plans together. But he's gone, Mel. You're still here, and he would want you to have fun.' Lydia grabbed her by the shoulders and gave her a shake.

No, he would want her to be Mrs O'Kane, with a baby on her hip, the way they'd planned. As would she. But fate had cruelly stolen that dream from both of them. Instead of a quiet family birthday celebration, she'd been whisked over to the remote Scottish isle of Innis Holm for a music festival she had no interest in attending. She was trying to enjoy herself for her friend's sake, but it just wasn't her scene. Slopping through the mud, sleeping in a tent, and the prospect of having to use those so-called communal toilets, was not her idea of a good time. Still, Melissa didn't have anyone else, and hadn't had since she was eighteen and her parents had moved abroad.

On the verge of doing her exams, and unwilling to leave everything familiar to her, she'd stayed in Scotland. Though choosing her own path hadn't made her feel any less abandoned or lonely. She'd had to work menial jobs to support her studies until she'd qualified as a midwife. Meeting Chris, finding someone who wanted to settle down as much as she did, had seemed like the perfect fairy tale ending.

Their five-year plan, building up a nest egg so they could get married, was just coming to fruition when he complained of an agonising headache and neck pain. Symptoms she didn't realise at the time were from a ruptured aneurysm, resulting in blood haemorrhaging into Chris's brain and killing him before they were able to get him into surgery, devastating Melissa.

It was irrational to think he'd abandoned her the way her parents had, but that was the way she felt, suddenly left to pick up the pieces of her life without him. She knew Lydia meant well organising this to get her out of the house, but she wasn't ready to move on. If she ever would be.

However, Lydia had gone to a lot of trouble. She was the only one who'd really been there for her, and Melissa reckoned she owed her. Even if it meant pretending to enjoy partying with a bunch of strangers in the rain.

'Come on then. We don't want to miss the headline act, do we?' She grabbed Lydia by the hand and pushed her way through the throng of people standing ankle-deep in mud until they had a good view of the stage. At least she knew a few of the band's songs so she wouldn't feel completely out of place.

In the end, Melissa was singing at the top of her lungs and dancing like everyone else. Temporarily forgetting her grief to lose herself in the moment. She had to admit, it felt good to be someone other than a bereaved fiancée for one day. Eyes closed, body swaying to the rhythm, she let go for once in her life. It was a feeling she could get used to.

'See? There is a party girl in there trying to get out. All we need now is to find you a man to remind you what else you're missing.' Lydia nudged her with her hip.

Sometimes Melissa wished she had her friend's confidence and outgoing personality. Lydia had already snogged three random blokes since they'd arrived and had indicated that she'd likely be sleeping somewhere other than their two-person tent tonight. She was someone who grabbed life with both hands and never wasted time on regrets or feeling sorry for herself. Melissa thought she should take a whole chapter out of her friend's book, but that didn't mean she was the sort of person to throw herself at a stranger.

'I'm not sure I'm ready for that, Lyds. Chris was the love of my life and I don't know if I want anyone else.' She couldn't imagine finding another man to replace Chris. Someone she could ever love as much as him.

Lydia rolled her eyes. 'I'm not talking about finding a husband. It's a music festival, Mel. I'm not sure the man of your dreams is standing waiting for you in this muddy field. But they do say the best way to get over someone is to get under someone else.'

Melissa couldn't stop her jaw dropping at the crass remark, watching agog as her friend pushed her way through to the makeshift bar at the side of the stage.

'Lydia! Chris isn't an ex who dumped me on a whim. He died.' The hysteria in her voice elevated that last fact to a level that stopped the bartender mid pour.

'I know that, Mel,' Lydia hissed through gritted teeth before flashing a smile at the man fixing their drinks. 'But the principle is the same. You have to move on, and it's okay to have a little fun with the opposite sex to do so.'

She handed Melissa a plastic glass containing some sort of orange-and-red concoction with a tacky paper umbrella sticking out of it. Melissa took a sip and winced. If this was what moving on tasted like, she wasn't sure she'd be overindulging.

'It's been so long, I wouldn't know what to do, even

if I did meet someone.' If the time ever came when she was attracted to another man, didn't feel as though she was betraying Chris's memory by pursuing it, and didn't make a complete fool of herself in the process, it would be a miracle.

It was Chris who'd made the first move the night they'd met in the local pub. He'd made it clear he was interested in her, so she hadn't had to worry about being rejected, only that they'd be compatible. She'd never been like Lydia, brave enough to walk up to someone and let them know she was attracted to them. The few men she'd been with before Chris had come on to her, and, perhaps flattered by the attention, she'd ventured into relationships that were never going to work. It only added to her sense of not being worthy of love when they inevitably dumped her because she was a homebody, and they were still in party mode. She doubted meeting someone here was going to change that pattern, though Melissa definitely wasn't looking for a long-term commitment. The heartache and loss that inevitably followed the initial euphoria of meeting someone were things she could do without going through again.

Perhaps Lydia had the right attitude with her love-'em-and-leave-'em approach to dating. She certainly seemed like the happier of the two of them.

'It's like riding a bike,' Lydia said, aiming a wink at the handsome barman. 'You never forget.'

'Unless you never learned how...' Melissa grumbled.

'You shouldn't have to work too hard, Mel. You've

got that glorious mane of red hair that makes you stand out in a crowd,' she said, undoing Melissa's ponytail to shake her tresses loose.

'And skin so pale it's liable to cause snow blindness.' She wasn't as fortunate as her honey-skinned, blond-haired companion who revelled in the sun when it made an appearance and wasn't forced to slather her entire body with factor fifty sun cream. A throwback to her Irish-born father's ancestors.

'You're a Celtic beauty. There's a guy by the burger van who certainly seems to think so. He hasn't taken his eyes off you in the last five minutes.' Lydia nodded somewhere over Melissa's shoulder as she sipped her drink through a straw.

Melissa almost broke her neck turning around to see who might be interested in her. There was the usual crowd of inebriated posers trying to latch on to any woman who crossed their path, which Melissa definitely wasn't impressed by. She was about to tell Lydia so when someone caught her eye. A tall, handsome someone with short, dark hair and a cute smile.

He acknowledged her with a raised bottle of beer, and Melissa turned away with burning cheeks.

'He is kind of hot.'

In his white T-shirt and tight jeans, he looked like every other man here, but there was something in the twinkle of his eyes and the cheekiness of his grin that was hard to ignore. Not least because he seemed to be surrounded by a group of both men and women who were hanging on his every word.

'He looks like he could show you a good time.' Lydia shoved her forward, then resumed flirting with her barman.

Melissa turned her attention back to the man holding court with one eye on her. He was laughing as he swigged his beer, lifting the bottle up and dancing to the loud music coming from the main stage. Everyone near him seemed to be having the time of their lives. In fact, Melissa realised, she was the only one who wasn't.

Perhaps it was time for a change after all.

She was coming over. Lachlan's smile faltered as nerves got the better of him. It was one thing showing off and flirting, quite another following through with anything. He hadn't been with anyone since his ex, or his surgery.

'Looks like you've pulled, mate.' His brother Duncan muttered, watching the attractive redhead approach their group.

'I'm just here for the music, Dunc. To celebrate life.' He clinked his bottle to his brother's.

'And I'm glad you're still kicking, bro, but don't rule out relationships altogether. Just because things didn't work out with Julieann, it doesn't mean there isn't someone else out there for you.'

'There speaks the voice of a happily married man. Seriously though, if this is my second chance at life, I don't want to tie myself down. I intend to live my life to the fullest.'

It was okay for his brother, who had a wife and kids,

and no cancer cells stealing away vital parts of his anatomy. But for Lachlan McNairn, staring death in the face had made him think about his mortality and the consequences it would have for those he left behind. He had grown up as the eldest in the family. When he was young, his dad had run away from his responsibilities and had left him to pick up the slack. He didn't want to be another absentee dad forcing the next generation to grow up too quickly in order to fill his role. As someone who'd given up his childhood, and a fair bit of his adulthood, to take care of his mother and siblings, he knew how unfair that was to ask of anyone.

Unfortunately, his ex hadn't seen his point. Family was still an important part of her future as far as she was concerned, so Lachlan had no other choice than to end their relationship. His treatment for testicular cancer had made it unlikely that it was still possible to have children. Even if he could have become a father, he didn't think it would've been fair at this stage to start a family. Not when there was always a chance of the cancer returning, perhaps more aggressively the next time.

So here he was, celebrating his recovery and the start of his new job as a paramedic in Glasgow. The next chapter of a life he hadn't been sure he'd get to experience. He certainly didn't need any complications of the romantic kind.

'Hey.' With the pretty dancer standing right in front of him, he promptly forgot all of that and went straight into flirt mode again.

'Hey.' She tucked a strand of hair behind her ear and fixed him with the most mesmerising pale blue eyes Lachlan had ever seen.

Suddenly the idea to spend this weekend at the festival getting drunk with his brother seemed a less attractive prospect than getting to know this woman.

'Lachlan.' He wiped the condensation from his beer bottle on his jeans and held his hand out.

'Melissa.' She shook it before he even had time to worry about how formal he was being, her smile reassuring him that he hadn't made a complete idiot of himself.

He was so out of practice when it came to being around the opposite sex. His experience was limited to his younger sister and Julieann, whom he'd been with since high school. Chatting women up wasn't something he'd had a lot of practice doing. When his teenage mates had been dating and going to parties, he'd been at home taking care of his siblings whilst his mum was at work. If he hadn't met his ex at the fast food restaurant he'd worked in to make extra cash to pay the family's bills, if she hadn't invited him out at the time, he might never have dated at all before his twenties. As it was, he'd only moved out of the family home once his little sister had grown up and sought her own independence. Now this was his time, and he was determined to make the most of it.

'Nice to meet you, Melissa. You seemed to be enjoying yourself in front of the stage earlier.' He'd been watching her dancing as though she hadn't a care in the world. Exactly how he wanted to feel. Preferably without the assistance of the toxic substances which most people here seemed to be taking to find that high. He'd had too many chemicals pumped into his body during his cancer treatment to even think about doing that. These days he didn't even drink more than a couple of beers because he didn't like that sense of being out of control of his body. Up close, he could tell Melissa wasn't under the influence of anything other than the determination to enjoy the atmosphere.

Her pale cheeks flushed a little pink, only making her even more attractive. 'You saw that, huh?'

'Couldn't take my eyes off you.' Lachlan leaned in and spoke for her ears only. Even though Duncan was giving him some space, using the moment to phone his wife, Lachlan wanted to make sure his brother didn't hear. If he crashed and burned, he could do without the added humiliation of his brother witnessing it.

'I'm just here with my friend, Lydia.' Melissa glanced back at the voluptuous blonde draped over the bar.

'Special occasion?' He nodded towards the sparkly cowgirl hat. It wasn't really in keeping with the dark clothing she was wearing. Unlike her friend's leopard print, her navy maxi dress with a starry pattern wasn't shouting for attention. He wondered if she was part of a breakaway faction from a large hen party.

Melissa reached her hand up to her hat, as though she'd forgotten she was even wearing it. 'It's my birthday.'

'Happy birthday. Your twenty-first?' Very smooth.

She narrowed her blue gaze at him. Clearly not easily flattered. 'Thirtieth.'

'Ah. The thirties are the best years of your life.'

'Speaking from experience, are we?' Those pretty blue eyes twinkled with mischief.

'Well, the first ten months have been good.' Getting the all-clear from testicular cancer, moving to the city and bagging a new job was a pretty good start to his new decade. Even though he'd have to have regular check-ups and blood tests to make sure the cancer didn't return.

'Well, old man, how about buying me a birthday drink?' She tilted her chin up with the tease.

He liked her confidence, and she certainly wasn't being coy about what she wanted. Although Lachlan wasn't looking for anything serious with another woman, this festival was about celebrating a new chapter of his life. If that meant sharing it with a beautiful, fun-loving stranger, then he wasn't going to say no. He was looking forward to getting to know her a little better.

'I was just about to suggest that. Although perhaps we should move somewhere a little more grown-up.' As a group of lads near them bounced along to the music, beer spilling everywhere, Lachlan moved closer to Melissa, feeling protective.

'That would be nice. It's hard to talk when you can barely hear yourself think.'

They abandoned what was left of their drinks on

one of the plastic tables in front of the burger van and began to walk away from the crowds.

'There's a pub across the road. If we're lucky, we might even get a seat to rest our thirty-year-old crumbling bones.' His grin was mirrored by Melissa, and he was glad she didn't seem to take herself too seriously. He didn't want to be with someone he'd have to tiptoe around. It was nice just to be himself, and have a laugh without any expectations.

Julieann had always wanted to talk about the future, settling down and having kids. Then there was Duncan. As much as he loved his brother, he'd spent most of this weekend listening to his marital problems or looking at pictures of his children. Some time kicking back with a drink and good company was exactly what he'd been looking for.

They were halfway across the field when the slight drizzle of the summer rain turned into a sudden downpour. Melissa let out a squeal and began running. He grabbed her hand and directed her towards the old concrete bus shelter at the edge of the road. Running and laughing, he felt like a teenager again. Or at least, he imagined this was how most teenage boys who hadn't had to grow up too quickly felt, hand in hand with a member of the opposite sex. Carefree, reckless…happy.

'I'm soaked,' she said through a bright grin as they sought shelter in the covered recess.

'No one else seems to be bothered. Are we wimps?' The rest of the festival-goers were still dancing, revelling in the rain and mud.

'I don't care. Give me a fire and a comfy armchair over that any day.' Melissa took a seat on the wooden bench with peeling red paint, and Lachlan sat down beside her.

'Add a hot toddy into that picture and I'm with you.' At this moment in time he couldn't think of anything better than sharing that cosy scene with her.

'Maybe some towels and a hairdryer too…' She tipped her head forward, sending a torrent of water running from her hat, then squeezed more out of the ends of her stunning russet hair.

He hadn't realised how drenched they'd got in such a short space of time, and despite the mild temperature, Melissa was shivering.

'We'll make a run for it once there's a break in the rain.' Watching it from their hidey-hole was like being behind a waterfall, sheet rain sealing them off from the outside world.

He put his arm around her shoulders, attempting to generate some body heat through the thin fabric of the dress clinging to her body. Melissa looked up at him, gratitude shining in her eyes. Along with something else.

It had been so long he'd failed to recognise it at first. Attraction. Longing. Need. All the same things currently pulsing in his veins too. With the break-up, not to mention the cancer, sex had been the last thing on his mind for a long time.

Now, with Melissa looking at him with such undisguised yearning, he felt like the luckiest man on the planet. He leaned down and pressed his lips softly against hers, needing to touch her, taste her, and believe that she was real. That this stranger had appeared and awakened part of him he'd worried had been gone forever.

Melissa melted under Lachlan's touch. She'd forgotten how it felt to be with someone, how good it was to be wanted. For eighteen months, she'd been on her own, mourning the man she loved, forgetting to think of herself in the process. Lydia had been right—she still had a life to lead, and Lachlan was reminding her of that. She had needs, especially when this man was kissing her, slipping his arms around her waist and pulling her closer into his warm embrace. One night with him could help her move on and mark the start of this new decade in her life. Without Chris. She had to get used to the fact he was no longer part of her life, and with every tender kiss from Lachlan, he was gradually fading into the past.

It didn't mean she was ready to get into another serious relationship, but she doubted that's what would happen from hooking up with someone at a music festival anyway. Years from now, he would just be part of the special memories she was making celebrating her thirtieth birthday.

She kissed him back with an urgency that seemed to ignite more passion in him. Until things were getting pretty steamy in the sheltered nook. The sound of blood rushing in her ears, the feel of his strong hands anchored to her body, blotted out every last ounce of her usual common sense. So all that remained was the all-consuming need for more of Lachlan.

When he eventually wrenched his lips from hers, she was left dizzy and bereft.

'I think the rain is dying down. We should probably make a run for it. I have some towels and a hairdryer in my room you can use.'

'Room?' Her head still spinning from his passionate kisses, she thought she'd missed some vital piece of information.

'I'm staying over at the pub. It's cheating, I know, but there was no way I was sleeping in a tent in a field.' He looked shamefaced at the admission, but Melissa was only sorry she hadn't thought of the idea first.

'Sensible.'

'So, what do you say? We can go to my room and get dried off. No funny business, I swear.'

Melissa looked at the pub across the road, then at Lachlan as he took her hand. The feel of him there was both comforting and exciting, and she didn't want it to end when this was the most alive she'd been in months.

'Spoil-sport. I was looking forward to the funny business,' she said with a wink, pulling him behind her as she made her way across the road to the pub. Her pulse raced and her mouth was dry with the uncharacteristic attempt at seduction.

If she was going to convince Lachlan, and herself, that she was the type of woman who could have a one-night stand and walk away as if it never happened, she had to fake a Lydia-style confidence. Goodness knew that she didn't want to let this opportunity slip through her fingers. This was her chance to put the past behind her, just for one night, and she couldn't think of a more fun, exciting way to do it than spend it with Lachlan.

Lachlan's heart was beating a quickstep as they walked into the elevator. As much as he liked Melissa's forward nature, ruling out the chance of any misunderstanding or worry of rejection, he was a tad apprehensive. Not of Melissa, or what they were about to do, but more about his performance. Certain parts of him had been out of commission since his cancer treatment. Even though he'd likely never see Melissa again, he didn't want to let her down or embarrass himself.

He certainly hadn't felt sexy or virile during his treatment, more emasculated by it. It had taken a while, and some counselling, to come to terms with everything he'd been through. Though he'd had a reconstruction of the testicle he'd lost, he still knew a part of him was missing. Illogical though it was, sometimes he worried he was no longer the sexual being he used to be.

A fear that began to subside when she started kissing him once the elevator doors slid shut. Running the palms of her hands up his chest, pressing herself tightly against him, Melissa was leaving him in no doubt about how much she wanted him. The ultimate aphrodisiac, if it was needed.

When the elevator pinged open, they stumbled towards his room in a frenzy of kisses and searching hands desperate to keep hold of one another.

'Are you sure you want to do this?' he asked, as much for himself as Melissa. Did he really want to engage in meaningless, passionate sex with someone he'd only just met and wasn't likely to ever see again?

The answer from both parties was an overwhelming, breathless, 'Yes!'

He'd done the long-term thing, committed to someone and something which ultimately hadn't been right for him in the end. People and circumstances changed, so it seemed pointless to do it all over again with someone else he would probably end up disappointing eventually. At least this way there were no obligations or expectations beyond this room. And, if it did turn out to be a disaster, he wouldn't have to worry about facing her again. The beauty of being on this island was that people travelled from all over to be here. It wasn't as though they'd met at a local party in the park, where the potential for running into each other would always be a concern. Beyond first names, this was anonymous. Just for fun. The way he intended to approach the next part of his life.

Once she'd ditched her fetching headwear, he pulled her dress up over her head, uncovering her pretty lace underwear and sexy figure. Her skin was cool under his touch, goose pimples appearing as he slid her bra straps down her arms.

'Are you cold?'

Melissa bit her lip as she shook her head, indicating for the first time that she might be as nervous as he was about this.

'Burning up,' she replied, denying the hitch of apprehension in her voice.

It should have been a sign that perhaps this wasn't as casual as she wanted him to believe. That she wasn't the sort of woman who could sleep with him and walk away without a second thought after all. Except he didn't want to heed that warning if it meant putting an end to this now. The urgency with which she stripped his shirt off obliterated any doubt. Everything in his body wanted more.

It was on the tip of his tongue to tell her he hadn't done this in a while, but that was personal, as were the reasons behind it. Rather than excusing himself before he let her down, he was hoping it wouldn't be too apparent. When she was touching him, kissing him, he certainly didn't feel as though he wasn't up to it. Where once he'd faced death, now he felt more alive than ever. He wished he could bottle this feeling.

Lachlan slowly undid Melissa's bra, uncovering her full breasts, which fit perfectly in his palms. She gasped as he kneaded the soft flesh and teased her pert nipples with his thumbs. So responsive and tempting. He dipped his head and sucked on the puckered pink tips until she was arching her body into his. He slid his hands into her panties and squeezed her round backside, pulling her flush against his ever-hardening body.

Melissa moved to unbutton his trousers, and for a split second, he forgot he was anything other than a normal hot-blooded man. However, as she touched him through his boxers, he froze.

'Wait!' He backed away, putting some space between them.

'Have I done something wrong?' she asked, a worried look on her face. He cursed himself, and his illness, for putting it there.

'Not at all.' A one-night stand wasn't exactly the right situation for a deep and meaningful conversation. It wasn't easy to say that part of what made him a man was missing. Despite it being a recent event in his life, having a testicle removed wasn't something that cropped up in everyday conversation.

'You're married.' She sighed, folding her arms across her chest.

'No. I…er…just wanted to make sure this was what you wanted.' He decided it was worth the risk of letting her decide for herself if she still found him attractive or not. If he was ever going to get back in the dating game, he had to start somewhere, and Melissa was the first woman in an age he'd wanted to be with.

She hooked a finger into the waistband of his trousers and pulled him back towards her.

This time he didn't stop her from unzipping him, though he was tense as she touched him. The first person other than the doctor and surgeons who'd treated him who'd had access to that part of him. Thankfully this was a much more enjoyable experience.

Perhaps it was simply a man thing, thinking that he'd lost his masculinity somehow, or that Melissa would notice and find him less physically appealing. Someday he mightn't care so much, but since he was still coming to terms with what had happened himself, every rejection would hurt that much more.

He held his breath as she completely exposed him, taking him in hand and stroking him until he forgot everything except her touch. Her acceptance reinvigorated him, gave him more confidence, as he pulled her towards the bed with him.

He almost felt like the old Lachlan.

Melissa swallowed nervously as Lachlan covered her body with his. He was kissing her all over, being too considerate for what she needed. She didn't want someone making love to her, giving her reason to read more into this than was there. Hot, passionate sex was all she wanted, to fulfil a need and prove that she was able to move on.

She ground her hips against his, eliciting a groan from Lachlan.

'If you keep doing that, this is going to be over before either of us is ready.'

'Maybe I don't want to wait,' she said in her best sultry voice, grabbing his butt with both hands.

Another groan. Then he sank into her, locking their bodies together, and taking Melissa's breath away. Eyes closed, she gave herself over to the sensations he was awakening inside her.

Tonight, she'd let herself enjoy her freedom, the anonymity of a one-night stand, because tomorrow she had to go back to her real life. She'd be out of here the moment Lachlan was asleep, leaving him as nothing more than a wonderful memory.

CHAPTER TWO

Three months later

'NONE FOR ME, thanks.' Melissa held up her hand before Lydia could pour her a coffee. 'I'll just have a glass of water.'

'That's not going to keep you going through another shift. I hope you're not coming down with the same thing Lisa is out with.'

'Trust me, I don't think Lisa has what's ailing me,' Melissa mumbled, knowing she couldn't keep this to herself for much longer.

Lydia frowned, studying Melissa over her cup of coffee. 'Come to think of it, you haven't been yourself for a while. Not drinking after work, skipping your caffeine fix in the mornings. Are you on some sort of health kick?'

Melissa wished that's all that was stopping her from joining her work colleagues at the clinic in their usual weekend wind-down sessions at the local pub. Life would be so much simpler for her right now if she only had to worry about calorie counting. She was putting on a little extra weight, sure, but not because she'd been overindulging. At least not in food.

'There's something I have to tell you…' Her stomach rolled at the thought of saying it out loud. Once she admitted to it publicly, she had to face up to the fact that this was really happening.

She could see the second Lydia finally figured it out as her frown morphed into an expression of shock and horror.

'You're pregnant!'

Melissa nodded, the relief of finally sharing the news, and the enormity of how much her life was going to change, making her well up. She was tearful a lot these days, though her hormones might have had something to with it too.

'I'm pregnant. It took you long enough to work it out. And you're a midwife…' Melissa attempted to make light of it, though she'd been covering her tracks well since the positive test turned her life upside down. It was probably more out of denial than worrying about sharing the news before the end of her first trimester.

'I didn't know you were seeing anyone.'

'I'm not.'

'Then how? Oh…' Lydia's eyes were like saucers when the penny dropped. 'Festival guy?'

'Festival guy.' So much for slipping away and pretending it had never happened. Now she'd have a life-long reminder of her recklessness.

Lydia pursed her lips. 'You're a midwife too. Did you forget how babies are made?'

Melissa deserved the sarcasm. It wasn't as though she hadn't beaten herself up over being so stupid.

'I know. I know. I was an idiot. When I was with Chris, I relied on the pill, and there hasn't been any need to take it since.' She and Lachlan had been too caught up in the passion of the moment to even think about contraception at the time, and now she had to live with the consequences.

'Well, what's done is done. How do you feel about it?'

'I don't know. Chris and I had always planned to have a family someday, and when he died, I thought that dream was over. I want to be a mum, but my emotions are conflicted about the way it's happening. I mean, I'm on my own. In all those daydreams I had, I never imagined I'd be raising a child alone after a one-night stand.' Her parents, though not actively involved in her life these days, weren't likely to be impressed either. She hadn't seen much of them since they'd moved to America when she was eighteen. It had felt as though when she went to university she was no longer their responsibility. Their duty as parents was over.

Perhaps they'd imagined she didn't need them any more, but she hadn't suddenly become an independent, self-reliant adult simply because of a birthday. That was something she'd had to work on becoming in their absence, because they'd left her no choice.

Contact with them since had been limited, and the shame of getting pregnant by a stranger was liable to drive them even further apart.

Then there were the practicalities of being a single mum. She had no idea how she was going to juggle motherhood and a career. It was still all so overwhelming to try and get her head around.

'I take it the father doesn't know?'

Melissa just about managed not to laugh hysterically. 'I don't even know his surname, never mind anything else about him. Besides, it was supposed to be a one-night stand. A bit of fun to get over losing the love of my life. I think this goes way beyond casual sex.'

Even if she did know more about the father of her unborn child than his first name, she doubted she would get in touch. It would turn his world upside down too. Lachlan hadn't signed on for fatherhood, just a roll in bed.

If she was honest, not knowing anything about him was a good excuse to keep him out of the picture when she was still trying to come to terms with the situation herself. The guilt of betraying Chris's memory by having another man's child was already eating away at her conscience without having Lachlan in her life to remind her on a daily basis. In different circumstances she'd be married to the love of her life, both overjoyed at the prospect of starting their family. Living out their dream for the future with another man seemed to make a mockery of everything she and Chris had together. As though it had been easy to simply transfer those plans to someone else in his place. The reality was so different she wanted to weep, and had done so frequently since that first missed period. So much for no-commitment fun.

This pregnancy was a mistake, but she would raise the baby herself, and do her best to honour Chris's memory. That wouldn't happen with another man crowbarred into her life because of one moment of madness.

'These things happen. We both know that, Mel. You'll make a fantastic mother.' Lydia opened her arms out wide for Melissa and enveloped her in a hug.

'I hope so. I really hope so.' She let herself be comforted for a few moments. Then she thought about the women waiting for her, and pulled herself together.

'You know you can come to me anytime. I like the sound of Auntie Lydia...'

'Thanks. I'm probably going to need a babysitter, and a friend.' Lydia was going to be the fun auntie who'd spoil the little one rotten, and goodness knew Melissa and the baby were going to require some sort of support.

Lydia gave her an extra squeeze before releasing her. 'I'm not going anywhere.'

Melissa felt the tears welling again, and inhaled a shaky breath to fend them off. 'Right. I'd better go and see to the other pregnant ladies.'

She had appointments to keep with women who were looking to her for reassurance and guidance. There were another six months for her to fret over her own situation.

Melissa left Lydia in the staff room and headed to the small room she'd been allocated for seeing her patients.

At least when she was working, she didn't have time for self-pity. It was her job which had saved her when Chris died, giving her a reason to get up in the morning and carry on, because these mothers-to-be were relying on her. As well as being the local community midwife, she often did shifts at the maternity wing in the hospital. She hoped her busy schedule would get her through this too and planned on working right up until the birth if possible. It was too scary to think about what would happen after that.

She pulled up her appointment list and patient files, glad to see Claire Burns was her first patient of the day. A chatty, friendly lady separated from her husband, and who was in the final days of her pregnancy. There was a comfort in knowing someone was in similar circumstances to Melissa's, that she'd gone through her pregnancy alone and hadn't fallen apart.

The knock on the door signalled her arrival.

'Come in,' Melissa called as she set out the usual bits and pieces she needed for these antenatal checks.

'Hi, Melissa. I'm not on my own today.' Claire beamed as she walked in.

'Let me get another seat.' Melissa turned away to pull a chair over for the extra guest, hoping that she'd managed to reunite with her husband for a happy ending.

When she looked up and saw the man walking in, she almost keeled over.

'This is Lachlan. Lachlan, this is Melissa.' Claire introduced the man who'd put Melissa in her current predicament, and who she hadn't got out of her head in three months.

Lachlan held out his hand as the introduction was made, though he looked as shell-shocked as Melissa felt. 'Nice to meet you,' he said.

For obvious reasons, he apparently didn't want to acknowledge that they already knew each other.

Understatement of the year.

She managed to croak out a 'Hello.' Then almost collapsed into her chair, her body dealing with a mixture of emotions all at once.

Her initial reaction to seeing him had briefly been happiness, remembering the time they'd spent together and the thought that she'd never see him again. That was quickly followed by the realisation that he was here because he'd fathered someone else's baby. He'd lied to her when he'd said he wasn't married. Worse still, he'd walked out on his wife when she was pregnant. Clearly he wasn't the good guy she'd assumed him to be in the short time they'd spent getting to know each other.

'How've you been, Claire?' She tried to keep her mind on the job, ignoring the flush of colour she'd noticed in Lachlan's cheeks when he'd recognised her. He should feel embarrassed, sleeping with a stranger when he'd abandoned his own wife and child.

Her own blood pressure was rising as she attached the cuff to Claire's arm to check hers.

'Great, now that Lachlan's here for some support.' The mother-to-be's smile made Melissa more nau-

seous than usual, seeing Claire fawn over a man who'd
betrayed them both.

'Better late than never,' she mumbled, drawing a
puzzled frown from her patient, reminding her to remain professional and set aside her personal feelings
on the subject.

'Why don't you pop up onto the bed for me so we
can check on baby's progress.' As Melissa pulled back
the curtain from around the bed, she offered a bright
smile to the couple.

Claire struggled to heave herself out of her chair,
her huge bump clearly proving a hindrance these days.
Lachlan stepped in and helped her up. Ever the gen-
tleman.

Melissa took over, assisting her onto the bed, shooting Lachlan the darkest look she could muster. She
didn't want to let him off scot-free. If she didn't get to
speak to him privately and let him know what a lowlife
she thought he was, she hoped she managed to convey
it with one glance.

With a jerk of her hand, she pulled the curtain around
the bed again, blocking out the sight of the man who'd
unknowingly turned her life upside down.

Claire lay down and pulled her top up over her
rounded tummy. 'I've been feeling a dull, heavy sort
of ache, and she hasn't been squirming around as much
as usual.'

After washing her hands, Melissa felt around
Claire's bump, checking the baby's position. 'I think
she's getting ready to come out. The head's engaged in

the birth canal, so it shouldn't be long until you meet her for yourself.'

The sheer joy she saw on Claire's face at the news was something Melissa hoped she felt herself when it was her turn. By the time she was at this stage, she trusted she'd have got over the initial surprise and made preparations for her impending motherhood. For now, she was still somewhat in a state of shock over what had happened. Seeing Lachlan today, in these circumstances, wasn't going to help her get over it just yet.

'I can't wait. Lachlan's built the cot and decorated the nursery for me. I don't know where I'd be without him.'

Melissa resisted tutting or rolling her eyes as Claire sang his praises. It was the least he could do considering how much he'd upset Claire, leaving her to go through the pregnancy alone. Melissa supposed she was in the same position, though Lachlan was unaware of the other baby he'd fathered, and there would be no happy family for her at the end. Though she would do everything in her power to make sure her baby was loved enough for both parents. She knew all too well how it felt to be abandoned. Lachlan might not be privy to their child's existence, but she didn't suppose it would make any difference if he was. Someone who didn't stick around for a child inside a marriage surely wasn't going to be involved in raising one with a woman he barely knew.

She let Claire adjust her clothes, and tested the urine sample she'd brought with her. 'Everything looks good.

I can't see you going far beyond your due date, so hopefully the next time I see you, you'll have your little girl in your arms.' That was the part she looked forward to most in her job. Although this one would be bittersweet, having to see Lachlan cooing over the baby. At least she'd be better prepared for running into him again in the future.

'I have my bag packed, all ready to go when the time comes.'

'And you have your birth plan... You might want to add your husband to that since you said you didn't want anyone with you in the delivery room.' When the time came, most women wanted a loved one with them, but Claire had been clear about doing it by herself because she'd have to get used to being on her own. Something Melissa admired and was thinking about adopting for her own birth plan. Although Lydia might have something to say about that one...

'What are you talking about? Why would I want to add my husband when I haven't seen him in months?' Claire was glaring at her, obviously upset by Melissa's comment.

Lachlan was scowling too, making it clear she'd messed up.

'Sorry. I just assumed Lachlan would want to be at the birth since he's here now.'

'Ew. Why would I want my brother at the birth?'

The room fell silent as the truth finally dawned on Melissa. She wanted to crawl into a hole and bury herself out of sight.

'Your brother?'

'Yes. He's just moved to the city, and he's been helping me get ready for the baby coming.'

'You thought I was the father? That I had walked out on a wife and unborn baby?' Lachlan was not as amused as Claire over the misunderstanding. His dark look indicated he wasn't happy that she saw him as someone who would easily abandon his family and sleep with a stranger.

'I—I'm sorry. My mistake.' In Melissa's defence, she didn't know him well enough to believe otherwise.

'No harm done,' Claire insisted, though Lachlan looked as though he was still brooding over the accusation. 'Actually, you might see more of my big brother from now on.'

'Oh?' Melissa's stomach was already swirling with the prospect of seeing him again in a professional capacity, pretending they didn't have intimate knowledge of one another. Their time together had been a one-off, out of character for her, but Lachlan wouldn't know that any more than she knew he was apparently the sort of man to step up and take care of his pregnant little sister.

'I've just started as a paramedic. Our paths might cross again from time to time,' Lachlan added, his jaw tense, giving an indication that he wasn't any more thrilled with the idea than she was.

'You've moved here? You're going to be working… here?'

His nod confirming her worst fears was all it took to start the room spinning.

Glasgow was a big city, but with her work as a local community midwife, they would be living and working in the same vicinity. Not to mention operating out of the same hospital. Something she hadn't anticipated when coming to terms with her future as a single mother.

'Melissa? Are you all right?' Claire's voice sounded somewhere in the distance, but Melissa's head was whirring at the thought of Lachlan being in her life and the consequences of that.

A million thoughts and emotions overwhelmed her.

She never thought she'd see him again, and part of her had been sad about that when they'd had such a good time together. For a brief moment, she'd been happy he was more than a distant memory. The attraction she'd felt towards him was clearly still there. There was even the fleeting notion that she wouldn't be in this alone any more, that maybe Lachlan was going to be there for her and the baby. She would have the support in her life which had been missing for so long.

Now, however, the reality of him being here was beginning to sink in. It had been easy to relegate her time with him to the past, to focus on her future. The one she'd planned for her and her baby, without him. Letting him be part of that upended everything, and along with that reminded her of the betrayal of Chris's memory. Of course, the baby was always going to be evidence of that, but if Lachlan became a constant presence in their lives, there was a possibility he'd arouse more than feelings of guilt. After all, she'd liked him enough to sleep with him soon after their first meeting.

She wasn't sure she wanted to run the risk of anything stronger than liking him developing.

It was probably safer to carry on as though he wasn't part of this.

There was no way she'd be able to hide her pregnancy forever. If he saw her again over the course of the next few months, it wouldn't take much for him to figure it out.

Her acceptance of her situation was in jeopardy now that everything appeared to be spinning wildly out of control. This wasn't how she'd planned things. She'd been preparing to do this alone and hadn't counted on ever seeing or dealing with him again.

Melissa felt as though she was being buried alive by the skeletons tumbling out of her closet.

She stumbled, grabbing for the desk, closing her eyes in an attempt to regain her composure.

Strong hands were suddenly holding her up, guiding her into a chair. A familiar deep voice asking if she was okay. One she heard in her dreams at night. Perhaps she was still asleep and this was a nightmare, all of her worst fears come true.

'Melissa? Should I get someone?' There it was again, that voice which had sweet-talked her into bed and changed her life forever...

It took her a moment to remember where she was and who else she was with.

'No. I'm fine.' She shook Lachlan off. It wasn't going to help her gather her composure if he was touching her, reminding her of the last time they'd been in close contact.

'Are you sure? You're looking a little green.' Lachlan's concern only irritated her and made her more determined to get rid of him.

'I skipped breakfast this morning. I'm sure it's just low blood sugar making me a little light-headed. I'll be sure to grab something to eat from the staff room before the next patient comes in.'

'It's the most important meal of the day, so they say. Although I couldn't face it in the early days of my pregnancy with the morning sickness. You're not pregnant are you, Melissa?' Claire laughed, and the best thing Melissa could have done was laugh it off too, but she couldn't, because there was nothing funny about it.

She just froze. Trapped in the headlights of the truth.

'Melissa?'

She could hear the unspoken question in Lachlan's voice, feel his eyes burning into her. What she said next could affect both of their lives forever.

There was nothing to be gained from telling him now except a whole lot of disruption for both of them. Lachlan was clearly starting some new stage of his life too. The last thing either of them needed was to be thrown together, forced to co-parent for the rest of their lives. She knew nothing about him, and though she should have thought about that much earlier, she'd learned her lesson. There was more than herself to worry about now.

'Very funny.' She gulped down the truth and tried to pass Claire's question off as a joke.

'Ignore me,' Claire said. 'I've obviously got babies on the brain at the minute.'

'No worries. It's understandable when you're getting close to your due date, but everything looks good, Claire. I'll make another appointment to see you, but hopefully you won't need it.' Melissa scribbled down the date and time on Claire's appointment card, in a hurry for the two to leave. She had a lot to process and needed some time on her own before she saw her next patient.

'I'll see you soon.' Claire got to her feet with her brother's assistance, and Melissa was ready to breathe a sigh of relief as they moved to the door.

With both of them working in the medical field in the same city, it was possible Lachlan would find out the truth anyway. She'd panicked being on the spot like that, but Lachlan hadn't questioned anything. In fact, he barely acknowledged her as he walked out the door, so perhaps she was worrying about nothing.

Melissa was shaking when they finally left. It had been a close call, but she hoped Lachlan was out of her life for good this time.

'She's lovely, isn't she?' Claire was extolling the virtues of her midwife, but Lachlan's mind was firmly trained on the woman he'd watched dancing in the mud, and kissed in the rain. He'd never believed he'd get to see her again. Especially since she'd ghosted him in the middle of the night, disappearing without a trace, except for the smile she'd left on his face.

And now that Claire had suggested Melissa might be pregnant, he couldn't get the thought out of his head. Was it his imagination, or was there a certain roundness in her curves that hadn't been there before? A glow that suggested perhaps it wasn't beyond the realm of possibility, despite her dismissal of Claire's comment.

Melissa hadn't directly denied the suggestion she might be pregnant, and she'd hesitated just a fraction too long. Ordinarily, she would have every right to keep that sort of information to herself. She wasn't obliged to share private matters with her patients. However, her reaction upon seeing him only raised more red flags. He could understand seeing a one-night stand in the workplace would be embarrassing for her, but she'd almost passed out when they'd come face-to-face and she'd learned he'd moved to the city. It gave the impression there was something more going on than regret.

What if it was his baby and she'd simply been afraid of talking to him about it in front of Claire?

Neither Duncan nor Claire knew anything about their tryst at the festival. When his brother had queried his sudden disappearance, he'd simply put it down to having too much to drink and going to sleep it off.

In hindsight, he and Melissa hadn't used any protection, but with his medical history, he hadn't imagined the chance of anyone conceiving his baby after one night was very high. It was still possible, though, and he needed to know for sure. Although becoming a father wasn't something he wanted, he wasn't going to abandon a child the way his own dad had readily done with his whole family.

Whatever the truth, he had a feeling Melissa was going to be a part of his life here in Glasgow. And the idea wasn't as scary as it should've been.

CHAPTER THREE

'AM I GLAD to see you. I had visions of having to deliver this baby myself.' An anxious-looking husband opened the door for Lachlan and his colleague.

'I'm Lachlan, the paramedic.'

'Gordon. The husband.'

He shook hands with the man, who looked as though he was about to start hyperventilating at any moment.

'What's your wife's name?'

'Marie. She's upstairs in the bedroom.'

'And there's no sign of the midwife arriving anytime soon?' Although they were absolutely the people to call in an emergency, when it came to births, that was the midwives' department. Lachlan and his colleagues only got involved when there was no other option. Like now.

'She's caught up in traffic and told us to call for you in case she didn't get here in time. I don't think this baby is going to wait.'

'Okay, well, we'll see how things are looking.' Lachlan made his way to the bedroom, with the husband close behind.

'Hi, Marie. I'm Lachlan. I understand baby seems

to be in a hurry. Was this a planned home delivery?' he asked the woman.

She nodded through panting breaths. 'Although we hadn't counted on a storm preventing our midwife from getting here on time.'

'I understand, and if she gets here soon, we'll certainly hand over your care into her capable hands. For now, though, I need to see how far labour is progressing, okay?' These days home births weren't uncommon. Sometimes going through labour in the comfort of their own homes, in familiar surroundings, made the birthing experience that bit more pleasant for mums. It could certainly be a calmer atmosphere than being under the fluorescent lights in a busy hospital ward, without the sound of machines, babies crying, and the general chatter. As long as they had support from their familiar midwives and hadn't been forced to call in the emergency services last minute.

Though Lachlan would do his best not to show it, he was anxious about the possibility of having to deliver this baby. It was a big responsibility, bringing a baby into the world, and was something he'd only done in theory until now.

'There's another one coming,' Marie managed through gritted teeth, sitting up in bed as the next contraction hit.

'Just breathe through it. We can wait until it passes. Deep breaths. In and out...' Lachlan took her hand and breathed with her, ignoring how hard Marie was squeezing, until the contraction began to subside.

Once it had passed, and the circulation was back in his fingers, Lachlan went to wash up so he could examine her.

'If you can slide your feet up and let your knees fall open, I'm just going to see how you're progressing.' He had hoped since this was her first baby that they might have enough time to transfer her to the hospital so they could deliver there, but it soon became apparent that wasn't going to be an option.

'You're almost fully dilated. It looks as though we're going to be welcoming baby soon.'

Marie looked relieved, but when Lachlan felt around her bump, there was more cause to be concerned.

'When you had your scans at the hospital, was there any indication that the baby might be in the breech position?'

'No. Why? What's wrong?' Marie grabbed for her husband's hand, understandably distressed that things weren't going according to plan.

'Okay, I don't want you to panic, but baby seems to have moved position. He's coming out feet first.' Lachlan tried to keep his voice calm as he delivered the information, not wanting to upset his patient. Even though he was feeling the pressure even more.

A breech birth made things trickier for him without the usual resources of the hospital should he need them.

'Is everything going to be all right?' Marie's husband asked.

'Yes. Baby's heartbeat is fine, but his position will just make the delivery a little trickier. Everything will be okay. We need to keep Marie calm and relaxed until then. You're both doing great.' Lachlan gave them his best optimistic smile, despite his heart trying to beat its way out of his chest.

Marie nodded and squeezed her husband's hand a little tighter when another contraction took over. Once it had passed, Lachlan was able to offer some pain relief. He needed the mother to be relaxed for the next stage.

When they heard the knock on the front door, there was a collective sigh of relief.

'That'll be the midwife.' Marie's husband rushed downstairs to let her in, Lachlan thankful his prayers had been answered.

'I'm so sorry. The storm brought down a few trees blocking the roads. I got here as soon as I could.' Melissa bustled into the room looking more than a little windswept as she shrugged off her coat.

'It's no problem. Marie's fully dilated, and baby is in the breech position.' Lachlan was glad to have her here for a multitude of reasons. The most pressing was the imminent birth, but on a personal level, he was happy to have another opportunity to speak to her. He hoped after this was over, they'd get a chance to talk about the time they'd spent together, so it wouldn't be the elephant in the room every time they did come into contact.

'Okay.' Melissa rolled up her sleeves and examined Marie for herself. When she'd got the call about Marie's labour starting, she hadn't expected to walk into this.

A breech birth was one thing—she could handle that—but she hadn't been prepared for Lachlan being on the scene too. Since seeing him again at his sister's appointment, Melissa had had a crisis of conscience about whether or not she should have told him about the baby. She was still undecided as to what action to take, but perhaps spending some time with him tonight would tell her more about his character and point her in the right direction. His job as a paramedic was a responsible one, as proven tonight by him taking charge in her absence. He'd also shown maturity in helping his sister out. The voice that had been nagging her about doing the right thing was telling her these were the sorts of qualities needed in a father figure. She simply wasn't sure if she was ready to have him in her life.

A conversation was definitely needed, but for now, her patient was the priority.

'When you feel the next contraction, I want you to push, okay?'

Marie nodded, and her husband mopped the sweat from her brow with a cold washcloth. Giving birth was very much on the mother, but those fathers who chose to be there for it generally did their best to help. Keeping their partners calm and offering support might not seem like a lot in the circumstances, but she knew it could make all the difference to a frightened woman.

It made her think about her own labour. She hadn't written her birth plan because she didn't want to think about it, or how lonely she would be. Even if Lydia volunteered herself to be her birthing partner, it was never going to be the same as having a significant other with her. Knowing she'd have someone to take her and the baby home, someone to share the responsibilities with. She supposed as long as the baby was healthy, that was all that mattered, but it didn't mean she wouldn't be a little down in the circumstances.

When she'd thought about starting a family, she'd imagined it would be with Chris. That he would be as excited and as anxious as she was about becoming a parent and meeting their baby for the first time. It wasn't the same falling pregnant to a stranger she knew nothing about.

Even if she confessed to Lachlan that he was the father, and he wanted to be there for the birth, it wasn't going to be the cosy family she'd always pictured. Worse still, she might come to hope for that possibility if Lachlan was on the scene, and she couldn't risk her heart on what could be a wasted exercise. Letting him into her life at all was leaving her vulnerable. She would have to remember that if Lachlan did want to be part of his baby's life, it would be because he felt obligated, not out of love. For her, that was the most important thing about being a parent. It wasn't something to go into half-hearted, because the child would feel it. She knew how it felt to be an afterthought.

It would be safer to keep Lachlan on the outside, but she knew it wasn't fair to leave him in the dark. The decision about whether or not he would be a father should be Lachlan's, not hers.

'Here we go again…' Marie gripped her husband's hand and bore down as the contraction took hold.

Melissa helped her breathe through the contractions until she saw the baby emerging.

'Okay, Marie, I need you to take it easy. It's best for baby to make his own way out now.' The hands-off approach wasn't something that came naturally to her, but letting the baby deliver itself in this situation was the best option to prevent any further problems.

Hopefully in this case, the only reason they would need transferred to the hospital would be for mother and baby to have a welfare check.

'Good, Marie. Just hold off on pushing for me so baby can come out himself.'

Melissa concentrated on catching the baby as he slipped quietly from his mother. Then she moved quickly to cut the umbilical cord and clean him up.

'Why isn't he making any sound?' Understandably, Marie voiced her concern.

'Sometimes babies need to adjust to their new surroundings.' Melissa didn't want to panic just yet. She knew the procedures. On occasion, babies were stunned by their sudden emergence into the world and needed their airways cleared or a little assistance before they started breathing on their own. She could feel the eyes of everybody in the room burning into her, relying on her to save this baby's life. Or start it.

'Lachlan, can you grab the aspirator from my bag, please?'

Without a trace of panic, or the slightest hesitation,

Lachlan placed the tiny mask over the child's mouth and nose, squeezing some air into his lungs. The pressure was even greater than usual when they weren't in a hospital setting, and failing here didn't just mean embarrassing herself. It meant the loss of a child. She was in charge, but Lachlan was such a confident and assured paramedic, she couldn't have asked for better backup in a potentially tragic emergency. This wasn't his field of expertise, but he wasn't afraid to step up when he was needed.

There was absolutely no reason she shouldn't tell him about his baby, except for her own issues over it.

When the newborn's chest started to rise and fall, there was a collective sigh of relief around the room, and tears from the new parents.

'Is he all right?' Marie asked as Melissa handed her son to her for the first cuddle.

'He's fine, but given the circumstances, it's best you both go to the hospital to get checked over. Lachlan will take you in the ambulance, and I'll follow in my car.'

'Can I hold him?' Gordon asked, clearly keen to meet his son.

'Of course. Why don't you take him for now whilst I get Marie ready for transfer.'

Marie carefully handed over her precious cargo to her husband. 'Watch his head. Make sure you've got him.'

'I've got him,' he assured her, the look of love in the man's eyes for his son making Melissa want to weep. Not only because it was such a lovely moment seeing him meet his child for the first time, but because she was preventing her baby from having the same welcome into the world from their father.

'Congratulations. We'll wait outside until you're ready to leave.' Lachlan and his colleague discreetly left the room, leaving her to deliver the afterbirth and ensure Marie was all right to be transferred to the hospital.

He gave her a smile and a nod before he disappeared out the door, and in that moment, her heart ached to tell him her secret. Despite not wanting to invite Lachlan further into her life, afraid of getting close to anyone again, she knew she couldn't deny him the chance of being a father to his own child.

Telling Lachlan he was the father of her baby left both of them open to hurt and rejection, but it was something she knew she had to do. What happened after that would be entirely down to him.

'You don't have to stay, you know,' Melissa said to Lachlan as he waited for news on mother and baby.

'It's fine. My shift's over. I just wanted to make sure they were all right. My first breech birth.' Not that he'd been actively involved in the end. Though he'd been ready to deliver the baby, he'd been relieved when Melissa had turned up to take over.

She'd been amazing, keeping her patient calm, and talking her through what was going to happen. Again, when the baby hadn't been breathing. It had been a scary time for everyone in that room, but Melissa hadn't once given anyone reason to panic. He'd been in awe of her.

Melissa smiled. 'Birth is an amazing thing.'

'So are you.' He hadn't known the words were going to leave his head and make their way out of his mouth, but they were true nonetheless.

It would have been easy to write Melissa off as some hippy-dippy free spirit from their first meeting at the festival, but she was far from that. She was a strong, capable woman who clearly didn't need him in her life. But Lachlan couldn't help being drawn to her. The memory of their time together at the festival hadn't left him, and wasn't likely to now that he was getting to know her a little better.

Since his cancer treatment, he hadn't thought much about getting into another relationship. But if he ever did, he imagined it would be with someone like Melissa. They'd had a connection from the first moment they'd met, and nothing since had made him feel any differently. Except he didn't want anything serious. The intensity of these last months during and after his treatment had left him emotionally and physically exhausted. He didn't have room for anything more in his life right now. Even if Melissa was interested in him as anything other than a fellow medical professional.

'I think we need a cup of tea and a debriefing... I mean, a chat about what happened. Even I don't see that many spontaneous breech births.' Melissa went a little pink, and Lachlan knew she was thinking about their night together too. The last time they'd 'debriefed'.

'Yeah, it's been one hell of a night.' Despite being aware of all the reasons he should say no and go home, he couldn't resist the chance to spend a little more time with her. He didn't know a lot of people in the city yet, and he was already aware of what great company she was. Okay, so they weren't likely to pick up where they'd left off, but it didn't mean they couldn't talk to one another at least.

Melissa led the way towards the canteen with Lachlan following, wishing it was a pub they were heading to instead.

The servery was closed, but the vending machines and seats were still available, so they waited for their paper cups to fill with what passed for tea and went to sit down.

'I'm glad you were there tonight,' Lachlan said honestly. Although he would've done his best for mother and baby, there was no one as experienced as the midwives when it came to delivering babies. Especially in circumstances like tonight when complications arose.

'I think you were doing okay on your own.'

'As I said, I'm glad you were there.' He took a sip of the tea, wishing it was something stronger. Both of their jobs had a high level of responsibility. People's lives were in their hands. But when it came to newborn babies, the pressure was so much greater. They were innocent souls just embarking on life. He didn't want to imagine how it would feel to lose one.

'So, you moved here to be with your sister?' Melissa shifted past the work stuff to the personal questions, but he supposed it was only natural for her to be curious about why he was here. Neither of them had expected to cross paths again.

'Partly. I needed a new start, and when this position came up, it also meant I could be here for Claire when the baby came. She doesn't have anyone else around her.'

'Won't your parents help out?'

'Mum lives out in the country and works in a farm shop. She doesn't want to move to the city, and Dad left when we were little. I barely remember anything about him, other than the mess he left us in. Mum had two jobs to keep a roof over our heads, and as the eldest, I pretty much raised my brother and sister. What about you? Have you got family here?'

Melissa shook her head, a sadness seeming to fall over her. 'No. They're living in America. Have done since I was eighteen.'

'You've been on your own all this time?'

'Yup. I don't have a lot of contact with them at all. I put myself through my midwife training and supported myself financially.'

'You're a strong woman, Melissa. You should be proud of yourself.' Lachlan didn't mean to be patronising, but if she didn't have her parents around, he supposed no one told her that very often.

'I'm not so sure about that. There are some things I'm not proud of. You know, seeing Marie and Gordon back there has given me some food for thought. There's something I need to tell you.'

Lachlan's heart was hammering against his ribcage as he waited for the response. He wasn't sure he was ready to hear whatever she had to say.

The way her gaze was locked onto his as though she was trying to communicate something telepathically rather than actually saying it out loud didn't help his anxiety.

'I'm pregnant.'

'Oh. Congratulations.' In that moment, he didn't know what else to say. He wondered why she was telling him now.

Melissa hung her head and let out a sigh, looking incredibly guilty about something. It occurred to him that she might have been in a relationship when they got together and was now remorseful, or worried he'd tell someone.

'If you're with someone, it's okay. I won't say anything about us.'

She took a gulp of tea before she spoke. 'I'm not with anyone, Lachlan. I haven't been with another man since the festival. In fact, you're the only man I've slept with in nearly two years.'

It took a moment for him to process what she was saying. The enormity of those few words eventually floored him. There was so much wrapped up in that night they'd spent together. It was always going to be more than a casual thing. Although he didn't know the details of Melissa's personal life, they'd clearly both been going through an emotional time. If she wasn't the sort of woman to sleep around, then he wondered what had prompted her to do so with him. He'd been breaking free from his old life, hoping to start all over again. Melissa must've had her reasons too.

'So…' He wanted her to spell it out for him.

'You're the father of my baby.'

'But you didn't say anything—'

'I know. I was surprised to see you that day. Claire put me on the spot, and I hadn't thought about how I was going to tell you. I didn't think I'd ever have to.'

Lachlan was sure that his spirit had left his body, that the shock of the information had killed him where he was sat. He was numb, the breath whooshing out of his lungs.

'I'm the father. Of your baby.' It wasn't so much a question, but a confirmation of what she'd told him so it might actually sink in. His one-night stand had suddenly turned into a lifetime commitment. However long that may, or may not, be.

'Yes.'

'And you wouldn't have told me if I hadn't walked into your office that day?'

She looked away. 'I didn't know anything about you. If I recall, that was the point of our time together.'

'I think having a baby negates the usual rules of a one-night stand.' He could feel the anger building inside him, replacing the shock. Melissa hadn't even been prepared to give him the chance of being a father. Okay, so it wasn't something he had planned for, but he suspected neither had she. He had the right to know she was carrying his baby and at least be given the option of getting involved. They'd conceived this child together, after all.

'I didn't even know your surname, Lachlan. I still don't.'

'McNairn. I'm sure you would have found me eventually if you'd tried.' It was clear she'd had no intention of telling him. He wondered what would have happened if he hadn't moved to Glasgow. The fact that he could have had a child out there that he'd never known about, all while thinking it wasn't possible for him to be a parent, seemed cruel. Of course, Melissa wasn't aware of his medical history, but it had still taken her until now to tell him, knowing he was in the city. He couldn't help but take that personally.

'It was quite a lot for me to get my head around too, Lachlan. My friend Lydia dragged me to the festival to celebrate my thirtieth birthday. It was supposed to help me get over the death of my fiancé, Chris, twenty-one months ago.'

'I'm sorry. What happened?' That went some way to explaining why she'd kept the news to herself. Getting over her loss would've been no small thing.

He'd been right in his assumption that their time together had been more than a casual hookup for her too. Especially if it had taken her this long to even try to move on.

'It was sudden. A brain aneurysm, they said.' There was a faraway look in her eyes, as though she was reliving the moment, and he could see the terror and pain residing within her.

It was the same look he'd seen on the faces of his family when he'd been going through his treatment. But his story had a happier ending. For now.

'That must've been horrific for you.' He reached out and took her hand to comfort her, the first contact they'd had since meeting again. Her skin was as soft and warm as he remembered.

She tried to smile through the tears filling her eyes, but her quivering bottom lip gave away her sadness. 'We'd planned to get married and have a family of our own. When he died, I thought that dream was over, so discovering I was pregnant after our night together was as big a shock to me as it is to you now. I'm still coming to terms with it.'

He was beginning to understand her motive for not coming clean sooner. Melissa, despite first impressions, was the settling down kind, and she'd realised pretty quickly that wasn't what he was interested in. Far from bringing a baby into a loving, established relationship, she was facing being tied to a man who'd picked her up at a music festival. And that was before she even knew he was someone who'd already had cancer once, and wasn't guaranteed to be around long-term. The question was where they went from here. He didn't want to scare her away by revealing his own health problems when she'd already been through so much.

'Why tell me now then?' He needed to know her motives for wanting him involved before he committed himself to anything. He didn't want to be another useless father like his own, or his brother-in-law, but he also needed to know she wasn't going to shut him out again if a better prospect came along.

Melissa was still holding his hand, so he took that as a good sign. 'I can tell you're committed to Claire and her baby.'

'Of course. She's my little sister. I've been looking after her for most of her life, and I want to make sure her child hopefully has the positive role model in their life that we didn't. I'll do my best to support them.'

'See. You're a good brother. I felt bad about not telling you the other day, but I was afraid of what it would mean for me to let you into my life. Then I saw you with the family tonight and realised I had to tell you. It's not fair to keep you out of the baby's life for my own selfish reasons. Now that you know, I'm hoping you'll make a good father too. Though it's entirely down to you if you want to be involved or not.'

'I want to be, if you'll give me the chance.' It was asking a lot of both of them, expecting Melissa to put her faith in him, and for him to commit to a family he never wanted.

'Claire's going to get a bit of a surprise, isn't she?' Melissa broke the tension with a smile, and a reminder that this wouldn't affect just the two of them.

'Have you told your parents?'

'Not yet.' Keeping this to herself for months went to show how much she'd been struggling with the news herself, but from now, on she wouldn't have to cope on her own.

'At least you know the name of the father of your unborn baby now.'

'Not funny, Lachlan,' she said, letting go of his hand to swat him on the arm, but she did so with a smile. They were making progress.

'Seriously, though, tell me what you want from me, Melissa. We're in this together.' He'd be lying if he said he didn't feel sick, that his gut wasn't churning with the prospect of becoming a father, and what that meant for the future. But they were both responsible for the situation they were in, and he'd never been one to walk away from his responsibilities.

'I'm not expecting anything from you, Lachlan. If you don't want to be involved, I'll understand.' Melissa was saying the words, but Lachlan wasn't sure she meant them. From everything else she'd said, he got the impression she was worried about going through this on her own, and he wasn't going to let her.

'I'm here. I'm involved. I'm the father.' Something he was going to have to repeat to himself until it finally sank in too.

'I've got my three-month scan coming up soon, if you'd like to be there?'

'I would.' Then finally they would both have to face the reality of the situation. When they saw their baby on the screen, there would be no denying this was happening, that it was more than just words and worries about the future. They'd created a life. One which they were both responsible for.

Only time would tell if they were up to the task ahead.

CHAPTER FOUR

'THANKS FOR DOING THIS,' Melissa said as they parked up outside the hospital.

It hadn't been easy facing Lachlan again after breaking the news that he was the father of her baby. Even less so having to ask him for a lift because she'd been feeling nauseated this morning.

'It's no problem.' Lachlan flashed her a smile, which she probably didn't deserve after almost denying him the chance to be a father.

'I just didn't want to take the chance of driving up here on my own and taking ill. It's probably nothing more than nerves, but I thought maybe I should have some company.' It had crossed her mind to go to Lydia first. She would have been the safer option, but Lachlan knew the scan was today, and it would've seemed churlish not to include him. Especially when he'd been hurt by her keeping the pregnancy to herself until now.

All things considered, he'd taken the news well. She'd dropped a baby bomb right in the middle of his world, and a lot of men would've gone running in the opposite direction. Not Lachlan.

'I told you I would be here for the scan.'

'You did.' Although she hadn't been one hundred percent sure he'd meant it, and a part of her had hoped he might not turn up. It would've made things easier for her if Lachlan decided he didn't want to get involved after all. Then she could just get on with things on her own the way she'd planned. Without worrying about having Lachlan in her life and the complications that brought.

Lachlan got out of the car and came around to open her door for her. 'Claire's excited about having a playmate for her little one.'

'You told her?' She couldn't help but wince at how that conversation might have gone.

It didn't make her look very professional getting pregnant by a patient's brother, even if they'd both been oblivious to the connection, or the consequences, at the time.

'Of course. I've told all the family, and they're thrilled. Although, to quote Claire, she doesn't know what you see in a "numpty" like me.'

That made her laugh. It was funny how grown adult siblings resorted to their childish selves when they were together. Chris and his brother used to engage in wrestling bouts at family get-togethers, and Lydia and her sister still fought like teenage girls over clothes and boys. Sometimes it made her glad she'd been an only child, but other times, like this, she wished she had that sort of bond with another family member.

It made her wonder about their baby, and if it would ever have a brother or sister in the future. If she could be in a stable, loving relationship where she would even think about having another baby. She certainly wasn't going to accidentally get pregnant with another stranger to do so. It was too emotionally complex and taxing.

'I told her, I'm handsome, fun, and currently looking after two pregnant ladies. I'm an absolute catch,' Lachlan joked, though every word was true. That was the problem. The very reason she was wary about opening up her life to let him in, if there was the smallest chance he would leave her the way everyone else in her life had.

It was plain to see that he had a special bond with his sister, teasing one another, but close all the same. Perhaps that was part of the reason she'd always wanted to have a family of her own. To have that security around her, ensuring she'd never be on her own again. Obviously, things hadn't worked out that way, and though she was happy she was going to have a child to share her life with, it was unfortunate she couldn't provide her offspring with the family she didn't have. Of course, Lachlan was going to be involved on some level, but it wasn't the same as having two loving parents raising their child in the same house. The chances of her having any more children to give this baby siblings were very low too, since this pregnancy hadn't been planned.

She supposed she should get used to feeling this level of guilt, since it seemed to be part of being a parent. Always worrying about doing the right thing for your child, and blaming yourself when things weren't perfect.

'Well, I'm grateful for your support, but I hope you've told her we're not a couple.' Melissa didn't want any misunderstanding on anyone's part. There was no way of knowing how things were going to play out in the future, but there was little point in getting carried away by the idea they were all going to end up being one big happy family.

'Yes. Although it was mortifying having to explain the circumstances.'

She could only imagine, and was glad she hadn't been there at the time, facing judgement of their reckless behaviour at the festival.

'Listen, I'll understand if you don't want to be here, or if you have something else to do. There'll be more scans for us to attend together. Or not. Whatever you decide.' Melissa didn't want to make things difficult for him, forcing him to be here if he wasn't one hundred percent on board. She hadn't left him much choice today when he'd had to drive her.

'Why would I want to miss seeing my baby for the first time? I thought you wanted me to be here.' A scowl marred his handsome features as they made their way towards the waiting room, and she knew immediately she'd said the wrong thing.

'I do, but I know you didn't ask for this. I'm giving you a way out.' She knew once they saw the baby together on the screen, there would be no going back for either of them.

Lachlan turned and fixed her under his dark glare. 'I said I'll be there, and I will. If this is your way of trying to push me out again, it's not going to work. This is my baby too, whether we like it or not.'

Far from being reassured by the statement, Melissa was reminded that he didn't want to be here at all. His involvement was merely because he felt a duty. She'd changed her mind about telling him about the baby after Marie's delivery because it was good to have his support and know he was there if she needed him. It made her think about her own labour, and if anything went wrong how nice it would be to have someone there with her. However, she didn't want that to be under sufferance. That wasn't how she wanted to welcome her baby into the world. It would be better to be on her own in that scenario in a room full of love, rather than regret and reluctance.

The shine of the afternoon was tarnished by Lachlan's words, her excitement at seeing her baby on the screen overshadowed by the thought that she'd strong-armed Lachlan into being here. That had never been her intention, but she couldn't help but worry that he didn't really want to be part of this. He was just the kind of man who felt compelled to step in when he was needed. Perhaps that was enough for some women, but Melissa would have preferred that he had a real emotional connection to their baby. With parents who acted sometimes as though she didn't exist, she didn't want the same for her child.

If Lachlan was only on the scene because he felt a

duty to be there, there was always a chance he could walk away too. Without any emotional attachment to her or the baby, it was only that sense of responsibility keeping him here. And goodness knew it hadn't been enough for her own parents to stick around forever. One day he might decide to follow dreams that didn't include being tied down to a child he'd never wanted, and then where would she be if she'd already made room for him in her life? Alone, wounded, and with a baby to take care of on her own. Exactly why she'd been reluctant to tell him in the first place. At least then she'd be doing this alone by choice, without having further reason to feel abandoned.

They sat in silence in the waiting room, an empty chair filling the distance between them. A stark comparison to the happy couples around them holding hands and chattering excitedly as they waited to see their babies.

'Melissa Moran?'

When her name was called, she got up and walked away without even looking to see if Lachlan was following her. She couldn't bear to see any trace of resentment on his face.

The sonographer checked her details, then asked her to get up onto the bed. It was the first time she'd looked at Lachlan since she'd been called, and was surprised to find him already sitting by the bed, watching the screen. Perhaps he wasn't as disinterested as she'd convinced herself he was.

'Can you just pop your top up over your belly for

me, Melissa, and pull the waistband of your skirt down a little bit?'

Melissa acquiesced, and the sonographer tucked some paper towel down the front of her skirt. 'It's just so we don't get any gel on your clothes.'

It was odd being on the other side this, when she was usually the one issuing instructions to anxious mothers-to-be. She'd have to get used to it with six months of her pregnancy to go. Although it would probably help her empathise more with her patients in the future. Their worries, and the extra problems pregnancy caused in a body. Her heartburn in the evening was even worse than the morning sickness had been.

'This will be a bit cold, sorry,' the sonographer apologised as she squirted some gel onto Melissa's tummy.

The little rounded swell had become a source of comfort, a reminder that her baby was growing there. Now, with that changing part of her body exposed to Lachlan's gaze, she felt self-conscious. He'd seen a lot more of her three months ago, but this was different, and she realised she still wanted him to find her attractive. Probably because she couldn't help but be drawn to him, regardless of the chaos they were dealing with in their lives.

He might have been joking about the conversation with his sister earlier, but he *was* handsome, and clearly loyal to his family. There was a big part of Melissa that wished his loyalty included her, that there was more between them so she could have that happy family she always dreamed of. But he was even less of a surety in her life than her parents, or Chris, had been.

She was still attracted to him, there was no doubt, but that only muddied things in her mind. It wasn't easy to separate thoughts of him as a father from the man she'd spent an amazing night with. Otherwise, she wouldn't be so afraid of having him around. The more she liked him, the more he could hurt her. That's why every time they seemed to get closer, she felt the urge to pull away. It was self-preservation. Preparation for the day he left, because experience told her that's what would happen the moment she dropped her guard.

It didn't help when they'd had intimate knowledge of one another. When she could still feel his lips on her, his hands caressing her body...

'Are you okay, Melissa? You look flushed.' Lachlan leaned across the bed to check on her, which only made her hotter round the collar as his warm breath tickled her neck.

'I'm fine. Just excited.' It was true on so many levels. Never more than when he gave her the soppiest smile possible.

'We're just looking to find baby's heartbeat,' the sonographer said. 'It might take a wee while, but don't worry.'

It was easier said than done to follow the medical professional's opinion, when Melissa knew better than anyone how many things could go wrong at this early stage of pregnancy. She felt as though she couldn't breathe until they had proof everything was all right with the baby.

As if sensing her anxiety, or maybe experiencing it too, Lachlan reached for her hand. That simple action of holding her hand in his, feeling the warmth and support in his touch, was enough to help soothe her nerves.

She felt the pressure of the Doppler moving over her belly, searching for signs of life like some sort of rescue mission. Melissa supposed that's what it was in a way, locating her baby's heartbeat to save her life and let her breathe again.

The air was heavy with anticipation, all eyes watching the grainy grey images, ears straining to hear anything which might put their minds at ease.

'There we go.' The sonographer smiled, and suddenly the room echoed with the pulsing sound of their baby's heartbeat.

She squeezed Lachlan's hand. This was real for both of them now. When she glanced up at him, he smiled and dropped a kiss on her head.

'I guess we're really doing this, huh?'

'There's no going back now,' she confirmed, though that niggle at the back of her mind wouldn't let her believe it one hundred percent.

Too many times she'd been let down, left to pick up the pieces from people who'd promised to be with her forever. Lachlan had never made such a big claim, and that's why thinking he would be here for her when it really mattered would be a mistake. For her sake, and the baby's, she had to keep those defences up a little bit longer.

Lachlan's head was completely taken up with babies these days. Talk about baby brain. He'd been so consumed by thoughts of Melissa and impending parenthood that he'd been unable to sleep after a long shift, and had gone food shopping instead. Only to forget to half the stuff he'd gone in for in favour of buying things for Melissa and the baby.

He knew she'd been struggling with heartburn because he checked in with her daily, either by text or with a call. Although he didn't want to be too full-on, he was aware that she didn't have any other support. He'd asked if she was all right with him keeping up with her, and she'd promised him it was fine. Telling him he had as much right to know what was going on with the baby as she did.

There had been a little tension at the scan, probably due to both of them being anxious. He'd also been afraid she didn't really want him there, but he thought seeing their baby on the screen for the first time together had brought them closer. She'd even let him hold her hand whilst they waited to hear the heartbeat. Progress.

When the baby arrived, he and Melissa would be sharing the childcare, juggling it around their shifts. He was determined to be a present father. Nothing was going to be more important than spending time with his child, and he wanted her to get used to having him around.

No, this wasn't where he'd ever expected to be, but he was committed to being a father, and he was sure he'd grow into the role. He was trying his best.

When he'd seen the baby at the scan, he'd felt a flutter of excitement. It was confirmation he was going to be a father. Thinking about what that would entail gave him more reason to get up in the mornings, and he realised he was looking forward to the prospect of having a child.

He could admit to himself now that part of the problem in his relationship with Julieann after his cancer treatment had been his fear that he'd never be able to be a father. Until he'd got sick, he'd always imagined having a family of his own. It hadn't seemed such an unrealistic prospect then.

However, when it became clear that fathering a baby mightn't be as straightforward as he'd always believed, he'd let fear take over, and it had ended his relationship with Julieann. He'd been afraid to fail her, to have to go through the pain and humiliation of not being able to do something as simple as getting her pregnant. And he'd had enough of hospitals and medical intervention to go through it in order to have a child.

With the decision taken out of his hands, he was allowing himself to get excited about the prospect of watching him or her grow up. Although an unexpected development in his life, this baby was going to be wanted and loved.

'Lachlan? What are you doing here?' Melissa opened her front door, pulling her fluffy pink dressing gown tighter around her.

'Sorry for calling late. I didn't wake you, did I?'

She looked tired and washed out without her make-up. Perhaps it was due to the knowledge she was carrying his child, but Lachlan thought she was even more beautiful now than when they'd first met at the festival.

'I wish. This little one is playing havoc with me.' Melissa rubbed her stomach and yawned.

'I know. That's why I picked up a few pieces for you while I was out shopping. Can I come in?' It was presumptuous of him to turn up on her doorstep at this time of night and expect her to welcome him in, but this pregnancy had awakened a need inside him to protect his family. Like it or not, Melissa was his family now.

He knew it couldn't be any more than that, even though they were having a baby. She'd made it clear she was still grieving the fiancé she'd lost, and he'd been the rebound. They'd been tied together because of a mistake and a lack of common sense. All they could do now was make the most of things and raise this baby as best they could.

The only serious relationship he'd been in had ended badly, and he couldn't afford for that to happen with a baby involved. He didn't want to prioritise his libido over his chance to be a father. If he did start something with Melissa and it didn't work out, it could impact his relationship with his child. Perhaps the only one he'd ever have. He didn't want to let down his son or daughter the way his father had done to him. As much as he liked Melissa, his relationship with the baby had to come first.

No one could possibly understand how much the absence of a father figure in his life had affected him. Probably because he'd spent his life protecting other people and hiding his true feelings. That responsibility had been heaped onto his shoulders at an early age because of his father, and was the very reason he couldn't afford to forget that the emotional well-being of his child was more important than his own.

'If you've got chocolate in that bag, you're very welcome.' She nodded towards the shopping bag at his feet and opened the door.

'Of course. I told you, I've got your back.' He grinned and followed Melissa into the house, stopping to collect the other gift he'd propped up against the wall.

'I wish you did. It's already hurting, and I've got six months and a few extra pounds to go yet.' Melissa collapsed onto the sofa, obviously feeling sorry for herself.

'You know if I could swap places with you I would.' He didn't want her to be uncomfortable or in pain, though having witnessed Claire in the latter stages of her pregnancy, it appeared to be part of the process.

'I know.' She gave him a half smile, but they both knew she was on her own when it came to dealing with the physical aspect of the pregnancy. Lachlan's role was to support her and make her as comfortable as he could in the meantime.

'Well, I'm hoping I've found something to help you

over the next few months.' He showed her the main reason he'd come over.

'What's that?'

'It's a V-shaped pillow. Apparently, they're good for helping your heartburn. They elevate you so you're not sleeping flat. I think it'll help your back too.' He eased her forward and positioned the pillow behind her back.

She shuffled in her chair and leaned back with a contented sigh. 'I'm taking this everywhere with me.'

Lachlan's cheesy grin was directly down to the fact that he'd been able to make her happy and comfortable even for a little while. 'I got you the fleece-lined one so it would be more cosy.'

'You didn't have to, but thank you. I appreciate you coming all this way to bring me a pillow so I can try and get some sleep. Can I get you a cup of tea or anything?' She went to get up, but Lachlan put out a hand to stop her.

'Stay there. I'll make us both a hot drink.' He wanted to make himself useful, to do something for her, because she didn't appear to have anyone else looking after her.

Melissa's parents had apparently taken the news well considering the circumstances, but hadn't mentioned coming back to see her. Lachlan's mum had been over the moon to hear there was going to be a new addition, and thrilled that he was going to be a father. Of course, she'd expressed her wish for him and Melissa to get together and live happily ever after. But he'd made it clear that wasn't on the cards. They had to be realistic.

As far as he could tell, relationships didn't last. His father had walked out on his family, Claire's other half had gone AWOL, and Melissa's parents had effectively abandoned her when she was barely an adult. Lachlan's relationship had ended eventually too. Even Melissa's long-term partner had died, robbing her of their lives together. Nothing could come of imagining that he had a future with her other than co-parenting their child, except heartache. Someone was always left behind, and, given his medical history, he was sure he'd be the one exiting the scene early even if it was against his wishes. Until that time came, he'd do whatever he could for his new little family, even if it required keeping something of an emotional distance. It would be best for both of them long-term. He didn't want to put Melissa through the pain of losing someone she loved again.

Lachlan carried his shopping into the kitchen. Melissa already had her eyes closed, though she had her hand on her chest, heartburn still in attendance. He unpacked the bits and pieces he'd bought to stock her fridge and cupboards, then heated up a cup of milk and added a spoonful of honey.

'Try that. It's supposed to help with the heartburn.'

'What is it?' Melissa inspected the cup as though he was attempting to poison her.

'Hot milk with a spoonful of honey.'

She took the cup and inhaled the smell. 'Mmm. It's so comforting. Reminds me of when I was little. Mum used to heat a little milk in the pan for me every night before bedtime to help me sleep.'

Lachlan was glad that not only had he succeeded in cheering her up, but also that she had some happy childhood memories. Sometimes those could get lost under later traumatic ones. That was partly why he'd worried so much about becoming a father himself. Having witnessed the effect of absentee parents, the toll it took on the children left behind, he didn't want to be responsible for inflicting that trauma on anyone else. Of course, circumstances made that more difficult now, but he would be here for his family as long as possible.

'I hope I haven't overstepped, but I've left some salads and things in the fridge. Apparently, it's better for your heartburn to eat little and often instead of big meals. I brought some bananas and almonds too.'

'You have been doing your homework.'

'Sorry. You're the expert. I'm sure you know all this yourself.' It dawned on him too late that Melissa was more than the mother of his unborn child. She was a qualified midwife who dished out advice to ailing pregnant women every day. He'd got carried away with the idea of providing for her, and had forgotten she was perfectly capable of taking care of herself.

'I'm not very good at taking my own advice, or I wouldn't be in this mess in the first place.' She set down her cup and rubbed her hands over her slight belly.

'I just wanted you to know I'm going to be here for

you both.' After the tension at the scan, he didn't want there to be any doubt about his involvement.

'And we appreciate it.'

In that split second, he imagined the sight of her sitting there with the baby in her arms, whilst he cooked dinner. A cosy domestic scene which, if they'd been in a relationship, wouldn't have been out of order. However, they were still virtual strangers, both with too much baggage to ever provide a stable home life for a child together. He needed to get that thought right out of his head. The baby was his, but its mother wasn't.

'If you've finished your drink, I'll take the cup in and give it a rinse.'

'You don't have to—'

'It's not a problem. You put your feet up.' He'd seen a couple of dirty cups and plates in the sink, so he took the cup into the kitchen and washed them all. At least this way he was doing something useful and still managing to keep a little distance.

Once he'd finished drying and putting away the dishes, he went into the living room to say his goodbyes.

'That's the dishes done. I'm going to head home and let you…sleep.'

Melissa was curled up on the sofa, hugging the pillow like a lover, eyes closed, fast asleep. He doubted it was the conventional way to make use of the present he'd brought, but she was asleep, which was all that mattered. They had a long way to go before they met the rascal causing all the trouble, and she was going to need all the rest she could get between now and then.

She looked serene, a soft smile on her lips that caused him to wonder what she was dreaming about that made her so happy. Probably the baby. Hopefully him too.

He was overcome with a swell of emotion, unfiltered because she was asleep and he was able to drop his defences for a moment. There was no doubt she was beautiful, her red hair spread around her shoulders like wildfire. But since meeting her again, Lachlan realised there was so much more to her. She was strong and independent, and he admired how much she'd achieved on her own. Melissa was an amazing woman and coping tremendously in difficult circumstances. There was no doubt she could manage this pregnancy and parenthood without him, and he counted himself lucky she was allowing him to be part of it.

He brushed a wayward strand of hair from her forehead and bent down to drop a kiss where it had lain. Taking the blanket draped along the back of the sofa, he tucked it around her to keep her warm, and crept out of the room, careful not to wake her. Capturing the picture of her sleeping peacefully with one last lingering look.

The hardest part of all of this was going to be stopping himself from falling for her, because he was pretty sure it had happened the first time he'd kissed her.

Melissa waited until she heard the front door shut before she opened her eyes and sucked in a shaky breath. It had taken all her strength not to pull Lachlan down beside her when he'd kissed her on the forehead. He was being so kind and attentive. It wasn't helping to stymie the attraction she still felt towards him. If anything, it was making it worse. Who wouldn't want a man who brought food, did the dishes, and made sure you had a comfortable pillow? He was certainly making her feel as though she and the baby were important to him. It would be a problem if she got used to it.

Lachlan was trying his best to be a father to their baby, but that only made her like him more. It was so long since anyone had thought about her feelings or looked after her, it was easy to get swept away in the romance of it. However, the last man she'd fallen for had been cruelly taken from her, and now she had even more to lose with a baby to consider. It was important to protect herself and the baby from being hurt, and not give in to some daydream that they'd be a happy family. She shouldn't throw caution to the wind again simply because Lachlan was an honourable man who didn't shirk his responsibilities.

That meant not turning into a puddle because he'd felt the need to kiss her. Regardless of whether that was a sign that he cared for her in some fashion and hadn't wanted her to know it.

It didn't matter that perhaps her growing feelings towards Lachlan weren't entirely one-sided. They absolutely couldn't act on the impulse that had upended their lives in the first place.

CHAPTER FIVE

'I KNOW IT'S early days in the pregnancy, but I thought it might be nice to get a few ideas for the nursery.' Lachlan opened the door into the store, a world of baby and maternity essentials that Melissa hadn't yet ventured into.

'I am superstitious, so I don't want to buy anything for the baby until closer to my due date, but we can window-shop. I'll probably need to get some maternity clothes anyway. It won't be long until I'm bursting out of everything.' In a short matter of time, her slightly rounded stomach would become the same boulder belly a lot of her patients were carrying, and she'd be needing to pee every few minutes too.

They all displayed similar symptoms around the time of the third trimester. At that 'fed up' stage of pregnancy when everything ached, and any movement was exhausting. When giving birth became just as much about having control of one's body again as meeting the baby. In the end, though, they were all happy simply to have a healthy baby.

'I'm sure you'll still be beautiful.'

Melissa knew he was just pacifying the mother of his

unborn child, but a simple compliment from Lachlan still had the ability to make her heart flutter. That was why she'd had to think twice about agreeing to come here with him today. In the end, she'd been forced to face the fact that she would have to make some concessions when he'd been so supportive at the scan. She didn't want to sabotage his relationship with the baby because she was afraid of getting too close to him. If she drove him away permanently, she would be setting her child off in life with the same sense of abandonment and rejection she'd been dealing with. Going on a shopping trip seemed a small price to pay to keep Lachlan happy in the scheme of things.

'Not as beautiful as I know this little one is going to be.' She rested her hands on her belly and put the focus back where it needed to be. On the baby, not her. It was safer that way.

'Well, it's blessed with a double helping of good looks and brains with us as parents. Though I'm not much for interior design, so I'll leave that up to you. I'll deal with the more practical side of things, like building the cot and painting the walls.'

'Suits me. I'll just supervise from an armchair with a cup of tea in my hand.' They were just joking around, but there was a part of her that was both excited by the prospect of them getting a nursery ready, and terrified that he would be so embedded in her life by that time. It suggested a level of intimacy along with the shared responsibility of parenthood. Everything that she was afraid of.

'As you should. Now, rainbows and unicorns, or trains and cars?' Lachlan held up a pink blanket along with a blue one.

'How about something more neutral?' Melissa countered with lemon teddies.

'Don't you want to know the sex? It would make things so much easier for this kind of thing.'

'I want it to be a surprise. Besides, I don't go in for gender stereotypes.' Melissa sniffed.

'Neither do I as a rule, but I'm desperate to know if I'm going to have a little boy or a girl.' Lachlan's enthusiasm was admirable, but it also set off alarm bells for Melissa.

'Wait, you want to know the sex of our baby?'

'Well, yes.'

'I don't want to plan out a name and a life for my baby before I've even had the chance to meet him or her.'

'Okay. It's not something we have to worry about now. We can discuss it later.' Lachlan dropped the subject and moved on to look at the pushchairs, but the conversation had unnerved Melissa.

They both clearly had different ideas, and though this wasn't a particularly big deal, she was sure they were going to disagree over a lot of decisions. They were sharing the parenting, and that entailed making those big choices together too. Not only now during pregnancy, but those affecting their child its whole life. She was beginning to realise the far-reaching implications of her actions three months ago, but it was too late now. The only way to survive this was to treat it as some sort of business deal, taking out any emotional attachment to Lachlan to safeguard herself and the baby. Not letting herself get too close to him because, like everyone else in her life, the day would come when he would leave her and she'd end up on her own. Dealing with the consequences of letting him get involved in the first place.

'I think I'll go up onto the next floor and try to find a pair of trousers with an elasticated waistband for my ever-expanding stomach.' Melissa excused herself to take the escalator and get a little space.

She'd accepted the invitation to go shopping as a chance to bond as parents over their imminent arrival, but now she was beginning to believe it was a mistake. Lachlan's enthusiasm to be involved was admirable, and would be celebrated if they were any other couple expecting a baby. But it only made her worry more. She didn't want to get drawn into his excitement and forget that they weren't actually together. Once she did that, she could kiss goodbye to what was left of her broken heart. First and foremost, this baby was hers. She'd be the primary carer, and Lachlan had simply been the sperm donor. He might want a relationship with the child, but that's where it had to end. For the sake of her own sanity.

A woman ahead of her was struggling to wrangle the baby on her hip and the youngster holding her hand. The little boy was trying to shake his mother off, and when he succeeded, he charged off up to the top of the escalator.

'Henry! Wait right there!' The harassed mother took off after him, but Little Henry was clearly keen to explore his surroundings, fascinated by the moving walkway. He'd made it to the top of the down escalator, letting his hand drift onto the handrail.

'Henry, that's dangerous. Please stay back.' The mother's tone was getting desperate as she rushed to try and grab him.

Unfortunately, the thrill-seeking Henry had decided to throw his whole body onto the handrail, apparently thinking it was some kind of ride. Melissa tried to make a grab for him as his mother screamed, but he was just out of her reach. She could only watch in horror as the child fell off, hitting the mechanical steps on his way down. He was lying lifeless on the ground floor as his mother's screams echoed around the store.

'Lachlan!' Melissa yelled to draw his attention to the situation. He was a paramedic, able to provide some first aid to the child until they could get him to hospital.

Once Lachlan understood what the commotion was about, he was immediately on his knees beside the boy, trying to rouse him.

'Phone an ambulance,' Melissa directed one of the young cashiers who'd come to see what had happened.

She took the mother's hand and guided her back down the escalator. 'Lachlan's a paramedic. He'll look after Henry.'

Someone brought a chair and a glass of water for the

shocked mother, and a first aid kit appeared at Lachlan's request. Melissa went to assist him.

'Is there anything I can do?'

'Unzip his coat for me. He's unresponsive but breathing. There's a head injury and significant bleeding.' Lachlan opened the first aid box while Melissa unzipped the child's jacket and loosened the top buttons of his plaid shirt to try and help him breathe a little better.

'Is Henry going to be okay?' The mother was understandably upset, but the store staff were keeping her at a safe distance from seeing her son and becoming more distressed.

'He's breathing. Hopefully it's nothing serious, but we'll know better when he gets to the hospital. Has someone called an ambulance?' Lachlan was very much in charge of the situation now. Although Melissa had medical know-how, he was the paramedic, used to dealing with such accidents.

'The staff phoned for one. Hopefully it won't take much longer.' Melissa checked Henry's pulse, relieved to find that it was steady.

Such a serious fall could cause all sorts of problems, from broken bones to spinal cord injuries or brain damage. The best they could hope for was that this was a simple concussion, leaving no lasting damage. Until they got him assessed at the hospital, however, they had to take precautions not to aggravate any injuries.

'I don't think there are any broken bones,' Lachlan said.

That was something, at least, but without X-rays,

there was no way of telling if there were any internal injuries.

'Pulse is steady, but there's swelling and bruising around his eye and cheek bone. Can someone get me an ice pack?' Melissa wasn't used to dealing with this kind of medical emergency. Usually there was a baby involved, and she had her bag of medical supplies with her. The one bonus was that she had Lachlan here with her. She was used to working on her own out in the community with the responsibility for the patient entirely on her shoulders. At times like this, she was reminded she didn't have to do everything on her own.

Something she could carry over into her personal life every now and then too. Goodness knew she was going to need the extra support when the baby arrived, and Lachlan would be more than capable of changing a few nappies, or giving a few bottles, if he could single-handedly deal with a medical emergency like this.

Someone handed her a medical ice pack from the first aid kit, and she broke the tube inside to activate it. Holding it against the child's face to try and reduce the swelling, she was struck by how much he looked like his mother. Melissa couldn't help but wonder if their baby would favour her or its father. She was surprised to find she was hoping for a mini-Lachlan. Even though that would mean a constant reminder that she'd gone on to have a family with someone other than Chris, it would be a reminder of Lachlan too.

For some reason, having a part of him in her life was

becoming more important than mourning a relationship that, if she was honest, wasn't as wonderful as she liked to remember. Yes, Chris had been her first real love, and she'd thought she'd spend the rest of her life with him, raising their family. But he'd also been a man who hadn't been great at expressing his emotions. Certainly, he'd never shown great enthusiasm when she'd mentioned having children. Lachlan, on the other hand, was here, involved, and ready to be a father.

'You okay, Melissa?' Lachlan was looking at her with concern for her welfare, even during this unforeseen medical drama.

'Yes. Just hoping the ambulance gets here soon.' She offered him a smile to reassure him that she was okay. This wasn't about her, though it was nice to know he was thinking about her, and how treating this small child might be affecting her.

It was difficult enough for all who'd witnessed the accident, including his mother. Though the boy would likely recover, she was sure the majority of those present would never get over the sight of the injury happening. She knew she wouldn't. Her heart was breaking for the mother sobbing nearby. Melissa already felt protective of her growing offspring and knew she'd be devastated if anything happened. Henry was so small and helpless lying here, it was impossible not to be moved.

'Henry? Can you hear me? Can you open your eyes for me?' Lachlan tried repeatedly to get a response to no avail. He cleaned away the blood at the boy's temple until he found the wound causing the problem, and covered it with a sterile dressing.

'He's probably going to need a few stitches, and the hospital will need to do some X-rays to make sure there's no fracture.' He kept the mother informed as he stroked the boy's cheek, trying to rouse him. Showing a sensitivity as well as his professional manner in his actions.

Melissa knew he was going to be a great father.

'Henry? Open your eyes so your mum knows you're okay.'

This time, as Lachlan spoke, the child's eyes began to flutter open.

'Mummy?' he croaked, drawing a sob of relief from his mother.

She dropped to her knees beside her son. 'I'm here, sweetheart. You've had a fall, but you're going to be all right.'

The woman stroked his forehead, ignoring the blood drying in his hair, her love there in every word and gesture.

It proved yet again what a huge undertaking parenting was, being responsible for a young life, emotions tied to the well-being of that tiny human.

Then Melissa thought about Lachlan, how good he was in a crisis, caring and competent. The kind of person she wanted with her to share the responsibility of parenting. Which was just as well when they were inextricably linked for the foreseeable future.

* * *

'That was full-on,' Lachlan remarked after Henry, his mother and younger sibling were driven away in the ambulance.

'Yeah. I think seeing a child in danger like that hits harder these days.' Melissa hugged her belly as they made their way back to Lachlan's car.

It was going to make her job even more poignant, bringing lives into the world, once she did it herself. On those rare occasions when a child didn't survive long-term, it was also going to be tougher than ever to deal with. These tiny beings were precious and, though she cherished every one, her own baby was going to be the most important thing in her life.

'I have to admit my heart was in my throat treating him.' Lachlan showed an uncharacteristic display of self-doubt. It hadn't occurred to Melissa that he would feel the same way. He wasn't carrying their baby, but clearly that paternal instinct was kicking in already. This baby was going to change everything for them.

'We've both had a shock.'

'We could probably do with some time to decompress after that. It wasn't the fun shopping experience I imagined when I suggested this outing.' Lachlan got in beside her, buckled his seat belt, and started the short drive home.

'Oh? What were you expecting? A line of shop girls catering to your every whim? Champagne and canapés while you waited?' Melissa couldn't help but tease when deep down she'd known the trip was going to end in disaster. Obviously, she could never have imagined the horrible accident which took place, but nursery shopping with Lachlan would never have been relaxing. Not when she was so torn between wanting him to be an involved father, and worried about getting too emotionally attached to him.

Lachlan glared at her out of the corner of his eye. 'No. I just wanted to spend some time together, making plans for our new arrival.'

His heartfelt reasons for today quietened Melissa's need to tease. She couldn't have asked for a more involved father for her baby, she supposed. It was difficult to work out whether that was a blessing or a curse in the circumstances. The complication was that the more she got to know him, the more she liked him. She was in limbo, with no clear idea of where she was going or what lay ahead. A perpetual state of confusion.

They spent the rest of the short journey in silence, but when they arrived at her house, it didn't seem right to simply send him on his way again.

'Why don't you come in for a cuppa?'

'Are you sure?'

'Yes. It's been a rough morning. Come in.' She got out and closed the car door, not giving him an opportunity to decline. In her experience, it wasn't easy to switch off after a fraught medical event. It seemed pointless for them to be sitting in separate houses, going over every second of what had happened and wondering if they could have done anything differently.

'My turn to make it today. Take a seat,' she called

over her shoulder, leaving him to make himself at home. She was glad she'd summoned enough strength to tidy up before she'd left that morning. Thankfully the morning sickness was beginning to ease off, so she was able to function a bit better these days.

When she walked back into the living room, Lachlan was looking at the framed photographs in her bookcase.

'Is this Chris?' he asked, holding up the picture from their engagement. It had become such a part of the furniture, she'd forgotten it was there. Even though Chris had been such a huge part of her life, she wished she had thought to put it out of sight. For both of their sakes—hers and Lachlan's.

Although they weren't together, she didn't want Lachlan to feel uncomfortable being reminded that he wasn't the one she'd wanted a family with. It was also jarring for her to see Chris staring back at her when he hadn't been at the forefront of her mind for some time. She'd been so focused on the baby, and batting away any feelings Lachlan was awakening in her, that she'd forgotten to miss him.

When she'd told her parents that Chris had died, their idea of consoling her had been to say she'd learn to live with her grief. At the time, she'd thought it insensitive to suggest she'd ever get over the loss. She'd even asked them not to come to the funeral. She'd been upset that they thought it would be so easy for her to forget a loved one, the way they seemed to have done when they moved away without her.

Now, however, she could see they'd been right. Life

had moved on, and whilst she'd never forget Chris, Lachlan and the baby were actively part of her life. Nothing was going to bring Chris back, and with a child on the way, she couldn't keep living in the past. Everything now was about the future, and unfortunately Chris was no longer a part of that.

'That was taken on our engagement day. We had a five-year plan of what we wanted to accomplish before we got married. As it turned out, we waited too long.' Whilst she would probably never get over losing him, or the unfairness of being denied their life together, Lachlan had helped her move into a new chapter of her life. Albeit unwittingly.

The pregnancy had been an accident, but ultimately she thought it was the best thing to happen to her. It had given her someone else to love, a future she hadn't wanted to look forward to until now. This baby had given her life meaning again.

'I'm sorry. And that was your last relationship before we...you know.' Lachlan turned a very becoming shade of red as he referenced their liaison at the festival. It was kind of cute that he was so coy about it. He certainly hadn't been shy at the time.

Melissa nodded. 'And you?'

Lachlan nodded too, the redness glowing brighter. He set the photo back and took the cup of tea offered before coming to sit on the sofa. 'I'd split with my ex about six months before that.'

'I'm sorry.' That would explain why he hadn't wanted to get into anything serious.

'Melissa, there's something I haven't told you…'

Although she had no way of knowing what was coming next, all the blood from Melissa's head seemed to drain down into her toes, leaving her light-headed. Whatever it was, it wasn't good. Despite all of the preventative measures she'd tried to take, if he told her now that he was backing off, she knew she'd be devastated. She'd got used to having him around, even if her growing feelings for him had made her uncomfortable at times.

'What is it?' She swallowed hard, bracing herself for what he had to say.

'Before we met… I underwent treatment for testicular cancer.'

'Oh.' It was a bigger shock to her system than the news she'd been expecting, and no less concerning. Not only for Lachlan, but because of what it meant for her and the baby too.

Although it seemed selfish to concern herself with thoughts of what would happen to them if they lost him now that she'd let him be part of their lives, she had more reason than ever to be afraid of the consequences. What if the same thing happened to him that had happened to Chris?

'I had a testicle removed. Went through chemotherapy and a surgical reconstruction. I know I should have told you sooner, but it's not something I casually drop into conversation. It was a difficult time, and when we met at the festival, I was celebrating the end of my treatment. I hadn't expected that we'd see each other again, and it didn't seem like something you needed to worry about. But since you've been honest with me…'

'I appreciate you telling me.' There was no logical reason for her to feel angry that he'd kept this information from her until now, but she couldn't help it. Whilst she was glad he'd come through it, and sorry that he'd had to deal with such a serious medical issue, she wished he'd told her sooner.

If she'd known he had serious medical issues, she would have been even more careful about getting too close. Melissa had every sympathy for Lachlan, but she'd already been through too much to face the potential of another loss in her life.

'I don't want any secrets. I know we're not a couple, but we are going to be in each other's lives for a long time. I hope.' Lachlan smiled, but his dark humour only served to make Melissa more concerned about what the future held.

It was a stark reminder that nothing was guaranteed, and she suddenly realised she didn't want to think of a life without him in it.

She could understand now what had drawn them together at the music festival, both having gone through a difficult time and looking for a new start. He was likely to have been carrying serious emotional wounds, especially if his partner had dumped him for something beyond his control. It seemed callous in the circumstances. Even if Melissa had known about Chris's illness, she would've wanted to spend every second possible with him. She wouldn't have abandoned him when he needed her most. Too bad she hadn't been given the chance to prove that.

Lachlan made a face. 'In a way…facing my own mortality like that made me think about what I really wanted in life. She was keen to start a family, and I decided I wasn't.'

The words were like a punch to Melissa's gut. As she had worried all along, Lachlan never wanted any of this. He was only here out of a sense of duty, and that did not seem the basis of a long-term relationship with his child. If his intention had been to remain foot-loose and fancy-free, he'd probably planned to travel and have fun. Now he was tied down to a baby. What if someone, or something, more exciting came along that he felt he couldn't resist? Or, worst-case scenario, he got sick again? Either way, there was no guaran-tee Lachlan would be here for the long haul. Another reason not to get used to having him around, saving the day.

'It's ironic, I know, given the circumstances. But what's done is done. We have to make the most of the situation now.' Definitely not the words of a man who seemed as ecstatic about the prospect of becoming a father as she'd thought. Melissa wondered if his ap-parent interest so far had been for her benefit. An at-tempt to make her think this was what he wanted so she didn't feel bad. He was a people-pleaser, but she wanted someone who would be honest with her about his feel-ings so there would be no unpleasant surprises down the line. She didn't think she could take any more.

'If your heart isn't in this, Lachlan, now's the time to back out. I don't want you disappearing when this baby is old enough to understand rejection. I can manage on my own.' She set down her tea, prepared to go into battle until she got to the truth. It was better to bring things to a head now, before the baby was born, so they all knew where they stood.

It felt as though he had as little interest in a family as Chris. Except they'd been left no choice in the matter. Lachlan hadn't been given the space to put off parenthood until he thought he was ready. He was going to be a father, and now she was more worried than ever that Lachlan would have second thoughts at some point between now and the baby's arrival.

He was frowning at her. She much preferred him smiling, but this needed to be said. There was no point in pretending he was on board if he was going to bail out when reality hit home.

'I thought we'd been through this, Melissa? I went to the scan, took you shopping today, because I'm a part of this. No, it wasn't where I thought life was going to take me, but I am one hundred percent committed.'

'You were so against starting a family that you ended your relationship. How can you change your mind over something so life-altering for a woman you barely know?'

He set his tea down on the coffee table and sank back into the chair, taking his time with how he answered. Melissa didn't know whether she should be pleased he was considering his reply so deeply, or worried he was about to let her down and thinking of a way to do it gently.

'I grew up without a father. My mum worked day and night to pay the bills, and as the eldest child, I had to step up. I took on responsibility for my brother and sister when I was little more than a child myself. I didn't want to carry on that legacy into another family.'

Melissa could understand that way of thinking. It would have been easy for her to do the same, forgo a family of her own so she didn't end up disappointing them the way her parents had. They simply chose different ways of dealing with their pasts and protecting their hearts. Now their mistake had disrupted all of their carefully laid plans.

'I was the opposite. When Mum and Dad moved abroad and left me behind, I was desperate to fill that void. I couldn't wait to have a family, but Chris wanted to hold off until we had our careers set and money in the bank.' Thinking about it now, he hadn't been as keen about starting a family, always finding excuses— they didn't have enough in savings, he wanted that promotion first, it was best to wait until after they got married so they wouldn't upset anyone. In the end, they'd agreed on their five-year plan, but she suspected that was only to stop her going on about it in the meantime.

Perhaps she had been trying to overcompensate for the void her parents had left in her life, but she'd thought Chris had wanted the same things she did. That could be why she kept doubting Lachlan's words, worried he was only saying things to keep her happy and didn't actually mean any of them.

'It wasn't a bad plan. Neither of you knew what was coming.'

'Hmm. I think he was just trying to put it off. In hindsight, I was the only one talking about a family in our future. I think I was projecting my issues onto our relationship.'

'I think we're all guilty of that. I let my feelings for my father destroy what I had with my ex.'

'Why were you so convinced you were going to stuff things up too? That you weren't going to be around?' Melissa wanted to know why he was so afraid of being a father himself, in case it came back to haunt both of them in the future.

Lachlan cleared his throat. 'The cancer. There's always a chance it will come back. I didn't want to have the thought hanging over my family that someday I wasn't going to be there. That I would be responsible for another child growing up without a father.'

Melissa swallowed down the sudden surge of bile rising inside her. Circumstances hadn't allowed them to factor that into any decision to start a family. She was just getting used to his support, and now he was reminding her that he might not be around forever. Everything she'd been afraid of from the moment she'd told him he was the father. It might have seemed selfish when Lachlan was the one who was dealing with health problems, but she'd already lost Chris, and she couldn't imagine going through it again. Didn't want to.

'But you're okay now? You got the all-clear?' Melissa tried to keep the rising hysteria from her voice, worried there was something wrong that he hadn't told her about.

'Yes. I suppose I'm just being paranoid.' His smile went some way to reassure her, but her stomach was still twisted into knots.

'It's understandable, but how does it make you feel knowing you *are* going to be a father now? That the decision has been taken out of your hands?' Melissa understood he had good reason to be wary of getting involved, given his own personal history, and not knowing what the future held for him. However, she didn't want him to end up resenting her or the baby, blaming them for trapping him in a situation he never wanted.

'Perhaps it's for the best things worked out this way. It's forced me to realise not everything is in my control. The truth is, I had wanted a family once. Before the cancer. But afterwards, I wasn't sure I could even have children. I told myself I didn't want a family, but I think I'd convinced myself of that because I couldn't spend the rest of my life trying and being left disappointed. Or worse, what if I did have children and ended up leaving them the way my father left us? It's my fault the relationship ended, because I was afraid. I might have beaten the cancer once, but that doesn't mean it won't get me in the end.' His wobbly smile was heartbreaking. Lachlan had been so strong for Melissa and the baby, and the whole time he'd clearly been worrying that the cancer would return. He'd been under tremendous strain, yet supporting them both when they'd needed it. Who'd been there for him?

'It doesn't mean it will either. I imagine we're both terrified about what's going to happen, but as long as we know we're in it together, I think we'll be okay.' She told herself his fear was not her reality. Mainly because it was her fear, too, that he'd be taken away, leaving her on her own with the baby.

'I'm here for as long as I have breath in my body. You both mean too much for me to go anywhere.' Lachlan leaned forward as he spoke, gazing so intensely at her, Melissa couldn't breathe.

She wanted to believe everything he said. Not only that he didn't intend on going anywhere anytime soon, but that she meant more to him than someone he was simply stuck with. Because, despite all the reasons she shouldn't, Melissa knew she was falling deeper for him every day. The way he was looking at her now made her think that everything was going to work out, and she might even get that happy family she'd always wanted. It was heady, and, when he leaned in closer, his eyes trained on her mouth, irresistible.

Lachlan knew he shouldn't, hadn't realised he was going to, but he was definitely about to kiss Melissa. He'd been wanting to from the second he'd laid eyes on her again, their time at the festival burned in his memory, and on every part of his body. As her eyes fluttered shut and she tilted her face up to meet him, he realised she wanted this too. That's when the last thread of his common sense snapped.

He sought her lips with his, the soft sweetness he knew he'd find there, and it was everything he remembered. Melissa relaxed into the kiss, and it only made him crave more. He cupped her face in his hands and deepened the kiss, gently coaxing her tongue with his. When his lips were meshed with hers, his mind full of thoughts of how she was making him feel, everything else melted away.

He wasn't thinking about the accident at the store, or his uncertain future. Not even worrying about what kind of father he was going to be. All he could think about was Melissa and how much he wanted to be with her.

Learning more about her background, how she'd lost her fiancé, only made him admire her more. Her strength and resilience were immeasurable, but he didn't want to let her down. Along with his sister, she was one of the most important things in his life right now.

When he'd moved to the city, he'd been prepared to face new challenges. Though he thought he would be living a life free from responsibilities. He never expected he'd have to step in to support his sister, or that he'd have to get used to the idea of becoming a father himself. The good part of all of this was that he'd got to see Melissa again. She was going to be a permanent fixture in his life from now on, and he didn't want to do anything to ruin that.

Kissing her when she was clearly still grieving for her fiancé probably wasn't the best way to keep her on side. She was vulnerable, especially after what they'd witnessed today. He'd be the worst kind of person to take advantage of her now.

Lachlan reluctantly pulled away, her dazed expression and kiss-swollen lips making him regret his decision already.

'Lachlan?' She blinked at him with big bush-baby eyes, which only served to make her look more vulnerable.

'Sorry. I shouldn't have done that. It's been a difficult day for both of us.' He scrabbled back in his seat, desperate to put some distance between them.

'It's not the first time we've kissed, Lachlan.' Melissa's hands went to her belly, reminding him they'd done a lot more than that in the past. But there was more to lose now.

He got to his feet. 'I know, but I think we should just put this behind us, like the festival, and carry on as we were. Focus on being good parents for the baby.'

Melissa nodded soundlessly, leaving him to ramble to cover the silence. She regretted having given in to temptation. 'If you need anything, just give me a ring, and let me know when your next appointment is so I can support you. Don't get up. I'll let myself out.'

Lachlan practically stumbled out the door in his desperation to get away from his latest faux pas. If he didn't reel in his attraction to Melissa, he was going to ruin everything. All being well, there were six months of this pregnancy left, and he needed to back off from any romantic notions he might have towards her. He'd lied when he referred to the festival, pretending that he'd ever been able to put that behind him. That was the very reason he couldn't keep on kissing her and saying it didn't mean anything. It would end in heartbreak somewhere down the line.

From now on, he'd have to try and limit his interactions with Melissa to public places, and preferably only regarding the baby. It was the only way to protect himself and ensure this baby had two parents present when he or she arrived. He didn't want to give Melissa any reason to give him the heave ho. If he hadn't done so already…

This wasn't a casual relationship between two strangers that could be set aside so they could go on with normal life. They were physically and emotionally tied to one another through the baby they'd conceived. A kiss was much more than a kiss now, and a failed romance could push him out of his child's life before it was even born. There was too much at stake to risk it on an attraction he couldn't be sure would last. He wasn't going to be another absentee father.

CHAPTER SIX

'I CAN'T BELIEVE you're back with your baby daddy and you didn't tell me until now.' Lydia had reacted just the way Melissa knew she would. Loudly. That's why she'd waited until they were outside of the workplace to tell her that Lachlan was back on the scene.

In hindsight, the end of a busy shift hadn't been the ideal time, when she was too tired to deal with her friend's resulting histrionics. Also, Lydia was driving home, her phone apparently on speaker, and Melissa didn't want her to crash the car in the process. However, given that Lachlan seemed a little more distant since that kiss, she thought she could do with the extra support.

He was still showing up for her when needed, but there was something missing between them. As though he was deliberately keeping her at arm's length. She was worried that he was gearing up to walk away, the kiss crossing a line he didn't think they could ever recover from. He was equally to blame for letting it happen, and she didn't see why she should be punished for it. Her hormones were all over the place as it was without him kissing her whenever the mood took him, and walking away when it didn't.

Melissa was aware the day in the store had been challenging, and, when they'd opened up to one another about their pasts, emotional. She didn't know if that was why he'd kissed her, because they'd shared deeply personal information. Neither did she know what had sent him scurrying from the house like a scalded cat other than regret, but she wasn't going to chase him. She'd told him from the start it was his decision whether or not to be in their child's life, and she wasn't going to force him to be in hers either. Not least because she didn't want him to think she was desperate for something more in their relationship. Regardless of how much she was missing the connection she'd had with him. These days he felt more like a stranger than ever. It was telling that she was already roping Lydia in as a replacement for the void he'd left in her life after such a short time.

'I wish you wouldn't call him that. His name's Lachlan.' It wasn't as though she'd had a string of lovers and narrowed it down to the one who'd actually fathered her baby. She knew exactly who she'd gone to bed with and when the baby had been conceived.

'So, where is he? When do I get to meet him?'

'One step at a time. I don't want to scare him off. We're still getting used to the idea of parenting together, and if things don't work out, I want to know that you'll be there if I need you.' She didn't want to use her friend, but having Lachlan in her life had made her realise she didn't have to do everything on her own. Lydia had offered her support, and Melissa had to get used to accepting help. When the baby came, she might need it.

'Of course. Auntie Lyds is on standby. I do hope things work out for you two though. You deserve some happiness.'

'I don't think it's on the cards for us, but as long as he's a good dad to the baby, I'll be happy.'

Lachlan had told her time and time again he would be here for her and the baby as long as he had breath in his body. It seemed selfish, and unrealistic, for her to want more now.

Melissa hung up and decided to take her weary body to bed. She'd just reached the top of the stairs when she realised she'd left her phone in the living room. The thought crossed her mind to leave it there, but she needed her alarm to get up for work in the morning. With a resigned groan, she turned around and began to make the descent. Unfortunately, she somehow missed the next step, her foot slipping off the edge and causing her to lose her balance. Before she knew it, she was mid-air, falling down the rest of the stairs, her head and back bumping hard against the steps until she lay in a heap on the ground.

It took her a moment to gather her thoughts, to process what had happened. Then her hands went instinctively towards her bump. She'd had a very hard fall, and though it was still early days in the pregnancy, it was possible that the baby had been hurt. Before she started to panic, she told herself her body was designed to protect the baby, as was the amniotic sac, but then her mind started to race. A placental abruption could occur in the event of a blunt trauma and restrict the baby's oxygen supply, or cause internal bleeding for the mother. Although she didn't think she'd hit her abdomen directly, she didn't want to take any chances. She'd never forgive herself if she didn't get checked out and something happened to the baby.

Unfortunately, she didn't have her phone at hand to contact anyone. Though she was afraid to move, she knew she had to. Melissa slowly got to her feet, bracing a hand against the wall, only for an excruciating pain to shoot up through her leg and collapse her again. She'd obviously injured her ankle if she wasn't able to put any weight on it without it giving way beneath her.

After a few more attempts to stand, and some swearing, she managed to drag herself into the living room. As she crumpled into an armchair, she was sobbing, both from the pain and fear. She grabbed her phone to call Lachlan, the only person she wanted here with her. He would hold her hand, talk to her in that soothing way he spoke to patients, and generally reassure her that everything was going to be okay.

She brought up her contact list, desperate to reach out to him, knowing he'd be at her door in minutes if he thought something was wrong. But she knew he'd only come because he felt a responsibility towards her, and that wasn't why she wanted him to be with her. She needed more than he was apparently willing to give.

Reluctantly, and with fear threatening to block her airways, she dialled 999.

'Hello. I need an ambulance please,' she said when prompted, holding her belly with one hand and praying her baby would make it.

Despite starting this pregnancy journey with a great deal of trepidation, her baby was the only good thing in her life right now. The only family she had here, and the only one she had a future with. To have it all taken away from her now would be devastating. This baby meant everything to her, and she was so looking forward to meeting him or her.

'Hang in there, jelly bean,' she whispered, hoping for once in her life, if she loved someone enough, they would stay with her.

'Pregnant woman has taken a tumble down the stairs. We should go and check her over.' Scot, the ambulance driver, relayed the basics of the call to Lachlan.

'Put your foot down, mate. I don't want to hang about on this one.' It hit hard, as everything mother- and baby-related did these days. Melissa was constantly on his mind. He wondered if she was okay and marvelled at how he'd managed to cock things up so badly by kissing her.

Perhaps he'd got so wrapped up in the idea of having Melissa and the baby permanently in his life that he'd forgotten all the reasons why he shouldn't give in to that attraction. His focus had to be on his relationship with his baby, not its mother. By kissing her, trying to take their involvement beyond simply being parents, he ran the risk of losing both of them. The last thing he wanted when everything he did was to try and be a present father to their baby.

To right his mistake in crossing that line, he'd had to back off, and make do with the odd text to see how she was. The next few months attending prenatal appointments and not being physically near her would be difficult, but a sacrifice he'd have to make to be the best father he could be.

Scot typed the address into the satnav, and Lachlan's insides seemed to plummet into his shoes.

'What was the name?'

'Moran. Melissa Moran.'

'I don't care how you do it, but get us there at warp speed.'

'You know her?'

'She's the mother of my unborn child, Scot.' Lachlan knew it was news to his colleague that he'd even been seeing anyone, never mind that they were expecting a baby, but nothing was more important than Melissa and the baby. If he'd thought he wasn't up to fatherhood, the panic, the complete fear that his child was in danger gripping his heart, was proof that he was a parent already.

Suddenly, it seemed as though the lights, sirens, and Scot's expert driving couldn't get them to Melissa's place fast enough.

'Sorry, mate. I didn't know. I'm sure they'll both be okay.' Scot did his best to reassure him, but Melissa was only just in her second trimester, and wasn't completely out of danger of miscarrying. Besides, they didn't know how serious the fall had been. Though she would've been concerned about the baby, he was sure she would've downplayed her own injuries. He couldn't bear to see either of them hurt.

'Let's hope so.' Lachlan grabbed his kit and jumped out of the ambulance the second they pulled up outside the house.

'She keeps a spare key under the flower pot.' He'd rolled his eyes when he'd heard that one. It wasn't exactly security-conscious, but she thought he should know in case of emergencies. Just like this one. Now he was grateful for her presence of mind.

'Melissa? It's Lachlan. You called for an ambulance?' he yelled into the house as soon as he unlocked the door. A desperate need to know for himself that she and the baby were all right spurred him on.

'Lachlan? I'm in here.'

He hated the sound of her sobbing and how small her voice seemed from the living room. It told of her fragility, of how frightened she'd been here all on her own, when he should've been with her. He'd been so caught up in his own fears and doing the right thing by the baby that he'd neglected to think of her and how she might need him.

Lachlan rushed in to find her curled up in a chair, her arms wrapped protectively around her bump. His throat was suddenly clogged with a lump of emotion at the sight of her so vulnerable and afraid. Despite everything he'd been trying to avoid recently, he had to reach out and hug her tight. She looked as though she really needed it.

'It's going to be okay.'

He felt her nod against his chest, heard her soft sob as her tears soaked through his clothes. Although he'd been fighting it for so long, there was no more denying he cared deeply for this woman. He would've done anything to make things okay for her. He held her like that for a moment, as much for his sake as hers, then let go to check her over.

Thankfully all of Melissa's vital signs were normal. Her heart rate was a little elevated, but that was to be expected in the circumstances.

'I checked the baby's heartbeat with my own Doppler,' she offered.

'Of course you did,' Lachlan said with a smile. Her first thought would always be for the baby, and he was relieved that both of them appeared relatively uninjured by the fall. Though he would still worry until they'd had the official all-clear at the hospital.

'We'll take you in anyway, and maybe get an ultrasound to put both of our minds at rest.'

Melissa nodded, offering no resistance as he helped her out of the chair, though he did notice her wince as she got to her feet. 'I think I hurt my ankle on the way down.'

'Why didn't you say? Scot, can you get the wheelchair, please?' He made her sit down again to rest up until it was in situ, wishing she'd stop being so damned independent.

Yes, he'd been guilty of holding back, of bottling up his feelings. But the thought of losing her had made him see just how damned important she was to him. He wanted to take care of her.

If they were to get back to the sort of camaraderie they'd had before he'd kissed her and complicated things all over again, they'd have to forget it had ever happened. The only important thing was that she and the baby were all right.

He and Melissa had a lot to sort out before their baby made an appearance. Important things like childcare and what financial contribution he'd be making. Hopefully he'd get over this crush at some stage so he could function as a present father, instead of a mooning teenage boy who couldn't keep his feelings in check.

Lachlan was as relieved as Melissa to see their baby on the screen, apparently unharmed by her tumble down the stairs. In fact, he got such a thrill out of watching the little heartbeat that he'd be permanently tuned in to that channel given half a chance. It was a constant reminder that his body hadn't failed him after all. That he was going to be a dad.

Only once Melissa was sure the baby was okay did she consent to getting checked over herself. She'd insisted on going to X-ray on her own, and he'd had to resist trailing after her.

When he finally saw her bustling through the corridor, he felt as though he could breathe again. She had that effect on him. Whenever she was around, his life just seemed so much better. That's why these past days had been so hard, not being around her.

'As suspected, just a sprain.' She showed off the bandage wrapped around her ankle.

'Don't scare me like that again.' Lachlan stood up from his chair and hugged her, wanting to cling onto her, and have that tangible reassurance that she was okay. He was forced to let go so she could sit down, before things got weird.

The thought of what could have happened was too devastating to imagine.

This woman carrying his baby was the most important person in the world to him. And he'd been doing his best to keep her at arm's length. Suddenly his logic seemed skewed. Instead of worrying about a cancer that might not return, or being as unreliable as his father, he should have been concentrating on the present. On the good things he did have in his life.

Melissa rubbed his back in that comforting way that reminded him he wasn't alone. Her touch was the contact he'd been longing for, not just tonight, but from the second he'd left her house the night they'd kissed.

'I'm sorry I haven't been around.'

'It doesn't matter.' The smile she gave him was too bright to be believable. He had hurt her by disappearing.

'I should have been there for you tonight.'

'It's all right. It would've been a little weird if you'd

been standing at the bottom of my stairs all night, waiting for me to fall. No harm done.'

Despite her reassurance, Lachlan wanted to make it up to her in some way, and to keep an eye on her. 'Have you had anything to eat tonight?'

'I was too tired after my shift to cook.'

'Why don't I go home with you and make sure everything's all right? Maybe we could make something to eat.'

'I told you, it's not necessary.'

'I don't want to be alone,' he finally said. If he went home, he knew he'd focus on the events of the night and worry about what might have happened. As well as wondering all night if she was really okay. Plus, he wanted to be there if she needed him.

'Okay then, you can come home with me and spend the night.'

Lachlan cocked an eyebrow at the invitation, drawing a sigh from Melissa.

'Don't worry, it's only so I can make sure you don't give yourself an injury beating yourself up. You'll be on the sofa, mister.'

She made him smile for the first time that night. Her assessment was spot-on. She clearly knew him well already.

Lachlan took her outstretched hand and let her lead him away. He couldn't think of anything better than spending the night with Melissa. In any capacity.

CHAPTER SEVEN

'DO YOU WANT to help me in the kitchen?' Melissa was worn out by the night's events, but she knew she wouldn't sleep.

Not with the added stress of Lachlan being in her house to keep her awake. She wasn't hungry either, but she had her baby to look after. Besides, making something to eat would give them a focus away from their personal issues.

He'd surprised her that night at the house when he'd kissed her. Though he'd been caring and considerate towards her, up until then she hadn't sensed that he might have had any feelings for her other than the need to take care of the mother of his baby. That kiss had said otherwise. It hadn't been a platonic peck on the lips, but a display of want which seemed to have been bubbling away for some time. She knew, not only because she'd been on the receiving end, but because she'd felt the same way. The feelings she'd been trying so hard to keep a lid on had suddenly burst forth, resulting in that spontaneous passion which seemed to take them both by surprise.

Tonight he'd shown the tenderness he obviously felt

towards her along with that attraction. Lachlan had done his best to reassure her things would be okay, and at the same time had been concerned for her well-being. This felt like more than basic lust, or a situation they'd been forced into. Melissa could see he actually cared about her. Something that was irresistible to a girl who'd been abandoned, and she was weary of fighting against every instinct making her want to revel in it.

'Sure.' He took his jacket off, hung it in the hall, and followed her into the kitchen.

They both needed the distraction after everything they'd been through together that night. The fear and uncertainty they'd both expressed waiting to find out if their baby was all right had brought them closer than ever. Though she knew it was probably a bad idea to bring him here in those circumstances, having him with her was all she wanted. In the end, her heart had won out over her head.

'I thought I could just make us some soup. Proper comfort food, and it'll warm us up. Is that okay?'

'Yeah. I don't think I could face a big meal.'

'Good. Well, if you're not going to sit down and take it easy, maybe you could chop the vegetables, and I'll rinse the lentils.' It would be filling and comforting, as well as nutritious. Just what they needed right now.

Melissa made up some vegetable stock and found some bacon in the fridge, so she chopped and cooked that to add to the onions, celery, and carrots Lachlan had cut.

'You're pretty nifty with a knife,' she said.

'Years of practice feeding everyone. Mum was always working, so it fell to me to make dinner most nights. I can get very creative on a food budget too.' The ghost of a smile teased his lips as he seemed to conjure the memories. Though Melissa was sure it must've been a struggle for him.

'That can't have been easy for you.' Despite her estrangement from her parents now, they'd been there for her when she was young. She hadn't had to worry about grown-up things like finances and feeding a family.

Her parents had been traditional; mum had been at home taking care of her and the housework, while Dad went to work to support them. That was why it had hurt so much when they'd moved abroad without her. They hadn't seemed to consider how lost and abandoned she would feel without them. Melissa supposed she'd taken them for granted, and perhaps she'd let her anger get in the way of maintaining a relationship with them.

In a perfect world, she would've had them here with her, but that wouldn't have been fair to them. She only wished she'd realised this sooner. Then she might have more support when their grandchild arrived. Hopefully she still had some time to make amends and find some way to have them back in her life, and her baby's.

'No. Dad leaving made me grow up pretty quickly. I felt responsibility for everyone in his absence, and I didn't want to let anyone down. Looking back, the burden shouldn't have fallen to me, and I do resent my father for leaving us like that. I think that's why the thought of becoming a dad myself was something that terrified me at times. I want to be part of my child's life, and the prospect of the cancer returning casts a shadow over that. I hate the thought that I won't be here for our baby someday, and that he or she might resent me for that.'

'I hope it never comes to that.' Even the idea of it sent shivers up and down her spine. She'd tried not to focus on his illness and what it could mean for the future. It was out of her control, but it was probably also why she'd been holding back her feelings for him. Afraid that even if he did want to be part of her life, that fate would steal him away from her just like Chris.

Except none of that was Lachlan's fault. It didn't seem fair to lay the blame at his feet for something he was powerless to prevent. Just like his father walking out. Not being honest about how much she cared for him seemed like a punishment neither of them deserved. Perhaps an even worse fate than if she gave in to those feelings and things didn't work out.

'Me too.'

'Do you see much of the rest of your family?'

'Probably not enough. That was my brother Duncan I was with at the festival. He's married with children, so we usually only see each other at special occasions. And Mum still works a lot. I think she's going to come and stay with Claire when the baby arrives, and I'm hoping we can convince her to move permanently. It will be nice to have her here when our little one arrives too.' Lachlan was clearly a family man who, despite his talk about starting a new life, wanted to gather all of his loved ones around him again.

Melissa still wasn't sure if that included her or not. She envied that close familial bond. On nights like this, she missed having her own family around her. Perhaps having Lachlan stay here tonight was as much for her benefit as it was his.

'I might try reaching out to my parents again. I haven't seen them in so long, and I might need them…' She didn't know if they would be willing to come back specially for her and the baby, but she wanted to open those channels of communication again at least. Maybe motherhood had made her grow up.

'I can understand why you'd want them around, but you know I'll be here for you regardless.' He held her gaze, conveying the sincerity of his commitment to her with one blue-eyed look. It was all she needed to be swept off her feet.

For a moment, that chemistry was back between them, simmering away like the lentil soup on the stove. Thankfully it bubbled over before she and Lachlan did.

'I'll get this. You pull out some dishes and butter some bread for us.' He took control of both situations, moving the saucepan off the heat and shutting down any notion of another kiss at the same time. Even though his gaze had lingered on her mouth a little too long to be considered disinterested.

On this occasion, Melissa let him boss her around in her own home because his actions were safer than the ideas her mind had conjured up. It didn't matter that getting personally involved now would lead to all sorts of complications. Today had been emotional and frightening for them both, and it wasn't over yet. Clinging to Lachlan was the easy way out, but she'd have to get used to dealing with the emotional stuff on her own if he didn't want that kind of relationship with her. Though his actions tonight said that he was involved as more than a victim of circumstance. She could tell he cared about her as much as the baby. Whether either of them wanted to act on that, and complicate things even further between them, was another matter. Next time she was in trouble, he mightn't be there for her, and it wouldn't do to think otherwise.

They sat down at the kitchen table, giving their late-night, post trauma dinner some sense of normality.

'This is so good,' Lachlan said after taking his first spoonful.

'Just what we needed.' The warmth filling her empty belly was a poor substitute for Lachlan's kisses, but it was tasty and comforting.

'There's still plenty left. Is it okay if I take some with me tomorrow?'

'Of course. I have some containers you can use.'

He yawned as he took his dishes over to the sink to wash up. He put her to shame—she'd happily have left the dishes until tomorrow. She supposed his attitude towards domestic chores was another throwback to his childhood, when he'd been expected to keep house in his mother's absence. It was a lot to put on a young boy's shoulders, and no wonder that he seemed to place everyone else's needs before his own. The difficult thing for her to figure out was whether his actions towards her and the baby were in the same vein. Was it out of responsibility he felt, rather than wanting to be there for them?

If it was the former, it mightn't prove sufficient for him to stick around long-term, despite his assertions. Someday he might feel a stronger responsibility towards someone else and follow it instead.

'You must be exhausted. I'll go and get some bedding and make up the sofa for you.' She left him to get settled and shuffled off to raid the cupboards for extra pillows and blankets. It wasn't often that she had anyone sleeping over. Only Lydia if she'd had one too many on a night out and crashed here. When she wouldn't have cared if it was a sofa or a doorway she was sleeping in.

When she returned to the living room, arms laden with bedding, she almost dropped the heap. Lachlan was sitting on her sofa, barefoot, bare-chested, naked apart from his boxer shorts. It took her a moment to regain her composure and wipe away her drool.

Was it her imagination, or had he got hotter in the three months since she'd last seen him naked? Perhaps it was because he was more than a stranger now. Or that he was the kind of man who looked after pregnant women and did the dishes. Most likely it was down to the sight of the patch of dark hair on his chest, and the taut abdominal muscles she could have played noughts and crosses on. The last time he'd shown this much flesh, she'd been too engrossed in what they'd been doing to pay close attention. She was making up for it now. It was all she could do not to go and make herself some popcorn to better enjoy the show.

'Sorry. I was just making myself comfortable,' he said, grabbing a cushion and clutching it to his chest. Probably to stop her ogling him.

It jolted her back out of her daydream.

'Of course. No problem. I guess I'm just not used to having half-naked men laying about my house.' She tried to make a joke out of it, but averted her eyes as she set about making a bed for him on the sofa.

He stood up to move out of her way, and she congratulated herself for managing not to stare at his backside. Hormones, she told herself.

'Thanks again for letting me stay here. I just want to be close. To be here for you and the baby in case you need me. At least for tonight.' His words might have been more comforting if he hadn't put a time limit on his need to be near her.

'It's not necessary, but thank you.'

'It's great living on your own until something like this happens and you realise you need people around you.'

'I can't say living on my own is all that great, but I suppose the house will be full again soon enough.' That would be the biggest blessing of all of this. She would never be on her own again. In a few months, the house would be full of baby things and a precious little one to give her the family she'd been missing. Then she could focus on what she had in her life, instead of what she'd lost.

'Sorry. I didn't mean to bring up any bad memories for you—'

'Night, Lachlan.'

She left him to get sorted for the night, not wanting to talk about losing Chris. Because she hadn't thought about him until just now.

Surprisingly, Melissa managed to fall asleep once her head hit the pillow. The events of the evening had apparently taken their toll. However, she was woken at all hours of the morning by that familiar burning sensation in her chest. Heartburn was the curse of her pregnancy, and very little seemed to ease it. Now she had the added pain of a sprained ankle to increase her discomfort.

She lay on for some time, trying to force herself back to sleep, but her body refused to cooperate. In the end she had no other choice but to creep downstairs on her injured ankle in search of some relief.

Not wanting to turn the light on and disturb Lachlan, she felt her way along in the dark until she reached the kitchen. She opened the fridge just a fraction to keep the light to a minimum, and reached in for the milk.

'You couldn't sleep either?'

The voice coming from the shadows made her jump, and she dropped the milk onto the kitchen floor. The contents spilled out.

Once she realised it was only Lachlan, she pulled

herself together again and turned on the light. He was sitting at the breakfast bar in his boxers, blinking at the bright light.

'Sorry. I didn't mean to scare you.'

'I thought you were asleep.' She bent down to pick up the container and stop any more milk leaking out, though the floor was already covered in the stuff.

'I tried. Here, let me get that.' Lachlan jumped up off his seat and grabbed the mop and bucket she'd failed to put away the last time she'd mopped the floor.

Too tired to argue, she perched herself on the seat he'd just vacated and let him do the clean-up. It was mesmerising seeing the mop slosh the milk back and forth until it gradually disappeared. Almost as much as watching the flex of Lachlan's muscles as he brandished the mop.

'I needed something for the heartburn,' she blurted out. Though it was her blood pressure now that was causing the problem, her body clearly responding to the sight of him in a state of undress doing housework. A kink she didn't know she enjoyed until Lachlan had come back into her life.

Perhaps it was the nesting instinct to provide the perfect home for her baby that made a man doing chores all the more appealing. Although she wasn't sure she would be as excited to see anyone other than Lachlan doing it.

'There's not much milk left, I'm afraid.' He filled the bucket with hot water and a squirt of detergent before giving the floor one last clean.

'But I do have ice cream in the freezer,' she remembered, pulling out a tub of her favourite chocolate chip and fudge swirl, and grabbing two spoons.

'You think this will help us sleep?' he asked, taking the spoon she offered and peeling the lid off the tub.

'No, but it'll make staying awake more enjoyable. And I don't have to worry about getting fat.' She dug her spoon in and helped herself to a large scoop of chocolatey goodness.

'No, because it's all for the baby, right?' His smile suggested he didn't believe it at all, but was happy to let her indulge.

'Naturally.' She took another spoonful and savoured the creamy taste on her tongue. 'Mmm.'

When she glanced at Lachlan, she was sure he was watching her the way she'd looked at him earlier. Maybe it was wishful thinking, but she thought she'd seen a hunger there for more than ice cream. She shivered. A delicious chill of awareness skated across her skin that, despite her lack of make-up and the sight of her pigging out in the kitchen, he might still be attracted to her.

'Brain freeze? Maybe we should step away from the ice cream.'

Melissa nodded. It was better to have him take away her comfort food than let him think she was reading something more into this than sharing a tub of ice cream.

He put it back in the freezer and came back to sit beside her.

'Everything's all right,' she assured him, believing that her and the baby's welfare was the reason he'd been sitting here in the dark.

'I hope so.'

'I think it's just shaken us both up a little tonight.' Melissa lifted the spoons and moved over to the sink so he couldn't see her face. She didn't want to look at him when she told him her deepest fears, though she thought he needed to know he wasn't the only one scared about what the future held.

She let her hands rest on the soft swell of her belly, which was probably imperceptible to anyone else, but she liked to think she could feel her baby growing in there already.

'What is it, Melissa? What's bothering you?'

'That I'm going to be alone. I don't have my family to hold my hand or worry about me. I'm afraid my baby is going to end up as lonely as I am.' The second she admitted her fears, the tears fell from her eyes.

She'd tried to convince herself she could do all this on her own, but as time went on, it was becoming clear she was going to need support. Someone she could rely on. It was what she always suggested to her patients— that they made sure they had a good support system in place—and now she realised the truth in that advice.

Emotions, as well as hormones, were all over the place during pregnancy. It was important to have someone to lean on, to give pep talks when needed, a listening ear, and a hand to hold. Melissa didn't feel as though she had anyone willing to do that. At least, no one who wasn't doing it under duress.

'You both have me.' Lachlan's voice sounded low in her ear, sending the hairs on the back of her neck to attention. Then he slid his arms around her and rested his hands on top of hers. Covering her belly.

She wanted so desperately to believe him. He'd said it often enough, but unfortunately his actions didn't match his words.

'How can I believe that, Lachlan, when you seem so distant lately?' She didn't even dare mention the kiss in case it sent him running again.

He dropped his head. 'I'm truly sorry. I never meant to hurt you, or mess you around. It's just… I'm afraid of doing something we'll both regret.'

It took Melissa a moment to process what he was talking about. 'The kiss?'

'Yes, the kiss. There's six months until this baby is born. I don't want to get into something now, only for it to fizzle out before the birth.'

'And I don't get a say in that? What about what I want?' Whatever did or didn't happen between them affected her too.

'I don't want to hurt you, Melissa, but more than anything, I want to be present in my baby's life. I can't jeopardise that for anyone. Not even you.'

It was difficult to hear, but it let Melissa know where she stood. She couldn't begrudge her unborn child taking priority in Lachlan's affections, when that's what she'd wanted. By telling him he was the father, she'd hoped deep down that he would step up and be the parent both she and the baby needed him to be. So their child didn't grow up feeling rejected the way they both had.

Still, it didn't stop her from needing to be a part of his life too. Especially when he made her feel the way he did. Even now, despite her upset, she was aware of him so close to her. Her fingers ached to touch the smooth skin of his chest. Her lips parted, ready to pick up from where their last kiss had ended. She still wanted him, wanted that same physical connection they'd shared at the festival. Even if it meant setting her feelings aside.

'Then why kiss me in the first place?' She didn't imagine Lachlan was the kind of man who couldn't control his impulses. After all, he'd managed to stay away from her for a week without any kind of contact.

Lachlan scrubbed his hands over his face. 'Because I wanted to. I like you, Melissa. You should know that at least. But what I want should come after what my baby needs. A father.'

'You don't think that part of what makes good parents is that they're happy? We both know there's an attraction between us, and I for one am tired of fighting it. It's exhausting pretending that I don't want to be with you. To relive what we had together at the music festival. Would it really be so bad to find some comfort in one another again?' When they'd first met, they'd been going through difficult, emotional times in their lives. Much like now. At least then they'd been able to forget everything outside of the bedroom for that night. She would like to have the opportunity to do the same now.

'Trust me, I want that too, Melissa. But there's so much else at stake now...' The push and pull of his emotions was obvious in the way he was reaching out to her, but still trying to keep his distance. She recognised the turmoil tearing him apart inside, because she felt it too. What she wouldn't do to be that carefree couple who'd thrown caution to the wind once more. It might be the last time they'd get the chance to do that before they became parents for real.

'We don't have to make promises to one another of happy ever afters. Acting on this attraction doesn't have to affect how we parent this baby. I need you, Lachlan. Even if it's only for tonight.' Melissa reminded him of the time frame he'd originally suggested. Stepping outside of the boundaries they'd set up when they'd reconnected for one night didn't seem as scary as anything more serious and complicated.

What she was suggesting wasn't necessarily everything she wanted, but she'd learned it wasn't possible to have it all. She wanted him to hold her in his arms for a little while. All she needed for now was to know he wanted her. To feel loved, even if it didn't last beyond the morning. The fear of losing him was gradually being blotted out by the fear of never really showing how much they felt for one another.

Lachlan didn't believe what he was hearing. He'd been up all night worrying not only about what could have happened to Melissa and the baby, but what he was going to do about his feelings for her. The conflict between doing the right thing by his child and what he wanted was tearing him apart. The next six months, not to mention the rest of his life, trying to keep the two separate was going to severely test him. It wasn't that he didn't want to try with Melissa, but he was worried that if—*when*—it ended, it would affect his relationship with his child. The last thing he wanted.

This way it seemed they could have it all. At least temporarily.

'It would be nice just to be together without worrying about the consequences...' He was tired of overthinking, of fighting his feelings for Melissa, denying himself the chance to be with her.

Today, when he thought there was a possibility that he'd lose her, had proven to him just how strongly he felt about her.

'It's how we met, isn't it? We were able to enjoy each other without a commitment, or even knowing each other's surnames, if I recall.' She teased him with the memory, colour rising in her cheeks, and the twinkle in her eye a little brighter. The idea certainly seemed to appeal to her, and Lachlan could see the benefits. In fact, he was struggling to come up with any cons.

'Getting pregnant kind of forced our hand though.' If he hadn't moved to the city, or come to Claire's appointment, he'd still be none the wiser about the baby. They wouldn't even be in one another's orbit now, though he'd still be thinking about her and the time they'd spent together.

'So now we get to take control. Decide what we want to do, instead of letting consequences, or our consciences, dictate our actions.' She placed a hand in the middle of his chest, scorching his skin and awakening his weary body. There was no denying he wanted to be with her. He ached for her. It was the consequences of giving in to those urges he worried about. Especially when the last time had caused such a massive upheaval in both of their lives.

'Are you sure?' His resolve was weakening with each second she was touching him, making him forget everything except how she made him feel.

If only he could manage not to get too emotionally invested in them as a couple, it was probably the best he could hope for.

His heart was trying to convince his head this was a good idea.

Then Melissa stood up on her tiptoes and kissed him, and the decision was made for him. He took her hand, and she led him upstairs to her bedroom, not another word spoken between them. A silent agreement to embark on this bold adventure together.

He slowly unbuttoned his way down her nightshirt, her earlier confidence apparently subsiding as she bit her lip. There was a hitch in her breath as he uncovered her body to his gaze, but she had absolutely nothing to be nervous about. Of course, there were subtle changes to her body from the last time they'd been together because of the pregnancy, but she was incredibly beautiful.

Lachlan kissed her on the mouth. Long and deep, trying to block out any negative thoughts she might have over her changing body. He cupped her breast in his hand, fuller than he remembered, and when he sucked on her nipple, it was clearly more sensitive.

He pushed her nightdress off her shoulders so she was totally exposed to him. Saw the goose bumps rise on her flesh, and her pink nipples stand to attention against her pale skin. It was too much to resist.

He kissed her hard, gripped her backside as he lifted her off the ground and wrapped her legs around his waist. His erection fought to escape the confines of his boxers as he pressed between her thighs, her soft heat teasing him through the thin fabric. He walked them over to the bed and laid her down gently, treating her like the precious cargo she was.

Though Melissa clearly wasn't feeling fragile when she reached between their bodies and stroked the length of his manhood, making him suck in a breath.

'I've missed you.' He buried his face in the side of her neck, kissing and nibbling his way along. Inhaling the sweet scent he'd been without for what seemed like an eternity.

'I've missed you too.' She slid her hands under the waistband of his underwear and grabbed his backside, leaving him in no doubt about that.

Melissa pushed his boxers down, baring him completely, and leaving their prone bodies skin to skin in the most intimate contact. It was torture and heaven all at once.

She took him in hand again and squeezed firmly, making his entire body tremble and his resolve shatter. Clearly she wanted him as much as he wanted her, and it had been way too long since the last time they'd done this. When he was with her, he felt whole again. One hundred percent masculine.

Lachlan claimed her with one thrust. Her gasp, his cry of triumph. He didn't want to think of her being anyone else's, even though the nature of this arrangement made it a possibility somewhere down the line.

Melissa slid her arms around his neck and pulled him down for a kiss. At the same time, she tightened her inner muscles around him, completely scrambling his brain and overwhelming him with sensations. All of them pleasant.

He loved her body, the way she made him feel, the connection they had. He loved...this. Lachlan was too afraid to continue down that emotional path and pushed inside her again so he couldn't finish the thought. Instead, he was completely consumed by the physical feeling of being with her. Those sensations he could allow himself to experience.

His hips drove home his insistence again, indulging his needs, and bringing Melissa closer to the edge with every move. Her building moans of ecstasy fuelled his pace, as well as his ego. He wanted her to feel as good as he did. For this to be as good for her as it was for him. Then she'd want to do it again and again, and there'd be room for him in her life in some safe capacity.

Melissa was the mother of his baby, the woman who'd made him feel like a man again, and he didn't want to lose her. He was just afraid that he'd want her too much.

The sound of her climax echoed around the bedroom, the shockwaves reverberating through his body from hers until he couldn't fight it any longer. It was the one moment when he didn't have to hold back. He poured all of those feelings for her he was afraid to say out loud into her with a roar. Until his limbs were shaking with the effort, and his breath came in heavy pants.

His chest rapidly rose and fell in synch with Melissa's as they recovered. Lying side by side, grinning at each other as though they'd won the lottery. In most people's books, he already had, starting a family with an amazing woman who still wanted to share a bed with him. The problem was that he wanted it all, but had enough experience to know that wasn't possible. He had to sacrifice something to make it work. If it had to be a proper relationship with Melissa, then that's what he would forfeit if it meant their child would grow up in a stable environment with two present parents.

He could give his love to their baby, but he couldn't risk giving it to Melissa when there was just too much to lose.

CHAPTER EIGHT

'MORNING.'

Melissa blinked awake at the sound of Lachlan's voice, wondering if she was still half-asleep.

'Morning,' she croaked.

'There wasn't much in the way of food in the cupboards. This was the best I could come up with. I can go grab a few things from the shops if you need anything?' He set a tray with orange juice, hot buttered toast and a bowl of cereal on the bed, and hovered expectantly.

'No. I'll get shopping in later. Sit down and help me eat this.' She moved the tray aside and pulled the covers back so he could get in beside her.

He was beaming as he helped himself to a slice of toast from the stack he'd piled high on the plate. Melissa took a sip of juice before tucking into some sugary cereal, certain she needed the energy boost after last night's antics between the sheets.

She hadn't expected Lachlan to even be here this morning, never mind make her breakfast. It was considerate of him, but not the actions of a man who was only here for the sex. She was glad he'd stayed the night, and well into the morning.

It was good to see him happy and a pleasant way to start the working day. At least neither of them felt the need to run away after giving in to temptation this time. And what fun it had been to simply enjoy being together!

Their first time together definitely hadn't been a fluke. They had a chemistry she'd never had in the years she'd been with Chris. An understanding of what they both needed, and a passion that fizzed in her veins with every kiss, every touch. It was a wonder they'd held out for as long as they had under the circumstances. At least this time they didn't have to worry about the consequences, because the baby was already on the way. It gave them more of a sense of freedom, even if she had to keep her feelings in check.

That soppy expression on his face was adorable, and Melissa could only imagine how he would look seeing his own baby for the first time.

Now that the initial shock had worn off, and she was sure Lachlan would stick around for his baby, she was beginning to look forward to the arrival too. Only time would tell if she and Lachlan would do this again. It mightn't be such fun against the backdrop of a crying baby, lack of sleep, and dirty nappies. They might struggle like any other couple with a newborn, even though they weren't actually together in the conventional sense.

So they should probably make the most of the time they had together now in case it all came to an end too soon.

'You know, in a few months, I'm going to be the size of a house. We mightn't be able to do this any more. You mightn't want to.'

Lachlan set down what was left of his toast and cradled her head in his hands. 'I will always want you. You will always be beautiful to me.' He kissed her, reawakening that need for him inside her.

Last night together had been special. Hot. She supposed because she'd suggested keeping things purely physical, he hadn't needed to hold back, or worry about her feelings. In that way, it was much like their time at the festival. For her, the thrill was in simply being with him. Kissing him. Touching him. Having him in her life, and her bed, in any capacity.

Perhaps that was pitiful, being so lonely she'd settled for sex, rather than run the risk of chasing him away if she admitted she had feelings for him as more than the baby's father. He wasn't just a convenient bed partner. Lachlan had become an important, present part of her life. But she couldn't tell him that. Not when he was so afraid personal feelings would affect how he'd relate to his child.

Melissa wanted to believe he'd always want her, that he'd still think she was beautiful when she couldn't see her own feet past her belly. But like their time together, nothing was promised forever.

She kissed him back, wanting to block out all of

those negative thoughts. If she only had him for a little while to herself, could only have this until it became uncomfortable physically and emotionally, then she'd enjoy it while it lasted.

She moved the breakfast things to her bedside table, hungrier for Lachlan than a piece of toast. He was certainly more satisfying.

With a confidence she had to dig deep for, Melissa pushed him back onto the mattress and straddled him. She was still naked, and aware the morning sunlight shining in through the window wasn't going to hide any imperfections. But she needed to convince him, as well as herself, that she could brazen this out.

'Feeling frisky this morning, are we?' Lachlan asked with a grin, grabbing her by the hips.

'Only when a man brings me breakfast in bed.'

'I'll have to make sure I do it more often, then,' he said, lifting his head to kiss her thoroughly.

The promise that this wasn't going to be a one-off after all only made her want him more. Melissa ground against him, testing herself as much as Lachlan. He pressed his thumb intimately against her, teasing, stretching, playing with her until they were both coated with her arousal. He slid easily into her then, filling her completely, as their bodies joined together.

She rocked her hips as he thrust up to meet her again and again, wishing they could stay like this forever. Where happiness was guaranteed and neither of them wanted to be anywhere else.

* * *

Lachlan was reluctant to leave Melissa's bed. It was too cosy, too tempting to give up everything to stay there with her and pretend the rest of the world didn't exist, and there were no reasons why they couldn't be together.

Unfortunately, they had to work to earn a living, and he was going to have a family to provide for soon.

'Why don't we have dinner when we're both free?'

'Sounds good.'

'I'll pick you up tomorrow about eight o'clock, then.' Lachlan leaned in and gave her a kiss.

He still needed to go home and get showered and changed before his shift. It was supposed to have been nothing more than a goodbye peck on the lips. But it soon developed into something more. Every touch between them seemed to be the catalyst for a greater chemical reaction. They slid their arms around one another, pressing their bodies tightly together as they deepened the kiss, bringing back vivid memories of everything they'd got up to in her bed last night.

It was like this every time. That was probably why he'd tried, and failed, to keep things between them to a minimum recently. He'd known his feelings for Melissa were growing stronger, and he'd been worried that by facing them, he was inevitably going to let her and the baby down if things didn't work out. Last night had been unexpected, and eye-opening.

They'd been vulnerable, the worry over the baby bonding them, making them cling to one another for comfort. He'd let his defences down, the thought of potentially losing Melissa or the baby drowning out any misgivings he had about being close to her. It had been nice to leave all of his worries aside for one night, having spent too long living on tenterhooks about what the future held because of his illness and becoming a father. Having the freedom to be with Melissa and simply enjoy their time together was something he could get used to. It also made him wonder if he should stop overanalysing everything in his life and learn to live in the moment when there was apparently so much to be gained. Certainly, he wanted to be able to do this again if he had the chance.

The dreaded alarm sounded from his phone, reminding him that he had to get out of bed, and he responded with a groan.

'I'm going to be late for work if I don't get a move on,' he muttered against Melissa's lips.

'I can give you a lift.' Melissa went to sit up, clutching the sheets to her naked body, but Lachlan pulled her back down beside him on the bed.

'No. You stay here and rest. I'll get my run in before work. It's not too far from here to my place.' Whilst it was true that he didn't want to inconvenience her, he also wanted to remember her lying here like this. It kept thoughts of the real world, and what complications their night together could bring, at bay for a while longer. In this room, he could pretend this was their whole universe.

'If you're sure, I could do with another forty winks

before I go in. I didn't get a whole lot of sleep last night.' Melissa's coy glance almost tempted him to stay, but her yawn reminded him that she needed sleep more.

'You rest. I'll text you later.' He gave her one last kiss before forcing himself to get up and grab his clothes.

She watched him dress, though her eyes were already beginning to close.

'I can't wait until our dinner,' she said through another yawn.

Neither could he, and therein lay the problem. The highlight of his days was being with her, and there was nothing remotely casual about his feelings for her.

In an ideal world, they'd be madly in love, raising this baby together in their home. He was beginning to wonder why that picture had to remain pure fantasy when they both seemed so happy together.

CHAPTER NINE

MELISSA MANAGED A quick change out of her uniform before Lachlan picked her up at work. He greeted her with a kiss on the cheek before taking her bag and placing it on the back seat of his car. She climbed into the front, glad he was driving since her nerves were getting the better of her at the prospect of another night with him. He'd been on her mind all day, along with thoughts of everything they'd done together.

'Are you sure you don't want a beer? I can drive us back.' Melissa knew if she could partake in some alcohol tonight, she would. For some reason, going out for dinner with Lachlan seemed more intimate than the time they'd spent in bed together, or the fact that they were going to be co-parents.

It marked a change in their relationship that part of her had hoped for, but that also brought more anxiety. Yesterday had been emotional and challenging, and apparently the catalyst for giving in to temptation again. They hadn't discussed what came next for them as a couple. If that's what they were now. But maybe that was for the best. What had happened the other night had been organic, and she didn't want to tarnish where they were by overanalysing everything again.

Those fears that Lachlan would leave her were always going to be there, regardless of whether she admitted she had feelings for him or not. Maybe she should just let herself enjoy their time together for what it was now, and see where it would lead...

'It's fine. I should keep a clear head if we're going to discuss childcare arrangements. Plus, I want other parts of me wide awake if we decide to make a night of it.' He shot her a lingering glance as though waiting for confirmation that she was agreeable.

Even the thought of sharing her bed with him again was getting her hot under the collar—and everywhere else. If it wasn't for the fact that she was responsible for the baby's nutritional needs as well as her own, she would've been tempted to tell him to forget dinner altogether and head straight home.

Instead, she simply reached across the front of the car and gave his thigh a squeeze, hoping that was enough to persuade him she was more than agreeable to the suggestion. Her reward came with the feel of his muscles bunching under her fingertips, and the visible clenching of his jaw. She gave a triumphant smile at the thought that she'd managed to get him as aroused as she currently was at the prospect of the night ahead.

'I haven't eaten since midday, so I'm looking forward to a good meal. None of that fancy fine dining stuff that wouldn't fill a hole in your tooth, you know. A proper plate of food. Are you hungry too?' Lachlan kept his eyes trained on the road straight ahead, and his sudden rambling, hardly pausing for breath, amused Melissa. It felt very much as though he was trying to steer his mind somewhere other than her touch, or spending the night together, when it was he who'd conjured the thought in the first place.

'Starved,' she said, willing him to turn around and see the desire she was sure was shining in her eyes for him.

The shaky breath he let out told her he could sense it.

Flashing orange lights up ahead in the darkness caught Melissa's attention, and Lachlan began to slow the car down.

'There's something going on...' he said, peering closely through the windscreen.

The rear lights of the cars ahead blazed brightly as they hit the brakes, traffic eventually coming to a halt. A flurry of activity around them and people rushing out of their cars suggested something serious had happened, putting all thoughts of romantic rendezvous out of Melissa's head for now. Lachlan's too, it seemed, as he pulled the handbrake on, switched off the engine, and undid his seat belt.

'I'll see what's going on. Someone might be hurt.'

She supposed it was his paramedic training kicking in that compelled him to help, and she wouldn't sit idly by if someone was hurt either. Lachlan likely expected her to wait, but that wasn't Melissa. Instead, she grabbed her midwife bag from the back seat in case there was anything in there that could help, and headed off after him.

It was a set of temporary traffic lights which had initially slowed traffic, but cars remained at a standstill even after the green light showed, and it was easy to see why. Heavy machinery involved in the roadworks had toppled into a ditch at the side of the road, but the panicked shouting confirmed it was more serious than a damaged digger.

Lachlan didn't hesitate to climb down and assess the scene, whilst Melissa took her time, making sure she didn't slip on any loose dirt. She didn't miss the look of disapproval on Lachlan's face as he reached out a hand to make sure she got onto safe ground, but rushed to cut him off before he could scold her.

'Don't start. We're both medical professionals, and I have some first aid supplies in my bag.'

In a sign that he knew her well enough not to argue, Lachlan simply led her over to the men in high visibility jackets and hard hats gathered around the upturned digger.

Lachlan introduced himself to the workmen. 'Hey, I'm Lachlan McNairn. I'm an off-duty paramedic. Is there anything I can do?'

'I've phoned for an ambulance, but one of our guys, Paul, is trapped under there. I don't know what happened. Maybe the road weakened and gave way... The driver got out, but Paul was digging in the ditch. Are we right to move this?' Lachlan assumed the man speaking was the foreman, since he was keen to place the blame elsewhere and was standing back watching as the rest of the men were attempting to shift the digger bucket, which appeared to have Paul pinned down.

'Yes.' If the weight was lifted after any more than fifteen minutes, it could lead to crush injury syndrome, a potentially life-threatening condition. Removing that pressure could release toxins into the system and overwhelm the kidneys, causing renal failure. There was also the possibility of the change in chemical balance leading to cardiac arrest.

He added his weight to the effort to shift the load off Paul's chest, and with a lot of grunting and straining muscles, they managed it. The man lying on the ground was deathly pale, but he was conscious.

'I—I can't breathe,' Paul managed through gasps.

'Don't try to talk. We need to see what damage has been done.' Lachlan set to work with his preliminary assessment of the man's condition. He was conscious and breathing, though it was clearly laboured.

'I might be able to help until the ambulance gets here.' Melissa came down beside him and rummaged in her bag to produce a manual resuscitator, a self-inflating bag used to deliver positive pressure ventilation.

'Thanks.' Lachlan shot her an appreciative glance, letting her get on with assisting Paul's breathing so he could continue checking the rest of the man's injuries.

Although Melissa was a midwife, she would have

first aid training, and he was grateful she was willing to help.

'How long has he been trapped?' he asked the crew.

'About five minutes. Not long.' Someone answered.

'Good.' Lachlan turned his attention back to the injured man. 'Paul? I just need you to point to where the pain is.'

He lifted a shaky arm and patted his chest.

'Nowhere else?' There was always the concern that there could be internal damage.

Paul shook his head.

Lachlan wished he had his usual equipment to hand so he could run an echocardiogram. With crush injuries, there was a chance of hyperkalaemia occurring—elevated potassium levels—and changes in these levels could be identified in this way, helping to give a better assessment of the situation, and therefore better hospital treatment after transfer. All he could do in these circumstances was keep the man as comfortable as possible and let the ambulance crew take over when they got here.

'We'll give you something for the pain, but you're going to need some X-rays. You might have some fractured ribs. We'll know better when we get you to hospital.' It was obvious Paul was in pain, his chest tender and badly bruised, but they wouldn't be able to see what was going on inside until he had a scan.

Paul pushed the mask off his face, beginning to come round a bit more thanks to Melissa's intervention. 'Am I going to die?'

'Hopefully you'll just need to rest up for a while.' It was a question Lachlan was often asked, and one he didn't like to answer when there were so many variables in medical emergencies. What seemed like a straightforward accident could end up with a fractured rib puncturing a lung and effectively drowning a patient. It was his job, therefore, to stabilise the injured party and watch him closely until they could get specialist medical care. Like the rest of his life, it meant he was tasked with a great deal of responsibility.

'We're going to have a baby,' Paul said, a smile lighting up his pale features.

Lachlan exchanged a conspiratorial smile with Melissa, knowing they shared the same secret.

'Congratulations. Now just lie still for me.' Lachlan knew something about wanting to tell the world about impending fatherhood. These last couple of weeks, he'd wanted to do the same. The baby no longer seemed like an inconvenience, but something he wanted to boast about. Whilst trying to navigate their path to parenthood, he and Melissa had yet to go public about him being the father of her baby.

He'd drawn enough awkward questions from his family trying to explain the set-up. It did make him wonder about when the baby arrived. Of course, he'd want people to know he was the father when he was determined to be a permanent part of his child's life. He wasn't sure how Melissa intended to handle that, and it was one of the things they needed to discuss.

'We've been trying for years to start a family.

They're my whole world. I don't want to leave them now.' Like Paul, Lachlan was beginning to realise he wanted to be here for his family as long as possible.

What he didn't want was to be emotionally absent, afraid to open himself completely to her and the baby in case he didn't live up to expectations. Perhaps being recognised as the father publicly would help him feel more part of that. What last night had made him realise was that it was pointless pretending he didn't already care for Melissa or the baby. It was only hurting everyone maintaining a distance because of things that might happen, that ultimately he had no control over.

'That's not going to happen, Paul. You'll see your wife soon.' He broke his usual stance to offer his patient some comfort, convincing himself it was better to give him something to look forward to than worry himself into a worse condition.

Advice he should probably take on board himself. He was so consumed by the thought of the mistakes he might make, it was possible he was missing out on something really special. Their pasts had prevented him and Melissa from exploring all aspects of a relationship, but he knew they had a special bond that went beyond impending parenthood. If they could be brave enough, there was a chance they could be more than good parents. They could be a family.

Every day Melissa became a greater part of his life, and she showed him more of the amazing woman she was. Even now, she tended to the superficial cuts on Paul's face, cleaning him up with antiseptic wipes and dressing the deeper wounds he'd sustained in the accident, highlighting her caring nature. This was going above and beyond her role as a midwife, and he knew it was part of who she was. Something that wasn't taught or learned from textbooks. In that moment, he knew she would be there for him should the worst ever happen.

It was down to him to be there for her until it did.

Thankfully, the sound of the ambulance sirens filled the night air, and it wasn't long before two of his colleagues were climbing down the bank to reach them. He gave them a quick rundown of Paul's injuries. Then, as carefully and as gently as they could, they moved him onto a stretcher and got him into the ambulance.

'I'll phone your wife, Paul,' the foreman called as the paramedics closed the doors. 'And thanks for all of your help too.'

'No problem.' Lachlan shook his hand, then assisted Melissa in picking up the debris from the first aid they'd administered on site. Once she'd repacked her bag, he gave her a hand back up onto the road.

She was shivering so hard he could hear her teeth chattering once they were in the car.

'You're freezing. I shouldn't have kept you standing around in the cold for so long.' He grabbed the jacket he'd tossed onto the back seat earlier and reached across to tuck it in around her shoulders.

'I make my own decisions, Lachlan.' She didn't need to give him the side-eye for him to realise that. Melissa had been doing that since the day he met her, and he admired her for it. He hadn't been able to act on his gut feelings without considering every consequence thanks to his father's actions and the impact they'd had on those around him.

Lachlan hoped the fact that he'd made a few more spontaneous decisions proved what a positive influence she was having on him. Maybe someday he'd be able to accept his father's actions and open himself up to the life he could have if he wasn't so worried about turning out like him.

'I'll put the heat on anyway. I'm feeling the chill myself now.' He turned the temperature dial on full while they waited for the traffic to begin moving again.

'It was probably only adrenaline keeping us warm out there,' she said with a smile. Then with more concern added, 'I hope he's going to be okay.'

Lachlan reached out and squeezed her hand. 'I'm sure he will be.'

Perhaps it was the bond he felt with someone else about to be a dad with an uncertain future ahead, but there was something illogical inside him that said if things worked out for Paul, everything would be okay for him too. And he wanted that more than anything. But how could he put her through the pain and suffering his treatment had caused him and his loved ones the first time around if his cancer returned? All he could do was keep his fingers crossed for him and Paul.

'You were impressive back there, taking charge and keeping him calm.' She yawned and leaned her head against his shoulder. It was a sign of how comfortable things between them had become now that they'd stopped fighting whatever feelings kept drawing them together. He should've been disconcerted by the fact that they were so close when he'd done his best to avoid that until last night. Except it was kind of nice. It was easy to imagine a different life, one where he was free of cancer and didn't have to worry about abandoning anyone. Where they could be driving home with their baby in the back seat. A nice, normal family life. The one he never had, and never thought he would have.

'You were pretty impressive yourself. We can reward ourselves with some carb-laden food at the restaurant. I'm sure they'll still be holding our table.' He'd already seen how Melissa handled her role as a midwife, but tonight had highlighted how supportive she was in general. It was nice to have her there for backup, to share the load with someone. Ironic, when that was the very thing he'd been trying to run away from. Determined to do everything on his own.

'Actually, I don't have much of an appetite any more. I'm just tired. Do you mind if we go home instead?' Another yawn hit the point home.

'Sure.' He headed towards Melissa's house, and it wasn't long before her steady breathing signified her lapse into sleep.

When they pulled up outside her house, he touched her gently on the shoulder. 'Hey. We're here.'

Melissa lifted her head and stretched out her neck. 'You want to come in?'

'I should probably let you get some sleep.'

'It's okay. You wanted to talk about the baby.'

'We can do that anytime. It's been an exhausting night, and you need to rest.' He wanted to take care of her, even if that only meant making sure she got enough sleep.

She undid her seat belt and got out of the car, not giving him time to argue. 'It's fine, Lachlan. Talking isn't going to tire me out.'

He wasn't so sure, but he followed her into the house regardless.

Once inside, Melissa kicked off her shoes and curled up on the sofa. It seemed like the most natural thing in the world to sit there with her. He lifted her feet and placed them on his lap to give her a massage.

'Mmm. That feels so good.' She closed her eyes, making little moans of satisfaction that didn't fail to call to his basest needs. Tonight, however, there were more important things to deal with than his libido.

'Glad I can do something for you.'

'You do a lot for me, Lachlan.'

'I hope so, and I want to do the same for the baby.'

'That's what you want to talk about?'

'Yes. I guess I just want to know what my role is going to be.'

Melissa frowned at him. 'Well, you're the dad.'

It sounded so simple when put like that, but he knew having a title alone didn't mean anything. 'Yes, but I also want to be a father. And not just an every-other-weekend one.'

'Okay.' She sat up straight, and he hoped he hadn't

gone too far in voicing his wants for the future. It was a topic they'd tried to avoid, because it likely meant facing whatever feelings they had for one another too at some point. Something he knew terrified them both, opening up their hearts and sharing their lives with someone again.

'I want to be actively involved. That means sharing the childcare equally, school runs when the time comes, parent-teacher meetings, holidays… I want to be there for all of it.' He meant that. Lachlan had no intention of shuffling off the earth anytime soon, and since he was trying to be the father he never had, he wanted to be there as much as possible in his child's life.

Melissa sat quietly, taking it all in. Probably contemplating the implications of that in her life. Only time would tell if the risk was worth taking, but now, from his point of view, they had to try and make it work for the baby's sake. Neither of them wanted the baby to suffer as a result of their personal issues.

Eventually she said, 'I'm sure we can come to an arrangement. I want to get back to work at some point, so having you on board would really help.'

That was easier than he'd expected, maybe because of the time they had been spending together.

'Great. So, we can make it official, then? It's okay for me to tell people I'm the dad?' Perhaps he'd been holding back on that too, afraid that once he acknowledged it outside of family, it made everything more real. Now that he and Melissa were working through their own hang-ups, however, he thought it was about time he went all in. Stopped holding back, and focused on the good things in his life instead of waiting for the worst to happen.

'Well, I'm okay with that if you are. It doesn't make any sense to sneak around pretending otherwise. I mean, we don't have to take out a full-page ad in the paper or anything, but feel free to share the news.'

She seemed at ease with the idea now. A far cry from those early days when she hadn't even wanted to tell him she was pregnant in the first place. It showed how far they'd come already.

'Thank you. Hopefully things will get easier for us from now on.' He didn't dare hope for too much, but he was enjoying just being in the moment with Melissa. That was enough for now.

'I hope so. Now, can we go to bed?' Melissa got up off the sofa and took his hand.

Lachlan let her lead him towards the bedroom, not caring if they spent the night making love or if she went straight to sleep. All that mattered was that she was in his arms. It had become so natural, comfortable, to be together like this, that he wished it wouldn't end. He didn't want to think about the reasons they shouldn't let their defences down when the alternative was so enjoyable.

CHAPTER TEN

MELISSA AND LACHLAN had had a couple of weeks of sneaking in and out of each other's beds, exchanging sexy texts and phone calls, and generally enjoying a passionate adventure together. Who knew how long it would last, but the intensity they shared in the bedroom showed no sign of abating. Nor did the feelings she had towards him. If anything, they were growing every day.

Along with their stolen moments together, and hot sultry nights, they were also becoming closer on a familial level. That's why she'd agreed to come to Claire's house tonight to celebrate the birth of her baby with the rest of Lachlan's family.

Melissa had met his mother a couple of times during postnatal visits, when they were visiting Claire. A potentially awkward situation apparently negated by the fact that his mother seemed to like her.

Lachlan wanted her to get to know his family so that when their baby came, they would feel a part of it. An idea she was on board with, since she'd grown up without an extended family. She wanted their baby to have people to turn to when needed. Something she hadn't had for a long time herself before Chris came along.

Perhaps she'd been guilty of clinging on to him in place of the parents she was missing at the time. He'd been a good man, but she hadn't felt about him the way she felt about Lachlan.

That was why, although she was enjoying this time with Lachlan, she was more worried than ever about being abandoned again. She'd been devastated by Chris's death when it happened, but she and Lachlan were about to become a family. Chris had never been as enthusiastic about the idea of becoming a father as Lachlan was. They were making plans for the future as parents, and given their current situation, it wasn't unreasonable to believe they could have a relationship beyond that. She had so much more to lose if Lachlan disappeared out of her life the way Chris and her parents had.

Although she may have seemed nonchalant about agreeing to Lachlan's want to be so involved in family life, it was so she didn't scare him off. Melissa didn't want him to feel as though it was a big deal to her, even though it was. It marked a turning point in their relationship, evidence that she was putting her trust in him not to break her heart.

Melissa rang the doorbell, her pulse racing, her palms sweating. Although she'd been to Claire's house on many occasions to check on her and the baby, this wasn't a professional visit. This was a 'meet the family' scenario.

'Hi, Melissa. Come on in. Is my brother not with you?' Claire opened the door with the baby in one arm.

'He got delayed at the hospital, but he'll be here as soon as he can.' When Lachlan had phoned Melissa to tell her he'd be late, her heart had sunk, knowing she'd have to come here on her own and meet everyone without him.

She followed Claire down the hall and into the living room, where her senses were assaulted by the sights and sounds of the family gathering. The loud chattering and laughter mixed with the happy squeals of children were overwhelming. When she was growing up as an only child, the house had been quiet save for the occasional friend she had over. She wasn't used to this level of noise, or the number of people gathered in one small room.

Once she got over the initial shock, she supposed it must've been nice to grow up surrounded by a big family like this, and wondered if their child would be part of it or remain hovering on the outside like her.

'Everyone! This is Melissa.' Claire announced her arrival to the room, refusing her the opportunity to back out.

'Hi.' Under the spotlight of the communal gaze, Melissa gave a little wave. Not knowing what else was expected of her.

Suddenly she was swamped with handshakes and introductions as the family came to introduce themselves.

'I'm Duncan, Lachlan's little brother. Claire and Mum have talked so much about you.'

'I'm Charlie.'

'And I'm Ava.'

The most adorable children sidled up to Melissa, and she bent down to say hello.

'It's lovely to meet you. I'm Melissa.'

'You're uncle Lachlan's friend,' the older boy with the beautiful brown curls said matter-of-factly.

'Yes.'

'Give her some space to breathe, guys. Why don't you come through to the kitchen with me, Melissa, and I'll get you something to drink.' Claire shooed every-one away, and though she wasn't thirsty, Melissa fol-lowed her, glad of a little breathing room.

The fact that she was wishing Lachlan was here for support, to ground her and stop her from becoming too anxious, said she'd already fallen too deep. She was relying on him too much. Attached to the idea of them being a couple. Already starting to think of them as a family.

'Thanks for that. I'm not used to big family gath-erings.'

'Yes, Lachlan said you're an only child and your parents live in Florida. Hold her for a minute, will you?' Claire handed the baby over before Melissa had the chance to reply, and began to pour out two glasses of wine from the many bottles littering the kitchen counter.

Melissa stared down at Lachlan's niece, feeling a surge of love for the little bundle sucking on her tiny fist. She always got broody over babies, but there was something extra special about this one. Whether it was because this baby was part of Lachlan's family, or from the vain hope that they could one day be related, Melissa couldn't be sure.

'Don't worry, it's non-alcoholic.' Claire nudged a glass towards Melissa and took one herself.

'Thanks.' The sweet sparkling grape juice was refreshing, and Melissa made a note to stock up on some herself, since she wouldn't be drinking anything alcoholic for the foreseeable future.

'We haven't really had a chance to talk since I found out you're having my brother's baby.'

Melissa almost choked on her drink at the thought that she was about to get a lecture from one of her patients. It had been something of a blessing that they'd only really seen each other on a professional level, often when her mother was in attendance, and the focus was always on the welfare of Claire and her baby, Melanie. There hadn't been a chance for her to quiz Melissa on her 'intentions' towards Lachlan, or the nature of their relationship.

'I know. It's not an ideal situation for either of us, but we'll try our best to be good parents.' She hoped that was vague enough that Claire would realise she didn't want to talk about her personal life. Apart from not wanting to jinx what they did have, it wasn't something she was ready to discuss with anyone. Including Lachlan.

They hadn't defined what their relationship was or what expectations they had. Likely because they'd have to face up to the fact that it probably wasn't a good idea. Neither of them was ready to do that when they were enjoying each other so much without all of the agonising over what it meant for them to be together. If they did stop to focus on the repercussions, it might all be over.

There was a commotion from the living room, saving her from having to respond further. The kitchen door opened and Lachlan walked in, sending Melissa's heart racing upon seeing him.

'Hi, bro.' It was Claire who greeted him first.

'Hey, you two. Should my ears be burning?' He frowned, glancing between Melissa and Claire, aware that he'd walked in on a serious discussion.

'I was just telling Melissa you need some baby practice. Could you change Melanie whilst I dish out the hot food?' Claire unloaded her daughter into Lachlan's arms, grabbed the changing bag, and slung it over Melissa's shoulder.

'Your sister doesn't take no for an answer, does she?'

'Generally, she doesn't wait around for an answer. Shall we go upstairs where it's quieter? I don't want an audience.' Clearly not one to hang around for a response either, Lachlan turned and walked out of the kitchen. Since Melissa had all the nappy-changing essentials, she didn't have any choice but to follow. She supposed it would give them some privacy away from his family to talk too.

They walked back through the living room towards the stairs, barely drawing a glance. The novelty of their arrival had seemingly worn off, with everyone's attention now on the table of food. It wasn't a bad thing if it meant she would no longer be under scrutiny from the rest of the family.

Lachlan walked into the pretty pink nursery room and set Melanie down on the waist-high changing table. 'Okay, gorgeous girl, let's get you all cleaned up.'

Melissa took out the baby wipes and nappies and handed them over, watching him get soppy over his baby niece. He moved deftly to take off the wet nappy and clean the baby up, all the while talking in a soft sing-song voice. He was going to make a good dad.

Despite her own experience dealing with babies, she let him do the change. Lachlan looked good with a baby in his arms.

'I hope work wasn't too harrowing for you tonight,' she said, noting he'd been held up. That usually meant there'd been complications.

Lachlan looked at her as though he had no idea what she was talking about.

'The hospital…' she prompted him.

'Oh. No. I wasn't working.'

It was Melissa's turn to be confused. 'But I thought—'

'I was at the hospital, but it wasn't because of work.' The clench of his jaw and the furrow of a frown told her something was wrong.

Melissa's stomach lurched with that feeling of foreboding she'd hoped never to experience again. 'Then why?'

'Let me put this one down in her cot for a sleep. Then we'll talk.'

She wasn't sure she really wanted to know the answer, but neither did she want him to keep anything from her. Surprises in her life tended to be unpleasant, life-changing dramas. Apart from the pregnancy, of course, but she could do without any more plot twists.

Lachlan placed the baby in her cot, waiting until she was settled before walking away, and led Melissa out into the hallway. He closed the door behind him and took a moment before he spoke. Everything in his body language told her he didn't have good news to share with her.

'Lachlan? What is it?' She could barely get the words out past the ball of fear lodged in her throat.

'I—I had the results of my most recent check-up today. I didn't tell you I was going because I didn't want it preying on your mind. But they're not happy with the bloods. The tumour marker tests showed some proteins usually made by testicular cancer cells. I had to have more blood work today. It's probably nothing, but, you know, there's always that worry.'

She did know. Her insides were tied in knots right now despite his attempt to reassure her it was nothing untoward. It was admirable of him to be concerned about her when no doubt he was going through emotional hell himself. Cancer was a tough journey, physically and mentally, and the prospect of facing it twice must've been horrific.

She felt selfish that after her concern for him, her thoughts turned to her own self-preservation, but this was a lot to process. 'So what happens next?'

'I guess I'll find out soon. They won't wait around if they think the cancer's back in case it spreads. Probably a whole battery of tests, scans…at worst, more surgery and chemo.' The more he spoke about it, the more deflated he sounded, and the more Melissa's heart sank.

If the cancer had returned, it most certainly could have spread, and the outcome might not be as favourable as the last time. Not only was he facing months of uncertainty, but there was a possibility he wouldn't survive. At the very least, he would be exhausted, sick, and no longer the Lachlan she knew now. He'd told her himself the cancer had made him reassess his life, and he'd ended his last relationship. One way or another, he was going to leave her. Sticking around, waiting for it to happen, falling for him more every day, was only going to increase her pain when he inevitably did go.

She hated that she was even feeling this way at a time when he would need her most, but she had to think about the baby as well as herself. Whatever happened, he wasn't going to be here to share the parenting, and she knew she couldn't cope with looking after him as well as a child. She wasn't heartless, but she was afraid. Losing Chris had broken her, and losing Lachlan would be even worse when they were about to embark on their family journey. All she could think of was getting out now before the cancer killed them both.

'I'm so sorry, Lachlan.'

'Hey. It's not your fault.' His lopsided smile only made this harder.

'You're going through a lot.' She cleared her throat,

trying to hold herself together. 'I think… I think perhaps we should cool things down between us so you
can focus on your health.'

'It might be nothing, Melissa.'

'And I hope that's true for your sake, but my priority has to be the baby. I think I'd forgotten that in all of
the excitement. You have your family to rally around
you, but I—I just can't do this again.'

'What about the baby?' The look of hurt in his eyes
was unbearable, but the least she owed him was some
reassurance there.

'If you're up to it, you can still be involved with
the baby, but we should end whatever it is we've been
doing. We both have other priorities.' She marvelled
at her ability to sound calm and rational, when inside
she was screaming. It seemed she was doomed to never
have the love she craved from anyone, but she'd rather
be alone than face losing her heart along with Lachlan.
She could only hope that with some space, it wouldn't
hurt as much.

'You're really doing this now?' The accusation in
his voice was justified. They were in the wrong place,
at the worst possible time for her to realise she should
never have got involved with him.

'We can talk over arrangements for the baby later,
but I think I need to go now. There's no point in drag-
ging things out or making things any more awkward
around your family than they already are. I'll make my
excuses and leave. Don't follow me.'

She practically stumbled out of the room, tears already blurring her vision, and her legs barely holding her up. The last thing she saw before she left was Lachlan looking at her as though she'd torn his heart out of his chest with her bare hands.

Melissa didn't know how she was going to survive without him.

CHAPTER ELEVEN

'WE'VE GOT A road traffic accident involving a pregnant woman,' Scot told Lachlan as he climbed into the ambulance.

'Then what are we waiting for?' Every time a mother and child were in danger he was going to think about Melissa and his baby.

Embarking on a relationship with her had been a big commitment for him, one he hadn't taken lightly. The days, and nights, they'd spent together had convinced him that they had a future as a family. He'd thought he'd made a breakthrough, letting go of his hang-ups about being around forever to focus on everything he had in the present. Or everything he'd thought he had. Perhaps he'd got so wrapped up in the idea of having Melissa and the baby permanently in his life, he'd been blinded to the fact that she wasn't as invested. They'd never had a conversation about being a couple, but he'd taken for granted that she'd felt the same way about him as he did about her. Certainly, her actions had made him think that. A mistake which had left him broken-hearted and alone again. When she'd ended things so abruptly at Claire's house that day, he'd felt his whole world collapsing in on the future he'd imagined.

Not only was he staring death in the face again, but the woman he'd imagined being by his side for a long time had cut and run when he'd needed her most. A reminder not to rely on anyone. He could only count on himself, and had done since the day his father left.

However, it had come too late. It didn't matter how much he tried to deny it or wish it was otherwise. He was in love with Melissa. The only thing worse than being dumped at his sister's house and pretending he wasn't devastated in front of his family was not being able to speak to her.

Waiting to find out the results of his tests was going to be as torturous as not being with her, but he understood why she'd had to distance herself. She couldn't risk him not being around for the baby. It wasn't what he wanted either. Perhaps he should back off altogether and let her do the parenting without him in the picture.

After all, it might be something they would both have to get used to.

'Melissa!' Her patient's yell spurred Melissa upstairs with her bag in hand.

From the tone of Tess, her young mother, it was apparent something was wrong. That this wasn't the straightforward birth she'd expected. Nothing could have prepared Melissa for the sight awaiting her upstairs. A trail of blood led from the bathroom into the bedroom. She found the woman who wasn't due for another three weeks on the edge of the bed, her face pure white. A stark contrast to the scarlet stain spreading quickly over her trousers.

'Is this normal?' The terror in the young woman's voice and in her eyes almost broke Melissa. She was pleading with her to say everything was going to be all right, to do something, but Melissa couldn't make the promises she needed to hear.

Sometimes it was necessary to feel the fear and push ahead, hoping for the best outcome. The irony wasn't lost on her that she hadn't been able to do that in her own life.

'Lie on the bed and take deep breaths. I know it's difficult, but I need you to calm down. Deep breaths.' She simulated the action first, encouraging her to follow. The last thing they needed was for the patient's blood pressure to rise. Once she knew Tess was beginning to regulate her breathing, Melissa pulled her phone from her pocket.

'I'm calling an ambulance as a precaution because of the amount of blood you're losing. I'll just be out in the hall if you need me.' Melissa didn't want her to hear the anxiety in her voice as she relayed what was happening to the emergency services. If her patient was haemorrhaging, time was of the essence for mother and child.

'We'll try to get the ambulance to you within the hour,' the despatcher told her, as if this was an everyday occurrence and not a life-or-death situation.

'That's not good enough. I'm not sure we have an hour,' she hissed through gritted teeth, trying to keep her temper, but emphasising how serious the situation was.

'We'll get an ambulance to you as soon as we can.'

It was all Melissa could do not to throw the phone at the wall when she hung up, knowing she was on her own. Tess and the baby's lives were completely in her hands.

'Melissa, is my baby going to die?' Tess was sobbing when she rushed back into the bedroom. The patient was deathly pale and clearly terrified for her baby.

'Not if I can help it. Now I need to take a look and see what's happening.' She washed up and did an examination, checking in on baby too, whose heartbeat was slowing down. She had to move fast.

'Melissa?'

She knew Tess wanted her to say everything was all right, but she couldn't. If this was a placental abruption as she expected, the baby might not survive.

'We need to deliver the baby now. How far apart have the contractions been?'

'Just a couple of minutes.'

'Good.' At least baby was ready to be born, and that should make the delivery easier.

There was a risk of her bleeding out. Colour was draining out of her with every passing moment, and though Melissa had put in a cannula to replace lost fluids, she needed to be in the hospital.

Tess was likely going to need a blood transfusion, and it was lucky she was even still conscious.

'The ambulance is on the way. They'll get you and

baby transferred to the hospital, where we can look after you both better. In the meantime, we just need to get baby safely out. Next time a contraction hits, I want you to push, okay?' At least once the baby arrived, she could concentrate on the mother.

Tess nodded and grasped for her hand. 'Don't let go of me, okay?'

'I'm not going anywhere,' Melissa assured her.

'If anything happens to me, take care of the baby for me.' It was telling of this young woman's situation that she was asking a relative stranger to step in if the worst happened. Given Melissa's current circumstances, it was triggering for her.

Tess hadn't had a choice. The father of the baby abandoned her the moment she'd become pregnant. Melissa had purposely pushed Lachlan out of her life. That action would affect her baby's life, taking away the chance for them to bond with their father. She was capable of doing all of this on her own, but it was the reality of seeing this new mother struggling that made her realise she didn't have to. Deep down, she knew she didn't want to either.

'Nothing's going to happen. You just concentrate on seeing this little one come into the world.'

Tess's face contorted into a mask of pain as another contraction wracked her body.

'I'm going to need you to push, Tess.'

'I'm tired,' she wept.

'I know you are, sweetheart, but we have to get baby

out. I'm going to need you to dig down deep. Your baby needs you to be strong for both of you.'

As her body contracted, Tess gritted her teeth and bore down with a scream.

'That's it. I can see baby's head. Focus on your breathing now for me.' Melissa could tell she was exhausted, her breaths interspersed with sobs, but they were nearly there.

Melissa coached her through the breathing techniques to stop her from pushing, leaving the baby to slither out on its own. She caught it quickly, wrapping it in a towel from the pile sitting at the end of the bed.

She cleaned the baby up, and the sound of it crying was the best thing she could have wished for.

'You have a little girl.' Melissa laid the child on her mother's chest.

Tess looked down at the baby with such undisguised love, Melissa was teary. Hoping she'd feel the same way about her baby too when the time came.

Tess gave a weak smile, barely able to open her eyes. 'A girl.'

'Stay awake for me. The ambulance will be here soon.' Although the bleeding was slowing, Tess needed a transfusion. She had to get to the hospital, and fast.

'Tess?' The new mother was beginning to lose consciousness. Melissa checked her pulse and found it was weakening.

This little girl needed her mother.

The weight off her chest when she heard the ambulance in the distance was short-lived. That pressure pushed down even stronger when she realised Tess was unconscious and had stopped breathing.

Melissa set the baby down in the crib at the side of the bed and started CPR on her mother. Arms out straight, fingers interlocked, she began pumping down on Tess's chest, counting out every compression. Then she stopped and looked for signs of life before continuing as long as her body would allow, her arms beginning to shake from the effort.

'One, two, three…' She kept going, stopping occasionally to listen to the heart, until eventually she was sure she detected a faint heartbeat.

Melissa put her ear to Tess's mouth and felt a little puff of air with the shallow breaths she was managing to take again.

She moved her into the recovery position and waited for help to arrive. Too tired to celebrate the rewards of her efforts, and too afraid in case it hadn't been enough after all.

'Hello?' a voice called from downstairs. Melissa ran out of the room to direct the paramedics upstairs as quickly as possible.

She relayed the seriousness of the situation as they rushed up the stairs, adding, 'She's lost a lot of blood.' As if they wouldn't see that for themselves.

Part of her wished Lachlan would be one of the crew in attendance to give her the sense of comfort and support she desperately needed. Disappointment settled in when he didn't appear.

The paramedics calmly set about preparing Tess for

transporting, leaving Melissa to gather up the baby and hold her to her chest.

'Mummy's going to be all right,' she soothed, knowing she wouldn't be able to hold back the emotion much longer.

Especially when she thought of everything that could go wrong in her own pregnancy. Having to go through it by herself like Tess, when Lachlan should be with her. She didn't want to even think of the possibility of leaving her baby on their own when the father wanted to be there for both of them.

If only she could move past the fear, she might still be able to keep him in her life. To have that family they both wanted.

Melissa wondered if she should get a pet to keep her company. Someone to talk to at the end of a difficult shift like last night's, even if it couldn't talk back. Despite living on her own for over a year and a half after Chris died, these weeks without Lachlan in her life had made her feel lonelier than ever. It had been nice to unwind with someone at the end of the day who understood the nature of her job, to swap stories with him, and simply have him to come home to. The house seemed bigger, emptier, without him filling her bed or making her cups of tea on demand. She missed him.

The nights were interminable at times. Never mind the physical side effects of the pregnancy keeping her awake—she also had thoughts of Lachlan swirling around her head. About the past they'd shared, and the future they could have had if things had been different. If there wasn't the possibility of him getting sick. If she'd been braver...

She'd given up trying to have an early night, regardless of how weary she was. She sat up late watching trash TV into the early hours in the hope that she'd doze off and get some sort of sleep. Although tonight was proving particularly difficult with her back hurting, and she kept getting leg cramps. It was going to be fun when she really started to put on the extra weight and the baby started kicking her insides like a football. She definitely would have more sympathy with her pregnant ladies in future. All the textbooks and study hadn't taught her as much about what pregnancy entailed as having her own baby.

Lachlan sent her a text message every day just to make sure everything was okay, but it was difficult getting used to not having him in her life.

Lydia had been very good about checking in with her, but even if she was with her twenty-four hours a day, it wouldn't fill the void Lachlan had left in her life.

At least she had her work to focus on until the baby arrived.

'Congratulations again,' she told the couple sitting anxiously before her after confirming their pregnancy with positive test results.

Despite their want for a family, there wasn't even a hint of a smile in their reaction to the news, only more hand-holding and worried expressions.

'I'm afraid to get excited about it just yet,' Abby confessed. 'You know, after last time...'

The young woman had experienced an early miscarriage over a year ago and was understandably anxious, but there was nothing in her medical history to suggest the same thing would happen again. She didn't have any underlying conditions which would have contributed to her losing the baby. It was just one of those unfortunate things.

'I know you're worried, but there's absolutely no reason to think this won't be a viable pregnancy. Losing a baby is a painful, tragic thing, but you didn't do anything to cause that. Sometimes it just happens. Please don't let it spoil this pregnancy for you.'

'I'm just worried about what might happen. I'm afraid to look too far ahead in case we're devastated all over again.' Abby squeezed her husband's hand a little tighter, her grief for the baby she lost and fears for the one she was carrying evident.

'I promise we'll keep a close eye on you. Don't let what's happened in the past spoil your happiness. Enjoy every second.' The irony of her words wasn't lost on Melissa. She was equally guilty of letting her fears ruin what could have been the best thing to happen to her.

As the expectant couple thanked her for her reassurance and left with smiles on their faces, Melissa's thoughts were of her own loss. Of everything she'd thrown away with Lachlan because of her fears. She was equally guilty of letting the past destroy something good. Perhaps even worse than that, she was letting Lachlan go through potentially the most difficult time of his life alone.

Okay, so he had his family around, but the rejection he must've felt when she walked out of his life would've been crushing. Melissa winced, knowing all too well how that sense of abandonment impacted every area of life. She'd been so self-involved she hadn't considered how Lachlan would cope with everything on his own. The same sort of behaviour she'd held against her parents for years. If she couldn't forgive them, how could she expect Lachlan to forgive her?

And she realised, likely too late, that that was what she wanted. Forgiveness. Lachlan. A family.

She was in love with him, and that's what she'd been running from, afraid to face it in case she lost him. However, the prospect of not having him in her life at all seemed worse than making the most of whatever time they could have together. They could be a family, even for a short while, and she hoped it wasn't too late to try.

She loved him and wanted to be there for him, if only he'd still let her.

Lachlan came out of the consultant's office stunned by the news of his latest results. He was in a kind of limbo, not knowing where to go from here now that he didn't have Melissa to turn to.

They should've been planning for the baby's arrival. Any other father-to-be would be painting a nursery and building furniture, but he'd been left on the outside, not sure if he would even have a part in his child's life.

He didn't know whether it would've changed things if he'd told her he loved her. Probably not, when it had been too much even for him to deal with. This time apart hadn't eased the situation for him. It had only served to prove the depth of his feelings for her. His sense of loss was very real. Not only because Melissa was no longer in his life, but his whole future, the family he'd realised he wanted after all, was gone with her.

He might never have another chance to have a child. Not that he would want one with anyone else anyway. She'd been the only person who'd managed to make him take that risk. Now he was grieving for the loss of it all.

So much so, he even imagined he could see her now walking towards him. Probably because all he wanted was a hug from her and a promise that everything was going to be okay. Too much to ask for, given the circumstances, but since it was his hallucination, he figured he could wish for the world.

Then suddenly she flung her arms around him, and he swore he could feel her warmth, smell her sweet perfume, and hear her voice in his ear.

'Claire told me you'd be here. I'm so sorry, Lachlan.' Melissa squeezed him hard enough he had to believe she was real, if only to tell her to let go.

'I can't...breathe,' he said, though he'd never been so happy to almost suffocate.

'Sorry.' She let go and took a step back.

'You're really here.' He couldn't believe his eyes, but his slightly bruised ribs would testify to the fact she wasn't a figment of his imagination after all.

'I am. I hope that's okay. I know I'm probably the last person you want to see right now.'

That simply wasn't true. She was the only person he'd wanted to see, but he didn't want to get too carried away when she'd made it clear the last time he'd seen her that she no longer wanted to be part of his life.

'Why are you here?' He moved out of the main corridor to a quieter area so they could talk in private.

'I'm sorry for how I left things. I've had time to think everything over, and I know I reacted badly. I should have been there to support you. Is it too late to do that now?'

Lachlan didn't know what had prompted this sudden act of conscience, and though he was grateful to see her, he didn't want her to be here simply out of guilt. It occurred to him that because of Claire, she was aware he was here to discuss the results of his cancer tests. He didn't want the outcome of those to influence her reasons for coming to see him.

'What do you want, Melissa? You made it clear that you no longer wanted to be involved with me on a personal level. What's changed?' He'd already been let down by her once, and he needed to know he'd be able to count on her in the future if the worst did happen. More than that, he needed to know she felt the same way about him as he did about her, or else he was always going to be the one to get hurt.

She hung her head, looking thoroughly ashamed. 'I panicked. When you said the cancer might be back, I thought of the impact that losing you would have on me and stupidly believed that if I backed away now, it would somehow lessen the pain. It was selfish of me to think that way.'

'So how do you feel now?' His heart was beating fast as he fought to control the hope that there could still be a chance for them. As much as he still wanted to be with her, he had to be sure of her motives and commitment. It wouldn't be fair on him or the baby if she decided again somewhere down the line that she didn't want him to be involved in their lives. As he'd said from the start, he wanted to be a proper father, and he had to value that over his own wants. If Melissa was only here because she felt sorry for him, they weren't going to be able to sustain anything long-term.

Melissa swallowed hard. 'I love you, Lachlan. That's why I was so afraid of losing you. But these past days without you have shown me that I still want you in my life for as long as I have you. I'll support you through your treatment, and we'll both be there for our baby as long as we can. That's all we can do, and more than I probably deserve.'

It meant a lot for him to hear her say that now, when the future seemed so uncertain and terrifying. She loved him. She wanted to be with him. And he knew how much that cost her to admit. Melissa was opening her heart to him, leaving herself vulnerable when there was a chance he could reject her. After everything she'd gone through with her parents and Chris, he knew this couldn't have been easy for her, and she wouldn't have said these things unless she meant them. Now it was down to him to be equally as brave. Even if it meant risking his heart again too.

'You deserve happiness, Melissa. Come to think of it, so do I.' He reached out and pulled her back into his arms, hugging her close to his chest, never wanting to let her go. There was no point in letting pride, fear, or ill health steal away what joy they had.

Melissa bunched his shirt in her fist. 'I just want us to be together. I'm sorry I was too scared to tell you that in the first place. But I'll be by your side for as long as you want me.'

'Hopefully, that's going to be for a long time to come.'

Melissa pried herself away from his chest to look up at him. For once he had some good news to share. He hoped it wouldn't change things between them except for the better.

'My test results were clear. It was a lot of worry over nothing. The cancer hasn't come back after all.'

He saw the tears welling in Melissa's eyes right before she buried her head in his chest again.

'I'm so happy for you, Lachlan.'

'That's not to say it won't ever return, but we'll cross that bridge if we come to it.'

'Together.'

That one word cemented their future. A promise and a commitment to each other and their baby. There would be no more looking back, only forward. To their life as a family.

Yes, he'd been guilty of holding back, of bottling his feelings. But losing her had made him see just how damned important she was to him. Melissa had never just been a casual lover, or someone he'd got pregnant by accident. She was the woman he loved. Someone he wanted to spend the rest of his life with. However long that would be. He would take a few years with her over a lifetime without her. If she'd have him.

Lachlan had spent his whole life doing the right thing, mindful of other people's feelings, and it was time to go for what he wanted. That was Melissa. The baby. A family.

Melissa reached out a hand and stroked Lachlan's cheek. 'I love you, Lachlan. You're here, now. That's all that matters. I can guarantee our baby would rather have you around for as long as possible than not at all. As would I. Besides, you're young, strong and incredibly handsome, and I will challenge cancer to a fight over you every day of the week. Please stay. Please love me.'

She sounded desperate, but if there was any chance they could be together, she was grabbing it and not letting go. If he loved her and wanted to be with her, then she was going to make sure they made this work. She wasn't losing anyone else she loved.

'I love you, Melissa. I think I always have, and I know I always will. We might have skipped straight from meeting into starting a family, but I'd like the chance to have that whole bit in between too. I want to be with you.'

'Honestly?'

'I honestly, truly, want to be with you. It's all I want.' He leaned down and sealed his admission of love for her with a kiss.

Melissa would be an idiot to say no now when he was giving her everything she ever wanted.

EPILOGUE

'WELL, MY PARENTS love you,' Melissa said as she manoeuvred herself into bed. At eight months pregnant, it wasn't becoming any easier. Nor was sleeping when she couldn't get comfortable at all. She was looking forward to having control over her body again almost as much as meeting their baby.

'Naturally. Old Jilly, Angus, and I get on like a house on fire. That's why they wanted to meet me so badly,' Lachlan teased, climbing in beside her.

He'd encouraged her to reach out to her parents and try to reconnect. After some soul-searching, she'd come to the conclusion that they deserved a second chance too, and thankfully they'd been overjoyed to hear from her. Apparently, they hadn't wanted to interfere in her life since they'd parted on bad terms, but loved her nonetheless. For the past few months, they'd been speaking a lot, clearing the air, and chatting over video calls. That was how they'd got to know Lachlan. She was pretty sure they'd come over as much to meet him as the baby. They were staying in the UK for the next couple of months until she gave birth, and hopefully beyond. There was even talk of moving back so they could see their grandchild, and Melissa, on a regular basis.

'You're so modest.' She cuddled into him as close as her huge bump would allow. There was nothing better at the end of the day than to be in his arms, feeling his love for her. In a few weeks' time, there would be an addition to their nightly routine, and she thought her heart would burst at the happiness coming into her life.

When Chris had died, she'd thought the idea of having a family was over forever. Thanks to Lachlan, not only was she going to have one of her own, but she had her parents here to be part of it. His recent oncology check-up had also been positive, giving him the all-clear. Everything was looking bright for the future.

'Hey, if I'd been shy, we might never have got together.'

Melissa nudged him with an elbow. 'Um… I think you'll find I was the one who walked over to you first.'

'Only because I'd been staring at you, and it was obvious I was interested. You knew it was safe to approach.'

'Well, I'm happy I did.' She tilted her face up to kiss him, glad she'd had the courage to finally move on from Chris, or else she'd still be on her own.

'Best day of my life was meeting you.' Lachlan dipped his head and kissed her again. 'Marry me?'

'What?' Melissa wrenched her mouth away from his, unsure she was hearing him right.

He twisted his body around so she could see his face.

'I mean it. Marry me. There's still time before the baby comes to make it official. We can be a proper family.'

Melissa eyed him with some suspicion. Though he showed her and told her he loved her every day, she still needed reassurance that he wanted to do this for the right reasons. Because there was nothing she wanted more than to spend the rest of her life with this man.

'And before you start questioning my motives, I'm asking because I love you. I don't want to waste another moment without you. I want nothing more than to make our family complete, and I'll spend my life proving to you how much I love you. Melissa Moran, will you marry me?'

'Yes, Lachlan McNairn. I would love to be your wife.'

Melissa looked into the eyes of the man she loved, the father of her unborn baby, and knew without doubt he was committed to her, body and soul. She was no longer alone.

* * * * *

WINNING OVER THE OFF-LIMITS DOCTOR

ANNIE CLAYDON

MILLS & BOON

CHAPTER ONE

FRIDAY EVENING. IT had been a long week in the paediatric
A&E department, and the only thing that stood between Dr
Mattie Graeme and the weekend was a visit to the medical
supplies stockroom.

'Mattie, do you have a moment?'

Mattie winced. She'd thought too soon and now two
things stood between her and the weekend. She turned to
find Dr Gareth Lewis, the head of A&E services, standing
behind her.

'I was about to go and check the stockroom. I think we
may be running low on a few things.' Mattie shrugged, not
wishing to get anyone into trouble. 'Maybe they're there
and I just couldn't find them earlier on...'

'I'm aware. I'm on my way there myself to see what's
going on.'

That was one of the reasons that Gareth was so respected
here. He kept his ear to the ground and addressed situations
before they turned into problems.

'What do you need from me, then, Gareth?'

'I've just had a call from orthopaedics. They've recruited
a new consultant for their trauma team who specialises in
paediatrics. Since he'll be working closely with this department, I mentioned a guided tour...'

Mattie grinned. 'And you'd like me to do the honours?'

'Would you mind?' Gareth glanced at his watch. 'It'll only take ten minutes, just a quick hello and looking forward to working with you, but I really need to get to grips with the medical supplies situation before the weekend.'

'My pleasure…' Mattie turned as Gareth's attention focussed over her shoulder onto a man who was making his way towards the admin station. 'That's him?'

Her surprise added an unfortunate squeak to the question. He looked like a movie star doctor who'd somehow got lost and ended up in a real hospital, where dazzling smiles and sex appeal weren't part of the job.

'Yep. You'll take it from here…?' Gareth was clearly concerned about the medical supplies situation and itching to get to grips with it.

'I've got it.' Mattie wasn't sure that she had, but her feet seemed to have made the decision for her, taking her on a trajectory that led straight towards Dr Amazing, cutting him off before he had a chance to reach the admin desk.

'Hi, I'm Mattie Graeme. Paediatric A&E. You're…um…' She probably should have thought to ask Gareth his name. '…the new doctor from orthopaedics?'

'Llwyd Morgan.' His voice was deep, with the almost musical lilt of a Welsh accent. 'I'm here to see Dr Gareth Lewis.'

'Gareth's busy with our medical supplies situation at the moment, and he asked me to show you around.' Finding yourself of secondary importance to a stockroom wasn't the most resounding welcome. 'Sorry…'

The apology came automatically, but when she looked up at him, Mattie really wasn't sorry at all. His smile was captivating.

'Whatever it takes to keep things running smoothly is

always most important. I'm looking forward to working as part of his team.'

'He's a good boss. Very supportive.' Mattie searched for a question that implied a casual interest, but didn't involve the colour of his eyes. 'You're new to Cartref Bay?'

'No, I was born here. Coming home to visit didn't include checking the hospital out, though, so this is new territory for me. I've been working in London for the last ten years.'

The Cartref Bay Hospital stood on a hill overlooking the bay and had replaced an older building, which catered to the needs of the villages around Cartref Bay. The new hospital still provided community care and in addition was a centre of excellence for a wider area of west Wales. 'You must remember the old cottage hospital, then. That was before my time.'

'Yeah. Largely in connection with the usual childhood accidents. How long have you been here?'

'Three years. Before that I was working in Sheffield.' Three years in one place was a record for Mattie, and mapping out the circuitous route that had led her here smacked of aimlessness.

'But you're from London?' His green eyes flashed with interest. 'Your accent…'

'Yes, I'm originally from London.'

It seemed like a long time ago, now. She'd packed her bags and her dad had driven her to university, on the first leg of a journey that had taken her through England and Scotland, and now to Wales. Mattie had always chosen the best work opportunities, because it didn't do to admit that what really kept her on the move was her own inability to settle in one place.

'Shall we start with the imaging suite? We have dedicated X-ray and CT scanning facilities here in A&E, which means we can work alongside radiographers to provide quick and accurate diagnoses...'

That sounded more like it. As if Llwyd's sand-blond hair, his broad shoulders and his green eyes were irrelevant details. As if the solid, dependable side of her nature had no careless alter ego.

Then Llwyd went and spoiled it all by smiling again. Mattie could very easily throw caution to the winds for that smile.

Doggedly, she introduced him to Irene, who sat at the admin desk and could invariably answer any nonmedical question it was possible to think of. His face lit up when she showed him one of the empty trauma rooms, and Mattie took her time in pointing out the technology available. When she led him into one of the unoccupied treatment rooms, he was similarly impressed.

'This is great.' He looked around at the spacious area, which boasted up-to-the-minute equipment and brightly coloured, comfortable seating.

'We can change the light levels...' Mattie flipped the dimmer switch, then quickly returned the light level back up to normal as shadows began to caress his face. 'And we have distraction packs and toys, along with a set of flip books, which visually explain most of the more common procedures, such as X-rays. They're available to every child, and they're often particularly helpful to autistic children.'

Mattie opened the door of a well-stacked cupboard in the corner of the room, and Llwyd moved a little closer, peering over her shoulder. Her breath caught suddenly in her throat, and she moved back a bit so he could see the range of resources available.

It was only then that she noticed his hands. The movement of Llwyd's right hand was deft and precise, but he wore a flesh-coloured fingerless support glove on his left hand, and the thumb and first two fingers were curled towards his palm. Mattie caught herself wondering...

Wanting to know all about him didn't make it okay to ask; if Llwyd wanted to mention it, he would. And right now, his whole attention was on the contents of the cupboard.

'You have stickers.' He grinned, pulling a box from its shelf, tucking it between his left wrist and his body so that he could open it and draw out one of the sheets inside.

'Yes, they're really popular and we have a range of them for various elements of the hospital experience. The kids like collecting them as they go.'

He chuckled. 'They're great, really nicely designed. Can I have one?'

Mattie smiled up at him, as she pulled an *I Visited A&E* sticker from its backing paper and tacked it onto his shirt. 'See what I mean? No one can resist a sticker.'

She stepped back, slipping her hands into her pockets, and found a sparkly pen that she'd used to draw stars for a little girl and forgotten to put back. She dropped it into a large box of pens in the cupboard and Llwyd grinned.

'Tough to resist sparkly pens, too.'

Sparkly pens and green eyes. 'Yes. Sparkly pens are my particular nemesis.'

Llwyd chuckled. 'Would it be okay if I took a set of these resources home with me, just to look at over the weekend? I'll bring it all back on Monday. I just want to go through what's available more carefully.'

'Sounds good to me. We have plenty of them. You didn't have anything like this where you were working before?'

'Yes, we did, but I've been working on the wards for the last nine months, so it was more the nursing staff's territory.' He raised his left hand, flexing it, and Mattie saw that he had very limited movement in his thumb and first two fingers. 'This happened eighteen months ago, and before that I was an orthopaedic surgeon, working with a trauma team. I switched to orthopaedic consultant, which is much the same set of medical skills, but I'm still working on the people skills.'

His people skills seemed just fine to her. The things that appealed so much to her impulsive instincts were ticking boxes with the more responsible side of her nature, too. His smile, his ability to listen and connect. Mattie could spend her time making bets with herself about how good a lover he'd be, or she could take a more rational approach and decide that he had all the skills necessary to calm a screaming child so that he could give them the medical treatment they needed. That was entirely up to her...

She smiled up at him. 'You'll need a bag. Irene usually keeps a few at the admin desk. I'll go and fetch one for you...'

Selecting a green cloth bag, that matched his eyes, was just a matter of choosing the one with longer straps that he could hook over his shoulder to leave his hands free. And raiding the cupboard to make sure he had everything was simply a case of covering all the bases.

'That's great. I really appreciate it. Your shift must have ended a while ago...' He made that seem like something he regretted, which prompted a jolt of similar regret in Mattie's chest. The much-anticipated weekend suddenly vanished down a rabbit hole of wanting Llwyd's company for just a little while longer.

'I saved the best for last. You want to see the Sensory Room?'

The look on his face told her that he did. 'I don't want to keep you...'

'It's of no interest?'

Llwyd laughed. 'I didn't say that.'

'I'll see if it's free.'

Despite the early-evening bustle in the department, the room *was* free, and Mattie led Llwyd inside, shutting the door behind them. Ignoring the mood created by coloured lights, and the swirl of stars and planets that were projected onto the ceiling, she plumped herself down on one of the squishy chairs, grabbing the control panel.

'We have fibre optic lighting, and the bubble tubes in the corner change colour when you touch them. There are several different programmes for the main lights...' She switched briskly from planets to bubbles and then on through the different light schemas.

None of it worked. She could see the same sense of wonder on Llwyd's face that everyone had when they saw the room for the first time. He walked over to the bubble tubes, reaching out to touch them.

'This is amazing. Don't you have kids in here all the time?'

'We'd love to, but we have to keep it for the children who need it the most. There's a lot of work being done on the benefit of extending this kind of thing throughout the whole department and we'd like to do that. There are options like sensory trolleys that can be moved around and used in any of the treatment rooms...'

For once, Llwyd wasn't listening. His right hand massaged his left thumb, straightening it, before he reached out to touch the bubble tube, watching as different colours scattered from his injured fingers. Mattie couldn't help smiling.

'Sorry...you were saying?' He turned suddenly and Mattie shrugged.

'Just that everyone can do with a sensory room from time

to time.' Despite all of his assurance, the sense that he was capable of meeting any situation head-on, she'd caught a brief glimpse of quickly hidden vulnerability.

'And the quantifiable benefits...' He thought for a moment. 'It must allow you to assess and provide medical treatment more quickly when a child isn't distressed. And if they're not traumatised by their visit to the hospital, then they feel much more positive about returning.'

Mattie nodded.

'This has always been here?'

'We raised the money for it. We had loads of volunteers and everyone chose their own challenge. We had an elderly lady who knitted thirty Christmas pudding hats one Christmas.'

Llwyd chuckled. 'You have one?'

'I do, as a matter of fact. It kept my ears warm for my challenge. I cycle to work so my five hundred miles didn't take me too long.'

'You cycle up the hill to the hospital every morning?'

Mattie laughed. 'The first hundred times were the worst. And going home's a piece of cake. I just freewheel down the hill and then take the cycle lane that runs around the bay...'

Stop. Now. No one here knew exactly where Mattie lived, and everyone assumed that when she said 'home' she was referring to bricks and mortar. Living in a converted bus, parked on a sun-drenched but frequently windy hillside, was something that suited Mattie but it sounded horrendously impractical. That in itself would be enough to fuel worried looks from her mum and dad, who valued stability and responsibility. They'd adopted her when she was just a baby and given her everything. Mattie loved them and if she couldn't tell them about her home, for fear of disappointing them, it was wrong to tell anyone else.

And then there was the boat… Another unstable thing that had been rocking gently at its moorings for the past year, ever since Mattie's biological father had turned up and then promptly disappeared again, leaving behind the lavish and wildly impractical present. If Mattie approached the question rationally, then selling the boat would be the obvious next step, particularly since she'd never had any interest in boats and had no way of actually using the craft.

But even though her biological father had never shown much interest in her, the lure of the idea that he'd never forgotten her was too strong, and Mattie couldn't bring herself to let go of his gift. Something so dedicated to movement was an unlikely kind of shackle, but increasingly it felt like something that tied her to Cartref Bay…

Her mind was wandering now, and perhaps the Sensory Room was getting to her, too. Mattie got to her feet, deciding that Llwyd had seen enough and it was time to move on. The combination of calming lights, a handsome guy whose gaze was capable of melting all her defences, and a rapidly approaching weekend was more than any woman could be expected to dismiss without a struggle.

'Are you going down to Y Llong?' he asked as he closed the door of the Sensory Room behind them. 'The Ship…'

That was one Welsh translation that Mattie *did* know, largely because the large sign outside gave both the Welsh and English versions of the name. The Ship Pub, which stood by the harbour at the centre of the bay, was a regular end-of-the-week haunt for hospital staff, and no doubt someone had mentioned to Llwyd that it was the best place for new staff to get to know everyone.

'I might pop in. It's on my way…' Suddenly, Friday evening drinks sounded a lot more attractive than usual.

'Care to walk down there with me, and let me buy you a drink?'

Mattie swallowed hard. Something about the warmth in his eyes made it easy to mistake that for an admission that he wanted her company. Or she could take the more rational approach and recognise that it was an obvious way to meet new colleagues.

'I need to get changed…' Her hand drifted to the hem of her scrubs top, just in case there was any question that she might be wanting to dress up for an entirely work-related rendezvous.

'I'll fetch my bag from my locker and meet you in reception…'

Outside, Llwyd was just as challenging as he was inside. Perhaps more so. His grey sweater and the small backpack slung over one shoulder smacked of the weekend, where time spent with someone was a matter of choice. Evening sun and a stiff breeze ruffling his hair, made him look even more deliciously outdoorsy.

'Any more questions?' Mattie asked as they walked together along the footpath that ran alongside the cycle track, Mattie pushing her bike.

'Only about a thousand. I'm reckoning on finding most of them out as I go.'

'It's a two-mile walk. Feel free to chip away at that total…' She grinned up at him and he laughed.

The hill that led down from the hospital had always been a cooling-off period for Mattie. Time to let the challenges of the day go. It seemed that Llwyd was working on the same principle, now a part of ruggedly beautiful landscape that surrounded them, and living only for the moment. As they talked, it seemed suddenly obvious that the colours of the open air should be reflected in his moss-green eyes, golden skin and sand-blond hair.

Two miles could teach you a lot about a guy, particularly if neither of you were walking too fast. Llwyd had grown up on the south side of the bay, and from their vantage point Mattie could see the small cluster of houses that he indicated. His first steps had been taken on a boat, and then he'd learned to balance on dry land, spending most of his time on one of the small beaches that were dotted around the mouth of the cove, or in his father's boatyard.

He'd gone to London to train as a doctor, and his soft Welsh accent was peppered with a few rhythms of the city. Llwyd left out the *hows* and *whys* relating to the injury to his left hand, but it had clearly played a big part in his decision to come home.

'Do you miss surgery?' Mattie could ask that, at least.

He laughed. 'Sometimes. Quite often at first, and the hospital where I was working bent over backwards to find ways I might continue surgical work. In the end it was my own choice not to. I realised what I'd been missing all these years and that kids can be more fun and a great deal more challenging when they're awake.'

'That's why I like working in paediatrics. Kids can be refreshingly unfiltered.'

He laughed, nodding. Instinct told her that Llwyd was holding things back, the same as she was. But here in the sunshine, she could forget all about those unknowns in favour of the quiet pleasure of just walking beside him.

CHAPTER TWO

LLWYD HAD ALREADY lost two of the things that were most important in his life—three if you counted the feeling that he'd taken for granted, that the world was largely a place of safety.

It was more than a year since he'd been mugged, in the hospital car park in London. It had taken a while to realise that his career as a surgeon was at an end, but the alternative had become surprisingly fulfilling. It had been more difficult to come to terms with the loss when his partner had walked out on him, but he'd accepted that, too. Maybe the scars and the disability, the nightmares, *did* make him a different person, as Hannah had claimed.

Coming home had seemed so obvious he'd hardly even thought about it. He'd started from here, and he knew that it was the place he could start again. A little differently, maybe, but home was solid ground when everywhere else seemed to be shifting under him.

He'd taken a month off in between jobs and steadied himself. And then Mattie had knocked him off balance again, in the most unexpected way.

She was clearly efficient and organised, and everything she did showed a commitment to her patients. But there was more—a quiet determination to do things her own way. A large proportion of his thousand questions—maybe as many as nine hundred and ninety of them—were things he wanted to ask Mattie.

He watched as she wheeled her bicycle over to the rack in the car park behind the pub. The bike had come as no particular surprise, a lighter version of a Dutch-style bike that had the benefit of gears to help her up the Welsh hills. Light turquoise, with a grocery basket at the front and a rack at the back, it wasn't going to outrun any of the racing bikes that were chained up in the car park, but he could imagine Mattie, in her Christmas pudding hat, clocking up the miles on the cycle tracks that ran around the bay.

The thought made him smile, and he turned away before Mattie noticed that he was watching her. From the first moment he'd met her he'd found it difficult not to stare. She was small—slight even—moving with a controlled grace that gave the impression she was dancing through life. Her short curls had exactly the same deep shine and colour as a horse chestnut, fresh out of its protective shell on an autumn day, and her dark blue eyes reminded Llwyd of the sea.

He wasn't ready for any of that just yet. Hannah had judged him irrevocably broken, and her verdict hung around his shoulders still, a weight that he couldn't put down, even if he had learned to carry it.

But a drink after work...that didn't cross any of the boundaries he'd set for himself. Llwyd entered the crowded pub by the back door, squeezing his way towards the bar and then turning to see Mattie in the doorway, looking around for him.

'What would you like?'

She didn't hear him above the din and plunged into the crowd, reappearing next to him and then stumbling forward as someone pushed her from behind. He felt her hand on his arm and automatically, protectively, drew her close.

'Oh! Bit crowded in here tonight...' She grinned up at him.

Llwyd nodded, ignoring the soft scent of her hair, which was currently trashing every one of his boundaries. 'What would you like?'

'Umm...' He felt her move against him as she turned to inspect the labels on the beer pumps and stepped back a little so that she could slide into the space between him and the bar. Mattie could take her time to answer. He felt that he had all that he wanted, right here, right now.

A smiling barmaid interrupted his reverie, and when he ordered a bottle of local brew, Mattie decided on the same. He handed a banknote over the bar and Mattie grabbed the bottles and glasses while Llwyd fiddled awkwardly with his change. She pushed her way through the press of people, heading for the main doors of the pub, which faced the bay.

'Phew! Busy this evening.' Mattie shook her head as the wind tugged at her curls, looking around at the groups of people who'd had the same idea as they had and spilled out onto the cobblestones that lined the quayside. 'Perhaps we'll start here. I can introduce you to a few people inside when it's thinned out a bit and we can hear ourselves speak...'

She was clearly on a mission, but Llwyd wasn't fully on board with that any more. The thousand questions that he'd said could wait were tugging at him, like a beckoning sea breeze. 'I guess... Have we covered everything already? Since we'll be working together...'

She smiled suddenly. Maybe Mattie wasn't quite done with him, either. 'Not even close, I'd say...'

There was one empty bench in the row that lined the top of the sea wall, and Mattie made a beeline for it, sitting down before anyone else could claim it. She set their drinks down on the seat between them, and Llwyd picked up one of the bottles, taking a swig from it. Mattie picked up a glass, filling it and then leaning back to sip her drink.

'This doesn't get old, does it?' She nodded towards the bay, curving on each side of them. 'Or perhaps you're used to it, and you don't notice it so much?'

'I'm still seeing new things about it. My father's lived here all his life, and any time he's asked he'll always say he's never seen the bay look quite the same as it did this morning.' Llwyd was beginning to wonder whether Mattie was in that same category. Things of beauty always seemed to offer something more, every time you looked.

Mattie nodded, clearly turning the idea over in her head as she looked out to sea.

Living in the moment seemed to suit Llwyd, and tonight it suited Mattie, too. Their conversation wandered through best cinemas they'd ever visited to best treatment strategies for fractures. Places in London that they both knew. Could Llwyd get his tongue around the London glottal stop, which softened her double Ts? And would it be better if Mattie didn't even try to reproduce the Welsh pronunciation of a double L?

'Voiceless alveolar fricative. At least I know what it's called now.' Since Llwyd's name involved a double L, Mattie had given it her best efforts.

'You're doing just fine. I'm impressed. Another year or so and you'd be able to fool a native Welsh speaker.'

In another year or so it most probably wouldn't matter, because she could be anywhere. But tonight that didn't seem to matter, because clocks and calendars had mysteriously stopped counting. The breeze that blew in from the sea was cooler now and made her shiver, reminding her that she should probably be making her way home. She reached for her jacket and put it on.

'It's been great talking with you, Llwyd...' He chuckled and gave her latest attempt at the double L a nod of approval. Now was the moment to get to her feet and go, but every time Mattie tried to reach for a goodbye, it drifted gently from her grasp, tangling with all of this evening's other moments, which seemed to hover in the air between them.

'Which way are you going?' Llwyd looked at his watch, clearly more practised in regaining a hold on the passage of time. 'It's getting late, I'll walk with you.'

It was a straightforward question, and answering it shouldn't be this difficult. 'Thanks, but it's okay. It's not far and the roads are all well lit...'

He grinned suddenly. 'Indulge me?'

Unfair question. Or maybe it was the intoxicating nature of his grin that was unfair. Who wouldn't want to find out every last one of his desires and indulge them? Mattie considered the alternatives. Her bus was parked on the other side of the bay, and the marina where her boat was moored was just a ten-minute walk. It occurred to her that spending time on a boat at the weekend might seem an obvious decision to Llwyd, and barely even open to question.

'That would be nice. I'll just go and get my bike...'

He nodded, shouldering his backpack and picking up the two empty glasses that sat on the bench. 'I'll return these. See you back here.'

The bench still stood empty as she wheeled her bike back towards it. Maybe it would be best to run now...

But she didn't want to run. Boats were a way of life here, and Llwyd didn't need to know the details of the complicated family situation, which made Mattie's boat a contentious issue.

The evening that had judged it perfectly okay for her to own a boat went ahead and opened up a second set of possibilities. If Llwyd had taken his first steps on a boat, then surely he wouldn't be so clumsy as Mattie was whenever she set foot on board. Maybe he knew how to tackle the intricacies of a more intimate kind of encounter...

She heard his voice behind her and jumped to her feet, her thoughts still snarled in the practicalities of making love on a moving object. It was all conjecture, anyway, because Mattie wasn't going to ask him in for coffee. That would be the kind of impetuous move that would be very difficult to explain away to herself when she had to face him again next week.

'Ready?'

'Yes.' Mattie waved her hand to indicate the direction they were going in. 'I'm going to the marina.'

'You live on a boat?' He grinned suddenly. His obvious approval of a choice that would make her mum and dad shudder with thinly veiled disapproval made Mattie shiver with pleasure.

'No, I don't live on it. I come down here at weekends, that's all. I'll be able to get up early tomorrow morning...' Maybe do a little cleaning. She hadn't come down here for a couple of weeks, and boats seemed to attract no end of splashes and peculiar stains...

'I always think that's the best time to go out. First thing in the morning, so you can watch the sun rise at sea.'

Probably. That sounded like something she'd enjoy, if she was capable of steering the boat out of the marina. If Llwyd had no difficulty in approving of the ownership of a boat, maybe not using it would be more difficult for him to understand.

She nodded, quickening her pace a little, and he fell into step with her. When they reached the narrow path that led down to the curved steel gates of the marina, Llwyd followed her, clearly wanting to make sure that she made it inside safely.

The security light flipped on and Mattie waved to the shadowy figure in the control cabin, receiving a wave in return.

'Good security here.' Llwyd clearly approved of that, as well. Maybe she should coax him down to London and introduce him to her mum and dad.

Then she went and spoiled it all, with the rashest question of them all. 'Would you like to come in? For... I'd offer you grog and hard tack but I'm afraid I only have coffee.'

He chuckled. 'I'd love to. But I need to get an early night tonight. I look after my nephew at the weekends.'

'How old is he?' Now Mattie was just playing for time. Putting off the moment when she'd see Llwyd walking away, because this evening had been just perfect.

'Eight. He's got a lot of energy. My brother and sister-in-law have their own restaurant, a little further around the bay. They made it through lockdown by creating a delivery menu, and they delivered frozen meals to people who were shielding at cost price. They're building things back up again but it's a struggle, and I've suggested I take Peter at the weekends so that they can both work.'

He really *was* a nice guy. Involved with his family and doing his best to settle back in here. Mattie felt a stab of guilt over having been tempted to involve him in the more chaotic side of her lifestyle.

'Another time, maybe. Does Peter like boats?' An eight-year-old would be sure to bring out her more responsible side.

Llwyd chuckled. 'That kind of goes with the territory in my family. I did mention to Peter that we could make a few trips at the weekends which didn't involve water, but he wasn't too keen on that.' He turned, looking through the steel railings. 'Which one's yours?'

Mattie pointed towards the sleek, ten-metre motorboat. The canvas deck covers didn't make it look quite so shiny, and the state-of-the-art console and leather seats in the cockpit were obscured from view, as well.

That didn't seem to stop Llwyd from recognising the craft. X-ray eyes would come in very handy in A&E. 'Nice choice. I'm told it's a very stable boat and easy to handle. Is that your experience?'

'I don't have much to compare it with really…' It was time to go, before she blurted out more than she should. 'Thanks for walking me back. I'll let you get on your way.'

He nodded, waiting for the security guard to open the gates and for them to click closed behind her. Then Mattie could trust herself to turn, as a kiss good-night was out of the question, and all she could do was give him a smile and a wave, before wheeling her bicycle along the quay to where her boat was moored.

Llwyd watched Mattie go, wincing as she awkwardly tried to lift the bike onto the boat, nearly falling into the water before she decided it would be better to remove the deck covers first. Anyone who made that kind of investment in a boat had to be pretty serious about it, and perhaps she was still getting to grips with a craft that was larger than she was used to.

So many questions, still. He would ask them, because so

far each answer had been a delight, even if some of them were a bit surprising. As he walked back up to the main path, the security light flipped off behind him.

'Sorry, mate.'

The man's voice came out of nowhere. Llwyd had stepped back onto the path that ran around the harbour before his eyes had adjusted to the darkness. Someone had brushed against his back and he was suddenly aware that he must have jumped about a mile.

'My fault. I wasn't looking where I was going.' His voice sounded thick, still clogged with panic. Llwyd focussed on the shadows in front of him and saw a young couple, clearly startled by his reaction. 'My apologies. Have a good night.'

'Thanks. You, too,' the woman replied and the two began to walk away from him, leaving Llwyd struggling for breath.

There was no point in running; he'd tried that before. The path was still busy with people walking home. It was well lit and safe. He didn't have far to go before he arrived back at the entrance to the mini-cab company, just a few doors away from Y Llong. He should wait, breathe and let the panic subside a bit.

Llwyd had almost forgotten this feeling—or at least he'd managed to push it away, into a place that couldn't hurt him. He avoided walking alone at night, and when there was no choice he kept his wits about him. But tonight, all he'd been thinking about was Mattie.

She'd made him feel whole, as if his partly paralysed hand wasn't the first thing to notice about him. Something had clicked between them, and he'd been entranced by her and lost track of time. Llwyd hadn't even felt the warning jab of nerves in his stomach as the sun went down, and insisting on walking her home had come naturally to him.

He could live with the physical repercussions of his injuries and was learning to adapt and rebuild. But the night-mares, the panic that triggered when he least expected it—that was something different. Mattie had allowed him to forget that he was broken for a while, but she couldn't mend him. The realisation was a new loss.

Concentrate. *Concentrate.*

Push the fear away, and look around. Stay in the light; stay where there are people. Llwyd forced himself to start walking, not too fast and not too slow. To *look* untouchable, even though he didn't feel it, fixing his gaze on the brightly lit mini-cab sign ahead of him.

He let a young woman, travelling home alone, go ahead of him in the queue, and there was a short wait. A little time to gather his thoughts.

He could do this. If he slept alone, behind closed and locked doors, no one needed to know about the nightmares. He didn't have to forgo the pleasure of spending some of his days with Mattie, just as long as he stayed within his limits.

'Llwyd. Harbwr Cottage?' One of the drivers opened the door of the small office and called his name. Llwyd raised his hand, feeling like a kid in school who had finally been asked a question he knew the answer to, and followed him to the cab.

CHAPTER THREE

MATTIE HAD SPENT a restless night in the luxurious cabin of the boat. The bed, which took up most of the space in the sleeping quarters, was a bit too large for comfort even if it was designed to give its occupants a good night's rest. Her bus might be a little cramped at times, but it had the advantage of not quite so much space to toss and turn if she couldn't sleep.

Then, slowly, the weekend had brought her to her senses. Dreaming of floating away with Llwyd, cutting all of their ties with the land and spending a night without consequences together—that was a bad idea. Thinking about him as a valued colleague—this was a much better idea, even if it wasn't quite so compelling.

Llwyd must have been at work early on Monday morning, because when Mattie arrived he'd already left a package for her at the admin desk, along with a note. He'd returned everything he'd borrowed from the resources cupboard, and since he'd be spending his first week familiarising himself with the orthopaedics department, he looked forward to starting work in A&E next week.

And then, on Wednesday evening, as she freewheeled down the hill from the hospital, all of Mattie's good intentions suddenly screeched to a stop. She applied the brakes on her bicycle, coming to a rather more controlled halt next to Llwyd, who was walking down the hill.

'Hi. Sorry, did I startle you?' He'd jumped, turning quickly as she stopped beside him.

'Uh… I was miles away.' Llwyd smiled, and Mattie promptly forgot about everything else, getting off her bike to walk beside him.

'You walked to work today?' Since he appeared to be walking home, that was an obvious enough supposition.

'Yeah, I was up early this morning. It's good thinking time. How's your week been?'

'Good. I needed some orthopaedics advice this afternoon and I missed you…' Mattie bit the words back, but they were said now and she had to own the amused quirk of Llwyd's lips that she got in response. 'Dr Chandra was excellent. As always.'

'She told me that she was looking forward to getting back to more complex surgery cases when her temporary role with the trauma team ends.' His eyes flashed with humour.

'Yes, she mentioned the same to me.' Now that any hint of a comparison between Llwyd and Annu Chandra's medical skills was out of the way, perhaps they could tacitly assume that the *missing you* was just a pleasantry.

'I missed you, too.' The warmth in his face seemed to echo the feeling of missing someone just for themselves, which had been tugging at Mattie since the weekend. 'I'm looking forward to taking over from Annu.'

That was settled, then. Mattie started to walk, feeling the warmth of evening sunshine on her skin. Or maybe it was just the warmth of seeing Llwyd again.

'Anything planned for the weekend?' He was strolling next to her, relaxed and smiling. That could just be a pleasantry, as well, although it didn't feel like one.

'Not particularly. You?'

'No, not really. I'm looking after Peter, as usual, so I expect I'll have to think of something other than catching up on my reading.' He shifted the backpack that was slung over his shoulder. 'Hospital procedures, mostly.'

Mattie wrinkled her nose. 'I wish there was an abbreviated version. Rather than having to work through all of the things that are just obvious common sense, to find the things you need to know.'

He laughed. 'Yeah. I suppose different people need to know different things.'

Always. Mattie needed to know a few different things right now. Whether Llwyd really did feel the same attraction that seemed to be tugging her closer to him. Or whether that chemistry was just her own reaction to a very attractive man who happened also to be a nice guy.

Whether a friendship between them would be enough. It would have to be, because Mattie couldn't back off now, and anything more would be a commitment that she didn't particularly want to give.

'You said that your nephew likes boats?'

Llwyd's chuckle sent shivers down her spine. '*Like* is a bit of an understatement.'

'I was wondering whether he'd be interested in coming down to the marina sometime. There are lots of different boats there, and I know quite a few people. He might like to have a look around.' Hopefully, he'd bring his uncle Llwyd with him…

'He'd love that. My father's boatyard maintains and repairs every kind of boat, but he specialises in traditional boat-building—'

Mattie caught her breath. 'Wooden boats? With sails?' She'd seen sailing boats on the bay, slipping elegantly past their more modern cousins, and always felt that they belonged on the sea in a way that hers didn't. But her biological father valued efficient speed, and his choice of gift had reflected that.

Llwyd shot her a puzzled look. Maybe he was about to ask but he didn't…

'Yes. Peter gets to clamber around on all types of wooden boat, but he'd really like the opportunity to see yours.'

That seemed to be settled, then. Mattie had something to offer, and surprisingly enough, it was the most awkward part of her life that had provided her with the chance to see Llwyd again.

'If you're free at the weekend… Either day's fine.'

'Saturday would be great, if it's not too much trouble.'

'No trouble.' Sunrise wouldn't be too early, but maybe she should sound slightly less enthusiastic. 'How does ten thirty suit you?'

'Sounds great. Can we bring anything?'

Mattie grinned up at him. Opportunities to play the hostess didn't come around every day, or every year, for that matter, and she wanted to make the most of this one.

'Just yourselves.'

They'd reached the bottom of the hill, and it was time to go their separate ways, Mattie to the right, and Llwyd to the left. But he hesitated for one delicious moment.

'I'll see you then.'

She nodded. 'I'll look forward to it.'

Mattie got back onto her bike, her head already swimming with questions about what was appropriate to offer guests on a boat. Since Llwyd's nephew was only eight years old, the endless supply of cocktails that had characterised her biological father's approach to sea-going hospitality was out of the question.

She needed to go now, since she had no excuse for hanging around just looking at him. Mattie gave him a wave, and concentrated her gaze on the route ahead.

But if she didn't react to his murmured words, she didn't miss them, either. They were something to keep until she saw him again.

'Missing you already.'

Mattie had missed Llwyd, quite ferociously, and was up at six on Saturday morning. That gave her four hours to decide what to wear and cycle around the bay to the marina, picking up some provisions from the local shops along the way.

The bus had limited storage space, and her policy of not owning any more than she absolutely needed was generally a time-saver when it came to deciding what to wear. But using a hair dryer on her curls instead of allowing the wind to sort them out, and choosing a pale blue linen shirt to go with her best jeans, had taken an age this morning. Similarly, although she'd decided on what to buy in the way of food, she'd changed her mind when she got to the bakery and smelled fresh pastries.

Then there were the boat covers to contend with. Mattie was proficient with rolling back the cover on the sundeck so that she could use the built-in table and soft seating, and less so with the cockpit cover, since she never took the boat anywhere. But finally, the covers were stowed away, the table was wiped and cushions were plumped. Then she stowed her purchases in the tiny kitchen area and went to sit on deck in the sunshine, waiting for Llwyd.

At half past ten, she saw a car draw up in one of the slip roads that led down to the sea. Llwyd got out, opening the back door for a small boy who was dressed in soft-soled shoes and a striped T-shirt, looking every inch the junior mariner. Mattie scrambled off the boat, almost losing her footing as it lurched slightly in the wash of another craft that was leaving the marina, and hurried to meet them at the gates, signalling to the security guard that it was okay to let them in.

'Hi. You must be Peter.' It felt a little easier to address the child, rather than look straight into Llwyd's moss-green eyes. 'I'm Mattie.'

Peter moved slightly closer to Llwyd, in response to the sudden presence of a stranger. 'Hello.'

'Your uncle said that you might drop by, for elevenses. It's nice to see you.'

'It's not eleven o'clock yet.' Peter hesitated. Like most children of Mattie's acquaintance, he clearly liked everything to happen in the right order.

Llwyd chuckled. 'It usually takes your grandad a good half an hour to make a cup of tea, doesn't it?'

Peter got the point and nodded sagely. Now that the necessary introductions were over and done with, the row of boats seemed to attract him like a magnet and he walked ahead of them, looking at each one in turn.

'Is he all right? He won't fall in or anything…?' Perhaps she should stay within grabbing distance of the boy.

'He's fine. He spends almost as much time in my father's boatyard as my brother and I did when we were kids. He's got a set of rules that he sticks to.' Llwyd grinned. 'When he knows someone's looking, at any rate.'

'And when they aren't looking?'

'He probably gets up to most of the things that Huw and I did.' Llwyd called ahead to Peter. 'That's where we're going…'

Peter stopped, looking at Mattie's boat with an appraising air. It appeared he hadn't grown in to his uncle's habit of taking things as they came yet, and was sizing the craft up.

'What do you think, Peter?' Mattie joined him, standing next to him, to survey the boat.

'It's nice. Is that your name?' He pointed to the flowing script on the hull. 'Matilda Rae.'

'Matilda's my first name, and Rae is my middle name. Only everybody calls me Mattie.' Mattie had mentioned a few times to her biological father that she preferred Mattie to Matilda, but clearly that hadn't sunk in.

Peter nodded, and Mattie decided it was time to move on. She scrambled onto the deck and turned, waiting for Peter and Llwyd to follow.

No one moved. Peter was solemnly waiting for something...

Llwyd chuckled, catching her eye. 'Permission to come aboard?'

'Oh. Yes. Welcome aboard, Peter.' That was probably a very good notion to instil in a child who spent time in a boatyard. Mattie smiled at him and the boy grinned, moving towards her. Maybe she should step forward and help him, but Llwyd already had his hand on Peter's arm as he negotiated the gap between the jetty and the boat, letting go as soon as Peter had a firm footing on deck. Then he stepped across, onto the boat, with the same ease as someone might walk from one room to another.

'Have you had breakfast?' Mattie tried to ignore the thrill that ran up her spine.

'It seems like a long time ago, now. Might have been yesterday.'

Mattie laughed. 'I've got some pastries, and...coffee and juice. I'm afraid I don't have any tea.' The mention of tea had reminded her that in her focus on choosing the kind of juice that Peter might like, she'd forgotten all about teabags.

'Coffee would be great. Thanks.'

Good. 'Right, then. Peter, would you like to come downstairs with me and choose which juice you'd like?'

Llwyd sat on deck, listening to the two of them talking. Peter didn't make friends easily, but Mattie was having no trouble in breaking through his reserve, and his nephew was starting to open up and talk to her. He appeared with a covered plastic mug of juice in his hand, planting it onto the table in front of Llwyd and then turning around again to go below deck.

It was a puzzle. A woman who owned a boat, which wouldn't have cost any less than a very generous deposit on a house, but which showed no signs of having seen much use. Who referred to the cabin below decks as downstairs, and who had almost slipped and fallen in the process of stepping onto her own deck.

Nerves, maybe? The thought warmed him, because he'd been as nervous as a kitten at the prospect of seeing Mattie again this morning. But that didn't account for all of it.

Peter appeared again, carefully carrying a stack of pastries on a melamine plate. Behind him, Mattie carried the coffee in two rather stylish cups, which were designed not to tip over with the roll of the boat. All thoughts of how and why she was here disappeared in the glow of her actual presence.

And Peter was turning into a great wingman. He sat next to Mattie on the comfortable banquette that ran around the table, the two of them chatting like old friends. It gave Llwyd a chance to watch her, which was the best enjoyment he'd had for a long time. Hair ruffling in the breeze, her cheeks a little pink in the sun. Her feel for the absurd, and her way of making Peter feel confident and happy around her.

The boy slid from his seat, ducking under the table to retrieve Llwyd's backpack and tugging at the zip. Llwyd leaned forward, opening it for him, and Peter withdrew one of his most treasured possessions, flipping open the small, hardback notebook and laying it in front of Mattie.

'These are all the boats I've seen.'

Mattie clearly wasn't under any illusions about the honour that Peter had just afforded her. She turned the pages, looking at each one as if this was a precious manuscript.

'You've seen a lot. And you've written down all the details.' Her tone conveyed admiration, and Llwyd wondered how many of the details meant anything to her.

'Can I put the *Matilda Rae* in?' Peter leaned against her, turning to the most recent entries.

'I'd be very honoured.' Her blue eyes flashed with mischief as she turned her gaze up to Llwyd.' Let's see if your uncle can get all the details right, shall we?

Llwyd handed Peter a pen, waiting for him to write down the name of the boat, and suggesting he include Mattie's name as captain, which she seemed to find amusing. Then he dictated the class and type of the vessel and added Cartref Bay as its home port for good measure.

'Do you want to write some of the other boats down?' Mattie was looking at the craft that were getting underway, slowly nosing out of the marina, and Peter nodded. 'Perhaps we could go up to the cockpit, where you can see better?'

Peter stiffened with glee. 'Yes, *please*. Can I sit in the captain's seat?'

'Um… You'd better ask your uncle.' Mattie shrugged at him and Llwyd chuckled.

'Peter doesn't usually get to do that with my father.' He indicated the seat behind the helm, just in case Mattie wasn't sure which seat Peter was referring to. 'He'll be okay there, if it's all right with you.'

'Yes, of course. You're very welcome if you'd like to, Peter.'

Peter was already on his feet, searching in Llwyd's backpack for the small pair of binoculars that he'd brought with them. Llwyd shepherded Peter forward, towards the bridge, and Mattie followed.

She stood back, letting Peter inspect the bridge carefully and perhaps listening to some of his answers to Peter's questions. But when Peter tried to climb into the leather seat behind the helm, Mattie was suddenly there, her soft scent blending with that of the sea, as she ducked between them.

'As it's the captain's seat, I'd better lift you up…' She made it sound as if this was her prerogative, rather than a matter of helping Llwyd, who could use both his hands to lift Peter if he had to, but it was awkward. Then she was gone, leaving him to crank the seat up so that Peter could see over the console.

Mattie had retreated back into the open air, sitting on one of the comfortable seats in the stern. Peter was clearly happy to stay put, while Llwyd joined her.

'Is he okay up there?' Mattie asked, nodding at Peter, who was now surveying the marina with the aid of his binoculars.

'He's having a great time, thank you. We may have a problem getting him back down again…'

Mattie laughed. 'I dare say he'll get hungry at some point.'

'So that's what kind of captain you are, is it? Starving the crew out?'

'Absolutely.' Mattie gave him a broad smile. 'It's really nice of you to come. I don't have many visitors.'

'You surprise me.' Being around boats had always seemed to Llwyd to be the most sociable of pastimes.

'Hmm. It's a conundrum, isn't it?' Mattie suddenly caught his gaze.

He supposed he could ask her what she was referring to, but that really wasn't necessary. And it would be a betrayal of the way that they just seemed to get each other.

'It is. I have several options under consideration. I'd be surprised if any of them were correct.'

She gave him a knowing half smile. 'So would I. How would an unexpected birthday present from a very rich, very absent, biological father strike you?'

'I didn't think of that one.' The conversation was turning into a complicated dance. Mattie was testing him, looking for his reactions, and Llwyd was trying to contain his curiosity and let it go at whatever pace she felt comfortable with. 'That's a little more awkward than a set of hideous mugs, I suppose.'

She laughed suddenly. 'Yes, it is. It came with the mugs, which I actually rather like, along with two years' worth of rental for the marina. And a set of storm wear, which I've never used because I can't sail it out of the marina.'

'Drive it.'

Mattie raised her eyebrows. 'Is that so? I thought you sailed a boat.'

'Only when it has sails. When it's a motor boat you drive it.' Bringing it all down to the small and manageable seemed to be reassuring Mattie. Llwyd couldn't fathom what she'd expected his reaction to be, but he didn't seem to be doing too badly.

'And when it has both?'

'Then you get the option of either driving *or* sailing it.' Llwyd clarified the situation. 'You don't have a lot of experience with boats, do you?'

'None. I've learned how to keep it clean and tidy, and when to have the engine serviced, but...' She shrugged.

Llwyd nodded. There was more to this. Maybe if he gave her a bit of time, Mattie would explain.

'My biological father doesn't have much contact with my family. It's all a bit complicated. My mum and dad are actually my aunt and uncle, so I suppose that Leigh might be classed as a rich uncle, but then my two older brothers, who are actually my cousins, have nothing to do with him—'

'Wait.' Llwyd held his hand up to stop her. 'I'm already confused. You want to start at the beginning and take me through it a bit more gently?' Mattie was already blushing furiously, and he reckoned that encouraging her to breathe might be good right now.

'Okay.' She took a breath. 'My biological father, Leigh, is American. He was doing a year out in Europe before he went to university, and he met my biological mother, Helen, in London. The next thing anyone knew was that they'd taken off together, and Helen was sending postcards from Rome.'

Llwyd nodded. 'Got it. I take it you're not close...?' There was clearly a 'mum and dad' somewhere in the mix, but that wasn't Leigh and Helen.

'No, by the time Helen knew she was pregnant, Leigh had gone back to America. And Helen died when I was just a week old. Complications from the birth.'

'I'm sorry you didn't get a chance to know her.'

'Thanks. I would have liked to...' Mattie's quick shake of the head was familiar to Llwyd. He did that, too, when he was trying to distance himself from the emotion of things that couldn't be changed. 'I got to know a bit about her, though, because Helen's older sister and her husband adopted me. They're my mum and dad.'

'I've got it now. And your brothers?'

'Mum and Dad already had two sons, Justin and Mark. Strictly speaking, they're my cousins, but…they've never been anything other than big brothers to me.'

'Did Leigh know anything about you?' They were working their way back around to the boat, but there were still a few missing links to clear up before they got there.

'Yes, Helen wrote and told him. He asked her to go to America and she told him she wouldn't. My oldest brother Justin was nine when I was born, and he remembers a bit about it all. He said that Leigh wrote to my mum and dad, offering a very generous maintenance payment for me—he came from a rich family who could afford it without even noticing. My dad wrote back saying that Leigh was welcome to come and see me whenever he liked, but he didn't need his money.'

'Your dad sounds like a really good man.'

Mattie smiled suddenly. 'Yes, he is. One of the best. And he knew exactly how to handle Leigh, because he never did come. He sent presents for my birthday and at Christmas, but…he was always too busy to visit.'

'What do your mum and dad think about the boat?' Llwyd couldn't imagine that they wouldn't have something to say about it.

Mattie grimaced. 'Actually…they don't know about it. Leigh was coming to England to meet with actors and directors about a big film project he was producing, and he came over in a sixty-metre cruiser and dropped anchor off the Welsh coast. I got a call from his secretary, who said that he'd be here for a week and would be thrilled if I was able to join him.'

'Did you?' Maybe Mattie hadn't seen that this was an invitation to yet more disenchantment.

She grinned at him. 'Don't imagine I didn't know what this was. He'd taken it into his head that he wanted to meet me, but if he'd been truly interested in me he would have come a lot sooner. I already have a father, and Leigh can't fit into his shoes. But I was curious, and…it was rash of me, but I'd heard a bit about him, and I just wanted to meet him. I was prepared to be disappointed.'

'How can it be rash? You weighed it all up and decided what you wanted to do.'

Mattie shrugged. It seemed that she stood by her rather harsh judgement of her actions. 'Well, anyway, I went. Leigh was really good. He respected the relationship I have with my mum and dad and seemed to know exactly how strange it all was. I stayed with him, the boat was marvellous and we spent a lot of time together. People were saying that I was like him in lots of little ways and I was…starstruck.'

Llwyd nodded. It must have been easy to play into Mattie's vulnerabilities, leaving her dazzled. Perhaps if Mattie's biological father had walked into A&E one day, taken the risk of approaching her on her own territory… He dismissed the thought as unnecessarily judgemental.

'And he gave you the *Matilda Rae*?' He leaned back into the soft cushions behind him, suddenly finding them rather less comfortable than they had been.

'It wasn't called that then. It was the boat they used for day trips and swimming. One evening Leigh took me out on it, just the two of us, and we sat on deck for hours, talking and watching the sunset. It was amazing.'

'And so he made you a present of it?'

Mattie rolled her eyes at the thought. 'Not there and then. I would have told him how impractical it was, and that

I couldn't keep a boat. I received all of the documents a couple of weeks after I got home, along with a note from Leigh, saying that the boat was in the marina, waiting for me. I came down here and just stared at it, every evening after work, for a week before I could summon up the courage to set foot on it.'

And Mattie was stuck now. Torn between wanting to keep something that her biological father had given her, and knowing she couldn't use it the way a boat *should* be used. Sitting on it on a summer morning, helpless in its grip.

'Would it make a difference…if you knew how to use it?' He couldn't help but ask, even if the question was a minefield. He'd known Mattie for barely a week, and it seemed totally wrong to advise her on something that obviously meant so much to her. And yet somehow, unexpectedly, completely right, as well. As if they'd been thrown together with a purpose that was only now becoming clear.

'I think… I don't know. Maybe…' She looked up at him, indecision showing in her face. Clearly, the rights and wrongs of the situation had occurred to her, as well.

They both jumped as the boat's horn sounded. Peter had leaned forward and was signalling to another vessel that was manoeuvring past their berth, and Llwyd got to his feet.

'Hold that thought. Please…' He just had to hope that Mattie would, because something was going on and he didn't have time to wait for her answer.

CHAPTER FOUR

MATTIE HADN'T BEEN aware that it was possible to slide back the overhead window at the helm, or that there was a foothold, which allowed Llwyd to swing himself upwards and wave to the other vessel, apologising for the misleading signal. The man piloting the craft saw Peter at the helm and laughed, waving and pipping his own horn in an *I heard you* gesture to the boy.

Being at home on a boat was clearly more than just a matter of spending the night here every once in a while and stocking up on coffee and pastries. Why had she thought that Llwyd wouldn't notice that the craft was a lovely, but ultimately useless, possession?

Because she'd wanted to see him. Today had been an opportunity to get to know him a little better as a friend, and she'd grabbed at it before she'd really thought it all through. And now she'd said too much, in an attempt to make all of this seem slightly less irresponsible than it looked.

She saw Llwyd curl his arm around his nephew's shoulders, talking to him quietly. Peter nodded, and Llwyd left him sitting in the captain's seat and walked back over to Mattie.

'Sorry. He got a bit overexcited.'

'No problem.' Mattie smiled. 'It's nice to see him enjoying himself so much. It took me ages to work out where the horn was.'

Llwyd's gaze softened. 'Do *you* get to have fun on your boat?'

Mattie twisted her mouth in an expression of remorse. 'I didn't mean… I'm sorry to bend your ear. That's not at all what I intended for today.'

Llwyd shrugged. 'I asked.'

Actually, he hadn't. But he'd listened, which in Mattie's experience was far more compelling than mere questions.

'Well…maybe I didn't really mean to answer. In such detail.'

He puffed out a sigh, rubbing his hand against the back of his head. 'Did you hold the thought?'

'You're not going to let this go, are you? I know it's irresponsible of me—'

'How so? It strikes me that it was an irresponsible gift, because it's problematic on a lot of different levels. But I can see how it must be difficult to let it go, and that you don't want to upset your parents by telling them about it. And that it's difficult to keep, as well.'

He understood. Mattie felt her eyes fill with grateful tears and blinked them away. 'What would you do, Llwyd? If it were yours.'

'I have no idea. Probably duck the issue completely and abandon it on someone's doorstep, in the hopes it might find a good home. At least you've taken a more responsible approach.'

That made her laugh. 'Okay. So what do you think *I* should do?'

He shrugged. 'I guess… I think that if you can use it, then you can make it yours. Then maybe your options would be a bit easier to think about.'

'Sounds like a plan. What would I need to do to learn?'

'I can take you out for an afternoon and show you a few things, if you'd like. If you think you want to take it a bit further, then my dad's a qualified instructor and he runs two-day beginner courses. They're pretty full-on, but after that you should be qualified to do the basics.'

'I'd get a certificate?' Mattie liked the idea of having something in writing. It seemed solid and responsible in a situation that felt out of control.

'It's an accredited course, so I think you must get something. It might not be a certificate...'

'That's okay. Something to carry in my pocket would be a bit more practical.' Mattie thought for a moment. 'You wouldn't mind taking me out?'

The spark of excitement she felt at the thought was mirrored in Llwyd's green eyes. 'Of course not. If you don't mind Peter coming along, then I'm free pretty much any weekend.'

'It wouldn't be any fun without him.' And one of the nice things about having Peter around was that she and Llwyd would be allowed to have fun together, without having to worry that this looked a lot like a date. '*This* weekend?'

He chuckled, clearly happy with the thought. 'Sure. How about now?'

Somehow, Llwyd made the impulsive decision seem more akin to decisiveness.

'Now's great, thank you.'

If she'd thought that he might just climb into the pilot's seat and switch on the engine, Mattie found that it was a little more complicated than that. Llwyd had flipped through the servicing documents, which were thankfully up to date, and Mattie and Peter had followed him from one end of the boat to the other, carefully keeping out of his way while he opened and shut things and switched other things on and then back off again.

'One hand for the boat and one for yourself.' Peter added his own piece of expertise to the situation when Mattie almost fell flat on her face while leaning over, trying to see what Llwyd was doing.

'Thanks. That's good advice.'

'Tad-cu told me that.'

Llwyd turned, grinning at his nephew. 'English, Peter.'

'Tad-cu means grandad. And mam-gu is grandma.' Peter added some extra information, and Mattie repeated both the words.

'Good to know. I'll remember that.'

She and Peter had both breathed a sigh of relief when Llwyd diagnosed the boat's condition as excellent. He reached into his pocket, giving Peter some pound coins, and suggested he take Mattie for some ice cream while he arranged for the boat to be fuelled.

They returned to the marina to find Llwyd sitting outside the reception area, watching as a small skiff towed her boat towards the fuel dock. Mattie handed him his ice-cream cone.

'Surprising what they'll do for you here.' He turned the corners of his mouth down. 'Or did they just think I couldn't manage it with one hand?'

'I doubt it. I have a deluxe membership package, which basically means I don't have to lift a finger. They just come along and do whatever needs doing. So I'm afraid that the offer was a matter of money being able to buy almost anything, rather than helping a guy out.'

He smiled. 'Silly me. I was about to tell them that I could manage perfectly well, but I'm glad I thought better of it now.'

Maybe she *should* ask. Llwyd's injury didn't seem to hamper him too much, but the grip in his left hand was obviously compromised. If he'd offered to do a little more than he could comfortably manage, now was the time to find out.

'You'll be okay driving the boat, though? I'm asking as a doctor who values helping people out. And a complete sea-going incompetent.'

Llwyd's laughter reassured her that she'd guessed right, and he'd far rather she was straightforward in her questions. 'I'll be fine. If I need you to help with something, I'll ask. Bearing in mind that suggesting you head for the safe water corridor at the mouth of the bay might not be particularly helpful.'

'Thanks. You can always just point to wherever we're supposed to be heading…' A thought occurred to Mattie. '*I'm* not going to be driving, am I…?'

He shrugged. 'I'll wait until you get to the point where you wrestle the helm from me.'

Llwyd left Mattie to think about the pleasures of wrestling with him while he fetched a pair of life jackets from the boot of his car. It seemed that they weren't going anywhere until Mattie had fetched her own life jacket and fiddled with the adjustments until it fit to Llwyd's satisfaction. When she'd protested that she'd never worn a life jacket before on the boat, Peter had observed solemnly that he and his uncle were setting a good example, and Llwyd had nodded in agreement.

Llwyd nosed the boat gently from the marina, and then it picked up speed as it headed around the bay. Peter pointed out his school and then the trees behind, where his uncle Llwyd's cottage lay. There was a cluster of boats around his grandfather's boatyard, and his parents' restaurant was at the top of a lookout point at the mouth of the bay. Then they were in open water, heading away from the land and towards a sparkling horizon. It was the same kind of exhilaration that Mattie always felt when she set off towards a new place, and she'd missed this sense of freedom.

This was a new adventure. She'd felt stuck for so long, but now she could feel the joy that had made her whoop with delight when Leigh had taken her on that first trip, out into the sunset.

She was learning to balance a little better against the movement of the craft and the roll of the sea. And then Llwyd asked whether she'd like to take the helm, and determined not to disappoint him, she'd agreed. Mattie made a few false starts, understeering and then oversteering, but under Llwyd's patient and watchful eye she finally got it right.

'This is marvellous. Thank you.' She'd used the very same words with Leigh when he'd taken her out on the boat, but this was something different. Mattie was no longer a cog in someone else's life, who could be put to use on their terms.

'Master of your own vessel?' he murmured quietly, and Mattie nodded. He didn't need to be told. He'd worked that one out all by himself.

'You'll give me your father's number? So I can give him a call and ask him about the course?'

'Yep. Or I could give him your number if you like and get him to call you.'

Mattie raised her eyebrows. 'You think I'm going to chicken out?' Hadn't he seen her excitement, the sense of triumph when she'd finally got it right and managed to steer the boat to the exact spot that Llwyd had indicated?

'No, I reckon not. He gives a discount for NHS employees, and if he knows you're a friend, he'll make it his personal mission to put you through your paces.' Llwyd's grin told her exactly which part of the deal he thought might attract her, and it wasn't the discount.

'In that case...' Mattie took the helm while Llwyd extracted his phone from his pocket and gave him her number.

CHAPTER FIVE

LLWYD HAD TEXTED Mattie on Sunday, telling her that he'd passed her number on and that his father would be calling her on Monday to discuss the course. It was only fair that if he had her number, she should have his, wasn't it?

And it was only to be expected that they would meet when he started working on A&E cases. The fact that he was looking forward to seeing Mattie again was entirely incidental.

It didn't hasten his steps one bit when the call came on Tuesday morning. A ten-year-old with a dislocated shoulder was quite enough to make him hurry down to the A&E department, and if there was a slight thrill in seeing Mattie's name on the board, as the doctor currently treating the patient, that was probably all about knowing that the child was in good hands.

When he entered the cubicle, Mattie was sitting beside a little girl dressed in football shorts and a vest. On the other side of the bed, a nurse was holding a mask attached to a nitrous oxide canister.

'I know it hurts…' Mattie nodded to the nurse, who leaned forward, offering the child the mask. 'You can take some more breaths, if you want to.'

The tenderness in her expression, as she gently smoothed a strand of hair from the little girl's face, left Llwyd almost breathless. Then Mattie turned, shooting him a smile, before winking conspiratorially at her patient.

'We've got Dr Morgan, Amalie. He's the best.'

She probably said that about all the doctors. But Amalie smiled, and that was all that really mattered. If she trusted her doctors, it would make the next steps a lot easier. Mattie introduced him to Amalie's mum, and Llwyd picked up the tablet that contained Amalie's X-rays and notes.

'Mrs Williams, I'm Dr Llwyd Morgan, from orthopaedics...'

Amalie's mother spoke to him in Welsh. As Llwyd replied, he saw Mattie's mischievous smile.

'What are they saying?' she asked Amalie.

'Just...hello.'

'Good. I wouldn't want to miss anything.' Mattie must know full well what the brief phrases meant; she would have heard them all the time in shops and pubs in the area. If people heard a local accent, they'd often greet someone in Welsh and then switch back to English. But Mattie's question had been a part of helping Amalie to focus on what was going on around her.

It wasn't helping Llwyd to focus, though. Right now, he needed to concentrate on Amalie's X-rays, and he couldn't take his eyes off Mattie. He murmured an *excuse me* and took the X-rays and Amalie's notes outside, where Mattie's tenderness couldn't assail him.

'What do you think?' She joined him a few minutes later, her manner a little more brisk and businesslike, now that she was out of Amalie's and her mother's earshot.

'Partial anterior dislocation. Did she fall?'

'Yes, she's in her school's football team and the PE teacher says that she took a tumble while she was training.

There was no blow to the shoulder but she threw her arm out in front of her to save herself.'

Llwyd nodded. 'Then I'll take a look at the shoulder, but I think that starting with a scapular manipulation is best, and if that isn't successful we'll move on to external rotation. How's she been getting on with the gas and air?'

'She seems fine with it. Amalie's a sensible kid and she's been using the pain ladder chart to show us how she's feeling and asking for more gas and air when she needs it.'

'Let's continue with that, then, unless she becomes distressed. You'll assist me with the reduction?'

Mattie shot him a grin, and Llwyd felt his stomach lurch in response. 'What makes you think I wouldn't want to see this through with her?'

'I'm not sure why I even bothered to ask. Can you point me towards the medical supplies store?'

'I could, but then I'd have to come with you to show you where everything is. If you want to get on with your examination, I can fetch a sling for Amalie and then give you the guided tour later.'

'Thanks. Anything else I need to know?'

'Just that she's really into football. She supports the Beachcombers, whoever they are...'

Llwyd chuckled. 'Our local team. Their women's squad did really well in the league last winter.'

Mattie had done a great job of reassuring Amalie and that was going to make a big difference in how well the reduction procedure went. Llwyd gently examined her shoulder, asking her how the Beachcombers were doing, and Amalie started to reel off match results and forecasts for the coming season with all the ease of a seasoned sports commentator. Mattie returned with an armful of boxes, and Amalie's gaze found her smile again. Llwyd gave in to the inevitable, and nodded to her in an invitation to explain to Amalie what was going to happen next.

Mattie sat down in front of Amalie. 'All this is a bit scary, isn't it?'

Amalie nodded, pressing her lips together.

'Well…do you know who's in charge here?' Mattie waited for Amalie's response, but the little girl didn't seem to want to hazard a guess. 'It's you. We need to move your arm so that the bone just gently slides back into the right place, as I explained to you, and that'll be a bit uncomfortable. But Nurse Emma is going to be right here for you, and if you feel any sharp pains, you speak up and we'll stop. Is that okay?'

'Yes. That's okay.' Amalie nodded, looking a little happier now.

'And Dr Morgan's going to keep an eye on you for a while, and make sure that you're able to play for your football team again.'

A tear ran down Amalie's face, and Mattie produced a tissue and wiped it away.

'That's what we're here for, Amalie. To make you well.'

'What are you going to do?' Amalie seemed more confident now.

'I'm going to hold your arm steady—' Mattie gripped her own forearm to demonstrate '—and you'll feel Dr Morgan pressing his fingers against your back and shoulder, right here.' She turned, pointing to her own shoulder blade.

'Okay.' Amalie nodded.

'First of all, Nurse Emma's going to give you the mask to put over your mouth, and you need to take a few deep breaths. Then I'll ask you if you're ready and we'll start.'

The procedure was faultless. Mattie gently flexed Amalie's elbow, pressing down slightly to apply traction, and then Llwyd carefully positioned his fingers on her shoulder, finding the tip of her scapula with his right thumb. He couldn't use his left thumb, but he'd practised the exact positioning of his left hand, which would allow him to use his ring finger to perform the delicate process of realignment, and it took little more than a minute of careful pressure before he felt the ball and socket joint slide back into its proper position.

'All done, Amalie. Does your shoulder feel a little better now?'

Amalie gifted him with a smile.

'Yes. Thank you, Dr Morgan.'

'It's my pleasure. You can rest a bit now, while I sort out a sling for you. I appear to have plenty to choose from...' He indicated the armful of boxes that Mattie had brought.

'They come in different colours!' Mattie protested.

Amalie's mum, who'd been sitting quietly in the corner, spoke up. 'Probably not red-and-black stripes. But Amalie has a red sweater and perhaps there's a black one...?'

Red and black? Amalie mouthed the words in Llwyd's direction, a puzzled look on her face, and he laughed.

'Beachcombers' colours...'

They had something. Mattie was quite capable of recognising a *something* when she stumbled across it, and she and Llwyd definitely had something.

It had been there on Saturday, and it was stronger now. A synchronicity, which meant Mattie didn't have to stop and think before she spoke; she knew that Llwyd would get her meaning. Sometimes he seemed to get it even before she said it, and sometimes she knew what he was about to say, too.

She didn't need to think too much about that. She could just take it for what it was, something that made her feel good when Llwyd was around, and when he wasn't around… she could just admit to herself that she wished he were and leave it there. Because however much Llwyd seemed to get her, he'd only seen one side of the coin. Doctor, boat owner. If the boat wasn't a wholly practical thing, then there was a reason for that, and Llwyd had seemed to understand that even the most sensible person might be in receipt of an unwanted present from an itinerant father. But her home…that was all her own doing.

She'd arrived from Sheffield three years ago, the excitement of making a new start in a new place heightened by the challenges that the new Cartref Bay hospital might provide. Mattie travelled light, and the boot and back seat of her car were enough to hold all of her possessions. She had three weeks to find a place to live and had made a tour of rental cottages in the area, all of which were practical, well furnished and affordable. And then…*then*…she'd seen the advert in the local paper.

Gwen and Owen farmed on land that overlooked the bay. Mattie had climbed a steep hill through irregular fields of crops she didn't recognise, to a stone-built farmhouse that was surprisingly modern and comfortable inside.

Their son and his then-fiancée had applied a novel approach to rising property prices and their own lack of savings. Gwen had told Mattie that she and Owen had been horrified when they'd seen the yellow school bus, which the couple had bought and had shipped from America. They'd gone along with the plan, reckoning that if the bus conversion didn't provide a suitable 'starter home' for when the two got married, they could always stay with them in the farmhouse.

Gwen and Owen may have had their doubts about the bus when they'd first seen it, but they'd clearly developed a great deal of affection for it. Now that their son and daughter-in-law had bought a house and were starting a family, they wanted the bus to go to someone who'd love it as much as they did.

'Goodness only knows where they got the idea from.' Gwen had offered Mattie another cup of tea from the pot. 'They wanted their own place, though, and this was something they could afford. My daughter-in-law's an engineer so she's the one who turns my son's wild ideas into practicalities...'

Wild ideas and practicality had appealed to Mattie. The bus was largely self-sufficient, thanks to solar panels on the roof and on-board water tanks, which could be replenished from a standpipe that had been installed next to the hard standing that Owen had created, halfway down the hill. In exchange for a small rent she could stay here, or there were other farmers in the area who might well be persuaded to allow her to park the bus in a more sheltered location.

Mattie had fallen in love. The bus had everything she needed: a small kitchen, a shower room, and there was plenty of living space for one. It could do with redecorating, but that just gave her the opportunity of making it hers. After living in a string of rental places, this was the nearest she'd ever got to having her own home, and it had the added advantage of being able to move with her.

Three days later, Mattie's offer had been accepted. She'd found a home.

She spent the first summer on Gwen and Owen's land, painting and repairing the bus in her free weekends. Mattie had bought a bicycle, and after two months of toiling up the hill to the farm had suddenly found she could make the trip home without wanting to collapse when she reached the bus. She'd sold her car, and in the winter she'd moved down to a more sheltered spot, on Kathy and Pete's farm, where the bus's small space heaters kept her warm through all kinds of inclement weather.

She'd been happy here, but her itchy feet had told her that she'd be moving on soon. Mattie had been looking at places where she and the bus might find a new base together, when disaster had struck. Leigh's impulsive gift was the one reminder she had that her biological father hadn't completely forgotten her, and Mattie couldn't contemplate selling it. It had tied her down, leaving her stuck here.

And then Llwyd had come along and shown her that there might be a way forward. Mattie didn't know what that way might be yet, but she could feel it, hovering in the air around her and loosening the bonds that she'd chafed against for the past year. Llwyd's father, Rhys, had texted her on Thursday morning, saying that if she wanted to do her course sooner than the date they'd booked, he had a cancellation for this weekend. Mattie had texted back, telling him she'd take the free date.

Llwyd had been in A&E for the whole of Thursday afternoon, working with a team of four other doctors on a child who had fallen from a first-floor window and sustained multiple injuries. Just the list of different specialties that had been called to the trauma room was enough to tell Mattie that the little boy was in a bad way.

'How is he?' She found Llwyd at the admin station, just as the evening shift started to arrive.

He looked up at her, his face drawn. 'Two broken legs, cracked ribs and head trauma, along with an injury to one of his eyes. He's on his way down to theatre now.'

Mattie nodded. One of the disadvantages of working with kids was that it hit you harder when something like this happened. They both knew that, and she didn't need to tell him that she understood just how he felt. 'Will he pull through?'

'Yeah, I think so. We managed to stabilise him, and the ophthalmologist is confident that he can save the eye. It'll be a long road for him, but...'

'You'll be with him all the way.' That was the most positive thing that Mattie could think of. That there *was* a future for the child, and he would recover in time.

'Yeah. Thanks.' Llwyd hit a few keys on the keyboard in front of him and then got to his feet. 'I'm finished now. Fancy a drink, or maybe a bite to eat before you go home?'

Boundaries again. Llwyd had made sure to mention the *going home* part of the evening, which was clearly as important to him as it was to her. She dismissed the thought that if a friendship was truly all either of them wanted, then there probably wouldn't be any need to set boundaries.

'Can I take a rain check? I've still got one patient left to see and I don't want to make him wait until the evening shift comes on—he was very tearful when he came in and I think he has a couple of fractured fingers. The X-rays should be ready any minute now, and hopefully the pain relief I gave him will be helping him to settle a bit.'

Llwyd smiled suddenly. 'Need any of my boundless expertise?'

She should have guessed that he might want in on this. Something practical to occupy himself with, and push back the helplessness he felt when he thought about everything that a badly injured child would have to face in the coming months.

'Just when I was thinking I could manage on my own.' She grinned back at him. 'But who could resist an offer of boundless expertise?'

She led Llwyd to the cubicle and introduced him to five-year-old Harry and his mum. Harry was a lot quieter now that the painkillers were beginning to take effect, and was starting to take an interest in what was going on around him.

'Hi, Harry.' Llwyd sat down on a chair next to the gurney, and Harry looked him up and down. 'I see you've been for your X-ray.' He indicated the sticker that the technician had tacked on to Harry's sweatshirt, and the boy nodded.

Llwyd reached for the pain chart stickers. 'Which one of these looks like you?'

Harry leaned forward, selecting a 'Hurts a little bit' sticker and Llwyd smiled, peeling it off the backing paper and offering it to Harry, who positioned it next to the X-ray sticker.

'Does *your* hand hurt?'

Llwyd hadn't had a chance to slip a surgical glove on over the fingerless support glove that he always wore on his left hand while working, and Harry's sharp eyes had seen it. His mother flushed and she apologised quickly for her son.

'Sorry, Dr Morgan Harry, we're not here to ask about that.'

Llwyd grinned. 'That's okay. Since I want to take a look at Harry's hand, it's only fair to let him see mine.' He turned to Harry. 'No, my hand doesn't hurt.'

Maybe this was one of the things that Llwyd had been referring to when he said that he liked working with kids. Harry's frank curiosity was a world away from his mother's embarrassment, and in Mattie's experience, the former was probably a little more refreshing than the latter.

'Can you wiggle your fingers?' Harry remembered the question that Mattie had asked him.

'These two, yes.' Llwyd demonstrated by wiggling his

ring finger first, then his little finger. 'The other three not so much.'

'They're all bent.' Harry reached out to touch Llwyd's fingers.

'Yep. I can straighten them if I want to...' Llwyd pulled his thumb and first finger straight, to demonstrate. 'But when I let go of them they curl back up again.'

Harry nodded sagely. 'My finger goes a bit bendy sometimes. Not like yours, though.'

'Yeah?' Llwyd glanced at Mattie. 'Which finger's that, then?'

He could so easily have allowed Harry's mother to quieten the boy's questions. But Llwyd hadn't, and Harry had started to talk now. Like all good doctors, Llwyd was listening very carefully.

'The one that hurts.'

'This one?' Llwyd indicated his own middle finger, and Harry nodded.

'How was Harry's hand injured, Mrs Davies?' Llwyd asked Harry's mother.

'He was running around in the kitchen while I was trying to get the dinner into the oven. So I asked him to go and watch TV in the sitting room until I'd finished, and he raced out of the kitchen, pulling the door behind him.' Mrs Davies turned her mouth down and Harry mimicked her expression. 'But you kept hold of the door by mistake, didn't you, Harry, and your fingers got shut in it.'

'And did you notice that he couldn't straighten his middle finger?'

'I tried to look at his hand but he was holding it inside his sweater and I had to coax him a bit. But when he did show me, all his fingers were quite straight.'

Llwyd nodded. 'Okay, that's fine. Harry, may I see your hand now please? I'll be as careful as I can.'

Harry had been protecting his injured hand fiercely, but he hesitated and then held it out. Llwyd cradled it gently in his, carefully probing his palm, and although Harry screwed his face up, he didn't pull away from him.

'All finished, Harry. You did really well there. I could see that it hurt you a bit.'

'Can I have one of those?' Harry reached out, touching Llwyd's support glove.

'It might not be the best thing for you. We'll have to look at your X-rays first, to see whether something different will be more comfortable.'

'Will it be *big*?'

Llwyd was clearly trying to keep his face straight now. 'Why? Do you want something big?'

Harry nodded.

'Let's see the X-rays first, shall we? Then we'll decide, but I'll do my best to give you a dressing that's as big as possible.'

'I hope so…' Harry muttered to himself, clearly not entirely happy with Llwyd's treatment proposals, and Mattie checked her tablet to see whether the X-rays had been sent yet. She wasn't sure how they were going to break the news that it was unlikely that Harry would be leaving here with his whole arm in plaster, and clearly Llwyd was wondering about that, too.

'Ah! The X-rays are back.' Mattie tapped the screen to call them up, and Harry's eyes lit up.

'Can I see…?'

'Wait a moment, Harry.' Llwyd got to his feet, moving over to where Mattie was standing. 'Let me look at them first.'

'But...'

'Simmer down, Harry. Show Dr Morgan that you can be quiet while he looks at your X-rays, and then if you ask very nicely he might let you see them.' Harry's mother took charge of the situation, diverting Harry's attention while Mattie showed Llwyd the X-rays.

He reached over, magnifying the image, and Mattie nodded. Two faint lines across the bones of Harry's index and middle fingers indicated that they were fractured.

'Anything else?' she murmured.

Llwyd moved the image on the screen, carefully checking the rest of Harry's hand. 'That all looks fine. I'd like to just keep an eye on that bendy finger, though.'

Clearly, he suspected that the swelling around the fractures might be masking something else. Mattie nodded. 'Trigger finger?'

He grinned suddenly. Llwyd must know that she'd seen the area of Harry's palm he'd been examining and put two and two together. 'How did you guess?'

The question didn't need an answer. In fact, it would be better *not* to answer, since that involved an admission that it hadn't been too difficult to get inside his head. Mattie pressed her elbow gently against his ribs and he took the hint, and he moved back to Harry's bedside, catching Mrs Davies's attention.

'There are minor fractures in Harry's middle and index fingers. There's no displacement there and they should heal well if we give Harry a cast to wear on his hand.' Llwyd proffered the tablet and Mrs Davies leaned over, looking at the X-ray. 'You see here...?'

'No! I can't see!' Harry protested loudly, and Mrs Davies smiled at him.

'Magic word, Harry.'

'Please!'

Llwyd leaned forward, showing him the image, and Harry subsided into open-mouthed silence. Mattie stepped forward, taking the tablet from Llwyd's hand so that she could hold it in front of the boy, giving Llwyd a chance to finish talking to his mother.

'This inability to straighten his middle finger may be a mild case of trigger finger. It's not easy to tell for sure right now, because the swelling and pain from the fractures make it difficult for me to feel for the characteristic bump in the tendon.'

Mrs Davies's hand flew to her mouth. 'I didn't notice...'

'No, you won't have done.' Llwyd reassured her. 'Even I can't tell for sure that's the case, and most of the time Harry's finger will be working just fine. It might just get stuck sometimes. The condition isn't all that common in children and often resolves itself. We'll be immobilising Harry's fingers in a splint for the fractures which will help alleviate the trigger finger, as well. But I'd like to see him again in a couple of weeks just to check on his progress. And meanwhile, if you're at all concerned, give me a call. Dr Llwyd Morgan, in orthopaedics.'

'Thank you, Doctor Morgan.' Mrs Davies smiled at him.

'My pleasure.' Llwyd turned to Harry. 'Right then, Harry. I'm going to go and find the biggest splint I can for you. It'll make your hand feel much better.'

Harry ignored him, fascinated by the image on the screen in front of him. Llwyd chuckled, leaving Mattie to explain what he saw to him, and disappeared to fetch a splint.

From then on, it was all smiles. Harry seemed happy with the size of the splint that Llwyd had chosen and watched carefully as Mattie secured the hook and loop fastenings around his hand and fingers, showing his mother how to make sure the fit was snug but not too tight, and giving her instructions on how to care for the hand.

Llwyd took over sticker duty, presenting Harry with a Cartref Bay Hospital sticker to add to the collection on his sweatshirt, and giving his mum a few extras for his room. Adults saw a brand-new hospital, efficiency and the latest medical technology. Kids saw kindness and stickers, and they were just as much an investment in the future.

'The I'll-show-you-mine-if-you-show-me-yours worked pretty well.' Mattie smiled up at him as they watched Harry and his mother leave.

He chuckled. 'Worked for me, too. You want to go and get something to eat now?' Llwyd's mood seemed to have lifted a little. Mattie doubted that the seriously injured child he'd treated earlier was very far from his thoughts, but Harry had reminded him that there was another side to their work.

'How do you feel about one of Hetty's burgers?'

He raised his eyebrows, obviously familiar with Hetty's organic burger shop down by the marina. 'You *are* hungry, then.'

'I reckon that stocking up on a few calories can't hurt. Your father called me this morning and he has a cancellation, so I'm doing his course at the weekend. It's a couple who cancelled, so there'll only be me and one other person there instead of three.'

'So you get to do three people's work between the two of you?' There was the trace of a challenge in Llwyd's smile.

'I was thinking more along the lines of your father having only two people to give his attention to, instead of three. But your version of it works.' She wrinkled her nose and he laughed.

'Hetty's it is, then. She'll be busy at this time.'

'I can phone and order a takeaway. We've got a boat to eat it on.'

He nodded. 'I've got my car with me today. Want a lift?'

'Thanks, but I have my bike. Tell me what burger you want, and I'll see you there.'

CHAPTER SIX

THE LAST OF the day shift were queuing to get out of the multistorey car park, and Llwyd wouldn't be surprised to find that Mattie was waiting for him down at Hetty's. It was three miles from here to the marina, but it was downhill all the way, and the cycle lane would cut half a mile from Mattie's journey.

When he arrived, she was standing outside the small shop, her bike propped up against the wall beside her and a cycle helmet dangling from her hand.

'I've got a ticket.' She waved one of the raffle tickets that Hetty gave her customers to indicate their position in the queue. 'Five minutes.'

'Let me go. If Hetty sees me standing outside, she'll never forgive me if I don't go and say hello…'

His entrance was accompanied by a small scream from behind the till. 'Llwyd Morgan, as I live and breathe… I heard you were home!'

'I'm not quite home until I've had one of your organic burgers.' Llwyd responded to Hetty's beckoning hand, leaning over the counter so she could plant a kiss on his cheek.

'Of course not. What would you like, bach?'

That was another thing that told Llwyd he was home. The Welsh endearment, which actually meant *small* but was used between family and friends of any size, was something he didn't remember missing, but now he realised he had. Hetty was focussed on him, completely ignoring the couple waiting to pay.

'It's already on order.' He handed the raffle ticket over to Hetty and stepped back, motioning the couple forward. She took the hint, ringing up their purchases and wishing them a cheery good evening.

The hatch from the kitchen opened and Hetty turned, grabbing the next bag and inspecting the number stapled to the top. 'Here we are. Two cheeseburgers, two salads and two rounds of chips… You're with that nice girl from the hospital?'

Llwyd knew exactly what that meant. Ever since he'd reached his teens, ordering two burgers from Hetty involved questions about who the second one was for. And she made the word *with* encompass all of the thoughts that had been intruding into Llwyd's mind over the past weeks.

'Mattie's a doctor, Hetty. We're colleagues.'

'Yes, of course.' Hetty managed to pour a liberal measure of disbelief into her words, and Llwyd ignored her. He knew that the more he tried to explain, the less Hetty would believe him.

Hetty handed over the bag and he propped it onto the counter, pulling a note out of his wallet. When he turned to leave, she called after him.

'Change, Llwyd…'

'Put it in the box, Hetty.' There was always a box by the till, collecting for a good cause.

'Thanks. We're collecting to resurface the children's playground in Stryd y Eglwys. Bonded rubber, which drains off to reduce pollutants…' Hetty always did favour causes to do with children and the environment, and this one clearly ticked all the boxes.

'Sounds great. Hopefully, you'll be reducing my work-load.' Llwyd tucked the bag under his arm, feeling in his pocket for some more loose change and dropped it into the collection box. 'See you later, Hetty.'

'Sooner would be better, bach…'

They walked down to the boat together, and Llwyd lifted Mattie's bike onto the deck before she and it tumbled into the water, securing it carefully while she unlocked the hatch that led to the kitchen area. Then she looked up at him suddenly.

'I don't suppose…can we take the boat out? Eat in the bay?' Mattie held the keys out in an obvious hint that *he'd* be taking the boat out for her.

'Sure. I'll cast her off while you deal with the burgers.'

Mattie raised an eyebrow. 'Who do you think I am, Long John Silver? I don't think I can balance chips on plates while the boat's moving.'

Llwyd laughed. She could charm the birds from the trees with just that one eyebrow. 'All right, then. If you're not going to do anything useful in the galley, then you'd better drive.

Mattie pressed her lips together and for a moment he thought she was going to chicken out. Then she walked up to the helm. 'You'd better watch me like a hawk. If I crash into anything here, there's going to be hell to pay.'

Mattie's progress out of the marina and across the bay might have been extremely slow, but she listened to his instructions and it was faultless. They anchored in shallow water in a secluded spot near the mouth of the bay, and Llwyd fetched a couple of plates from the galley while Mattie unwrapped the foil around the burgers and arranged the napkins.

'Mmm.' Mattie took a bite from hers. 'Hetty's cheese-burgers really *are* the best. You and she are old friends?'

'Yes, I've known her ever since I was a kid, she and my mum are very friendly. I remember them both sitting at our kitchen table, working out where Hetty could source fresh, organic ingredients, and how to cook them without using too much fat. She used to experiment on Huw and me with her recipes. I think that's where he got the idea of going to culinary school.'

'That's nice. To know people that you grew up with.' She stabbed at her salad with a fork. 'Are you happy to be home?'

He'd come back from London because after the attack, Llwyd had felt himself redefined by forces out of his control. He was alone and hurt, and as the world seemed to close in on him, there was only one place left to go. And his family needed him. Looking after Peter while Huw and Georgina got their restaurant back on its feet was too much for his parents, and helping out was the only way he could make a difference any more.

But then his relationship with his nephew had started to become more important in his life. He'd begun to find some peace in remembered places and people. And then he'd met Mattie. As he sat with her on a gently rocking boat, surrounded by the bay that he knew every inch of... *This* felt like home.

'Right now, it feels really good to be back.'

Mattie looked up at him. She seemed to know that something wasn't right, and that there were things that he'd chosen not to say.

'Right now is what really matters, isn't it?'

Llwyd nodded. 'Yes, it is.'

They ate in silence. Llwyd could almost feel himself

soaking up the relaxed rhythm of the water. Letting the warm breeze gently tease the worries of the day loose and blow them away.

'Brachial plexus injury.' The past felt as if it was hovering between them, and Llwyd wanted to sweep it aside. To be able to reach past it, to Mattie's smile.

She nodded. 'Motorbike accident?'

There was a roughly fifty percent chance of her being right. 'Good guess, but no. I was stabbed and the nerve was severed.' Now that he'd actually gone past the point of no return, it was almost a relief. Saying it was easier than he'd thought it might be.

'And they operated to repair it?'

She was self-possessed, calm. Almost clinical. But Llwyd could feel Mattie's warmth, see it in her eyes. She'd found the only way that he could talk about this without drawing back from it, and it made him feel more in control. Stronger.

'I'm guessing it was your median nerve that was affected.'

Llwyd nodded. He didn't need to explain that the wound that had caused all this was at the back of his shoulder, where the nerves ran from his spine down his arm. That he might never regain the full use of his hand, and that any recovery that was possible might take years.

'How's the pain?' Mattie knew, too, that the pain associated with an injured nerve could be long-lasting, and often didn't respond to traditional painkillers.

'It took a year, but apart from waking up occasionally with what feels like pins and needles in my arm, I'm completely pain-free now.'

'And you sleep?'

He knew what that question meant. 'I have nightmares. Every night, at first, and now…from time to time.' He shrugged. 'Darkness can be challenging.'

She nodded, never breaking eye contact with him. It was touching that Mattie could hear all of this and accept it. 'What happened, Llwyd? All of it.'

She knew there was more. Mattie wanted the whole story, not just a piece of it.

'I was walking across the car park of the hospital where I was working in London. It was late, I'd been operating all day and I was tired, and not taking any notice of anything that might be going on around me. I didn't see them until they were on me. Three or four of them, I'm not sure.' He shrugged. 'All I felt at first was the shock. I didn't realise I'd been stabbed. I felt it when I hit the ground and they started kicking me, though...'

'I'm so sorry that happened to you.' Llwyd thought he saw tears in Mattie's eyes and tried not to look at them.

'It was...' He took a breath, realising that he was trembling. 'I had a collapsed lung, and my spleen was ruptured. I was losing blood from the stab wounds...'

Mattie reached forward, the tips of her fingers just a shiver away from his left hand. When he moved to touch her fingers he felt hers curl around his. Reaching for the hand that had been injured felt more intimate than anything, as if Mattie was there to protect him at his most vulnerable.

'Take a breath, and say whatever it is you want to say.'

He *should* know how to do this, but he wasn't listening to the professional voice in his own head. The one that was used to dealing with these kinds of situations. 'Sorry, I...'

Mattie twisted her mouth in a gentle rebuke. 'I know. We're doctors, we deal with things. Only we're human beings, as well.'

Suddenly, he was strong again. 'I was lucky. They took my car keys along with my wallet, and the receptionist in the main building saw them burning rubber out of the car

park and reckoned it couldn't be me at the wheel. She sent a
security guard over, and he found me and raised the alarm.
I remember seeing a nurse that I knew in A&E and thinking *Okay, I'm going to be all right now*. She stayed with me
until they took me down to theatre…'

Mattie nodded. 'That's nice. Someone to hold on to.'

She was the one who was there for him now. In Llwyd's
experience, people who were there for him didn't always
stay, but he'd take this moment, even if it was all there was.

'I woke up hurting…'

'Yeah, I bet you were.'

Llwyd grimaced. 'Panicking a bit, too.'

'Of course. You'd been through a lot.'

'I didn't cope with it all that well.'

She leaned forward, her gaze catching his and holding
it. 'No one does, Llwyd. The emotional fallout from something like this isn't an optional extra, it's real. It takes time
to get over it, and a lot of support.'

He shrugged. 'I had… I was in a relationship when it
happened. The cracks were beginning to show and I'd felt
it was only a matter of time before Hannah and I decided
to call it a day. But she stayed with me and looked after me
really well when I made it home.'

Mattie nodded, wordlessly. Waiting…

'I was just so grateful for that. I thought maybe we'd
turned a corner, somehow found each other again. It felt like
a new beginning, but it didn't last. She told me that she'd
stayed because she felt she couldn't face our friends again
if she left. But *I* was different and things were never going
to be the same as they were.'

Something stopped in his throat. He'd known that things
wouldn't be the same, but Llwyd had felt that he was at least
working his way back to the life he'd known.

Suddenly, Mattie lost her cool, staring at him with a look of undisguised anger on her face. Then he felt her hand tighten around his, keeping hold of him.

'I'm so sorry that all those things happened to you, Llwyd. But do they make you a different person?'

'I have scars. Nightmares…'

Mattie pursed her lips. 'I don't underestimate how hard that must have been, for you and the people around you. But there's another way of looking at it.'

Maybe he should have known that Mattie would see past it all, in a way that Hannah couldn't. Maybe he *had* known and he'd just been waiting for her to say it.

'What's that?'

'Maybe you were a complete pain in the neck when you were recovering. I have no way of knowing. But why Hannah thought that it was a good idea to let you think that the relationship had rekindled, when she could so easily have just looked out for you as a friend…' Mattie shook her head. 'That's beyond me.'

'Maybe she just made a mistake. Or changed her mind, when she saw the realities of the situation.'

Mattie frowned, clearly angered by the suggestion. 'If she had a guy who's as willing to give her the benefit of the doubt as you obviously are, she might feel that making it all your fault was a cruel thing to do.'

Something lifted from him. Maybe it had all been in the telling of a story that he'd tried so hard not to tell. Maybe it was just Mattie, and the way she didn't pull her punches, but still ended up making the world around her seem a little brighter.

'So it's a no-blame situation?'

'Why not? If you want to leave someone or something, then that's enough. You don't have to come up with a load of reasons to convince yourself and everyone else that you have no choice. You have to own your decisions.'

Mattie had thought about this. Probably not quite in this context, although it seemed that she had plenty of practise in leaving places and people. That should make Llwyd wary, but somehow it didn't.

'I'll have to think about that. Later, perhaps. I really appreciate having been able to talk about it but... This is enough.' Suddenly, he wanted to wash the taste of words from his mouth and just appreciate the peace and quiet of a summer evening on the water. 'I don't suppose you have any juice in the fridge, do you?'

She smiled. 'I'll go. Call it yet another learning exercise. Practising getting drinks out of the fridge and into a couple of glasses without throwing them all over the place.'

Llwyd chuckled. 'This I've got to see...'

Listening to all that had happened to Llwyd had been hard. But as much as he'd seemed to need to say it, he also needed to stop. Know that he could leave it behind for a while and step back into the present. When he'd smiled, it had seemed so much easier for her to leave it behind, too.

She'd insisted on going to the galley alone. Mattie had managed to extract the ice cubes from their holder without anything slithering away from her, but then she'd knocked over the measuring jug and sent everything crashing onto the floor. She'd cleared up the mess and got ready to start again, when she heard Llwyd making his way below deck.

'I can manage...' She frowned as she saw him appear in the doorway of the galley. 'Shouldn't you be upstairs in case anyone tries to crash into us?'

'It's unlikely. And you have a proximity sensor, which will alert us if anyone gets too close. I've switched that on.'

'Oh. That sounds like a handy thing.' Mattie tried not to look too surprised. 'Actually, I may have gone a little overboard with this. If you're allowed to mention *overboard* when you're on a boat.'

He chuckled. 'You can mention it, but try not to put it into practise. What are you making?'

'Lemon and lime, soda water, grenadine...with cocktail cherries and straws. I got the cocktail cherries and straws when I first had the boat.'

Llwyd nodded approvingly. 'Keeping up appearances?'

'That was the general idea. Only I never quite got around to sipping cocktails on deck and watching the world go by. Takeout coffee and sandwiches were about my limit.'

'It's about time you christened her properly, then.' His lips twitched into a smile. 'May I...?'

They'd touched before. Plenty of times when Llwyd had been helping her drive the boat for the first time, and when they'd been working together. But maybe this time he was acknowledging that a little pleasure might be involved, and the thought that physical contact meant something more to him than the practical made the idea even more thrilling.

'Please do.'

His feet were planted a little apart, and he was as steady as a rock in the soft roll of the craft. All the same, he reached up with his right hand, gripping the handhold that was set into the ceiling. Mattie smiled up at him. One hand for the boat, and one for her...

His left arm curled around her waist, cradling her against his body. She could lean back against him, with both hands free to work. And it was delicious, her thoughts somewhere far from the practical, savouring the feel of this almost-embrace as she opened the cupboard above the small counter, taking out the things she'd need.

'How do I do this when you're not around?'

'I heard you did an emergency tracheostomy the other day. If you can do that, you can do this, Mattie. It's all just a matter of practice and technique.'

She wanted so much to turn and see the tenderness in his voice mirrored in his eyes. Fall into his embrace and forget about everything else. Being on the water seemed to encourage the feeling that the bonds to their everyday lives were somehow loosened and they could do whatever they wanted.

But they'd both packed for the trip, bringing along their own vulnerabilities. Whatever happened between them, however far they dared go, it needed to be on dry land. Where everyday life was a little closer, and fantasy a little further away.

But she could still enjoy. When the boat rolled a little she instinctively grabbed hold of the countertop, and Llwyd let go of her waist for a moment, steadying the bottle of grenadine before it toppled over. A heady synchronicity that balanced each of their movements into one flowing action.

'Stand by. I'm going to mix it all up.' She was almost done. Mattie felt Llwyd's arm tighten around her again, and she let go of the countertop, relying on him. The mixture swirled and rattled in the measuring jug, and she poured it into two wide-bottomed tumblers. They were done.

'Put everything away, or it'll be all over the floor before we've finished our drinks,' he reminded her softly. Mattie cleared up the mess, putting everything back in its place, and allowed herself to turn the corners of her mouth down. Soon, there would be no more need to touch, and she suspected that neither of them was ready to do it without a good excuse.

He let her go, just slowly enough to allow her time to consider the idea of turning to kiss him. Maybe that was on his mind, too. Maybe he'd be the first to break and kiss her. But it was far too soon to even think about that. There was a lot for both of them to clear out of the way before they could even contemplate a proper embrace.

Cocktails on a boat were the perfect way to wind down after a long day at work. When the sun began to near the horizon, Mattie took the step of suggesting that she could bring the boat back across the bay, if Llwyd would manoeuvre it back to its place in the marina. She stood on the dock, watching as he checked the moorings and then lifted her bicycle back off the boat.

'I want to say sorry…' Now that she was back here, something was nagging at the back of her mind.

Llwyd gave her a querying look. 'Whatever for?'

'That evening—after we met at the pub—I let you walk me back here and just didn't think about how you were going to get home.'

He shrugged. All the same, she could see in his face that *he'd* thought about the problem. 'It wasn't late. There were plenty of people around still, and the dockside's pretty well lit. I got a taxi at the place by the pub.'

That was all good to know. 'All the same. I looked at you and you're a lot bigger than me, and stronger. I fell into the trap of thinking that it was okay for you to walk with me, and not really necessary for me to wonder how you were going to get home.'

He was silent for a moment, looking down at the bicycle that was standing between them. Then his green-eyed gaze caught hers. 'Thanks. I… It's probably a little crazy.'

'No, it's not. No one's invulnerable, and friends should look out for one another. How are you getting home?'

Llwyd chuckled. 'Same way I got here?'

'Sounds logical. I'm doing the same.' Mattie started to wheel her bicycle towards the exit gates of the marina.

'Can't I give you a lift?'

No. Absolutely not. Someone who had a boat she hardly knew how to use was one thing—she'd not had too much choice in the matter and Llwyd had already accepted it. Someone who chose to live in a bus was another thing entirely, and she wasn't quite ready to show him the secret that she'd kept from everyone.

'I'll be fine. I take the cycle path that runs around the bay and then cut up into the village.' She gestured towards the other side of the bay, and the houses that spread out up the hill towards Gwen and Owen's farm. The last leg of the journey was a technicality. 'It takes me twenty minutes and it won't be dark for another hour.'

Llwyd hesitated, clearly assessing her route home.

'And since you don't have a bike rack, I'll have to leave my bicycle on the boat. Then I'll have to walk to work in the morning, and I'm really *not* going to thank you for that.'

He nodded, and Mattie waved to the security guard, who opened the gates for them and wished them a good evening.

CHAPTER SEVEN

LLWYD'S COTTAGE HAD been in the family for generations, and since his parents and brother both had homes of their own when his gran had died, they'd decided to do the place up and let it out as a holiday home. When Llwyd had first started to think about moving back here from London, he'd asked whether he might buy his father and brother's shares out, and it had seemed like an ideal solution. Gran would have liked the place to stay in the family, and Huw and Georgina were glad of a lump sum, which had finally enabled them to reopen the restaurant.

Everything had fallen into place. He knew every inch of the village and the bay that it overlooked, and practically everyone who lived here. He could help look after Peter while Huw and Georgina were getting the restaurant back on its feet, and he quickly managed to secure a job offer at the hospital. The one thing he hadn't factored into his thinking was a new relationship, because Llwyd had come here to heal his wounds, not to risk opening them again.

He'd tried so hard to think of Mattie as a friend and a colleague, because that was what fitted into the life he'd carefully chosen for himself. Someone who'd accept a steadying arm without either of them having to think about it. But when he'd put his arm around her, he'd felt his own shiver of delight echo through her body.

Maybe. Just maybe… Llwyd dismissed the thought. Everything about Mattie betrayed a restless spirit and she couldn't want someone like him, who'd deliberately tied himself to one spot. Chemistry was just…chemistry. Something that might intrude from time to time and then fade soon enough if it wasn't nurtured.

Maybe he was avoiding Mattie, and maybe she was avoiding him. And maybe if they truly *were* just friends he wouldn't have even noticed that their paths didn't cross at the hospital on Friday. As Llwyd ended his shift, he gave in to the inevitable and texted her.

Hope everything goes well with your course. Cwtch…

Llwyd backspaced. Hugs were okay at the end of a text and he'd seen Mattie looking up Welsh words she didn't know on her phone before.

Actually, it was the use of Welsh that made it seem so intimate. The language he'd grown up with at home always seemed to express the warmth of family ties to Llwyd. It was something special and if it meant something to him to share that with Mattie, she probably wouldn't even notice.

Cwtch.

He typed the hugs in again and sent the text before he changed his mind. Llwyd put his phone back into his pocket, pulling it back out again ten minutes later when he felt it vibrate.

Am I going to need hugs?

She made her point with a scared face emoji.

Can't wait to show you what I've learned. Cwtch.

Llwyd couldn't help smiling. Maybe Mattie *did* understand.

He and Peter had spent most of Saturday at the boatyard. Llwyd couldn't help but glance out over the bay from time to time, and he spotted the powerboat that his father used for the beginner's courses, too far away to see who was at the helm. If it was Mattie, she seemed to be doing well...

He'd decided to cook a proper Sunday lunch and asked his mother over since she was on her own today. Llwyd was just congratulating himself on having managed to peel everything without too much help, and was stacking the plates in the dishwasher, when the call came. He glanced at his phone, wondering who wanted him and whether he could reject the call, and then answered immediately.

'Yeah. Dad?'

'We've got a situation.' Llwyd stiffened. That meant an emergency in the language that his father always used when he was teaching. 'We're aground off Tywod Beach, one person taken ill. Mattie says it's... What was it, Mattie?'

He heard Mattie's voice in the background. Calm and cool, which concerned Llwyd even more. It was the tone of voice she used when she was working.

'Supraventricular tachycardia.' His father repeated Mattie's diagnosis. 'I have a call in to the coast guard but they're pretty busy this afternoon and it might take a while for the nearest boat to get to us.'

'I'm at home. Mum's here, I'll ask her to look after Peter. Tell Mattie I'll be with you as soon as I can.'

His father relayed the message and heard Mattie's voice again, saying that was great and everything was going to be fine. She was clearly managing her patient's expectations and keeping everything calm.

But supraventricular tachycardia was an emergency—a heart arrhythmia where the two sides of the heart had stopped beating in sync, and the heart began to race to correct itself back to a normal rhythm. If the boat had run aground on the long, sloping shelf off Tywod Beach then there was no way that they could get to the shore.

'There's someone on standby with the recovery boat?' The boatyard's recovery craft was usually called out at least once during summer weekends, and his father always made sure that someone was on duty.

'Tom's there. I'll call him now and tell him to wait for you.' His father ended the call abruptly, and Llwyd turned to find that his mother had heard his side of the conversation and already gone to fetch his windcheater and life jacket from the hall.

The boatyard was ten minutes' walk from his cottage, and five if you ran. Llwyd sprinted, arriving to find Tom at the helm of the recovery boat, waiting for him.

'If they're where I think they are, they're on the shoals, a bit further out from the beach.' Tom was already thinking ahead, as the craft gathered speed. 'Depending on how fast they were going, we should be able to get in reasonably close and just pull them off. What's this supra...whatever?'

'It's a heart arrhythmia. Mattie and I can try to stabilise the patient, but we'll definitely need to get them to hospital as quickly as we can.'

Tom nodded. 'So I'll take extra care not to run aground.'

'Yeah. And I want to get across to them as soon as I can.'

'Understood.' Tom nodded, and as they turned out of the

mouth of the bay, Llwyd saw his father's craft, immobile on the far side of the shoals.

They made a wide arc, keeping well clear of the shallow water, then Tom edged the boat carefully towards the stranded craft. He could see Mattie now, bending over a burly-looking man, who was lying on the cushioned bench on the main deck. His father was at the stern, leaning over to gauge the depth of the water.

For now, Llwyd had to wait, although he was impatient to get to Mattie and the man. His father and Tom were calling to each other, assessing how close they might get, and the recovery craft edged gingerly towards the other boat.

'That's it, no closer,' his father called across, and Tom nodded, keeping the recovery craft steady in the water about four feet from the stern of the stranded boat. 'Can you make it, Llwyd?'

He was going to have to. There was no way that Llwyd wasn't going to try. He threw the light, strong tow rope across to his father, who secured his end of it. Tom moved the recovery craft forward a couple of feet to keep the line taut.

'Don't get your feet wet, bach,' his father called over to him.

It wasn't going to be easy to keep his feet dry, but that was the least of his worries. Llwyd slid across, winding his left arm around the rope and gripping it with his right hand. His father caught him, manhandling him on board. It was ungainly, and his shoes were now squelching with water, but it worked.

He left his father to discuss the next step with Tom and stepped onto the small main deck. Mattie shot him a grin.

'This is Llwyd. He's a doctor.' Mattie spoke to the man. 'Llwyd, this is Euan.'

Euan seemed quiet and comfortable. In these circumstances the best that Mattie could have done for him was to keep him calm, and since the heart rate monitor that was clipped to his finger was hovering at one-ninety bpm, and they were stuck almost a mile from the shore, that can't have been easy.

'Hi, Euan.' Llwyd smiled.

'What's happening…?'

Mattie grinned down at him. 'We'll be moving soon and on the way to the hospital. In the meantime, Llwyd and I are both here to make sure you're okay. Give us a moment.'

Euan nodded, and Mattie drew back from him a little, turning to Llwyd. 'Euan's heart rate is steady.' That sounded like a positive, but when it was steady at one-ninety bpm, it wasn't. 'He's feeling dizzy and light-headed, but he's remained conscious and responsive and his blood pressure is stable. He has no history of any other heart problems, and I've checked for any signs of heart disease.'

'Valsalva manoeuvre?' That might not work, but it was a technique sometimes employed by ambulance crews to 'reset' a patient's heartbeat back to normal. There would be drugs at the hospital, which would do the same thing with a higher degree of certainty, but they weren't currently at the hospital.

Mattie nodded. 'That's what I was thinking, but I couldn't do it on my own, and your father's been busy keeping us afloat.' She turned to Euan. 'We're going to do a procedure that involves you blowing into an empty syringe to push the plunger out, if you can. Then we'll tip you backwards while lifting your legs. It sounds a little weird, but it's completely safe and a good first option for getting your heart back to normal, before we get to the hospital.'

'All right.'

'Would you like us to demonstrate first?' Llwyd grinned at him.

'That's okay. I trust you.' Euan glanced at Mattie and she nodded. He trusted *her*. Llwyd hadn't done anything yet to earn that trust.

'Right, then.' Mattie reached for the boat's medical kit and withdrew a wrapped syringe.

Llwyd rose, moving aft to tell his father that they didn't want any sudden movement on the boat for a few minutes. Mattie arranged cushions on the deck and they both helped Euan to sit down on them, his legs out in front of him. Calm, cool and seamless. Mattie showed Euan how to breathe into the empty syringe, while Llwyd supported his back.

'On my count?' she murmured softly and Llwyd nodded. The plunger of the syringe began to move slightly as Euan tried to push out a breath, and Mattie mouthed a silent *three—two—one...*

As Llwyd tipped Euan's body back, so he was lying flat, Mattie raised his legs. After fifteen seconds they returned Euan to a sitting position for a minute, then Llwyd allowed him to relax back against the cushions.

'I think... that may have worked.' Mattie's gaze was fixed on the heart monitor.

Euan's heart rate was beginning to fall now. Llwyd checked his blood pressure and nodded to Mattie.

'Are you feeling a little more comfortable?' Mattie smiled at Euan.

'I'm okay. Feeling a bit better.'

'That's great. Looks as if your heart rate is beginning to get back to normal now. We'll still be taking you to the hospital, because you need to be checked over, and doctors generally prefer a roof over their heads when they do that.'

Euan smiled suddenly, reaching for Mattie's hand. 'You did just fine. Thanks, Mattie.'

'It was our pleasure. You did pretty well, yourself.' Clearly, the two of them had hit it off in the past couple of days, and Llwyd's father's team building had helped lay the foundations for a good outcome.

'I expect Dad and Tom have a plan to get us back to shore by now.' Llwyd grinned at her and Mattie nodded, catching his arm before he could get to his feet. He looked down, noticing that his windcheater was torn on the inner side of his left elbow, where he'd wound his arm around the tow line.

'It's okay...' Suddenly, he didn't care. He wanted Mattie to take a look and decide how his arm was for herself.

'Let me see.' Llwyd straightened his arm and she brushed the torn material to one side. Underneath, the skin wasn't broken. That was good to know, because being without a spleen meant he had to be diligent about washing and dressing cuts and grazes.

'That's all right. Any pain?'

'No.'

'You can move your fingers okay?'

'Not entirely. But there's no change there.' A flash of intimacy suddenly bound them together and Llwyd smiled.

She shot him a look that would have melted the heart of an iceberg. 'All right. You can go.'

Llwyd stood up, walking over to his father. They'd achieved their first goal, and the second was getting Euan back to dry land.

Once Llwyd had given the all-clear to try dislodging the boat it hadn't been too difficult a task. His father's boat can't have been going at full speed when it hit the shoal, and a little extra traction timed to coincide with the swell of the waves had pulled it free quickly.

All the same, they'd transferred Euan over to the rescue boat, in case there was any unnoticed damage to the other boat. Mattie went with him, slithering across the deck in the unfamiliar roll of the craft, and Tom caught her arm, helping her to the seat next to Euan's before the boat moved away. They headed straight back towards the boatyard, to continue their journey to the hospital by car.

Llwyd and his father had nursed the speedboat back to the boatyard and were now sitting in deckchairs on the jetty, with his mother and Peter, who'd come up from the cottage. Llwyd had taken off his wet shoes, putting his feet up to allow the hems of his jeans to dry off in the warm breeze, and his father had gone to fetch two bottles of beer, handing one to him.

'So… What made you run aground, Dad?'

'Llwyd! You could be a little less hurtful about it. When did your father last run a boat aground?' His mother admonished him.

'Sorry. What made—whoever—run aground?' Llwyd was hoping that it hadn't been Mattie, as that might have dealt a severe blow to her confidence.

'Mattie did exactly the right thing. I think we'll be making a sailor out of her.' His father pre-empted Llwyd's next question. 'I'd taken them over to Tywod Beach to show them how to spot shallow water, and where to place the boat to stay clear of it. I demonstrated how far they needed to stay from the shoals and asked Euan to take the helm on the way back. Mattie asked a question and I just turned for a second…' His father shook his head, and Peter followed suit, clearly following the conversation closely.

'And?'

'Suddenly, the boat veered round, almost sent me flying. Mattie was hanging on with both hands…'

'Advantage of not quite having your sea legs yet.'

His father nodded. 'Yes. Euan had felt suddenly dizzy, and he instinctively hung on to the helm, pulling it hard to port as he fell. Mattie took over and tried to steer away from the shoals but even I couldn't have managed that. She did a near-perfect emergency stop, putting the throttle into neutral and then reverse while she hung on to the wheel for dear life. It's always the first thing I teach people, and she remembered it.'

Llwyd nodded, warm admiration for her flooding his veins. He should have known that Mattie was resourceful enough to make the best out of any situation. He grinned at his father, who silently pointed one finger in his direction and then away. If Peter hadn't been around he would have voiced the question.

You and Mattie? Anything going on?

Llwyd shook his head, glad that Peter *was* around. If he'd had to answer out loud, he might have started to over-explain…

'Did Mattie save you?' Peter looked up at his grandfather.

'I believe she did. She made sure that the crew were all safe. That's the first thing you have to consider when you get a boat of your own, *bach*.'

Peter began to interrogate his grandfather about *when* he might have a boat of his own, but Llwyd wasn't listening any more. He'd heard a car pull through the gates of the boatyard, and when he turned, he saw that Tom and Mattie were back. Perhaps this wasn't quite the right time to rush towards her and gather her into his arms, and Llwyd stayed in his seat.

'Ah. Here they are.' His father got to his feet. 'Peter,

would you like to come and help me print out Mattie's certificate of competence?'

'Yes, okay, Tad-cu.' Peter used the Welsh word for grandad. 'I think you might need a bit of help.'

His mother caught Llwyd's eye. 'You stay there. I'll go and keep an eye on them. That young woman deserves something a little more presentable than your father's best efforts at word processing, and we can't rely on Peter to keep him under control.'

'Thanks, Mum.' Llwyd smiled up at his mother. His father had many talents, but computers weren't one of them.

He watched as his father exchanged a few words with Tom and Mattie, and Tom joined the party who were heading for the boatyard's office—leaving Mattie alone and on a trajectory that led straight towards him. Llwyd went to fetch another of the faded deckchairs from the pile in the workshop, setting it down next to his.

'How's Euan?' Llwyd resisted the temptation to fall wordlessly into the depths of her blue eyes, and managed to get the question out.

Mattie smiled. 'He's fine. They saw him immediately and checked him over and he was still going at a steady sixty bpm. They'll be referring him on to an arrhythmia specialist, but this may be an isolated incident.'

He nodded. 'My father tells me that you did pretty well out there.'

'Did he?' Mattie looked a little surprised. 'I couldn't help running aground.'

'Dad said you did a near-perfect emergency stop. You know that you risk breaking the prop shaft if you don't get it right?'

Mattie flushed. 'Well, no, I didn't. I didn't break the prop shaft, did I?'

'No, you'd know all about it if you had. Dad said that he couldn't have made the turn to avoid the shoals, either.'

'Did he?' Mattie was all smiles now. 'I wonder if I'll get my certificate.'

'You might.' Mattie's face fell and Llwyd grinned. 'Dad's gone to print it, and Peter's helping him, which means you may get a piece of dog-eared paper with his signature on it. But Mum's keeping an eye on them, so we can hope for the best.'

She gave him a luminous smile, flipping her finger towards his bottle of beer. 'Have I earned a sip?'

He could have gone and fetched her a drink, but he'd rather share. Llwyd handed the bottle over to her and she took a mouthful.

'Mmm. That's nice and cool.' She handed the bottle back, leaning back in her deckchair, the sunshine caressing her face. Llwyd could have kissed her, right then and there. But sitting in the sun, passing the bottle lazily back and forth between them, was a more than adequate second best.

His father returned, presenting her with a manila envelope, and Mattie withdrew a laminated sheet. Dad didn't usually laminate certificates, and the course that Mattie had completed was for the lowest level of competence. Llwyd made a mental note to thank his mother for doing Mattie proud.

'I passed!' Mattie squealed with excitement, thrusting the certificate towards Llwyd so he could see it. 'Ten out of ten for everything! Thank you so much!'

'You earned it.' His father sat down on the deckchair next to her, balancing a folder on his knees. 'Are you still going to do the follow-up course on navigating after dark?'

Mattie grinned. 'Yes, please. But won't you be putting that off? I doubt that Euan's going to be making it next weekend. He'll be fine, but he had a scare and he'll probably be taking it easy for a little while.'

'That's all right. I thought that as it's just you, you might like to go out on the *Matilda Rae*. It wouldn't do any harm for you to learn on your own boat. It won't take us long to go through everything you need to know, and if we have time we can go for a spot of night fishing afterwards.'

Night fishing. His father must like Mattie. Llwyd smiled.

'I've never been fishing…' Mattie hesitated.

'About time you tried it then, eh?' His father glanced over at Llwyd, and he nodded in agreement.

'I'd love to, then. Thank you. And if you don't mind, I'd really like it if we could do it on the *Matilda Rae*.'

'Right, then.' His father handed Mattie the folder. 'Have a read through that, and I'll see you next Saturday evening.'

'I'll look forward to it.' Mattie clutched the folder to her chest, giving an excited smile.

His father left them alone, again, eager to check the speedboat over for any scrapes on the hull. Mattie leaned back in her deckchair. 'It's been a great weekend.'

Llwyd smiled. It hadn't *just* been a great weekend. Mattie had made it a perfect one.

CHAPTER EIGHT

'WHAT HAVE YOU GOT?' Mattie found Llwyd at the admin station on Monday afternoon.

'Broken arm. I'm just waiting for the X-rays. You?'

'A new mum. She brought her baby in because she was convinced that he was crying differently and trying to tell her something. I've given him a very careful once-over and he's fine. She's not coping, though, and she's really anxious about everything. I've given her health visitor a call, and I'm just waiting for her to call me back, so that we can arrange some extra support for her.'

Llwyd nodded. 'Since we both have an idle moment... I don't suppose you're free one evening this week?'

'I was hoping you might be. I wanted to try my driving skills out on you.'

He chuckled. 'I think that it's my turn to play host. Dinner at my place?'

'Oh... Yes, okay. I mean...' Mattie hadn't been expecting that. 'Dinner would be very nice, thank you. How about Wednesday?'

'Wednesday's good for me.' His phone beeped and he glanced at it. 'Sorry, the X-rays are ready. If I don't see you before then, I'll text you to arrange a time...'

Had Llwyd just asked her out on a date? Dinner on Wednesday evening *sounded* like a date, but asking in an odd moment between an X-ray and a health visitor sounded more like an afterthought.

But then Mattie had always been at pains to make her invitations sound casual. Even if the time they spent together was shifting—slowly but surely—from two people who enjoyed each other's company, to two people who wanted to get to know each other a great deal better.

She had to go carefully. Llwyd was a man capable of almost anything he set his mind to, but he was vulnerable, as well, and Cartref Bay was the one place in the world that could heal him. And she was torn, between the stability of the family she loved, and the irresponsible free spirits of Leigh and Helen, the two people who'd made her. Always moving, always searching for a home that might reconcile the two sides of her nature. She and Llwyd couldn't be more incompatible if they'd tried, but somehow they seemed to fit together perfectly.

Risk and reward. Something special was growing between her and Llwyd and it outweighed all of the risks. Despite all of her reservations, Mattie couldn't say no to this. She trusted him and they'd handle the difficulties one by one, as they came to them.

Mattie had left her bicycle at home and booked a taxi to take her into work on Wednesday morning. She'd decided to take a taxi home again this evening; that would be natural enough. She made a beeline for the locker room, changing into her scrubs and hanging the dress she'd chosen for this evening carefully in her locker. So far, so good.

Llwyd was working in A&E for most of the day on a whole string of cases that required his expertise. They finished the shift by working together, with a child who had a stress fracture in her foot. Llwyd had fitted her with a supportive boot, and spoken at some length with her mother.

'She seems to have got the idea of walking with crutches at least.' Mattie watched as the thirteen-year-old girl and her mother walked slowly together out of the department.

'Yeah. She really doesn't want to give up her ballet classes, but I think I've made it very clear to both her and her mother that she must take a complete rest from them for a while. I'll be seeing her again, and we can put together a sensible plan to minimise the risk of future injuries.'

Mattie nodded. 'Maybe she'll have decided she doesn't want to do ballet any more by then.'

'Maybe. I wouldn't bank on it, though. She's quite obviously been in some discomfort for a while and been trying to work through it.' Llwyd allowed himself a frown, before the process of leaving a patient behind and moving on to the next thing on his agenda kicked in. 'You have someone else to see, or are you ready to go?'

'No, I'm finished for the day.' Mattie looked at her watch. Usually, she didn't think twice about leaving work thirty minutes late, but this evening it had deprived her of a whole half hour of Llwyd's company. 'I'll meet you in reception, in fifteen minutes?'

That would give Mattie time to shower, do something with her hair and maybe even put some makeup on. Preferably giving the impression that she'd just changed back out of her scrubs, the same as she did every evening.

'Sounds good.' His grin gave the impression that Llwyd might actually miss her while she was away. Mattie turned her back on him, so that he couldn't see the smile that sprang to her lips, and hurried away.

He was waiting for her in reception, wearing a shirt and a pair of chinos. Casual but smart. Llwyd had made an effort, too, and the understanding that tonight was something special for both of them brought an awkwardness to their greeting. As they walked through the high-capacity revolving doors, they found themselves alone for a moment in the large, slowly moving compartment.

'I'm just glad I didn't make the effort to dress up.' He leaned over, murmuring in her ear.

Suddenly, the tension broke. Mattie started to laugh, nudging her shoulder against his arm as they headed for the multistorey car park. 'Yes, that would have been embarrassing, wouldn't it?'

'Very. You look gorgeous, by the way.'

'You mean this old thing?' Mattie could be happy with the compliment now, and tease him a little.

'Yeah, that old thing.'

They were still laughing together when they reached his car. Somehow, Llwyd's opening the front passenger door made them both chuckle, and as they drove down the hill towards Cartref Bay, the evening seemed to open up before them, like a heavy-scented flower. Llwyd took the road that led towards the boatyard, turning into a narrow set of gates and parking outside a stone-built, whitewashed cottage, the high slate roof climbing from two-storey level at the front, and then sweeping down to one-storey height at the back. There was an air of tranquil solidity about the place, and a feeling that it had belonged here for so long that it had become part of the landscape.

'Is this yours? It's lovely, Llwyd.'

'It's mine to look after for a while. The place has been in my family for generations. We let it out for a while as a holiday home. When I came back here from London I bought Dad and Huw's shares out.'

'How old is it?' Mattie followed him to the wooden front door and they walked together into the hallway.

'It was built in about 1750, by my four-times-great-grandfather. He farmed here, but the land's no longer connected with the house. It's been passed down through various branches of the family, but there have always been Morgans here.'

'May I look around?'

Her request clearly pleased Llwyd, and Mattie decided to try the door on the left first. That led into a comfortable sitting room, with an inglenook fireplace and windows set deep into the thick, stone walls.

'What's this?' She ran her hand around an alcove, cut into the wall, which seemed to take pride of place in the room.

'That's where the family bible was kept. My dad has that for safekeeping. It tells the story of our family for a couple of hundred years.'

'It must be wonderful to have something like that. We have my grandad's papers, but nothing from before then.' Unless Leigh had family papers. Mattie had never thought to ask.

She walked back across the hallway to find a cosy, white-washed dining room, with a small study beyond. 'What's through there?' Mattie indicated a newer-looking door at the far end of the hall.

'This is the more recent part. It was added in the late eighteen hundreds.' He grinned, opening the door. Slate floors were replaced by seasoned oak floorboards and there was a step down into a long room, split by a square-shaped arch in the centre. It was flooded with light from the garden, with a kitchen on one side and a second living space on the other, lined with empty shelves, with an assortment of boxes stacked in the corner, a reminder that Llwyd had only recently moved in.

'My grandmother told me that when they inherited the house, it was really dark in here, so they opened up the back wall and added the extra windows. As she got older, Dad had thermal windows installed.' He smiled. 'Everyone's added something.'

'And you?'

'Not yet. Give me time.'

Mattie looked around. The kitchen was in need of a re-vamp, but maybe that would be Llwyd's contribution to the cottage. She opened a door that seemed to lead back towards the front of the house, and found a wooden stairway.

Llwyd flipped on a light, motioning for her to go up if she wanted, and she found a gleaming bathroom at the end of a long passage. Just one of the bedroom doors was open, clearly not in use because it contained just a bed and more boxes, but Mattie could see the potential. The high ceiling, which followed the shape of the roof, was criss-crossed by beams, pegged together with wooden staves, and she could imagine waking every morning to find new and different shadows playing across them.

She walked quickly past the closed doors, not daring to open them. Maybe this was why Llwyd had let her come up here alone—to allow her to explore without having to decide whether to take the step of showing her his own bedroom. That did feel like a step, over a line that was becoming in-creasingly blurred, and Mattie decided not to take it.

It was beautiful. Not just picture-perfect beautiful, al-though Mattie imagined that it would be when Llwyd settled in here. It was the story of a family, who had expanded the cottage up and back over the years, as times changed and people changed with them.

'This is more than just a place to live, isn't it?' She'd gone back downstairs and found him fiddling with the controls on the old range stove. 'It's your roots.' Roots that grew deep into the earth here.

'Yeah, I guess so. I didn't notice that much growing up,

but when I went to London… For a long while it was vibrant and exciting, with new opportunities. But after I was hurt, this place seemed able to curl around me and protect me, in a way that London never did.' He shrugged. 'I guess if you'd grown up in London, you'd feel a little differently?'

Maybe. London had seemed to wind around her, strangling her. 'Did you speak Welsh at home, or English?'

'A bit of both. My grandparents both came from Welsh-speaking homes, and they taught my dad and uncles. My mum's from South Wales where English is more prevalent. She only learned Welsh after she married Dad. By the time Huw and I came along, Welsh was being taught in schools again.'

'So…it's more than just a language, isn't it?'

He smiled, nodding. 'Very much so. Much of the love I had from my family when I was growing up was in Welsh.'

Mattie considered the idea for a moment. A language to express love. 'So which language do you dream in?'

Llwyd chuckled. 'A bit of both. Depends what I'm dreaming about, mostly.'

What *did* he dream about? Maybe the freedom of the open sea, which had begun to feature in her own dreams recently. But they were still different. His freedom was here, while Mattie responded to the rootless freedom of the open road.

'Do you miss London?' It was an innocent-enough question, but there was a trace of uncertainty in Llwyd's voice.

'I…' Mattie shrugged. 'London's a difficult place for me.'

He looked up from the hand-wrapped packages that he was taking from the refrigerator. 'How so?'

'A lot of expectations.' She almost wanted him to ask, even if the answer was challenging. But he didn't. Mattie watched as he transferred some part-baked bread from the freezer to the oven.

'My parents…my mother in particular, didn't want me to turn out the same as my biological parents. She didn't like Leigh much at all. She thought that he was trying to buy his way out of his responsibilities. She was mostly furious with Helen, though.'

Llwyd was suddenly still, looking at her thoughtfully. 'For getting pregnant?'

'Partly. No one thought that running off to Europe with Leigh was a great idea, but they all assumed she'd be back in time to take up her place at university. But she wasn't. The family had just about got used to that, and then the idea that she was pregnant and that Leigh had already gone back to America. The final straw was when she took off to see Leigh, two weeks before her due date.'

Llwyd leaned back against the worktop, his brow creased. 'She flew?'

'Yes, she managed to lie about how far on she was. Apparently, she had this idea that she'd turn up on Leigh's doorstep, have the baby and it would be a happy-ever-after. But she never got that far. She had pre-eclampsia, which she knew about but hadn't heeded any of the warnings, because this was a great love that would conquer anything. She was taken ill on the plane and rushed to hospital when it landed. I was born thirty minutes later, but Helen… They couldn't save her. Leigh hadn't known she was coming, and he wasn't there.'

Llwyd knew it all now. That she'd been brought up by parents who constantly feared that nature might overcome nurture at some point. Maybe he would have those fears about her, too. He seemed to be struggling with his thoughts.

'I have to admit that on the face of it her actions seem very rash. Did anyone ever ask why?'

Relief washed over Mattie. No one *had* asked that very simple question. 'I have some of Helen's sketch pads that my mum saved for me. I think there were diaries, as well, but I've never seen them. But from what I know of her she was talented and imaginative—and being the youngest child by quite a few years she always got her own way. Maybe she just needed someone to say *no* to her once in a while. A bit of direction, to channel all of that creative energy.'

Llwyd nodded. 'I can see now why you've never told your mum and dad about the boat.'

He understood. And he hadn't turned his back on her yet.

'They'd be… I don't know. Furious. Disappointed. They wouldn't understand that I can't let go of it, because… Helen and Leigh are a part of me. It's impractical but so were they. As far as Mum and Dad are concerned, I may move around a bit, but I'm gaining valuable experience and seniority by doing so, and that makes them happy.

'But not you?'

Another of Llwyd's insightful questions. And hard to answer.

'I don't know. I'm trying to find my balance, still. Maybe I'm a bit more like Helen than I'd like to admit.'

A smile played around his lips. 'Or maybe you're like *you*. Genetics and upbringing can be really important, but they don't rule your life. You do.'

'Thanks. That's a nice thing to say.' Now that she'd heard it, Mattie could let this go for a while. 'What are you cooking for dinner?'

'Nothing. You're cooking your own.' He bent down, taking an electric Raclette grill out of one of the kitchen cupboards. 'I'll just have to run an extension lead outside, and we can eat in the garden...'

Sliding back the doors that led from the kitchen to a small paved area outside, turned the whole garden into an extension of the cottage. Llwyd filled the table outside, vegetable kebabs and slices of salami and garlic sausage for the large top grill, with peppers, mushrooms and cheese for toasting in the individual Raclette trays beneath. Fresh bread, a green salad and potatoes rounded it all off.

It was a perfect getting-to-know-you meal, even though Mattie felt that she already knew Llwyd better than anyone else in her life. For two hours, they caught up on all the things that had been missed in their heady plunge into intimacy. Favourite foods and places, best books and films, childhood adventures and friends. Bucket lists...

Finally, they'd eaten as much as they could and Llwyd started to clear the table, putting the fresh food back into the refrigerator and stacking the dishwasher. He switched the coffee machine on and fetched a large bowl of strawberries.

'So...what's the thing you most want to do next?' Mattie picked up a strawberry, taking a bite from it.

He turned suddenly, his green eyes a mixture of tenderness and fire. Mattie caught her breath. She'd been considering a near future that ran to weeks, months even, but Llwyd lived in the moment. And suddenly she knew *exactly* what he most wanted for this moment.

Then he looked away, smiling. 'Strawberries...'

She could go outside with him, and they could eat strawberries. There had already been moments like this, and she knew he wouldn't push her. They could accept them and move on, or they could take what they both wanted. She could be his for the night, and he could be hers. Suddenly, there was no choice in the matter.

She stepped forward, brushing her fingers against his arm and he turned. There was no going back now, and Mattie reached up, winding her hand around the back of his neck and standing on her toes.

He was still too tall for her to reach his mouth, but that was resolved in seconds. His fingers gently skimmed her cheek and he bent towards her. Mattie kissed his lips, and the beginnings of a delicious fire began to spark between them.

'Cariad…' he murmured softly, then seemed to realise he'd slipped into Welsh. 'It means—'

Mattie put her finger across his lips, silencing him. She could see in his face exactly what it meant. She'd felt the way his body reacted to her, and she knew that Llwyd wanted this. She kissed him again, and this time he responded.

'It means this?'

Darling. My love.

And the very fact that the word that had sprung to his lips was in the language he'd grown to understand love in, made it even more meaningful.

'Yes.' He drew back a little. 'But I don't have much to offer you, Mattie.'

She ran her hand down his chest, to the spot where she knew the scars would be from the operation to remove his damaged spleen. A flutter of uncertainty crossed Llwyd's face.

'Says who? If what you have to offer is exactly what I want, then I can take you just as you are. If you'll take me as I am.'

The sliding doors that led out into the garden slammed shut behind her, the lock engaging with a click. Llwyd kissed her again, holding her tight against him. She caught his hand, leading him to the door that opened onto the stairs, and they stumbled up them together. Stopping on the way to kiss, as the boards creaked beneath their feet and the touch of Llwyd's fingers made her gasp. He lifted her up the final two steps, backing her against one of the closed doors and kissing her again, before he twisted the handle, slowly propelling her into his bedroom.

It seemed like a nice room, with more of the exposed beams... She'd look at those later. Right now, she didn't even need the soft bed or its collection of pillows, although that would make things more comfortable. All Mattie really cared about was the raging passion that she couldn't control, rising within her.

He gasped as she ran her fingers across his chest. He was feeling all of the same things as she was, about to give her everything...

Mattie came to her senses, suddenly. If Llwyd was going to make this step, then the very least she could do was tell him the whole truth. He'd been careful, showing her everything about himself and waiting until he was sure that this was what Mattie wanted. Honesty and consent went both ways, and she had to do the same.

'Llwyd... Wait.' He must have heard the urgency in her voice, and when she stepped back he let her go.

'Whatever you want, Mattie.'

She felt herself wince. He was such a nice guy, and that only made her feel worse. He was vulnerable and unsure, and she'd convinced him that this would be okay. But he hardly knew her and really didn't know what he was letting himself in for.

'I want...to go home...'

He nodded. 'I'll take you. Or I can call a taxi if you prefer. Would you like to go downstairs and have some coffee first?'

'I mean that I want you to take me home. See where I live. Then you can leave or you can stay, that's up to you.'

He stared at her. Anyone in their right mind would start asking questions right now, but Llwyd just nodded.

'Okay. I'll go and get my car keys.'

The drive around the bay took no more that fifteen minutes at this time in the evening. She directed him through the village and out the other side, and he said nothing. When she indicated the track that led up to Gwen and Owen's farm, he got out of the car and opened the access gate without comment.

'You can park right there. Beside the...'

'Large yellow bus?'

'Yes. Beside the bus.'

Mattie opened the passenger door before he had a chance to do it for her, almost running towards the bus in her eagerness to get this over with. The exposed hillside, overlooking the sea, was a little cooler than the sunshine in Llwyd's garden, and Mattie shivered as she took her keys from her bag, unlocking the door and pulling it back. He was waiting quietly behind her, and she motioned him inside.

Llwyd climbed the steps, coming to a halt behind the driver's seat. The light was beginning to fail now, and Mattie switched on the low-level LEDs that lined the top of the windows, where the luggage rack had once been.

'You live here?' Llwyd's voice gave no clue about what he was thinking.

'Yes.'

'For how long?'

'Nearly three years. I was looking at flats when I first came here and saw this advertised. I just fell in love with it. I still love it, I have all I need, and I can take my home with me wherever I go…' Mattie should stop talking now. Let him take it all in and weigh up the pros and cons of it for himself, even though every nerve was begging him to say something. Anything.

He turned towards her, grinning suddenly. 'It's wonderful, Mattie.'

CHAPTER NINE

LLWYD HADN'T BEEN sure what to expect, and so he'd tried not to think too much about where they might be going. This wasn't a horror film, and he was as sure as anyone ever could be that Mattie wasn't a supernatural being. Whatever else she felt she had to admit to, he could handle.

It was a surprise when they turned into open farmland, and she indicated that he should park next to a really nice American school bus. Even more of a surprise when she showed him the inside of it, because why on earth was Mattie ashamed of living here? There were a few practical questions, but he was sure there must be an answer to all of them, and the place was both quirky and delightful.

'You don't think…' She was shifting uneasily from one foot to another. 'It's small.'

Llwyd nodded. 'Looks as if you have everything you need within reach.'

'Not very responsible, though.'

Suddenly, the penny dropped, with an almost deafening crash. 'You haven't told your family about the bus, either, have you?'

She shook her head. 'They'd be horrified. They'd probably break all the rules they've set for themselves and *tell* me that they're horrified.'

'And living in a bus—you could leave tomorrow.' Perhaps it was best to get right to the point, rather than circling it.

'I guess so. Not actually tomorrow. I'm not thinking of doing that.'

He turned to her. If Mattie needed to leave then he'd deal with it. But Llwyd knew now that he wanted to spend some time with her before that happened.

'In that case, we can come to some decision about to-night.' Mattie was staring up at him and he realised he needed to make this very clear. 'Neither of us can predict the future, Mattie. But if we don't do what seems right in this moment, then neither of us *has* a future.'

'You're sure?' She was trembling now.

He could take her to wherever her bedroom was, which couldn't be far and there was only one direction to go in, and show her how sure he was. Or he could show her that this wasn't just lust. If sex was going to work between them, then they had to trust each other. He was relying on her honesty, because Hannah had shamed him by letting him believe that she could accept him as he was, when she couldn't. He had to let Mattie know that he could see everything about her, and accept it, before being together could ever mean anything to them.

'I'm sure.' He took her hand, curling his fingers around hers. 'Will you show me your home now?'

Mattie had shown him the sitting room and the kitchen, which were within a couple of steps of each other in the front half of the bus. The study and dining room were two bench seats, which looked as if they'd been salvaged from the original interior of the bus and re-covered, on either side of a table.

'I really like the pictures.' He pointed towards the framed

cards, which ran the whole length of the front section of the bus, above the windows.

It was nice he'd noticed them. 'They're from my brother Justin. We have this thing going, that we take turns to send a card every month, with a bit of news about how we're doing. We both go out of our way to find something a bit different and when I bought the bus I picked out the best ones to frame.'

'Makes the place feel like home.' Llwyd studied the cards carefully and then turned his attention to the more practical question of her electrical supply. They went outside with a torch so he could stare up at the solar panels on the roof, and then Mattie showed him the battery and backup generator in the rear luggage compartment.

They'd both needed to trust each other enough to share the things they kept secret. And now they needed each other. When Llwyd coiled his arm around her waist, she felt confident now. Driven by more than just a reckless wish to forget about all the reasons why they shouldn't take what they wanted. They had an understanding, and when he pulled her close and kissed her, it felt even more exquisitely arousing.

She took him by the hand, leading him back onto the bus, closing and locking the door behind them. Safe and sound in their own small world.

Mattie pulled back the sliding door that led to the back of the bus. 'Bathroom. I have hot water and… Oh!'

Llwyd was kissing her now, clearly not caring what temperature the water in the shower was. Mattie reached for the far door, sliding it back. 'Bedroom.'

He grinned. 'It's bigger than I thought.'

That was because most of her clothes were folded neatly into the deep drawers under the bed, and the rest were in the slim wall cupboard that formed part of the partition be-tween bedroom and bathroom.

'I have everything I need. Not a lot of things that I don't.' Right now, she needed him. And he knew that. He sat down on the edge of the bed, pulling her onto his lap, one arm behind her, the other hand straying from her cheek to her neck, and then further still to cup her breast.

'Be warned, Llwyd… I like that a lot.'

'Yeah?' Apparently, she'd just waved a red rag to a bull, and he kept teasing until she cried out. 'You be careful, too. I like *that* a lot.'

They were both on a knife edge now. Wanting to make this last, but passion wouldn't let them. She pulled at his shirt, undoing the buttons and running her hands across his chest. Llwyd clearly felt that scars and a partially paralysed hand might matter to a lover, and Mattie had wondered how she might show him that they didn't. But she didn't need to, because desire overwhelmed all of that, stronger and clearer than all of their uncertainties.

Buttons and zips were no barrier; they were both too eager to see and feel each other to worry about who undid what. The only thing that Llwyd hesitated over was when she took a condom from the drawer of the small cabinet by the bed.

'May I?' He was sitting on the bed and she knelt in front of him, resting her elbows on his knees. Llwyd smiled down at her.

'I haven't had a great deal of practice putting these on one-handed—' He cried out, his head snapping back, as Mattie showed him that wasn't why she'd asked. Watch-ing him, seeing the desire in his eyes, was potently erotic.

'Come here.'

Mattie knew just what to do. Sitting astride him, her

legs tucked on either side of his, meant they each had both hands free. They were face to face, able to see everything.

He supported her weight while she guided him inside her. Slowly, gently filling her in an action that made them both cry out. Mattie felt a tear roll down her cheek and he wiped it away with his thumb. He knew. Llwyd knew that this was too overwhelming for words.

One arm around her waist stopped her from moving too suddenly. As he kissed her, his hand found her breast.

'I said…' Mattie couldn't remember exactly what she'd said now, but Llwyd knew that doing this for too long would make her come.

'I heard what you said. It's time, Mattie. There's more for us to do later.'

She couldn't stop it now. 'What…? Tell me what.'

He laughed softly, whispering in her ear. Her imagination, one of the most erogenous zones of all, made the muscles that cradled him tighten and he groaned, loosening the pressure of his arm around her waist so that her hips were free to move with the orgasm that gripped her. When Llwyd let out a cry it seemed a long way away, but she felt every delicious pulse as he came inside her…

They clung to each other for long moments. She could feel his heart racing against hers, every gasping breath. And then the slow, sure winding down, feeling safe in his arms and unable to move. When they did, and she slowly and carefully shifted from his lap, a final stir of feeling made her shiver.

And then those precious moments, curled in his arms, the warm afterglow of feeling still thrumming through her body. Llwyd kissed her forehead.

'Mattie…'

'Yes, I know. I felt it, too.'

He chuckled softly. 'Good. Because I don't have the words for it. You are the most beautiful free spirit. And the most sensible…'

Mattie laughed. 'That's nice of you to mention but coming from a man who's just had sex in the back of a bus, I'm not sure it's going to convince anyone.'

'*Great* sex in the back of a bus. And it's an extremely practical bus. That has to count for something.'

She snuggled against him, feeling his warmth envelop her. 'You see here?' She stretched her hand out, her fingers pulling at the curtain that covered the glazing at the back of the bus.

'Yeah?'

'It's an emergency escape door. Just in case you wake up in the morning and find you've changed your mind.'

'I don't need it.' He brushed his lips against her cheek. 'Tomorrow morning's going to be fine. I promise.'

Mattie felt Llwyd wake with a start, just after midnight. She switched on the night-light and found him sitting up in bed, rubbing his hand across his eyes, as if to clear his head.

'Were you dreaming?'

'Uh… Sorry I woke you.' Llwyd lay back down again, clearly trying to pretend that nothing had happened.

'What's happening, Llwyd?' She snuggled up next to him, feeling his arm curl around her.

'I guess… A sound, maybe. Or perhaps I became aware of being in an unfamiliar place. It just gave me a start.'

She hugged him tight. 'I should have thought about the fact that you'd sleep better in your own bed.'

He rolled over suddenly, covering her body with his. 'You don't have to think about every little thing. If there's something I need, I'll tell you. If you need something, then you tell me, right?'

The sudden expression of dominance made her smile. 'Got it. There *is* one thing I need.'

'And what would that be?' She felt his body harden suddenly against hers. He knew exactly what she needed.

'A little more time with that gorgeous body of yours?'

Llwyd grinned. 'That would truly be my pleasure. We can take as much time as you want.'

He was true to his word. Mattie stretched out beneath him, languorous in the pleasure of his caress. She liked his rhythm, the way they found a position they liked and Llwyd stayed with it, exploring every possibility that it offered. The way he valued the connection between them, his gaze holding hers as he made love to her. He knew all about the persuasive power of words and imagination, and how to coax her body way past mere arousal and into a state that felt a lot like bliss.

And then there was the fire. She'd thought that the desperate longing she'd felt the last time must be something that hit once in a blue moon, but here it was again. Llwyd shifted a little, finding that sweet spot of almost agonising pleasure. The orgasm made her whole body jolt this time, and Llwyd demanded yet more of her, pushing her past her limits and into unknown territory.

'Llwyd...' Mattie wanted him to feel the shattering pleasure that she'd felt. Tilting her hips a little further, she felt his body stiffen. A little further still and he cried out, his body convulsing in the grip of something that he seemed powerless to resist.

He was still suddenly, his hands planted on the bed on either side of her. Breathing as if he'd just run a marathon, a soft sheen of sweat on his body. Mattie reached up, caressing his cheek.

'Hey there. I'm Mattie.' It felt as if she'd finally met the man who'd taken up so much of her attention for the past few weeks. These moments together had crowded in on them, stripping them both of their fears and hesitancy. They were still there, still jostling to be heard, but for now, they could be ignored.

He smiled suddenly. 'Llwyd. I've heard all about you, and I can't tell you how good it is to finally meet you.'

He bent his arms, dipping down to kiss her. She could run her hands across his shoulders now, one perfect and finely muscled, the other still perfect, but bearing a scar. They'd shown each other what their bodies could do, and he could be under no illusions about how much she adored his.

When he lifted his left hand, brushing his thumb and first finger against her cheek, it seemed natural and right. 'You feel me?'

He nodded. 'I feel you.'

'I suppose we're not looking at a miracle cure here, though.' If he had a little more feeling in his thumb and fingers than usual, she supposed there might be some physiological reason for that. Her whole body felt acutely sensitive to his touch.

'No, we're not. It's the same as it's been for months now.' He shot her a wicked look. 'Shame. Imagine the headlines.'

Mattie laughed. *'Doctors claim breakthrough in nerve regeneration techniques!'*

'You can take all the credit for the research.' He teased her, carefully lifting his hips away from hers, breaking the last vestiges of their connection. But still, it hovered between them. Mattie had all that she wanted, right here and right now. Tomorrow could take care of itself.

* * *

Llwyd had had better nights' sleep. But when he woke at five in the morning, he couldn't remember feeling any more ready for the day in a long time. He was stretched out in the bed, and when he looked for Mattie she was squashed against the emergency exit window of the bus. Feeling a little guilty he moved her towards the centre of the bed, and she half woke, falling straight back asleep again as he covered her with the duvet.

He should go. He needed to get home for a change of clothes, before going on to work this morning. And however convenient and practical Mattie's shower was, it might not be up to washing the memory of her from him, and letting him concentrate on the day.

But first, he had a promise to keep. He'd told Mattie that this morning would be fine, and he was determined to make it so.

He slipped out of bed, careful not to wake her, and picked his clothes up from the floor. He was used now to the extra time and concentration it took to button his shirt, but somehow that felt strange this morning. As if during the night he'd been whole again, and woken to find that nothing had changed. The surgical scar on his side was still there, along with the reddening of the skin over his ribs. He puffed out a quiet breath as he fumbled with the button on the waistband of his trousers, then slipped his feet into his shoes.

Instinct told him that he should expect the rolling motion of a boat, and he smiled to himself, remembering that Mattie's compact home was on four wheels. The sliding door that led to the front of the bus moved silently, and he closed it carefully behind him.

Realising that he wasn't entirely sure where he was, he moved to the front of the bus. Through the windscreen, he could see the village below them, and the curve of the bay. On the other side, the lush green of fields and trees, a stone farmhouse nestling amongst them at the top of the hill. Everything was quiet, and there were no signs of movement, but he nodded to himself, happy to find that Mattie wasn't entirely alone here.

Moving back to the small kitchen area, he opened the cupboards, finding a cafetiere but no coffee. There was tea, though, and he switched on the kettle. There were two mugs in another cupboard, stowed in a crockery organiser that looked as if it was designed for a boat, and he made the tea. Realising he couldn't carry the mugs at the same time as he slid the door that lay between him and Mattie, he made two journeys, setting the mugs down on the small table next to the bed.

Taking a moment to watch her as she slept was sheer self-indulgence. But preserving this vision of her, locked away in his head for safekeeping, seemed important. Finally, he reached over, pressing his fingers on the soft skin behind her ear, so that she'd wake without starting.

'Hey there.' He smiled as her eyes fluttered open, focussing on him. One more thing he wanted to keep.

And then she realised where she was, and that he was here. The spell broke as she gathered the duvet around her and sat up, her face twisting into a look of uncertainty.

'What's the time?' Her gaze flipped around the small space, as if she was trying to check what had changed and what was still the same.

'It's early. I have to go home for a change of clothes, and I didn't want to leave…' Leave her to wake up alone, wondering where he was. He'd reckoned that a note wouldn't be enough, and Mattie's startled look had just confirmed that.

'I made you some tea.' He indicated the mugs and saw Mattie's shoulders relax slightly.

'Thank you. I… I'm out of coffee.' She risked untangling her arm from the duvet to reach out for the mug, watching him warily as she did so.

He'd thought that this would be a lot easier. That maybe just a kiss, along with a cup of tea, would be enough to convince them both that the world hadn't changed last night. Their lives had just touched, with such overwhelming consequences that it was easy to think that everything would be different from now on.

'I took a look outside. I didn't notice the farmhouse when we arrived here last night, but as far as I can see the village is still in the right place and so is the bay.'

She smiled suddenly, tweaking the curtain that covered the back window of the bus and peering out. The duvet slipped a little, and Llwyd tried not to notice the soft curve of her shoulders.

'So it is.'

'I'm still someone with roots and responsibilities here, and my weekends are booked for the foreseeable future. You're still a woman who owns a boat, a bus and a bicycle, so I get that you haven't found a place to settle yet.'

That made Mattie laugh. 'I suppose…if we'd set out to avoid any romantic entanglements, we couldn't have organised things much better.'

'Not unless I'd been a Montague, and you were a Capulet…' Llwyd grinned at her. 'But I still wouldn't have changed one thing about last night, Mattie.'

'Me neither.' The duvet slipped another inch. 'Thank you, Llwyd. You said that this morning would be fine.'

He nodded. Llwyd didn't want to leave now, but he had

to. Maybe one more promise would make it easier. 'I'd love it if our paths were to cross again…'

'They will.' Mattie's sudden certainty made him shiver at the thought. 'How long exactly does it take you to drive back home, get changed and then on to the hospital?'

She could work that out by herself. She probably already had. 'An hour.'

'So if you leave at seven…?'

'I'll be there by eight.' He took the half-empty mug from her hands, putting it with his on the table. 'Are you going to make me get undressed again?'

'That's only fair, isn't it?'

She let go of the duvet and Llwyd couldn't help staring now. Morning light was streaming through the thin curtains and her skin was still flushed from sleep. Her eyes seemed a brighter blue than they had in the half-light last night, and… Llwyd reached for her and she shifted back, laughing.

'No touching. Not until we've looked.'

She knew that was a challenge for him. Maybe she knew that he was equal to it now. Llwyd let out a mock sigh and reached for the buttons of his shirt…

They couldn't be together every night. Llwyd had known that from the start, and Wednesday night in her bus, followed by Thursday night at his cottage, was enough, wasn't it? All the same, he'd missed Mattie on Friday night, after he'd picked Peter up to spend the weekend with him.

At seven o'clock on Saturday his phone rang. Peter was outside in the garden, and appeared to have decided to dig a hole for some reason. Llwyd stood at the window, watching him as he flipped the answer button.

'Hey there. Ready for your night driving—'

'No! I can't do it, Llwyd.' Mattie sounded as if she was panicking.

'Which bit can't you do?'

'I was just thinking about getting ready to go down to the marina, and your father called me and said if I came a bit early for my lesson he'd show me the boat he's working on. I'd been asking him about the wooden boats. I said yes, and he said he'd see me in an hour at the boatyard and just hung up.'

'Yes, he does that. When he's said everything he has to say, he hangs up. It can be unsettling at first, but just call him back…'

'No, Llwyd, I can't. How am I going to tell him that I can't get the Matilda Rae out of the marina?'

Llwyd sighed. His father's strategy was becoming clear now. 'Okay. Breathe. You've done this before, and you did it perfectly.'

'Yes, but you were with me.'

'Purely as an interested spectator. Are you ready for the course?'

He heard Mattie puff out a breath.

'Well—yes. I had a nap after lunch and then I drank three cups of coffee, so I'll probably be awake until this time next Thursday. I've read everything in the folder he gave me, printed out the weather forecast and plotted courses around the whole of the bay.'

'Right, then. And you've seen Dad's teaching certification?'

'What? No, of course not. Llwyd, it would be rude to ask…'

'It's your boat, Mattie. You're the captain.' There was a silence on the other end of the line. 'Mattie…?'

'Okay. I get what you're saying. It's what all this is about, isn't it? Taking ownership of the *Matilda Rae*?'

'Yes. And when you're at sea, you don't assume that the person with you is going to pick up on anything you've forgotten. You're the one in charge. And by the way, Dad's got about a hundred certificates for all kinds of things. They're pinned up on the noticeboard in the office.'

Llwyd was aching to tell her that he'd meet her at the marina, and that he and Peter would hitch a ride with her over to the boatyard. But he trusted his dad, and if he thought Mattie was ready then she was.

'I'll take your word for it. And I'd better check my lights and navigation before we leave.'

Now she was getting it. 'Good idea. Don't let him interfere, and if he stands around looking at the sky, don't fall for aged mariner act. He'll have checked the weather forecast, and show him that you have, as well.'

'Okay. Gotcha.' Mattie's voice took on a teasing tone. 'So what are your qualifications for driving the Matilda Rae, Llwyd.'

Now she was *really* getting it. 'How about I'm completely besotted with you, and I'd never let you get your feet wet, cariad. Oh, and I actually do have a qualification to teach, although my insurance has lapsed, I used to help Dad out during the summer holidays when I was at university. I didn't mention that because I had designs on you and I thought it might be a conflict of interest if we had a tutorial relationship.' When he thought about it, that might be less of a joke than Llwyd was making it out to be.

'Sensible.' He could tell that Mattie was smiling, now. 'I think I've got it, thank you. I'm ready to go and show your dad what I can do.'

'That's the spirit. Spare a thought for me tonight, eh?'

Mattie laughed. 'Lots of them, sweetheart. Only not when I'm driving...'

Llwyd ended the call, standing for a moment, watching Peter in the garden. This was more than he could stand. He called to his nephew, who came running back to the house.

'Do you fancy a walk up the hill before bedtime?'

Peter shook his head. 'Not really.'

Llwyd tried again. 'Well—would you mind coming along with me, then? Mattie's taking the *Matilda Rae* around to the boatyard this evening, and we'll be able to see her from there.'

'Okay.' Peter agreed immediately and Llwyd made a mental note to be a little more transparent with him in the future. 'You only needed to say...'

Mattie had made a perfect departure from the marina, even if she said it herself, and a slightly less than perfect arrival at the boatyard, needing two tries to line herself up neatly against the jetty. She'd decided that attack was her best form of defence, and launched straight into showing Llwyd's father the weather report, inviting him on board to see the routes she'd plotted around the bay, and demonstrating her mastery of the boat's navigation lights.

'Very good, Captain. Would you like to see my latest project now?'

'Yes, please.' Mattie grinned at him, conscious of the honour he'd just bestowed on her by calling her *captain*. 'So... For tonight, we're both in charge?'

'There's only one captain. Everyone around here calls me Rhys.'

Mattie followed him off the boat, swallowing hard. Maybe she'd bitten off a little more than she could chew. But she had an hour before it began to get dark, and that was taken up with the workshop, where an elegant wood-framed hull was under construction. Rhys showed her the shaped wooden struts and supports, all as smooth as silk when she ran her hand over them. Another smaller boat, which was almost finished, boasted gleaming wooden fittings, finished off with brass.

'These are so beautiful. They're like works of art.'

Rhys chuckled, obviously pleased with her reaction. 'These are working boats. They belong in the sea.'

'I imagine…you could listen on a boat like this, couldn't you? Hear the wind and the water.'

'Yes. You see that one, over there.' Rhys pointed to a hull, which was stored in a frame against the wall. 'That's Llwyd's.'

'He never said he had a sailing boat.' The hull was part covered by a tarpaulin, but Mattie could see the same elegant lines and gleaming woodwork.

'He didn't use it so much when he was living in London.' Rhys gave her a twinkling smile. 'Llwyd's a bit more interested in speed right now.'

Mattie turned the corners of her mouth down. 'He has been spending a bit of time showing me how to get started with the *Matilda Rae*. If I'd known…'

'Nothing wrong with that. She's a good craft. You made an excellent choice with her.'

'It wasn't actually my choice. She was a gift, from a family member with a bit more money than sense. That's why I need you to teach me.'

It was so easy. Mattie could just say it now, and if Rhys asked any more questions about Leigh and his gift, she could answer them. Llwyd had helped her free herself from the weight of keeping it all a secret.

Rhys nodded. 'She's a good boat.'

'I'm just really grateful to Llwyd and you for helping me to understand that.' She looked at her watch. 'Is it time to go out now?'

'I think so.'

Under Rhys's patient tuition, Mattie carefully manoeuvred the *Matilda Rae* around the bay, getting the feel of using her lights and navigation system in the dark. She practised entering and leaving the marina in the dark, and then they left the bay, moving parallel to the lights along the coastline.

There was a lot to take notice of, and she had to concentrate. But Mattie was feeling more confident now, and Rhys was there to guide her through things she was unsure of. He let her make her own mistakes, stepping in whenever it looked as if she was getting into any trouble, but giving her the chance to correct herself first. At one in the morning, he finally called a halt to the session.

'We've done enough for tonight. Any more and you'll be getting tired and forgetting things.' Rhys must have seen Mattie's look of disappointment. 'We're not too far from Ogof Briallu, if you still want to do a little fishing?'

'That sounds like a great place to go. Although I don't know what it means.' Mattie was learning to ask about Welsh words that she didn't understand.

'Primrose Cavern. There aren't any primroses there at this time of the year, and we won't be going into the cavern. You need a smaller boat for that. Best place for night fishing along this stretch of the coast, though.'

'You have time?'

'I always have time to fish. Find it on the chart…'

They nosed into a tiny, sheltered bay, rocky outcrops on each side of them, and a small beach up ahead. Rhys had pointed out the sea entrance to the caves, and they'd dropped anchor in the centre of the bay. He'd brought along an easily manageable rod for Mattie, and they sat together on deck, waiting in the darkness for the fish to bite.

'You brought Llwyd to fish here?' Mattie murmured.

'Yes, he and his brother Huw used to come here a lot when they were young. You should ask him to bring you to explore the caves.'

Mattie nodded. Maybe she would, although she'd like it better if Llwyd had the idea of showing her this childhood haunt without being prompted.

'It must be good to have him home.'

Rhys nodded, pulling on his line to reel in a fish and taking it carefully from the hook, before releasing it back into the water.

'You don't want that one?'

'Too small. We'll take what we want for the table and return the rest—young fish that haven't had a chance to breed yet, protected species.'

'I don't think my table can cope with anything other than fish fingers. If I catch anything you can throw it back.'

'You're missing out. But if you're sure I'll take any extras up to Huw. He'll be able to use them at the restaurant.'

'Sounds good. That'll give me a reason to try and catch something.' Mattie jumped as something tugged at her line, and Rhys reached over, helping her to reel the fish in. 'Is that one big enough?'

'It'll do nicely.' Rhys removed the hook. 'You might want to look away.'

Curiosity got the better of good sense, and Mattie watched as Rhys expertly stunned and spiked the fish. She had the stomach for all kinds of medical procedures, but killing a fish to eat made her feel slightly queasy and she decided to turn her back next time.

'Llwyd told you about what happened to him in London?' Rhys's question came out of the darkness as they sat, waiting for the next fish to bite.

'The attack? Yes, he did.'

'I expect you know more about it than we do. Being a doctor.'

Llwyd hadn't talked to his parents? A sliver of alarm trickled slowly down Mattie's spine. 'He hasn't told you about his injuries?'

'He tells me and his mother that everything's all right. That makes her worry.'

It sounded as if Rhys did, as well. Mattie couldn't blame them. *Everything's all right* wasn't the best kind of reassurance, particularly when everything clearly wasn't all right.

'I…um… I don't tell my parents everything.' She felt suddenly guilty, wondering if her mum and dad really did believe the reassurances that she gave when she went home to celebrate birthdays and Christmas with them.

'Neither did I when I was young. But you're a doctor, Mattie. Can't *you* explain it all to us?'

Rhys was clearly desperate to know, and this was a grey area. Mattie wasn't Llwyd's doctor, so professional confidentiality didn't apply, but Rhys was asking her to comment in her professional capacity. Mattie took a breath.

'I really want to help, but since I haven't seen Llwyd's medical records I don't have the full picture, and I could say something that's misleading. But it strikes me that you don't need information from me. You need Llwyd to tell you.'

Rhys nodded. 'You're right, there.'

'Would you mind if I suggested something that you might do?'

'I'd be grateful if you could.' Rhys's voice quavered a little with emotion.

'How would you feel about making up a list of questions, specific things you want to know, rather than just asking how things are in general? Sometimes breaking it all down and giving someone a question they know how to answer makes things much easier.'

'That sounds sensible. We'll try it. Thank you.' Mattie's line began to pull again, and Rhys reached out to steady it. 'Looks like you've got another one...'

They'd fished for an hour, and then Rhys decided that there was more than enough in the ice cooler for both the restaurant and his own table. 'You're sure you don't want to take one?'

'Positive. I really wouldn't know what to do with it.'

'All right. I'll come back with you to the marina. My car's parked outside.'

Mattie caught her breath. 'You mean...you parked your car outside the marina and then let me come to your boat-yard on my own!'

Rhys gave a slow grin. 'You were fine, weren't you?'

Yes. It had been well within her capabilities, and handling the boat alone had felt like a significant step forward.

'And you're asking me how to talk to your own son. Maybe I should mention that you know exactly how to get the best out of people, and just tell you to get on with it.' Mattie walked to the helm, switching on the navigation lights and starting the engine, gently turning the boat in the water as Rhys had taught her. When she looked around he was laughing.

'Seems we both learned something tonight, then.'

CHAPTER TEN

MATTIE HAD INTENDED to go back to the bus as soon as it was light, but there was no alarm clock on the boat and she'd slept late. Instead, she was woken by her phone.

'Uh…?'

She heard Llwyd's chuckle.

'Sorry, did I wake you?'

'No, I was just lying down with my eyes closed, pretending to be asleep. What time is it?'

'It's gone eleven. Huw's called me. Do you fancy eating one of those fish you caught last night?'

'Do I have to clean it? Or cook it?' Mattie didn't want to think about either of those things at the moment.

'No, the restaurant's not busy today, so Peter and I are going to have a late lunch there at around two. Can I call Huw back to let him know you'll be joining us?'

'Thanks. That would be really nice.' Mattie answered before she could think too much about the idea that this was a family Sunday lunch, which seemed a little daunting. Or consider the dream, still fresh in her mind, where she'd been trying to navigate the *Matilda Rae* through the darkness to find him. That was probably because her unconscious mind had registered the movement of the boat, and had nothing to do with the lingering feeling that hurting Llwyd might be a lot easier than she'd realised. That Llwyd wasn't talking to his family, who were the very people he *should* be talking to.

'Are you still there, Mattie?'

'Um... Yes, sorry. What time's lunch?'

'Two o'clock.' The humour in his voice told her that this was the second time he'd said it. 'I'll come and pick you up at a quarter to two.'

'Great, thanks. I'll see you then.'

Mattie surveyed her clothes, which where all piled on the bed. The bus didn't have much storage space, and she'd worked her way through almost all of the nicer outfits since she'd met Llwyd. She'd consulted the restaurant's website, which showed pictures of informal dining amongst splendid views of the bay, and decided that her only summer skirt with a light, lace-knit sweater that she hardly ever wore would have to do. Maybe she should consider going shopping and using some of the boat's empty storage for clothes.

When Llwyd arrived, he was alone. 'Where's Peter?'

'I left him at the restaurant. Show an eight-year-old boy a bus that you can live in and there'll be a queue of kids outside, wanting to see it, by tomorrow lunchtime.'

'I suppose so.' It didn't seem quite so vital to keep that secret now that Llwyd knew it, and didn't think it was too impractical for words. But it was nice that he did; it seemed like their own private place that only a few people knew about.

'I hear you went to Ogof Briallu for the fishing.' There was a note of regret in his voice. Maybe he'd wanted to take her there for the first time.

'It was dark by that time.' Mattie wound her arms around his waist, kissing him. 'I'd like you to take me back sometime, so I can get to see it properly.'

That seemed to be the right thing to say. 'Didn't Dad give you the talk about being the one in charge on your boat?'

'Yes, he did. *You're* the one in charge of going to new places that I haven't seen before, so I'm officially deputising you—' Llwyd silenced her with a kiss. She'd obviously made her point.

'You look beautiful today.'

'You're going to have to stop saying that. I've worked my way through pretty much all my wardrobe...'

Llwyd's grin broadened. 'Did I mention your clothes?'

He'd made his point, too. Mattie wriggled free of his embrace, before that became impossible and they ended up skipping lunch.

'Let's go, shall we?'

When Llwyd ushered Mattie into the restaurant, looking around, he could see that the place was only half-full. Georgina was at the reception desk and introduced herself to Mattie.

'I haven't heard anything about you at all, so I'm looking forward to finding out for myself.' She glanced at Llwyd and he smiled, passing over the soft drinks and bottle of wine he'd brought with him. Georgina's easy, friendly manner was one of the things that was helping make the restaurant a success. Along with the food...

'Come and meet Huw. He's skulking in the kitchen as usual.' Georgina whisked Mattie away from him, leaving Llwyd to follow the two women.

'Not so busy today?' Llwyd asked his brother. Georgina was now showing Mattie around the kitchen, leaving Llwyd with Huw, who was keeping a close eye on Peter.

Huw shrugged. 'We were very busy on Friday and Saturday, and this is the third weekend in a row that we'll be making a profit. We're definitely getting there.'

'I'll take a few more pictures for your social media.'

Huw shook his head. 'We need variety, Llwyd. You're getting to be a familiar face on there.'

'I'll take one of Mattie.' Peter settled the question and Huw smiled.

'Anything we ought to know there, Llwyd?'

'Remember when you and Georgina first got together?'

Peter's head turned towards his father, clearly wanting to know the answer to that question, too.

'Right, okay. Back off and give you some space. We're not going to ask again, are we, Peter?'

Peter shook his head. 'No. I suppose not.'

'We'll let you get on, then.' Llwyd shepherded Peter out of the kitchen, and Georgina and Mattie joined them a few moments later, Georgina showing them to one of the outdoor tables and sitting down with them to take a short break.

'What an amazing view!' Mattie sat down, looking around. The restaurant was situated on the headland at the mouth of the bay, and they were sheltered from the wind by glass screens.

'Take a picture,' Peter instructed her. 'Dad doesn't want Uncle Llwyd on our social media any more.'

'Oh! That's a bit harsh, isn't it?' Georgina laughed.

'It's good to get a bit of variety. If I'm on there too much, it's going to look as if I'm your only customer.' Llwyd settled back into his seat, watching as Mattie got to her feet, carefully framing her picture, before sitting back down again and fiddling with her phone to post the image.

The afternoon began to take over. There were no menus for family, Huw and Georgina just cooked whatever they had, and it was always delicious. Huw appeared with three plates, the fish freshly caught and now cooked in a beer batter, with triple-cooked chips. Mattie was encouraged to try hers before Huw went back to the kitchen, and when she rolled her eyes with sheer delight at the taste of the fish, he nodded, satisfied with the results of his efforts.

Georgina went back to the kitchen while they ate, and Huw joined them for coffee, laughingly bowing when Mattie gave a round of applause for the treacle tart that Georgina had made for dessert. His father called, wondering whether Peter would like to come over and try out a radio-controlled model boat that he'd been making, and when Peter nodded excitedly, Huw said that Georgina would pick Peter up from his grandparents' later on and take him home.

They'd gone to the kitchen to say goodbye, and Llwyd had slipped a note from his wallet under one of the door magnets on the fridge, while no one was looking. Huw and Georgina always refused offers of payment from family, and this compromise avoided any lengthy discussions on the matter.

Then, finally, they were alone, walking along the sloping path that led down to the car park. He felt Mattie's fingers brush the back of his hand, and he curled his arm around her shoulders, falling in step with her.

'That was gorgeous. I never knew fish could taste like that. And the restaurant's just beautiful.' She reached up to her shoulder, catching hold of his hand as if to keep it in place. 'Is it so very wrong of me to be glad it's all over and that I have you to myself now?'

'Probably. But since I feel exactly the same, I'm not going to judge.' He swerved off the path, leading her across the grass to one of the benches that lined the lookout point next to the restaurant. Llwyd didn't want to drive just yet; he just wanted to look at Mattie. The wind teasing her curls across her face, her eyes bright.

'Mattie, I…' The words might be difficult to say, but not so much that he couldn't say them. 'Will you be my partner?'

She looked up at him. Mattie knew exactly what Llwyd meant by that. 'You mean… We know what's going to happen next now?'

'Yeah. I think we do.' Pretending that they were just two people spending a little time together wasn't going to wash any more.

'I like that. Yes, I'll be your partner.' She leaned over, kissing his cheek. 'Thanks for asking.'

They'd made the step of trusting in a future that they might have some control over, and that wasn't easy for either of them. She shifted closer to him, and he put his arm around her.

'I was talking to your dad last night, while we were fishing. It appears we have more in common than I thought.' It wasn't so much her words, more the deliberate way that she said them, which made Llwyd realise that he was probably in for some uncomfortable truths.

'That sounds…challenging.'

'I think it is quite challenging for him and your mum. He mentioned that when they ask how you are, you just tell them everything's all right.'

Llwyd frowned, beginning to feel uncomfortable now. 'And what did you say?'

'I suggested they make a list of specific questions they want to ask, because then they might actually get the information they want.'

Good advice. When it didn't apply to him. 'Sometimes

it's better not to know anything, Mattie.' He heard a note of defensiveness creeping into his voice.

'I don't think your dad would have asked if it wasn't really bothering him. Have you ever really tried to explain what's going on?'

Llwyd didn't answer. Mattie would probably, quite rightly, take that as a *no.*'

'I'm quite aware of my own hypocrisy. I keep a lot of things from my mum and dad, and just tell them that everything's going well. Maybe I need to readjust my attitude a bit, as well.'

Mattie didn't pull her punches, especially with herself. 'I'd be far more inclined to give you the benefit of the doubt on that particular issue. I just don't want to hurt them.'

'I'm going to have to make a leap and assume that if she's married to your dad, your mum's capable of dealing with the truth.'

Llwyd puffed out a breath. When Mattie said it like this it did all seem horribly obvious. 'Yes. If anything, Mum's the one who keeps Dad on his toes.'

'Then tell her. Show her the scars.' Llwyd opened his mouth to protest, and Mattie silenced him with a stern look. 'Do you think for one minute she hasn't imagined what they look like? That's worse than anything.'

He held up his hand. 'I'll give Dad a call and go and see them one evening next week.'

'And you'll talk to them? Answer their questions?'

'Yes, I will. Maybe I'll explain that I wasn't in a good place after Hannah left, and I just wanted to deny everything that had happened.'

She leaned over, kissing him. After two nights apart, she was as hungry for him as he was for her.

'Is that a sympathy kiss? Or are you offering me sex because you got what you wanted?' He grinned at her. 'I have to tell you that I'm not particularly comfortable with either of those options.'

'Neither am I. And I'm not offering you anything, I'm letting you know what *I* want. Is that okay?'

'Yeah. I'm very comfortable with that.' Llwyd kissed her again, feeling her melt against him. 'Feel free to tell me what you want anytime you like, cariad.'

The past three weeks had been idyllic. Slowly falling into the kind of deep emotional connection that allowed them to explore how they might both break the rules they'd set for themselves and make a future. Mattie hadn't allowed herself to think about what might happen if they were mistaken, because believing in a future made her so much happier than believing in no future.

Once or twice a week they'd go out on the boat for the evening. Mattie was gaining confidence and beginning to use all that she'd been taught. Balance was no problem any more and even when she was moving around in the bus, she sometimes absent-mindedly reached out to hold on, even though the bus wasn't going anywhere.

'Where are you thinking of this evening?' Llwyd usually expected her to plot her own course.

'Ogof Briallu?' Her preparations had involved getting the pronunciation of the words exactly correct, and his grin showed her that he'd noticed.

'You want to go fishing?'

'No, I'd like you to show it to me.' She reached into her pocket, taking out the printout of the weather forecast and giving it to Llwyd. 'Will you captain my ship for this evening?'

His smile told her that he knew exactly what she had in mind. 'It would be my pleasure.'

'You'll plot a course...'

He chuckled. 'I think I know the way.'

They sped towards the setting sun, out of the bay and then slowing as Llwyd followed the rocky coastline. The cliffs around Ogof Briallu rose in the distance, and as they turned in to the sheltered cove and dropped anchor, the motion of the boat steadied to a gentle rise and fall in time with the waves.

'Now, milady.' He turned off the boat's engine, and suddenly all Mattie could hear was the sound of the water. 'Since I've succeeded in carrying you away to this deserted spot, you have a choice. I could have my way with you, or set you to work scrubbing out the bilges.'

Mattie pretended to think about it. 'Don't we have a bilge pump?'

'Not tonight, no. Which is it to be?'

She put her arms around him, pulling him close. Swaying together with the motion of the craft. 'Have you had sex on a boat before?'

'Pass...' She liked that Llwyd would never answer questions like that. *Then* and *now* were two different worlds to him. 'We'll put the perimeter lights on and engage the proximity sensors. Hardly anyone comes this way after dark, anyway, and if Dad sees our lights, he'll head a little further down the coast. There are plenty of other good fishing spots.'

'No chance of a rescue, then?'

'None whatsoever.' He kissed her. 'What's it to be?'

Mattie wasn't quite sure what sex on a constantly moving object might entail, but Llwyd seemed confident enough about it, and he was captaining the ship tonight. She followed him down to the cabin, and they both sank down onto the bed. Slipping off his shoes, he propped himself up against the headrest and drew her into his arms.

'Close your eyes,' he whispered softly into her ear.

Llwyd knew that she could do this without her head swimming; he'd shown her how closing her eyes would allow her to feel the motion of the boat and gauge the movement of the tides. This was different, though, far more sensual.

'Have you got it?' he asked.

'Yes…' She could feel the gentle rise and fall of the waves, and Mattie started to relax into the movement.

'Concentrate.' One arm was supporting her back, and she felt his other hand skimming her body. Gently pulling off her sweatshirt and sailing shorts.

It was gorgeous. Wonderful. His caress moved in time with the waves, and it felt as if there was no difference between them. He was as unhurried as the path of the sun in the sky, as warm as its rays. The temptation to open her eyes and focus on him was almost overwhelming, but somehow she could feel so much more of him like this. He knew her rhythm now, and he was using it, along with the rhythm of the sea.

At just the right moment, he lifted her gently, laying her down again on the pillows. He was gone, but his words still flowed over her, telling her all of the things she needed to hear, so that she could embrace the vulnerability of letting him do this.

Then she felt his skin against hers. Gently moving her limbs, letting her feel what was about to happen. When it did, it was overwhelming in its intensity, and Mattie couldn't hold back the feeling that rolled over her.

When she opened her eyes, he was there. The cabin was

almost dark now, and she reached for the light, both of them blinking in the sudden glare.

'You're sure you want to do that, cariad?' Llwyd had come to terms with the idea that sex meant showing yourself to someone, but he was generally more relaxed in a softer light.

'Will you close *your* eyes for me?' Mattie knew what she wanted to do now, and that if he wasn't comfortable with it, he'd tell her. He'd known how vulnerable she'd been, allowing him to see everything while she saw nothing. It was one thing to look at each other, but this was entirely another, and maybe it was a step too far for him.

'I don't know if I can give you all that you gave me in keeping them closed.'

'That's okay. Just do it moment by moment.'

He rolled onto his back, pulling her on top of him. Then he stretched his arms above his head, closing his eyes. Mattie kissed him, hoping that she could give him just one small part of what he'd just given her.

'Concentrate.' She ran her fingers down his chest and he flinched. Too much, maybe...

But then she saw his lips form the shape of her name. 'Mattie. Please don't stop...'

They'd been at anchor in Ogof Briallu all night. Mattie woke early the next morning to find that the alarm and proximity sensor lights that glowed on the control panel beside the bed indicated the system had been switched off. Quiet footsteps above her head told her that Llwyd was keeping watch now.

She got out of bed, pulling on her clothes as she made coffee. That was one advantage of the kitchen being so close to the bedroom. When she carried the mugs up, she found him on the main deck.

'Hey. I was about to come down and wake you.' He smiled at her as she put the cups down onto the table. 'Thanks.'

They had time. Half an hour before they needed to start back. And that half hour was suddenly precious. Llwyd was wearing boat shoes and jeans, but his T-shirt was hung across the back of one of the seats. The scars on his back and side were plainly visible, as were his strong shoulders and slim hips.

'What's this?' She moved closer and he wrapped his arms around her. 'Working on your tan?' She'd seen him at the boatyard and on deck so many times. Not once without his shirt, even when the sun was at its hottest.

'I guess… I couldn't work out how it would make things any better for Mum if she saw them, but you were right and she says that it has. I still don't know why you don't see them. But you don't seem to.'

'I see them. But I don't see them as something which marks you out as having failed. They show that you survived.'

He bent to kiss her. 'From the first day I saw you, I thought that you were someone I could easily fall in love with. I *do* love you, Mattie.'

'I love you, too.' They were hard words to say. If they didn't love each other, then they'd never have the chance to hurt each other. 'What are we going to do?'

'There's always time, Mattie. We can work on it, eh?'

The thought of what they could be if they succeeded overwhelmed everything else. 'Yes. We'll work on it.'

CHAPTER ELEVEN

'I'VE GOT AN eight-year-old boy. He's here with one of the teachers from his school. His mum's been called and is on her way, although she'll be a little while. I'm pretty sure his ankle's broken.' The triage nurse met Mattie on her way back to the admin desk. 'Are you free?'

'Yep, I've just finished with my last patient. Where is he?'

'Room three.' The nurse thrust the notes into Mattie's hands and hurried away.

Llwyd wasn't around and maybe she should page him. She'd take a look at the boy first. Mattie opened the door of the cubicle, switching on her most professional smile, and then stopped and stared.

Peter.

He was lying on the bed, his left shoe and sock off and a temporary box splint around his ankle. Beside him was a young woman, who looked very relieved at Mattie's arrival.

'Hi, I'm Miss Grant. This is Peter Morgan. He fell over in the playground and he says that his ankle hurts…'

'Okay, thanks for coming with him. I know Peter. You have his school healthcare plan?'

'Yes, right here.' Miss Grant handed a sealed envelope to Mattie, and she turned to Peter as she opened it.

'Hi there, Peter. How are you doing, sweetheart?'

'Okay.' Peter's face was streaked with grime and tears. 'Is Mum coming?'

'Yes. I'm going to take a very quick look at your ankle and then I'll find out exactly where your mum and your uncle Llwyd are.' A prickling at the back of her neck told Mattie that it would be best if she found out a bit more before she called Llwyd.

Peter managed a smile. 'Thank you. It hurts…'

'I know and I'm going to give you something to make it feel better. Now, is it just your leg that hurts…?'

Peter nodded, and Mattie carefully undid the hook and loop fastenings of the splint and examined his ankle. It looked as if it might well be broken. She read through the form from the school, which gave all of Peter's medical details and bore Georgina's signature, then opened the door of the treatment room and beckoned to one of the nurses.

'Are you free? I need you to fetch some medication and then get Peter here into a gown.'

'Yes…' The nurse took the details of which painkillers to fetch and hurried away.

Georgina's mobile number was on the school's form, too, and Mattie pulled her phone from her pocket and dialled, smiling at Peter. Georgina answered almost immediately and Mattie heard the sounds of a car engine thrumming in the background.

'Georgina, it's Mattie. I'm with Peter and he's okay. We're looking after him.'

'Oh, thank goodness. Mattie, I'm so glad it's you. May I talk to him?'

'That's why I called. I can hear you're in the car, so I want you to pull over and call me back.' From the noise in the background, Georgina was using a hands-free phone, but just talking to her son while driving was too much distraction at the moment.

'Thanks. I understand, safety first...'

Mattie's phone rang again just as the nurse returned, and she passed it over to Peter while she checked the medication. She could hear Peter talking to Georgina.

'There's a big boy in the top class. He made my face all dirty and he kicked me...'

'Peter, may I speak to your mother please?' Miss Grant had been sitting quietly but now she reached for the phone and Peter held it tightly against his chest, a tear dribbling down his cheek.

'Not now. Peter's talking to his mum.' Mattie stepped in. 'May I have a word with you?'

She shepherded Miss Grant out of the room, leaving the nurse with Peter.

'I think Peter has things wrong. I just wanted to tell his mother what really happened.'

'You saw him fall?' Mattie asked.

'I'm assured he did. Maybe I should call the headmaster.'

'Did *he* see Peter fall?'

'No, but he's directly in charge of any child who gets hurt on school premises.'

That sounded like a threat and Mattie smiled at her. Peter was under *her* care, and if he had something to say about how he got hurt, Mattie wanted to hear it. 'We have dedicated space for carer's use, and perhaps it would be better if you made your call there.'

Miss Grant gave Mattie one of the most insincere smiles she'd ever seen. 'Of course. Thank you.'

Peter was looking a lot more cheerful when she returned. He'd finished his call and the nurse was keeping him company, talking to him. Mattie signed off the medication and took the tablets over to Peter with a glass of water.

'Miss Grant got it wrong. He *did* kick me and then I fell over...'

Mattie sat down in the chair next to the bed. 'Here's how this works, Peter. I'm here for you, no one else. I believe you, and I want to hear what you have to say. Understand?'

Peter nodded.

'Good. Now the nurse is going to help you into a hospital gown and look after you while I go and order an X-ray for you and find your uncle Llwyd. Is that okay?'

'Where's Miss Grant?'

'I've asked her wait in another room while we look after you.'

'Okay. I don't like her.'

Mattie gave Peter a smile and quitted the room before she was tempted to agree with him out loud. She called Llwyd first, and before she'd finished writing out her instructions on the X-ray form he came spinning through the doors into A&E. Mattie waved her hand to catch his attention.

'Is he okay? Does he have someone with him?'

'Yes, I asked the nurse to stay with him so I could find you. Georgina's on her way. She'll be a little while. She's driving back from somewhere.'

'I expect she went to pick up some supplies for the restaurant, from their specialist suppliers in Aberystwyth. Which room?'

'Wait a moment.' Mattie beckoned Llwyd into an empty room and closed the door.

'What's the matter?'

'Since you're Peter's uncle, I want you to act in loco parentis. Which means you're not attending as a doctor.'

Llwyd frowned. 'I know what it means, Mattie. Are you

telling me that I'm too emotionally involved to treat a broken ankle?'

'Yes, you are. The guidelines are quite clear on this point. There are other staff available, and you're Peter's uncle so you need to step back.'

Llwyd puffed out a breath. 'You're right, of course. What do you need me to do?'

'I need you to just talk to him. He was a little upset because when he came in his teacher was saying that he fell over in the playground, but Peter says that one of the other kids kicked him. When he spoke to Georgina and told her, the teacher tried to take my phone away from him.'

Cold, hard fury showed in Llwyd's eyes. 'What did you do?'

'I threw her out. Not bodily, I'm afraid she didn't give me a reason. She's in the carer's room, calling the headmaster.'

Llwyd grinned suddenly. 'Are we scared?'

'Not even a little bit. I don't answer to him over how I treat my patients. The thing is, Llwyd, you know better than I do that there's an emotional difference between being accidentally hurt and deliberately hurt.' Mattie just wanted to hug him right now, but she needed to stay focussed and professional. 'I need you to be his uncle, not his doctor.'

'Okay. As Peter's closest available relative until Georgina gets here, I'm requesting that this teacher has no further access to him.' He took Peter's notes from her hand and started to write in the special instructions box. 'What's her name?'

'Miss Grant.'

Llwyd scribbled a few more sentences and signed his name. 'That do?'

'It's more than enough.' Mattie put her hand on Llwyd's shoulder. 'I'm sorry that this happened to him. You know I'll do everything to make sure he's all right.'

'Yes. Thanks, Mattie.' He sank down onto the bed, reaching for her and then suddenly seemed to remember where they were. 'Maybe I'm not the right one to get him to talk, and you should call one of the hospital counsellors.'

Mattie shook her head. 'You are exactly the right one to talk to him, Llwyd. First, because you're his uncle but also because you know how it feels to be hurt by someone. Thankfully, he's not hurt as badly as you were and we can put this right.'

He got to his feet, brushing a kiss against her cheek. 'Thank you, cariad.' Llwyd's sense of purpose was back with a vengeance and he swept out of the cubicle, leaving Mattie to finish the paperwork for the X-rays.

Llwyd was not only an outstanding doctor, he made a great job of being a relative. He was the guy that every patient wished they had sitting beside their bed, kind and encouraging, and so solid that it seemed impossible that any harm could come to anyone in his presence. Peter seemed keen to tell the story of the older boy who'd pushed a handful of dirt in his face and Llwyd had been just right, listening carefully and responding, letting Peter know that he was believed and safe.

When Georgina arrived, Llwyd explained everything that had happened, leaving Mattie to speak to the senior consultant in orthopaedics, who reviewed the X-rays and said he would come down to A&E to do the very minor procedure that was needed to realign the fracture and then plaster the ankle.

Mattie popped her head around the door of Peter's room and was greeted by three smiling faces.

'You'll turn a blind eye?' Llwyd shot her an innocent

look. Georgina was perched on one side of the bed, her feet supported by a plastic chair and her arms around her son.

'To what exactly?' Visitors weren't usually allowed to sit on beds, but Llwyd had arranged things so that Georgina could hug Peter without any danger of disturbing his injured leg, or of falling off the bed herself. Sometimes a hug from their mum was the best medicine a child could have.

'Thank you, Mattie.' Georgina grinned. 'Any news on the X-rays?'

'Yes, Peter has a fractured ankle. Dr Edwards will be coming down from orthopaedics to check the alignment of the bones and either give Peter a boot to wear or apply a plaster cast. In either case, we'll be giving you some guidance on how to care for Peter's ankle and he should be able to go home with you this evening.'

'Can I see—?'

'No, Llwyd, you can't see anything,' Georgina interrupted him. 'Thank you, Mattie. This Dr Edwards…?'

'Head of orthopaedics.' Llwyd answered before Mattie could. 'He's excellent, extremely experienced and a very fine doctor. We're lucky to have him.'

Georgina nodded. 'Mattie, you couldn't show me where the drinks machine is, could you? I'd kill for a cup of tea, and I expect Llwyd and Peter could do with something, too.'

'There's a coffee bar in the main reception hall. You can get cold drinks and tea there, too. Come with me.' Mattie suspected that Georgina might want a private word with her.

She led Georgina to the door of A&E, pointing across to the main building. 'Just go through those doors there, past the reception desk, and you can't miss it. Is there anything you wanted to ask me?'

Georgina laughed. 'I just wanted to say thank you. Llwyd's very good at what he does, and I doubt it was all that easy to keep his nose out of Peter's case.'

'Llwyd knew exactly what he had to do. I just pointed it out to him, in case he was tempted to stray across the line.'

'Thanks, anyway. And for believing Peter, instead of this teacher. I didn't realise that she tried to take the phone away from him and that you stopped her.'

'In my experience, children will give you a very good picture of what's going on if you let them. It's one of the reasons I do this job. Now, if there's anything you need, or you have any questions, I want you to call me…'

Mattie had been busy for the rest of the afternoon, but Dr Edwards had caught her, telling her that Peter's procedure had gone well and that he was discharging him. Then Llwyd had found her.

'I'm going to take Georgina and Peter home.' He seemed restless. Nervous almost. At some point he'd changed out of his scrubs and perhaps that was it. He looked like any other worried relative now.

'He's okay?'

'Yeah, I think so.' He managed a smile. 'Thanks, Mattie. For everything.'

'Make sure you text me later and let me know how he is.' She wanted to know how Llwyd was, as well.

'Yeah. I don't suppose…' He pulled his house key from his pocket, already disconnected from the bunch on his key ring. They'd arranged that Mattie would spend tonight with him at the cottage. 'I will be home. I don't know what time.'

'You want me to wait for you there?'

Warmth flooded into his green eyes. 'Would you mind?'

'Absolutely not. Your TV's a lot bigger than mine, and I can raid your fridge.'

He pressed the key into her hand. 'Thanks.'

This wasn't right. He was a doctor. He'd been a surgeon. A cool head was a prerequisite of the job, wasn't it?

And Llwyd had managed to keep a cool head while he was with Peter and Georgina. He'd called Huw, who'd taken the train to Cardiff today for an important meeting with an up-market tour operator, who was thinking of including the restaurant on one of its itineraries, and managed to be truthful and yet reassuring. He'd spoken with the headmaster of Peter's school on Georgina's behalf, curbing his frustration and finding that he, too, was concerned about how Peter had been hurt.

But he'd taken one look at Mattie and fallen apart. Maybe because a rather better version of that was one of the finer aspects of their relationship. Falling apart and then feeling her put him back together again. There was nothing that he could conceal from her.

He'd taken Peter and Georgina home, waiting for Huw to return before he left. When he got back to the cottage, he saw Mattie's bicycle, leaning against the side of the house, beckoning him home.

She was sprawled on the sofa in the family room, watching TV, eating toast and peanut butter. The dimly remembered feeling of finding someone there waiting for him at the end of the day hit him hard.

'Is that all you've had for dinner?' He found a smile for her, sitting down on the other end of the sofa as she flipped the TV off.

'No. I've had a banana, a pear and I heated up one of those chicken pies from the farm shop. That was really nice.'

Fair enough. The toast was whole wheat and he supposed that, taken together, it approximated a reasonably balanced meal. Mattie had a tendency to graze rather than sit down and eat, probably the result of doing a demanding job and having a very small kitchen.

'Have you eaten?' She offered him the toast and he waved it away.

'Georgina pulled something out of the freezer that turned out to be the best comfort food I've ever had. Peter's headmaster popped round to see how he was.'

'Yeah? How did that go?'

'It was good. Nice man, and I was really impressed with his commitment to sorting all of this out. He asked if he might speak with Peter for a few minutes, and he sat down with him and listened to everything he had to say about what happened, then reassured him that nothing bad was going to happen when he went back to school. He's even going to video call with some lessons each day so he doesn't fall behind.'

'Ugh!' Mattie made a face. 'When we were at school, you broke your ankle and you got to stay home and play. It does sound as if he's making a real effort for Peter, though. What about this teacher?'

'He took full responsibility for that and apologised, although I really don't think it was his fault. Apparently, when he heard what had happened, he said that everything had to be done carefully, because it involved an assault by one child on another. Miss Grant took that to mean that it would be better for the school if it was an accident.'

Mattie sat up straight, indignation on her face. 'I suppose it would have been, but it wasn't. You don't silence a child because what they're saying doesn't fit in with your agenda. She's a teacher, for goodness' sakes…'

Mattie's unswerving commitment to her child patients always made him smile. The way she listened to them first, and everyone else later. 'Simmer down. You're preaching to the converted.'

She flapped her hand at him dismissively. That was another thing he loved about her; if she thought that something wasn't right, she didn't let it go. 'So what's happening, then? She gets a ticking off and a hundred lines?'

'The headmaster didn't say exactly. He's been talking to everyone who saw what happened and to the other boy's parents, as well, as a first priority. But he told Georgina that Miss Grant would be barred from any contact with Peter until further notice. Huw and Georgina will have a chance to meet with him formally and their views will be taken into consideration in deciding what further action needs to be taken.'

'Hmm. I suppose that's the best he can do at the moment and it sounds as if he's taking it seriously.' Now that she was happy with that aspect of the situation, she moved on to the next. 'And how about you?'

'Me?' Llwyd pretended he didn't know what she was talking about.

'You don't fool me.' She shifted towards him on the sofa, giving him a hug.

This was what she'd given Peter. Warmth, understanding and a chance to say what was on his mind. Right now, it seemed that Peter knew how to respond to that far better than he did.

'You were quite right. I was able to use what happened to me in speaking to Peter.'

'Hard, though. I respect you for doing it.'

That meant a lot. He put his arm around her shoulders, holding her tight.

'What was it that chimed with him?'

Llwyd knew exactly what she was doing. Mattie was breaking everything down into bite-sized chunks. One question at a time made it all seem more manageable. But their relationship had always been inextricably fused with their shared professional goals, and right now, Mattie's approach didn't feel like a technique; it was an act of love.

'Peter told me that he'd tried to run away, but the other boy wouldn't let him go. I tried to let him know that I understood how frightened he was, that something was happening to him, which he couldn't stop. But that he was safe now.'

'From what I saw of him, he heard you.' She shifted in his arms. 'Since I'm happy that we've done all we can for Peter, I can turn my attention to you now. Tell me one thing about when you were attacked. Something you may not have mentioned before.'

There were a lot of things. All stored away in his head, as clear still as if it were yesterday. Then he knew. The sensation was so immediate that it made him shiver, and he felt Mattie's arms tighten protectively around him.

'I was…only half-conscious. I tried to work out what injuries I had, and whether they were survivable.'

'Sounds like an obvious first step.' She wasn't fazed by the hard practicality of it, because it was what they'd both been taught. Basic triage.

'I couldn't do it properly. I could feel something running down my back, and I told myself that was okay because it must be raining. Stupid…'

'Well, you couldn't *see* your back. You were in shock and had a collapsed lung, so your oxygen levels would most likely have been falling fast. Your body was probably starting to shut down in order to survive. In those circumstances thinking isn't a priority. That's why we examine people who are injured instead of just asking them what the matter is. And it does rain a fair bit in winter...'

'So it's all perfectly normal, then.' Thinking about it, maybe it was, although this was the first time he'd come to that conclusion.

'Well, no, thank goodness, that kind of thing doesn't happen every day. But in that situation it's a very predictable reaction.'

He kissed the top of her head. Mattie seemed to know that he'd said enough for the time being, and shifted in his arms to kiss him back.

'What do you say we watch the rugby? There's a match on tonight, isn't there?'

Llwyd chuckled. 'Now I *know* you're just being nice to me.'

She grinned at him. 'I am not. I just want to know how half the hospital can get so fired up about a game that involves so many injuries. There has to be something I'm missing.'

'If you've lived here for three years and still don't get it, then maybe you never will.'

Mattie thought for a moment. 'I've never actually slept with anyone who likes rugby. Maybe something's rubbed off.' She left him with the thought, getting to her feet. 'Tortilla chips...?'

'No...' Suddenly, he *could* eat something. 'Yes. Are there a couple of bottles of beer in the fridge?'

'Only one. We can share it, while you explain the rules to me...'

CHAPTER TWELVE

MATTIE STILL DIDN'T fully understand the rules of rugby, and Llwyd had frowned at her a couple of times for cheering at the wrong time. But it had been good to share, in lots of different ways, and when they'd curled up together in bed, he'd gone straight to sleep.

Maybe that was why she was wide-awake at two in the morning. Then she'd realised that Llwyd was sitting bolt upright in bed, and the cry that she'd thought was somewhere in her dreams was real. She sat up, curling her arm around his shoulders and found that he was shaking.

'Go back to sleep. It's nothing…'

It was always nothing. Nothing to worry about. Nothing he couldn't handle. Mattie held him tight, waiting for *nothing* to loosen its grip on him.

'You were dreaming?' He'd stopped shaking now and reached for her, rocking her gently in his arms. As if that was the one thing that would bring him comfort.

'Yeah.' Llwyd paused, still halfway between his dreams and reality. 'I was in the rain. But I wasn't on my own. Peter…'

'He was there?'

Llwyd nodded. That would have been the real terror for him, that Peter might be hurt.

'He's got a lot of things going for him, Llwyd. A lot of support.'

'Yeah, I know.' He took a breath. He seemed to be actually breathing now, not just fighting for air. 'I guess... It just stirred up a few memories.'

'I'm sorry if I made it worse for you.' Mattie had felt that he needed to talk, but maybe she'd pushed him a little too hard.

'It happened. It doesn't get any worse or better, it's just there. I think talking just lets it out...'

'That's the general idea. It's not a bad thing.'

Mattie wrapped the duvet around him to keep him warm. Llwyd was beginning to wind down again, and he lay back on the pillows, holding her close.

'Can we talk again? Not now...'

'On the water somewhere?' That was the place where Llwyd always seemed less troubled. There, and at the hospital, but that wasn't really the place for heart-to-hearts.

'I'd like that.' He kissed her cheek. 'Thank you.'

'You know that just you and I... We can't do everything on our own.'

'You think I need to talk to someone...?' He wanted so badly to move on, for Mattie's sake as well as his own, and stirring up old memories didn't seem to be the way to do it. 'It's been a while since it all happened.'

'Hey.' Mattie tapped his chest with her finger, to emphasise the point she was about to make, and he chuckled.

'I'm listening.'

'Feeling something is reason enough.'

He nodded. 'Maybe. I'll think about it.'

Mattie had stayed awake for a while, watching over him, but Llwyd slept peacefully and she'd finally fallen asleep.

She woke early the next morning to find him propped up on one elbow, returning the favour.

'Stop! I could have been doing anything.' Mattie frowned at him. 'Snoring. Muttering… How do I know what I might have been doing? I was asleep.'

'You were beautiful. You wrinkled your nose a couple of times, but you did it quite adorably, cariad.'

She jabbed him in the ribs. 'Don't you *cariad* me.'

He winced. Clearly, her abuse of the Welsh language was more painful than anything she might inflict physically on him. She tried the pronunciation again, and he smiled.

'Perfect. Something's rubbing off.'

'Really? You want to try improving my vocabulary?' She trailed her fingers across his chest and then downward. Slowly, so that he could think a little about where they were going.

'Always happy to help with it.' He pulled the duvet off them both, letting it slide down onto the floor. He'd stopped trying to hide his body, and his insistence on seeing everything was incredibly sexy. Particularly since Mattie got to see everything, too, and watching him in the early-morning light had become one of her favourite occupations.

It could be a little chilly, though. But when he rolled over, covering her body with his, warmth started to thrum in her veins. Carrying them off to a place where thought was left behind and couldn't hurt them.

The past three weeks hadn't been easy. Mattie had been on a set of CPD courses, which meant that she was away for a day each week. Llwyd had been spending time with Peter.

That wasn't really the problem.

Llwyd had thought that the nightmare, after Peter had been hurt, was a one-off. Something that Mattie had accepted and guided him through. When it had returned the following night she'd stayed and guided him through that, as well. But how many more broken nights would she tolerate before she left? How much longer before she came to her senses and accepted that some things were beyond repair?

Peter was doing well, and Llwyd knew that his fears for him were out of proportion. Huw had taken him for a drink and carefully suggested as much, and Llwyd had denied it. But he'd asked his parents to take Peter for the weekend so he could get his head straight. Even though he'd only seen Mattie for one evening the previous week, he hadn't corrected her when she assumed that he was busy and Llwyd spent the weekend alone.

Somehow, he managed to thrust it all to one side. He could work with her during the day, and on the few nights he allowed himself to stay with her, he didn't sleep for long enough to dream. The nightmares still troubled him when Mattie wasn't there, but he could handle that. Just as long as she never saw them.

And then, life began to return to normal, like a boat righting itself after a storm. He found himself thinking about all the good times and rejecting his fears. He'd called her and they'd fixed a date. Peter would be staying with his parents on Friday evening, and perhaps she'd like to come over. He'd make dinner.

She seemed to realise that this was a new start. Mattie was wearing a blue summer dress that he hadn't seen before, and which she laughingly dubbed 'this new thing' when he told her how nice she looked.

Georgina had given him a recipe for an easy salmon salad, which had proved quite complicated enough for Llwyd, but was a big hit with Mattie. They were back on track.

'Mmm.' She tried a spoonful of the chocolate pudding that he'd heated up for dessert. 'Georgina made this, didn't she?'

Llwyd feigned outrage. 'You think I can't cook?'

Mattie shrugged. 'You're a perfectly fine cook, a lot better than I am. But crushed vanilla pods are Huw and Georgina's territory.'

'You found a piece of crushed vanilla?' Llwyd investigated his portion with his spoon and realised that Mattie's shoulders were shaking with laughter. 'You've seen Georgina, haven't you?'

'Yes. Sorry, she brought Peter in to see Dr Edwards the day before yesterday, and texted me to see if I was free for coffee afterwards. It just so happened that I was, because I hadn't had lunch yet. And I love it that you made such an effort with dinner, even if it didn't involve any crushing on your part. Thank you.'

'You're welcome.' A victory was a victory. 'Should I go and crush some coffee beans?'

'No! Not yet, anyway. It's no fun savouring a pudding on your own.'

After he'd made coffee, they went outside to drink it.

'Peter seemed very well when I saw him. Apparently, Dr Edwards was very happy with the way his leg's going.'

'Yes, I've been keeping an eye on it, too. Completely unofficially, of course. He's back at school now and doing well. It turned out that this was the tip of the iceberg in regards to the other boy's behaviour, and he's at a different school now, where they can give him the help he needs.'

'Very sad situation all round, really. How are you doing?'

'Fine.' One inaccurate word didn't cover it but Llwyd really didn't want to go there. 'I hear that you popped in to the boatyard yesterday evening.'

'Yes, I took a spin around the bay, just to practise. Your

dad must have seen me and he texted asking if I wanted to drop in for a cup of tea. I've been meaning to give him a call. I was wondering if he knows anyone who'd be able to sell the *Matilda Rae* for me.

'You're selling her?' A chill travelled down Llwyd's spine. The thought that Mattie had discussed this with his father before him didn't make him feel overly happy. Nor did remembering that Mattie had once felt that the only thing keeping her in Cartref Bay was the *Matilda Rae*.

'I don't know yet. What you said about learning to use her and making her mine… You were right, and now that I do feel that she's mine I can do what I like with her. She's beautiful, and I love having her, but my membership at the marina is going to run out next year, and I'm not sure I can afford to keep her on my own.'

'I'm sure Dad wouldn't mind if you moored her at the boatyard. There's plenty of room there.'

'Yes, but the marina does everything…repairs and up-keep. Your dad said that if I sold the *Matilda Rae* I could use half the cash to buy a very nice boat and the other half I could spend on actually using it a lot more. Fuel costs for longer trips and so on.'

Thanks, Dad. That was an eminently sensible solution.

'Or you could put some money down on buying a place. You can't live in the bus forever.'

Mattie pressed her lips together. 'No. I don't think I'm ready to do that right now. The bus is fine.'

'So you're leaving…' It was the one thing that Llwyd had dreaded and so the first which sprang to mind. The past three weeks *had* taken its toll, however much Llwyd tried to deny it.

She turned, looking at him steadily. 'No. I never said I

was leaving. If I was, I would have told you.' Her tone was cool now. Verging on icy.

'Maybe that's exactly what you're telling me. You don't want the boat any more, that's fine, I can see your point. But if you are planning on staying, why keep the bus?'

'Because it's my *home*, Llwyd, and I like it. And while we're asking questions, I've got one for you. Why have you been avoiding me?'

'I have family commitments, Mattie. You know that.'

She looked at him thoughtfully for a moment. Llwyd had the uncomfortable feeling that she could see right through him. 'I wasn't going to mention this because… I knew you were going through a hard time, and I just wanted to be there for you whenever you needed me. When I saw Peter the other day, he told me what he's been doing the last few weekends. Turns out that he was with your mum and dad for two of them.'

Guilt flashed through his chest. He should have known better than try to keep secrets in a close-knit community. 'I needed some time on my own.'

'I appreciate that, and I understand. But I was really hurt because if you'd said something I would have given you whatever space you needed. You didn't need to lie to me.'

'I'm not aware that I did.' Llwyd hadn't acted particularly well, but he hadn't lied.

'Well…you didn't tell me the truth. You *knew* I'd assume that you were spending the time with Peter.'

There was no space left for him any more. Between the nightmares and the worry that Mattie would find out that he wasn't enough to make her stay, he couldn't breathe.

'Mattie, I can't have a relationship where I'm constantly on edge, wondering whether you're going to even be here tomorrow.' Llwyd realised too late that he was making it sound as if that was her fault. It wasn't; it was his.

'And *I* can't have a relationship with someone who doesn't trust me.' Mattie sounded really angry now. She jumped to her feet, swiping at the half-empty coffee cup that lay on the table beside her. It spun into the air, an arc of liquid spilling from it, and crashed against the corner of the patio, smashed pieces rolling onto the lawn.

For one moment, Llwyd wondered whether it was all going to be okay. Whether she'd laugh, and then he'd laugh… But Mattie was already in motion, marching around the side of the house. He heard the wheels of her bicycle crunch on the gravel and then silence, broken only by the solitary song of a thrush.

Now he knew. He'd driven Mattie away and now there really wasn't anything to keep her here. He might see her again; he probably would. But she was already gone.

Mattie pedalled as hard as she could along the cycle track that led around the bay. She'd missed Llwyd over the past few weeks, sensing a distance between them that had worried her. She'd been hurt when she'd found out that he'd been deliberately avoiding her, but she'd made excuses for him, and decided that tonight could be a fresh start. But it had turned out to be an ending.

An ending that hadn't given her a chance to speak. She'd *said* things, a few of which she regretted now. But he hadn't heard any of it. He didn't trust her, and he'd all but accused her of being as careless as Leigh was, and as rash as Helen.

She lifted her bike over the gate that led onto Owen and Gwen's land. The cup hadn't helped. Why had she resorted to throwing crockery? It had felt good at the time, but now she was just trying to remember whether the mug she'd been drinking out of had been part of a set.

She locked her bike into the rack next to the bus and climbed aboard. Almost tore off the new dress she'd bought especially for tonight, because she wasn't going to be wearing it again. Mattie climbed into sweatpants and a T-shirt, and sat in the driver's seat of the bus.

She could load the generator into the rear luggage compartment. Secure her bike in the space behind the driver's seat and then just go. She reached forward, twisting the keys in the ignition, half hoping that the bus wouldn't start—she hadn't taken it on its usual run last weekend. But the engine choked into life, settling down into a smooth growl. She had petrol in the tank and…

Mattie wasn't going anywhere. If she didn't turn up at the hospital on Monday morning, A&E would be one person down. She had leave saved, and if she didn't take it soon HR had threatened she might lose it, so perhaps she could persuade the head of department that she really did need some time off soon. But just walking out wasn't an option.

She switched off the engine and locked the doors of the bus. Stepping over her wrecked dress, she walked back to her bedroom, closing the sliding doors behind her. Then Mattie flung herself onto the bed and cried.

Llwyd had spent the weekend putting on a happy face for Peter. It had been exhausting, and then the first thing that he saw when he turned in to the hospital was Mattie up ahead of him.

The bike racks were to the right, and the car park to the left. He slowed the car, keeping his distance, and annoyingly she decided to turn left. She must have seen him, but she betrayed no sign of having done so, making a smooth arc onto the slip road that led around the car park to the admin offices beyond.

Llwyd didn't want to think about what that early-morning visit meant. Mattie was already gone, and all he was seeing were ghosts.

As the week wore on it became increasingly obvious that Mattie didn't want any contact with him at all. A&E doctors would often help each other out and share their workload, and Mattie was clearly ducking and diving a little to make sure she didn't end up treating the same patient as he was.

It might all have turned into a game, but for one small detail. Llwyd's heart was broken. Hannah might have stripped him of his confidence, pointed out the way that things were going to be from now on, but he'd never lain awake thinking about her. Mattie was different, like a light burning brightly in the darkness, which he could never reach.

And then, on Friday afternoon, just as he was reckoning that this week would have been the worst, and things only had to get better from now on, he found her right in his path on his way out of A&E. He slowed, and she shot him a half smile.

Still radiant. Even though she looked as if she hadn't had a good night's sleep in a while. Llwyd imagined that he wasn't looking his best, either.

'Llwyd, I want to let you know… I've taken some leave and I won't be here for the next couple of weeks.'

She'd said that if she was thinking about leaving she would tell him, but there was no need for her to keep that promise now. Llwyd tried to summon a smile.

'Thanks, Mattie. I appreciate your letting me know.'

She nodded. 'Take good care.'

'You, too.'

Mattie stepped back, out of the way, and there was nothing else that Llwyd could do but keep walking. Back up to orthopaedics, then back home and finally, after restlessly pacing the garden, back to his empty bed.

But her words echoed in his head. *Take good care.* And in the soft, clear light of the morning, he knew exactly what he needed to do in order to take the best care of himself. He drove around the bay, and up to the farm, parking in a lay-by at the side of the road and walking up the track. Even before he reached the hard standing he could see that Mattie's bus wasn't there and he continued up the hill to the farmhouse, where Gwen was surveying the morning, a cup of tea in her hand.

'Morning, Llwyd. You're looking for Mattie?' The presence of his car, parked beside the bus, hadn't gone unnoticed, and Mattie had made sure to take him up to the farmhouse to introduce him to Gwen and Owen.

'Yeah. Do you know if she'll be back later?'

Gwen shook her head. 'She left last night. Said she was going, but she didn't say when she'd be back. Mattie comes and goes as she pleases. She hasn't been away at the weekend for a while, and I expect she's decided to take a trip.' Gwen regarded him thoughtfully. 'Give her a call, why not?'

'I will. Thanks, Gwen.'

'You want a cup of tea, love?' The concern in Gwen's voice told Llwyd that his dismay must have shown in his face, and he forced himself to smile.

'No, thanks, but I've got to get on. Have a good day.'

As he walked back down the hill, those words echoed again in his mind. *Take good care.* It was also the kind of thing you said when you weren't expecting to see someone again.

CHAPTER THIRTEEN

MATTIE HADN'T PUT a lot of thought into where she might go, just that she'd go somewhere. But when it came to the point of leaving, there was nowhere else. She'd called her older brother, Justin, on Friday morning, and asked if she might stay with him for a little while in London and he'd agreed immediately.

Justin and his wife, Caroline, received her with warmth, and the bus with surprise. But Caroline came to the rescue, gathering up baby James and taking three-year-old Tess by the hand, and demanding that Mattie give them all a guided tour. When Justin had inspected the engine and the electrical system and taken a look at the bathroom and cooking facilities, he'd come around.

It was only then that Mattie had realised what she'd done. She'd been heartbroken and alone, and she'd run home. Llwyd had shown her something after all.

They'd had a Sunday lunch with all the trimmings. Visited the theatre. Mattie had gone shopping in Oxford Street with Caroline, and there had been visits to a few museums and galleries. She'd done a lot of walking, and reacquainted herself with the city that she'd left, but which still seemed to be waiting for her to return.

No one had asked what she was doing here. Justin and Caroline had accepted Mattie's vague references to a few *work things* she needed to follow up on, and insisted that she stay for the full two weeks of her holiday. And when Tess had pleaded to be allowed to sleep on the bus, Caroline had asked whether she might, too, to make sure her daughter didn't get into any mischief.

It had taken Justin and Mattie several careful manoeuvres before they managed to get the bus onto the small driveway in front of the house. Caroline had observed that if they got any closer, they'd actually be *inside* the house, and Mattie had shown her how to operate the alarm, which would no doubt wake up the whole street if anyone dared lay a finger on the vehicle. Tess had said goodbye to her dad, and that she'd be back tomorrow, and Justin had taken charge of baby James, who really didn't care whether he was sleeping on a bus or in his own cot.

'Do you think Caroline's all right out there on her own? There isn't a great deal to do on a bus, it's a bit of a one-trick pony. Once you've got over the fact that it's a bus, that's it.' Mattie asked Justin when he came back downstairs to the sitting room, after settling James down to sleep.

'Are you kidding? She's fine. I dare say that Tess will run out of energy at some point, and when Caroline's put her to bed, she'll be sitting down with her book and a mug of hot chocolate, and having some time to herself. That's a rare treat when you have kids.'

'I suppose so. Perhaps I should text her and tell her to call me if there's anything she wants.'

Justin shrugged. 'If you like. Or you could just pull the curtains back and give her a wave…' He walked to the sideboard, fetching a bottle and two glasses, which he put down on the coffee table in front of Mattie. 'You want a drink?'

'Just a splash. Thanks.'

Justin poured the drinks, handing one glass to Mattie

and sitting down next to her on the sofa. Mattie nudged her shoulder against his.

'This is nice.'

'Yeah. It's good to be able to share a bit of quality time, Mats. It's been too long since we've done that.'

'Busy lives. I really appreciate you having me here.'

'It's our pleasure. Always.' Justin took a sip of his drink. 'Do Mum and Dad know about the bus?'

'No. I keep thinking I should be a bit more honest with them, and then it all goes to pieces when I realise that they'd be furious with me.' A thought occurred to Mattie. 'You're not going to tell them, are you?'

'Not if you don't want me to. *You* could, though.'

Mattie was beginning to wonder whether she'd been set up. Caroline and Tess away for the night, and a bottle of good whiskey on the table, to loosen her tongue. Or maybe Justin had simply seized his opportunity.

'Seriously, Jus? You know that Mum would think I'm being as irresponsible as Helen was. And I don't want to worry her. You've seen for yourself that the bus is a perfectly good home for me.'

'It's a great home. I'm actually a bit worried that Caroline and Tess might decide to drive off in it tonight.'

'They won't get far. There's not a great deal of petrol left in the tank. I'll have to go and fill it up before I take it anywhere.'

Justin chuckled, putting his arm around her shoulders. 'Thanks for that. There's something you should know…'

A murmur of anxiety tugged at Mattie. 'Am I going to like it?'

'Maybe. Probably not. You ought to hear it, though, because you have no way of remembering what happened when Helen died.'

Mattie took another sip of her drink. 'Go on…'

'Mum was devastated. She went upstairs to her room and didn't come back down again. Dad said she had a nasty cold and that we weren't to go up to her, because we'd only catch it. But she was crying. For days. When Grandma and Grandpa brought you home to us a week later, she could barely hold you without bursting into tears, Dad was the one who looked after you in the first month or so.'

'But… I didn't think that Mum and Helen were that close?'

'They were different, and they used to have the most terrible rows. But they loved each other and they always used to make up again afterwards. I can just imagine Aunt Helen bringing a bus with her when she came to stay, and Mum and us kids going out to sleep in it for the night.'

'You mean…' Mattie could feel tears beginning to form and wiped them away impatiently. 'I thought that Mum disapproved of Helen.'

'She was angry with her. For dying. And she made a big mistake, because it hurt too much to see you growing up and being like her. Can you forgive her?'

'There's nothing to forgive, Jus. Mum and Dad… They took me in and I'll never be able to thank them enough for that. I thought…' Mattie shook her head, trying to get her thoughts into some kind of order. 'Trying to be more responsible than Helen is just my way of showing them that I *am* grateful. How do you know all this?'

'I didn't, not until recently. I knew what had happened, of course, but I was only nine years old and I couldn't put it all together. Dad said something that started me thinking last Christmas, though. We were sorting through the tree ornaments, and I found some really nice ones that I hadn't seen before. Dad told me to put them away, because Aunt

Helen had given them to Mum, and it would only upset her if we put them on the tree.'

'But… Mum gave me things of Helen's. She told me all about her…'

'I think that must have cost her a lot. She tried to do the right thing, but it came out all wrong because she could never quite let go of her grief.'

The realisation hit Mattie like a punch in the stomach. 'I'm so sorry… I didn't know…'

'Don't be. You were never meant to know. I can see now that was the wrong decision, and that you should have known.'

Tears started to roll down Mattie's cheeks. When Justin hugged her she tried to push him away, but he refused to let go of her.

'Stop it, Justin. This is *my* fault.'

'Don't be such an idiot. I didn't tell you this to hurt you, I told you because I think you need to know. I asked Caroline what she thought—'

'What! You told Caroline?' Mattie really liked Caroline and the suspicion that she might think the worst of her was uncomfortable.

'You think she didn't know about it already? Mattie, it's glaringly obvious that Mum never got over losing Helen, and that you've been staying away, pretending that you're nothing like Helen and Leigh to make Mum feel better. No one ever said it, though, and that's on us. When Mum and Dad adopted you, Mark and I did, too, and we promised to look after you and be your older brothers.'

Mattie couldn't think about this any more; her head was spinning. Justin hugged her, and she hugged him back. Her big brother, comforting her, just as he had when they were kids and he could make everything in her world all right.

'I've got a boat, Justin.'

'Yeah? What sort of boat, a rowing boat?'

'No, much bigger than that. It has a downstairs, with a kitchen and shower room… It's almost as big as the bus. It's been moored in the marina in Cartref Bay for almost a year because I couldn't use it.'

'Okay, so you have a large boat that you can't use. Tell me there's something more to this, Mattie, or I'll have to take back everything I said about you being a responsible human being.'

'Leigh gave it to me.'

Justin rolled his eyes. 'Leigh. He turned up, gave you a boat you couldn't use and then… He's not still hanging around, is he?'

'No. I didn't really expect him to have the staying power to actually keep in touch. It hurt when he didn't but…' Mattie shrugged. 'The one thing about Leigh is that he's consistent.'

'Yeah, consistently thoughtless. Why didn't you tell me, Mattie? I can see how you wouldn't be able to let go of it yourself, but I could have come and sorted it all out for you. Scuttled it perhaps, while you weren't looking.'

'It's a really expensive boat. It would have been better if you'd sold it when I wasn't looking.'

Justin shrugged. 'Whatever. Mum and Dad don't know about this, either, I assume.'

'What do you think?'

'I'll take that as a no. Okay, you've got a bus. I think I'm pretty up to speed with that and we both agree it's a pretty cool place to live. You also have a boat that you can't use but you can't bring yourself to get rid of, because Leigh gave it to you and he's your biological father.'

'I *can* use it now. I met someone and he taught me.'

'Gotcha. Bus, boat, guy… Who's the guy, Mattie? Do I need to know that?'

'His name's…' Mattie couldn't even say it. She'd told herself that she wasn't going to cry again, but she couldn't help it.

'Hmm. Do I need to play the big brother and come and sort *him* out?'

'No!' Mattie jabbed Justin in the ribs. 'Don't you dare. He's a good person. He's a doctor and we work together. He's really great with kids, he doesn't mind sleeping in a bus, and…' She loved Llwyd. And she'd run from him.

'Mattie… When are you going to stop trying to be someone you're not?' Justin hugged her tight again, and then groaned as the sound of James fretting in his cot came over the baby monitor. 'James, *please.* Just settle down, sweetheart. I need to talk to your aunt Mattie.'

'Go. I can't talk about this any more. I need a bit of time to absorb it all.'

Justin got to his feet. 'I won't be long. Don't go anywhere.'

'Where am I going to go? Caroline has the keys to my bus.'

'Good point.' Justin slid the bottle across the table towards her. 'Help yourself. Although I doubt it'll make you think any straighter.'

Probably not. Right now, she didn't want to think at all. Mattie reached for the bottle and then changed her mind.

Everything that Justin had said made sense, like a truth that had been hiding in plain sight. She'd been so afraid of disappointing her parents that she'd run from them. And it had become a habit, something that she needed. She was free to go at the first sign of discord, but the one thing that she'd never been was free to stay.

Sooner or later she was going to have to stand and fight. Maybe now was a good time to start doing just that.

It had been more than a week since Mattie had left. Llwyd had raged at her, and then taken every word of it back, because he loved her. Wept at his own stupidity in driving her away. Then the weekend had rolled around, and he'd pulled himself together, for Peter's sake. They'd spent most of their time at the boatyard, where Llwyd's father was beginning to sketch out a plan for Peter's first boat. It would be a small skiff, with oars and a sail, sturdy enough for two at first but light enough for Peter to manage on his own when he got a little older. Llwyd expected that later on in the summer, he'd be spending his Saturdays taking Peter to the local boating lake.

'Have you thought about what colour you want?' his father asked Peter.

'Yes. I haven't decided, though.'

Peter was taking this seriously, as well he might. Llwyd well remembered the pride and excitement when his father had announced his intention of building his own first boat. But even this milestone failed to engage him quite as it should. Without Mattie, nothing tasted quite the same.

'It's not an easy choice.' His father nodded in agreement. 'Mam-gu's in the office. Why don't you go and take a look through the ideas book with her?'

Peter nodded, getting to his feet and hobbling towards the office, where his grandmother was tidying up. The ideas book contained photographs of practically every boat his father had built, organised by size and type. Peter might be some time.

'Not heard from Mattie?' His father's question came as a surprise.

'She's on leave at the moment.'

'Shame. I thought you two might go the distance.'

There was no point in denying it. He and Mattie had been spending increasing amounts of time together and now they weren't.

'It just…didn't work out. To be honest, I'm not even sure that she'll be back.' A thought occurred to Llwyd. 'You haven't heard from her, have you? About the *Matilda Rae*.'

'No. Mattie called me a couple of weeks ago, thanking me for the advice, and saying she was still thinking about what to do next. The *Matilda Rae's* still in the marina, isn't she?'

Llwyd shrugged. 'I expect you're right. I can't imagine where else she'd be.'

His father thought for a moment. 'Look, bach…'

'Dad… It won't make any difference.' Whatever his father was about to say, Llwyd didn't really want to hear it. He'd gone to pieces and tried to push Mattie in a direction she didn't want to go, and she'd been right to leave him.

'That's just the problem, isn't it?' His father picked up the sketches for Peter's boat, putting them back into the plan chest that stood in the corner of the workshop. Llwyd began to wander aimlessly towards the jetty, wondering whether borrowing a skiff and rowing around the bay might work off a bit of his disgust with himself.

Then he turned, walking back towards his father. 'What *is* the problem, Dad? I can't work it out.'

'You never can when you're sitting right on top of it.'

Llwyd raised his eyebrow. Dad was quite right, but he was hoping for something a bit more substantive.

'I've always been proud of you, Llwyd. Never more so than when you were injured.'

'I did the wrong thing, Dad. I didn't talk to you and Mum about it.'

His father nodded. There had been a lot of tears when Llwyd had finally spoken about it with his parents and shown them the scars, and not all of them had come from his mother. But they'd been closer, ever since.

'Did Mattie ever tell you that you were less of a man because of your hand? Or your scars?'

Dad was fishing, but he was exactly right. Llwyd decided not to ask how he knew, because he obviously *did* see rather more than he ever admitted to.

'No. She never did. But she's gone, Dad. She left me and…' Llwyd puffed out a breath. 'To be honest, she did exactly the right thing. I was having a bad time, the nightmares had come back for a while and I tried to hide that from her. I should have just told her and asked for some space, but I didn't. Mattie's a free spirit, and I tried to shackle her because I was afraid of losing her. I ended up driving her away.'

His father nodded. 'Your mother and I thought as much. I know that business with Peter being bullied at school hit you pretty hard. Do you love her?'

'I'm not even going to answer that one, Dad. It doesn't matter, because it's over. If Mattie's gone, there's no way I can follow her.'

'Why not? Because of Peter? Don't get me wrong, Llwyd, what you're doing in helping Huw and Georgina out is marvellous. But you're underestimating your mother if you think she can't work something out to make sure the boy's properly looked after. You and Huw didn't do so badly when you were boys, even though I was busy developing my designs and your mother was taking care of the office.'

'The cottage?' Llwyd knew the answer to that, but he wanted to hear his father tell him that the new possibilities that were glimmering through the cracks in his resolve might become realities.

'Don't be perverse, Llwyd. You know full well that it's been rented out before. You have to look at this the way you always looked at things when you were growing up. You worked out what it was that you wanted and then took it.'

There was no point in telling his father that he couldn't do that any more, and if he was honest, Llwyd was beginning to feel that it was just an excuse. *Can't* had become a comfortable word, protecting him from all of the things that Hannah had thought of him.

But Mattie had always seen him as more than just the sum of his injuries. She was the bravest person he'd ever met, terrifyingly honest and wholly beautiful.

'Maybe I should take a leaf out of Mattie's book.' If he had the self-assurance to even contemplate trying to win Mattie back, that was largely because of her.

His father laughed. 'You could do a lot worse, bach...'

CHAPTER FOURTEEN

LLWYD HAD SLEPT badly on Saturday night, but his head had been too full of impossible dreams to contemplate nightmares. He took Peter to the cinema on Sunday afternoon, dozing through the film. On the way back, the boy demanded that they drop in on his grandmother and grandfather.

'Why do you want to go and see Mam-gu and Tad-cu?'

'Because I've decided what colour I want my boat to be.'

'Okay.' Clearly, the information couldn't wait, and no doubt it would be received with a degree of relief. 'Do you like staying with them?'

'Yes.'

Sometimes Llwyd wished that Peter would give a bit more insight into his reasoning. 'More than me?'

'Do I have to choose? Mum says that you can like two things and that you don't have to choose between them.'

Maybe Georgina had been talking about food. Although it sounded as if she'd given Peter a piece of good advice, which might be applied to any number of situations.

'Your mum's right. Sorry I asked.'

'That's all right.'

Maybe actions spoke louder than words. The way that Peter tumbled out of the car and ran up the path to give his grandmother and grandfather a hug, left Llwyd in no doubt that he was looking forward to seeing them. His father suggested that Peter stay for tea, so that they could finalise Peter's exact specifications for the colour scheme, and told Llwyd that he should go home. He'd call Georgina and get her to pick Peter up from here.

'You look tired, bach. Get some sleep.' His mother followed him to the front door, unexpectedly reaching up to kiss him goodbye.

'What was that for?'

'Too grown-up for a kiss from your mother?' She rebuked him. 'Go home, Llwyd. We can take Peter whenever you need us to.'

So Dad had been talking to Mum. That wasn't unexpected. And even if he didn't have all the answers yet, he had some of them.

He was considering the possibility of making a list, and wondering whether that wasn't a too clinical way to make the most important decision of his life, when suddenly the answer presented itself. As he turned in to the driveway, he almost slammed into the back of Mattie's bus.

She came tumbling down the steps, running towards him. It wasn't the meeting that Llwyd had envisaged in any of his dreams, but suddenly there were no decisions left to make.

'Sorry...sorry. Are you all right?' She wrenched open the door of the car, bobbing down to look at him.

'I'm fine.' Llwyd released his seat belt, getting out of the car. 'It's my fault, I was thinking about something else...'

He'd been thinking about this moment. Not quite *this* moment, because Mattie was clearly still upset and embarrassed. A moment like it.

'I didn't think. When you drive a large yellow bus, it's easy to imagine that everyone can see you.'

Llwyd took a few paces back, turning to look at the bus,

which was partly obscured by the trees in the driveway but not entirely. 'I can see it from here. I should have been taking more notice.'

Mattie frowned. 'Do you have any difficulty moving your head?'

'If I had whiplash, I'd have mentioned it before I got out of the car.' This was not the way he wanted this to go, and he was pretty sure that Mattie hadn't turned up here to discuss whiplash. 'It's good to see you, Mattie. I'm grateful you came.'

She smiled suddenly, her cheeks reddening. 'Thank you. It's good to see you, too. I don't suppose... Would you like to come in for coffee?'

The cottage might be a more obvious place for coffee. But then Mattie would be able to slam the front door behind her and drive away, and it was encouraging to know that she didn't have that in mind. And the bus didn't leave much space to avoid each other, so whatever it was that Mattie had come to say would have to be up-close and personal.

Only... Maybe he needed a little time to think first. Work out how he might apologise to her. But now that Mattie was here, he felt a little more confident about winging it.

'Thank you. That would be really nice.'

The bus was as clean and tidy as it always was, although Llwyd noticed that everything was secured for a journey. He could only hope against hope that Mattie had reached her destination now.

He slid into one of the seats by the table and allowed himself to just enjoy her presence for a moment. She had coffee and milk, along with biscuits, and although he didn't really want to drink or eat anything more, he accepted everything she offered. Then she sat down opposite him.

'Llwyd, I came to say that I'm sorry. I should never

have just disappeared like that without telling you where I was going.'

'Apology not accepted, Mattie. You have nothing to be sorry for. I drove you away. I did it because I couldn't believe that I'd ever be able to be enough for you. It was wrong of me and I'm deeply sorry.'

He jumped as Mattie brought her fist down onto the table. 'If you're not going to accept *my* apology, then I won't accept yours.'

'Mattie…!' He'd almost forgotten how delicious it was to be exasperated with her. 'Okay. Can we agree on a no-fault expression of mutual regret?'

Mattie thought for a moment. 'Only because I have more to say, and because I want to see things through.'

A quiver of dread gripped him. *Seeing things through* sounded horribly final, and he'd reckoned that persuading her to come back to him might be a lengthy business.

'You want to do that now?'

Maybe she saw the terror in his face. She slid her hand across the small table towards his, and Llwyd took it.

'What I really want to say to you, Llwyd, is that we're both trying to find our balance. In different ways…'

He nodded. 'That's fair.' Mattie was trying to balance out the creative, headstrong side of her nature, with all the pressure she was under to act responsibly. And he was trying to rebalance himself, come to terms with a new physical reality.

'But there's one thing I know for sure. I love you, and I'm hoping you might still love me. Because if that's the case, I believe we can find our balance together.'

Llwyd felt a tear run down his face. *'Cariad…'*

She let go of his hand, reaching to caress the side of his face. 'I know what that means, Llwyd.'

She leaned across the table, kissing him. Suddenly, everything was stunningly simple. They loved each other and they were going to work things out together.

Mattie hadn't expected this. She'd known that Llwyd would be kind, but hadn't expected him still to want her, after the way she'd behaved. But he did; she could see it in his eyes. He was willing to give her a chance, and she was determined not to blow it this time.

She told him about going to London. About Justin, and the things he'd told her about their mum and Helen. How she'd realised that never being able to settle in one place was just a way of avoiding the rejection she'd always felt over Leigh, and the desperate need to be accepted by her mum and dad.

'I wasn't running from you, Llwyd. I was running from all the things that I thought they wanted, and that I'd never really challenged. So I went to see them.'

He looked at her steadily. 'Please tell me you took the Tube.'

'No, I took the bus.'

His green eyes flashed with humour. 'How did that go?'

'They were horrified. Mum burst into tears, and Dad was giving me this thunderous look. But I stood my ground. I told them how much I loved them, and that I owed them everything. That it must be hard for Mum in particular, seeing me do the same kinds of things that Helen did, but that I wanted to be honest with them.'

'That sounds good to me. How did they take it?'

'Surprisingly well. Mum didn't stop crying, but she hugged me and told me that she loved me. That it really hurt sometimes to see how much like Helen I was, but that she loved me for that, as well. Dad asked if he could take a look at the bus, and I let him take it for a spin.'

She saw Llwyd's eyebrows shoot up and grinned at him. 'Dad's got a full Driver CPC licence. He drives the coach for the local Green Urban Spaces group.'

'And he approved?'

'I had a bit of trouble getting the keys back from him afterwards. I told them about the boat, as well. I reckoned in for a penny, in for a pound. I blamed that all on Leigh.'

'Fair enough. It's entirely his fault. Does your dad want to drive your boat, as well?'

'They're coming down for a visit in a month or so. I'm going to keep it for that long, just so I can give them a spin.' Mattie took a deep breath. 'Llwyd, you were right. I don't need to keep moving to find my own identity. I just need to stand my ground.'

'Yeah. Would you like to go back to London, so you can be nearer your family?'

Mattie would never ask him to leave Cartref Bay. 'I want to be with you, Llwyd. And you need to stay here.'

'No, I don't.' He grinned at her. 'Surprising how families can come up with the answer if you let them.'

'What?' She hadn't been expecting this. 'What have you done, Llwyd? This is your home.'

'Yes, and it always will be. But my dad told me in no uncertain terms that I was using my ties to this place as an avoidance tactic. I didn't want to confront my fears that I was somehow less than I'd been before I was attacked, and so I dug myself in deep. I bought this place and made a decision to take Peter every weekend—'

'No. Llwyd, you can't. I've seen you and Peter together and he's not just a way of avoiding commitment. He loves you...'

'And I love him. Huw and Georgina need some help at the moment, but I'm not the only one who can give it. Dad's made it very clear that he and Mum will pitch in a bit more, and honestly… Huw and I grew up together at the boatyard, and I can't think of a better childhood. All I ask is that we make our decisions about where we want to go, together.'

That made things very easy. 'I like it here, Llwyd, and if you don't mind, I'd like to stay. Peter's a great kid, and we'd really be missing out if we passed up the chance of having our weekends with him. And we can visit London and see my family. Have them come here.'

He stared at her. 'You're not just saying that, are you? Because you think it's what I want.'

'I'm saying it because it's what'll make us both happy. Don't you want to be happy, Llwyd?'

He leaned across, kissing her. All of the passion, all of the hopes that they'd dared not hope, in one sweet gesture, that left them both trembling.

'I want to be happy with *you*, cariad.'

That was all she could ask of him. Everything that Mattie could want.

'Your place or mine, then?' She grinned at him, laughing as he pretended to think about it.

'Yours. Then maybe mine…?'

There was something more binding than a ring. More precious. Llwyd hoped that Mattie would understand that. Mattie still had another week left of her holiday, but Llwyd was working, and he'd called in on his father on the way home to collect the finely carved wooden box, securing it carefully on the back seat of his car. Mattie was in the cottage kitchen, wearing a pair of shorts and a T-shirt, sorting through bags of shopping.

'I've got steak, or some chicken. Plenty of vegetables, and lemons for the chicken and some peppercorns for the steak…'

'Will it all keep for another day?'

'Yes, it'll keep till the end of the week. You want to do something else?'

'On a Monday night there are plenty of spare tables at Huw and Georgina's. Would you like to go there?'

Mattie turned, kissing him. 'That sounds really nice. Only this time we pay the bill, yes?'

'Yep.' Hopefully, they'd be drinking champagne.

'What shall I wear? This old thing, or that old thing?'

'Surprise me.' He caught her hand, stopping her before she could open the doors into the garden, and make her way to the bus, which was now parked alongside the house, making them next-door neighbours.

He kept hold of her hand, falling to one knee. 'I can't wait a moment longer, Mattie. I promise to always love you. Will you marry me?' Llwyd had thought about a longer proposal, but they were the only words that really mattered.

She let out a little scream. 'I love you, too, Llwyd. Yes!'

Mattie pulled him to his feet, and he took her in his arms, kissing her. 'Whatever comes next…'

'Whatever.' She kissed him again. 'I love that you couldn't wait. Now was just the right moment.'

'There's something I'd like you to see….' He took her hand, leading her to the sitting room at the front of the house. Somehow, that had felt appropriate. The wooden box was on the coffee table in front of the sofa, and Llwyd sat down, with Mattie at his side.

'What a beautiful box,' she murmured, reaching out to touch the carved wood with her fingertips.

'Open it.'

Mattie lifted the lid and one hand flew to her mouth when she saw what was inside. 'Oh! Is this your family bible?'

'Yes.' He took a pair of white cotton gloves from the box, putting them on and lifting the bible out, opening it on the table. 'You see here, at the front? Births, deaths and marriages, the story of the Morgan family for the last three hundred years.'

'I can't read it.' Mattie was peering at the faded lettering. 'It's in Welsh—tell me what it says.'

'Later…' He carefully turned to the newer pages that had been stitched into the bible when the family had grown past the confines of the original blank pages at the front. 'Here's my mum and dad.'

Mattie leaned forward, reading the lines that he indicated. 'Rhys Morgan and Annalise Evans…what's the next bit?'

'It says *"Declared their intention to marry."* And further down is their marriage, a year later.'

'So they put their engagement into the book as well as their marriage?'

Llwyd nodded. 'Yes, some of the very earliest entries include intentions of marriage. Would it be too soon for us to write in here? You don't have to…'

Mattie's eyes widened. 'Can I? Would your dad mind? I'd be so honoured.'

'I told him what I wanted the bible for when I went round to fetch it on my way home this evening. He couldn't get the safe open quickly enough. I don't have a ring for you yet, but I do have this.'

'This is just…it's wonderful, Llwyd. Please, I'd love for you to put my name with yours. I think we should say 'solemn declaration.' It sounds a lot more as if we mean it.'

Llwyd laughed. 'Solemn declaration it is.' He took the fountain pen that his father had given him from his pocket, writing their names, along with their intention to marry. Then he blotted the entry carefully.

'That's so beautiful, Llwyd.' She fanned her face with her fingers. 'I can't even look at it properly because I'm crying and I don't want to get the page all wet.'

'There's plenty of time. This is parchment so I need to leave the book open for a little while so the ink doesn't smudge. What do you say we go to London this weekend? I'll book a nice hotel and we can find a ring you really like, and then take your mum and dad to dinner. That way they'll be the first to see it.'

She flung her arms around his neck. 'That's perfect, Llwyd. Thank you so much. My mum will love that. Can we watch the ink dry?'

Right now, watching ink dry was the one and only thing in the world he wanted to do. His name and Mattie's. Together, with a solemn declaration of their love.

EPILOGUE

Nine months later

TOMORROW WOULD BE one year to the day since Mattie had first met Llwyd. And his father would be removing the family bible from his safe and taking it down to the chapel to be inscribed along with the official wedding register.

Mattie was so proud of Llwyd. He'd worked every day to restore more movement and feeling to his left hand, using electrical stimulation and exercise. Although his grip was still compromised, there had been a significant improvement in his thumb and fingers. When the hospital offered him the chance to return to surgery he'd turned it down— he enjoyed being able to interact with his young patients.

Slowly, painstakingly, he'd recounted the full story of his attack to a therapist. It had been hard, and Mattie had held him through nightmares and terrors, which worsened at first, and then slowly but surely disappeared.

Life had been good. They'd worked hard and loved each other faithfully. Mattie had decided to keep the *Matilda Rae*, and it was now berthed at the boatyard.

They'd asked Leigh to their wedding, but made it clear that he would be coming as a welcome guest and that Mattie's dad would be giving her away. Leigh had replied that he wasn't sure he'd be able to attend, and said that he would be looking at a house in America for a wedding present, which Mattie and Llwyd could use as a holiday home. Llwyd had written back, telling him that they already had more than they needed, and that any guests who wished to mark their wedding day were being asked to make a small donation to one of four favourite charities. Leigh had acquiesced gracefully, and Llwyd had promised Mattie that he would make sure that a proposed visit to America would be done on her own terms.

'What do you think they're doing in there?' Mattie was sitting in the front seat of the bus in her nightdress, craning her neck, trying to see into the back windows of the cottage. She'd insisted on staying here for the night before her wedding, and Caroline, Georgina and Tess had decided to make it into a slumber party.

'Cooking, probably,' Georgina suggested. 'At least Huw is. He just texted me to say that they'll be sending a selection of savoury crêpes followed by rainbow fruit sorbet.'

'Mmm, that sounds good. It must be wonderful to have a husband who cooks.' Caroline grinned.

'Yes and no. There's a fair bit of washing up involved.'

'I hope they're not getting drunk…' Mattie squashed her face up against the windscreen. 'Perhaps I could just take the handbrake off and roll the bus forward a couple of feet.'

'No, Mattie. What happens if you overshoot and crash into a tree or something? I'm not risking you ending up in A&E on the night before your wedding. We're here to make sure everything goes smoothly.' Caroline admonished her.

'Anyway, they're not going to be getting drunk. They have Peter and James to look after. I'll bet you anything you like that they'll all be having an early night, and they'll be as fresh as daisies in the morning.' Georgina seemed very sure of herself, and Mattie had to admit that she was probably right.

Mattie tried to ignore the list that was forming in her head, of all the possible things that could go wrong. 'Do you think my dress will be all right?' Her simple wedding dress, made from cotton and lace, was hanging in the bedroom.

'It's absolutely you, Mattie, and you look just beautiful in it. And you don't want anything too frou-frou if you're going to be climbing into a boat later.' Caroline admonished her.

'And the parents…?' Her mum and dad were staying with Llwyd's parents tonight.

'They'll be fine.' Georgina rolled her eyes. 'They all get on like a house on fire, so you can't possibly be worried about them.'

Mattie took a breath, trying to think of anything else that might go wrong. 'Is this wedding nerves?'

'Yes!' Caroline and Georgina chorused, and Caroline reached for a large paper carrier bag. 'We're both old hands with wedding nerves. As soon as you see Llwyd standing at the altar, you'll be fine. And for the meantime we've brought along some soothing candles—'

'Uncle Llwyd!' Tess was standing on one of the seats next to the table, banging on the window, obviously trying to catch Llwyd's attention. Caroline and Georgina abandoned any attempt at soothing, hustling Mattie from the driver's seat of the bus, back into the bedroom.

'What's he doing?' Mattie asked Caroline, who was standing guard by the sliding doors.

'Making faces at Tess… Come here, darling. Don't encourage him.' Caroline raised her voice, calling out. 'What are you doing, Llwyd?'

'Crêpes…' Mattie heard his voice outside. That was enough to calm all of her fears. Whatever else happened tomorrow, she was going to marry Llwyd, and that was what really mattered.

'Leave them by the door. And go away!' Caroline called back, and Mattie heard Tess giggling and running to the front of the bus. Then silence. 'Okay, he's gone. You can come out.'

Georgina collected the food, which was plated and neatly wrapped in two large carrier bags. Everyone found a place to sit, and silence fell as they ate.

'Mmm. That was just gorgeous.' Caroline put her plate to one side. 'Should we start with the tranquil breathing?'

'I'm fine. I feel pretty tranquil already.' Maybe it was because Tess was already leaning against her mother, her eyes heavy with sleep. Maybe because Mattie knew that Llwyd was barely a hundred feet away, dreaming the same waking dreams as she was. This time tomorrow they'd be alone, on the *Matilda Rae*.

'Me, too. Perhaps we should just have an early night, eh?' Georgina suggested.

'You're sure you don't want to go across to the cottage? It's a bit cramped in here and I'll be fine.' Mattie yawned behind her hand.

'No, Tess and I are good. I'd rather be here.' Caroline had caught the yawning bug now.

'Me, too.' Georgina gathered up the plates. 'We'll stay here and keep you company, if you don't mind.'

Her bridesmaids had advised her well. When Mattie and her father walked together into the chapel the place was full to bursting, but the only person she saw was Llwyd. Standing waiting for her at the altar.

'Steady on, love. You'll be there soon enough,' her dad whispered in her ear as she started forward. Huw was clearly giving Llwyd the same advice, because he seemed ready to run down the aisle to meet her.

'You look beautiful,' Llwyd murmured as she finally reached him, his green eyes bright in the sunshine that streamed through the windows. 'Marry me quickly, before you change your mind.'

'I've made up my mind.' She smiled up at him.

Mattie's vows were just for him, and Llwyd's just for her. Their home was with each other now, and change would never part them. Her ring was inscribed inside with his name, and his with hers.

Mattie had always known she wanted her reception overlooking the bay, but when Llwyd's father offered the boatyard she'd wondered whether the ambiance there would be quite right. Llwyd had said that Huw and Georgina had held their reception there, and that Mattie would be surprised at how the place scrubbed up and she'd decided to trust him. She'd made the right decision there, too.

The main shed had been emptied completely and temporary flooring installed. The high ceiling twinkled with lights, giving the whole space an atmosphere of nautical chic combined with a liberal sprinkling of magic. Huw and Georgina had overseen the food, and there was a magnificent wedding cake, which Georgina had made herself to Mattie's specifications. The huge space meant that everyone could circulate freely, and there was room for large statement plants in massive containers, amongst a riot of flowers.

As darkness fell, Llwyd's father climbed aboard the *Matilda Rae*, taking her a little way out into the bay. She bobbed at anchor, the lights that were strung around her reflecting in the water. Peter waited impatiently with Huw, at the end of the now-empty jetty. Everything was ready, and it was time to go. Mattie and Llwyd hugged everyone, thanking them for coming.

'Ready?' Llwyd grinned down at her. This was a family wedding tradition that he'd clearly been looking forward to.

'Yes.' Mattie had changed her wedding shoes for a pair of white plimsolls, which Caroline and Georgina had decorated with glitter hearts.

Everyone cheered as Llwyd picked Mattie up, cradling her in his arms. He carried her down the jetty, to where Peter was now waiting in his boat. Llwyd set her back onto her feet and his brother helped her down into the small craft.

Peter was clearly conscious of the honour he'd been afforded, and started to heave on the oars almost before Llwyd had a chance to settle himself behind Mattie. Llwyd grabbed at his set of oars, and they started to move more smoothly across the water towards the *Matilda Rae*.

His father helped Llwyd moor the skiff securely to the bathing platform, which had been lowered at the back of the *Matilda Rae*. Then Mattie and Llwyd stepped aboard together. Another cheer went up from the shore, as Llwyd's father boarded the skiff and he and Peter started to row it back towards the jetty.

'Aren't you supposed to kiss me now?' Fireworks began to shoot up from the boatyard, exploding above their heads.

'That's the plan…' Llwyd took her in his arms, and suddenly they were alone. The centre of everyone's attention, but all she could see was him.

'And now you're going to carry me away for my wedding night.' They'd booked a hotel a few miles along the coast, the first stop on their honeymoon.

'That's also the plan. Although since this is the twenty-first century, perhaps you might carry me away?'

'Tempting. I think I'll stick with tradition, though. Perhaps we could stop off, before we go to the hotel, though.

At Ogof Briallu. Maybe see if we can start on the family we've been talking about?'

He kissed her again. All she wanted and everything she needed. 'I'll go wherever you go, Mattie. And if you're ready to make babies…' She felt his chest heave with emotion.

'I'm ready. We've found our home, Llwyd. Let's make a family.'

* * * * *

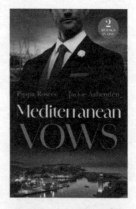

COMING SOON!

We really hope you enjoyed reading this book.
If you're looking for more romance
be sure to head to the shops when
new books are available on

Thursday 18th July

To see which titles are coming soon, please visit
millsandboon.co.uk/nextmonth

MILLS & BOON

MILLS & BOON®

Coming next month

HER SUMMER WITH THE BROODING VET
Scarlet Wilson

Eli's hand lifted and rested on Aurora's hip, just as her own palm tightened on his arm, almost like she was willing him even closer.

They moved in unison. Lips brushing together for the briefest of seconds before they locked entirely. Her hands wrapped around his neck, the length of her body pressed up against his.

His lips moved to her face, her ear and her neck and she let out the tiniest groan. He could taste her perfume on his lips, feel it with every inhale.

She let out a breath, and stepped back, nervous laughter filling the air between them. Her pupils were dilated, the green of her eyes nearly invisible.

'Whoa,' he said, trying to catch his breath.

'Whoa,' she repeated, a broad smile across her face.

Continue reading
HER SUMMER WITH THE BROODING VET
Scarlet Wilson

Available next month
millsandboon.co.uk

LET'S TALK
Romance

Follow us:

f Millsandboon

🐦 @MillsandBoon

📷 @MillsandBoonUK

♪ @MillsandBoonUK

For all the latest titles and special offers, sign up to our newsletter:
Millsandboon.co.uk

afterglow BOOKS

Afterglow Books is a trend-led, trope-filled list of books with diverse, authentic and relatable characters, a wide array of voices and representations, plus real world trials and tribulations. Featuring all the tropes you could possibly want (think small-town settings, fake relationships, grumpy vs sunshine, enemies to lovers) and all with a generous dose of spice in every story.

♪ @millsandboonuk
📷 @millsandboonuk
afterglowbooks.co.uk
#AfterglowBooks

For all the latest book news, exclusive content and giveaways scan the QR code below to sign up to the Afterglow newsletter:

SCAN ME

Never Date A Roommate
PBO 9780263322897 £8.99
Ebook 9780008938420 | Audio 9780263324860
For publicity enquiries please contact
millsandboonpressoffice@harpercollins.co.uk